WRATH

A SINFUL EMPIRE DUET

EVA CHARLES

QUARRY ROAD PUBLISHING

This book is a work of fiction. Any references to historical events, real people, or real places are used fictitiously. All other names, characters, places, and incidents are products of the author's imagination. Any resemblance to actual events, places, organizations, or persons living or dead is entirely coincidental.

Murphy Rae, Cover Design

Dawn Alexander, Evident Ink, Content Editor

James Gallagher, Castle Walls Editing, Copy and Line Editor

Faith Williams, The Atwater Group, Proofreader

Virginia Tesi Carey, Proofreader

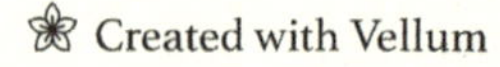

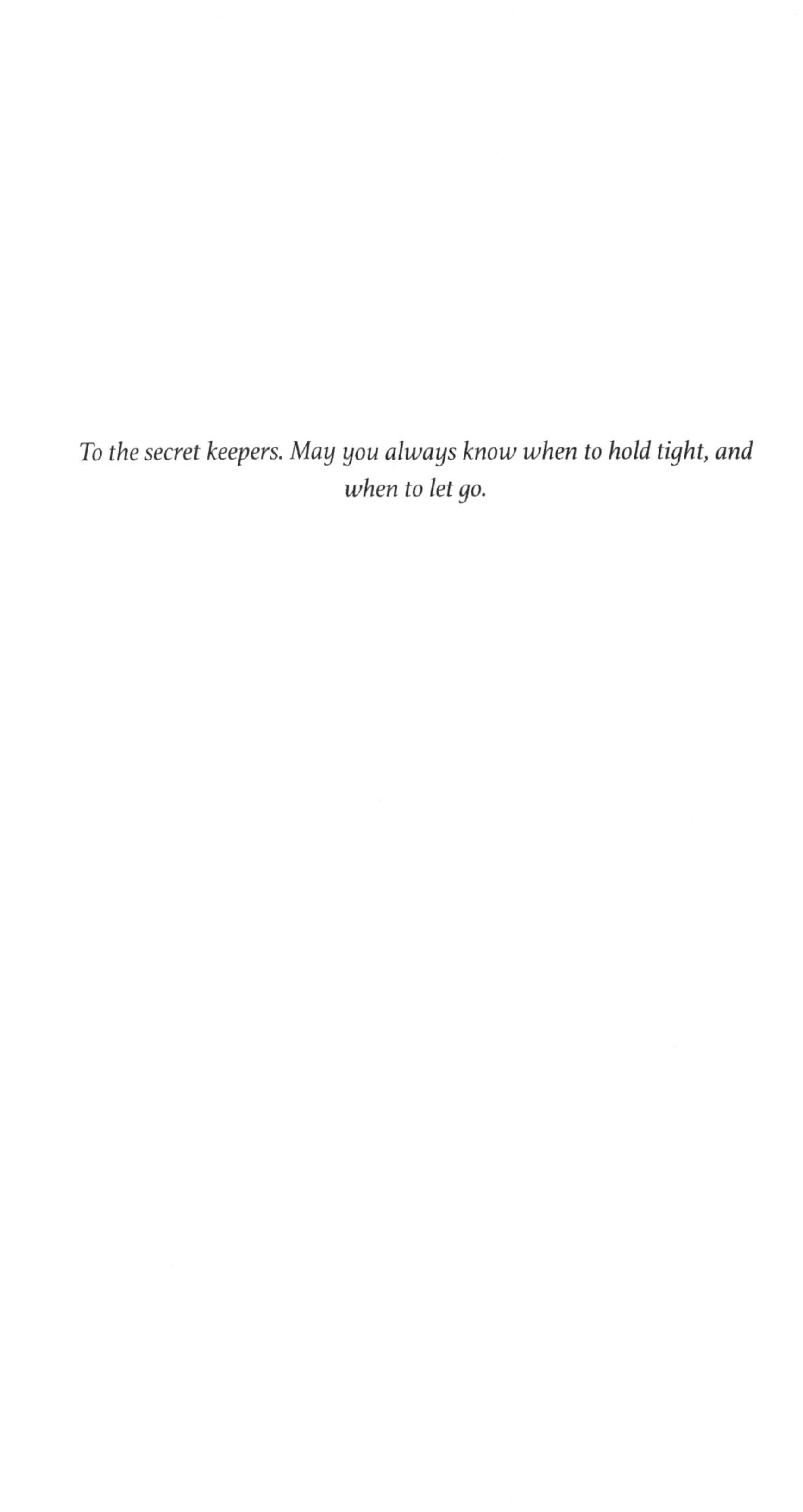

To the secret keepers. May you always know when to hold tight, and when to let go.

Sometimes it's the princess who slays the dragon and saves the prince.

— SAMUEL LOWE

Sheltered Heart
Noble Pursuit
Double Play
Unforgettable
Loyal Subjects
Sexy Sinner

ALSO BY EVA CHARLES

STEAMY ROMANTIC SUSPENSE

A SINFUL EMPIRE SERIES

TRILOGY (COMPLETE)

Greed

Lust

Envy

DUET (COMPLETE)

Pride

Wrath

THE DEVIL'S DUE (COMPLETE)

Depraved

Delivered

Bound

Decadent

CONTEMPORARY ROMANCE

NEW AMERICAN ROYALS

AUTHOR'S NOTE

DEAR READER,

Welcome back to Porto! Thank you for reading Wrath, the final episode in the Huntsman family saga! This book, like the others in the series, is equal parts romance and suspense. Wrath is not a standalone. I trust if you are here, you have read Pride, the first book of the duet.

Wrath has two epilogues. One completes an arc that began in Greed, although it's not necessary to have read Greed, and the other gives you a glimpse of Lexie and Rafael's life eight years later.

I love everything about Rafa and Lexie—their growth and passion, and the way they bring out the best in each other, even when the world is crumbling around them. They are exactly who the other needs to thrive—at least I think so, and I hope you do too!

While "dark romance" means something different to each of us, please be aware that there are dark elements in this story. I don't shy away from difficult topics. If you have any concerns about the subject matter, please contact me. I want you to feel safe while you read.

Are you still here? *Good.*

Buckle up, and let's take a ride!

xoxo

Eva

PROLOGUE

Where we left off...
Rafael

"TAMAR, can you activate a tracking device from the plane?"

"Sure. What am I looking for?"

"Lexie's on a flight destined for—somewhere. It's a long shot, but she might have a tracking device on her. One of the new prototypes that can be retrofitted into a piece of jewelry."

"A tracking device on land is one thing." She glances at me warily. "But we'll need a satellite to track something on a moving plane."

A satellite? "Where the hell are we going to get a satellite?"

"I know where to find one, but if we're caught, it's going to cost you. Not money, but a big favor to a foreign agency. Maybe even to a foreign country."

"Whatever it takes."

I don't ask a single damn question about the satellite while Tamar sends a message. I assume it's to someone affiliated with her old agency. I don't care—to ensure Lexie's safety, I'd make a deal with the devil himself.

While we wait to hear back, I take out my phone and pull up the information about the tracker on the angel wings. *I'm the only one who has it. The wings were between me and her. Our special thing. I didn't even share it with Zé.*

"We're set," she says, "but it's going to take a little time for the stars to align."

"How much time?"

"Five or ten minutes. In the meantime, give me the tracking information."

"Here." I hold my phone while she inputs the data, my eyes glued to the clock on the computer screen. Five minutes come and go.

"It's activated," she announces exactly six minutes later. "It'll need another minute or two before it can get us the codes we need to proceed."

"Put it up on the monitor," I instruct, pointing to the large screen on the wall.

You don't even know if she has the wings with her. Maybe she dumped them in the trash on her way out.

While I wait, I pray the signal won't come from somewhere in my damn apartment. It's been so long since I prayed, that I've almost forgotten how. I'm not a believer, but I'd get on my goddamn knees and kiss a ring if I thought it would help me find her.

"Look," Tamar says, relief resounding in her voice. "The plane's over the Atlantic, skirting the European coast. It's definitely not on its way to London," she adds. "Or if it is, it's taking a strange route. Right now, it looks like it's headed toward northern France. But that could change."

"Northern France? What the hell?" I stare at the blip on the screen. It's so much more than a blinking point on a map. *It's everything.*

They have her. The monsters have her.

I can't think. My mind is racing in circles. Chasing all sorts of nightmare scenarios. *I'm never going to see her again.* I kick over a chair, and Tamar startles.

Pull yourself together, Rafael. You're not going to be able to help her like this.

I clasp my fingers behind my neck and dig my thumbs into the muscle until it groans. "Okay." I draw a breath. "Let's go through what we know.

"Lexie boarded a plane in Porto with a flight plan filed for London. Somewhere en route, the flight plan was modified." *I've done this myself many times.* "And a code indicates that the destination was changed."

"Maybe to northern France," Tamar adds, "but we don't know for sure. Why do you need her location?" she asks.

Fuck. I haven't briefed her. I was in the cabin when I spoke with Zé, and she was here.

"Do you remember Francesca Russo?"

She nods.

"She was murdered earlier today."

"You think the flesh traders are involved?"

"I do."

"Alexis has guards with her," Tamar assures me. "Giana contacted me earlier. She wondered if I needed her to do anything. She had some downtime because Ms. Clarke had her own security when she left."

A lot of good security did the Russo girl. "Did she say anything else?"

Tamar shakes her head. "No. But I doubt Will Clarke has fools protecting his daughter."

Don't bet on it.

"Francesca Russo was killed along with an experienced guard. These bastards don't fuck around."

My eyes and my heart are trained on the screen, studying the small dot as though my life depends on it. *In many ways, it does.*

Where are you, Lexie? Maybe it's somewhere totally innocuous, but that's not what my gut's telling me.

I go over to the screen on the wall and touch my fingertip to the lit speck, blinking on an image that represents her plane. I touch it gently, like it's Lexie herself. *I'm coming for you, Angel. I'll find you wherever you are.*

When I lift my trembling finger, the tiny dot is no longer blinking. It's gone. *Gone.*

"Tamar!"

"I see. We lost her," she replies, the strain in her voice palpable as she bangs on the keys.

"The satellite or her tracking device?"

"The satellite is still on line. It's functioning. We lost the tracking device."

"What about the plane?" I ask, eyes glued to the large monitor. "I don't see the plane."

She shakes her head frantically. "It's gone."

1

RAFAEL

My phone beeps, and without wasting a single second, I connect the call through satellite Wi-Fi and snarl, "It's about fucking time."

"What the hell are you up to, Huntsman?" Will Clarke roars back.

"Have you heard anything from Lexie or the plane in the past ten minutes?"

"None of your goddamn business."

Like hell it's not. "Francesca Russo was murdered along with a seasoned guard less than a mile from home."

Will draws a sharp breath. "Is that so?" In a beat, his tone shifts from outraged daddy to ruthless crime lord. "And you know this how?"

"The prime minister's assistant contacted me."

He pauses for what feels like an eternity, the silence screeching loud enough to make my blood curdle.

"The flight attendant who was scheduled to be on Lexie's flight is dead. Her credentials were used by another woman to board the plane," he says, finally.

My heart drops into my stomach. Will's voice is icy and

tightly controlled, without a hint of the emotion one would expect from a father under these circumstances. Although I have no doubt his pulse is hammering as hard as mine.

"Have you identified the impostor?"

"We're on it."

"We're on it"? That's all you're going to give me? I don't think so.

"What have you heard from that plane, Will, and when did you last have contact with Lexie?"

"My daughter is on her way to London, where she belongs, and is no longer your concern."

"Bullshit!" I bark, because we don't have time for games. "We tracked her plane headed for northern France."

"The satellite monitoring the flight—that was you?" he growls, every word a poisonous dart.

If you didn't want me tracking the plane, you should have answered your damn phone. "After I learned about the Russo girl. But we lost both the plane and Lexie about ten minutes ago." We're wasting precious minutes. I'm done answering questions. "For the third time, when was your last communication with that flight?"

"Not that it's any of your fucking business, but the plane's on course to northern France, as planned. I had the signal scrambled so that it's impossible for fuckers like you to track my daughter."

He scrambled the signal. Every muscle in my body unfurls, including the one in my chest. But it's a brief respite, because Francesca Russo's killer is still out there, and Lexie's life is still in danger.

"Where is she going?"

"You were tracking my daughter's every movement, without her consent, like a lowlife predator."

Just answer the question, you insufferable bastard.

"I'm going to put a bullet in you before the day is over."

"You do that. In the meantime, tell me exactly where Lexie's going so I can get some men on the ground before she deplanes." When I couldn't reach Will, we pulled together a couple of teams. Kept one on standby and sent the other to northern France. They're not on the ground yet, but they're close.

"Everything's under control. Stay in your lane, boy," he warns. "The one that's far away from my daughter."

Ricocheting from crime boss mode to daddy mode is a dangerous way to operate. Too dangerous.

I won't allow him to sideline me.

"Like hell it's under control." Now I'm the one with ice water running through my veins, tempering the boiling blood so that my words emerge steely, with none of the bluster of a hothead.

"The plane with *your* daughter is over the Atlantic, skirting the European coast, with at least one insurgent on board, maybe more. You have no idea who the perpetrator is or who sent her. And I'd bet my last euro that you still don't have a damn clue how deep you've been infiltrated. *Your* daughter's life is on the line, and like it or not, I'm the best friend you have right now. So swallow your fucking pride and let's make a plan."

More silence.

I just crossed *every* line with him, and I'm one step closer to that bullet he promised. But I don't give a shit. Those animals are not getting to her on my watch. *Cost be damned.* A bullet is a relatively quick death compared to what those monsters will force Lexie to endure until they're done with her.

"Quimper," he replies gruffly. "The flight is headed to Quimper."

I scribble a note and hand it to Tamar. *Have Zé alert the teams and tell our pilot to file a new flight plan.* She nods, swiveling toward the keyboard.

"Is there anyone on the plane you trust without reservation

—the pilot, the guards?" *Please tell me there are guards on that plane.* "Getting a message to someone could change the outcome. Just giving Lexie a heads-up is better than nothing. Otherwise, they'll be blindsided."

Trained guards should never be blindsided. They should anticipate trouble at every turn. Although it doesn't always work out that way. If the guards are taken by surprise, the likelihood of her falling into the hands of the monsters is high. *Too damn high.*

"The pilot is loyal, and a capable soldier," Will replies confidently. "We've been vetting him and the dead flight attendant for the past eighteen months before transitioning them to Lexie and Samantha's flight crew. They were on separate crews before today, and their paths never crossed."

"This was to be their maiden voyage together?"

"Yes. They were going to begin to work as a team next month, but Lexie wanted to come home as soon as possible, and the usual crew assigned to personal flights was on a mission. We brought the new team in early and without much notice."

She wanted to come home as soon as possible. Whose goddamn fault is that? *No time to dwell on it now.* "When did Lexie contact you to come home?"

"Sometime before noon. Whoever put out the hit on the flight attendant and had her replaced is nimble, with plenty of resources."

They also had help from the inside. There's no way they could have operated so quickly without someone feeding them information. He doesn't admit to it, but Will knows he has a traitor in his midst. It's a direct shot at his power—and because his daughter is on that plane, it's a bold attempt to emasculate him, too.

"What about the guards?"

"The guards are also highly capable, and loyal, as far as I know. But their loyalty hasn't been tested."

Then why the hell are they protecting your daughter? I don't say it, because even well-tested guards can turn. There's a certain amount of luck involved in assigning protection. No one likes to talk about it, because leaving anything to chance when it comes to a loved one's safety is chilling. But Lady Luck always has her say.

"Even if the personnel are trustworthy, Rafael, the communication channels could be compromised. We have a problem, but we're still searching for the rotten root."

Will's voice is hollow, with the twang of defeat. Men like him never admit weakness. His candor is a testament to what's on the line. Not that I need a fucking testament to understand the stakes.

"After the crash with Edward and Lydia," he continues, "we put measures in place that make it virtually impossible to sabotage our planes. So the bastards did the next best thing. They got an insurgent on board." Before the final word is out, there's a loud crash and the sound of glass shattering through the phone.

Tamar peers up at me, brow raised.

Given the chaos, I should ask if everything's okay, but it would only embarrass him.

Will isn't prone to throwing tantrums in the middle of a shitstorm. He lives by the adage revenge is a dish best served cold. Either he's slipping, or this is more than even he can shoulder. Regardless of the reason, his ability to make sound decisions feels off.

"I'm going to put you on speaker," I tell him. "One of my best soldiers is with me." I glance at Tamar. "She's smart, Mossad trained—and loyal. You can speak freely."

"Tamar Sorin, sir. I assume we're on a secure line."

It's correct procedure to check, but there's no way he would be talking so freely if the line wasn't secure.

"The most secure. I hope you can say the same, Sorin."

"Without reservation, sir. What exactly is the plane's destination?" Tamar cuts right to the chase without taking a breath, and her voice doesn't waver as she questions the notorious William Clarke. She's got a lot of balls.

"Quimper. Cornouaille Airport," he replies curtly.

A midsize airport just a few miles outside the city.

"Why is Lexie going to Quimper?"

"Shopping for wedding gifts or some other nonsense."

Oh, Angel, you can fool your father, but I don't buy it. You could have purchased wedding presents online. Quimper might be an old city, but it has twenty-first-century capabilities. Porto. Oslo. Quimper. They're connected. I feel it in my bones. What are you chasing, Lexie?

I weigh the possibilities. It's not the first time I've mulled them over. They all lead to one place. Somewhere dark and sinister, where there's no escape if she's snared in the net. *I have to get to her before that happens.*

"Anything else Tamar should know before I take her off speaker so she can focus on getting a team on the ground?"

"No."

I glance at Tamar, who shakes her head.

"Why didn't you reroute the plane to London as soon as you learned about the dead flight attendant?" I ask once the phone's off speaker.

"Now you're questioning my decisions?"

Yes. "I'm trying to understand what the fuck is going on so we can get Lexie to safety."

He clears his throat. "My first instinct was to bring the plane to London—until we discovered the flight was being tracked by satellite. At that point, keeping it airborne seemed too risky. And..."

His voice trails off, as the guilt creeps into my chest, but I don't let it throw me off course. "And?"

"My men discovered the flight attendant while attending to another matter."

"What kind of matter?"

"It's been a hell of a night here. Bedlam in all corners of the city. Mostly small problems, but it's eaten up a lot of manpower." He mumbles something to someone in the room with him before continuing. "It's a distraction—a prelude to something bigger," he adds coolly. "Samantha's in a secure location, but I wasn't certain we could get Lexie back and secure before the shit really hit the fan."

Bedlam in all corners of the city. Jesus Christ. You couldn't have mentioned this earlier?

"Do you think the mess in London is related to the traffickers?"

"Until I heard about the Russo girl, it didn't even occur to me. But even now, I doubt it."

You doubt it? Really? Because it's fucking suspicious.

"Hours, maybe less, after Francesca Russo was killed, someone wanted on Lexie's flight bad enough that they murdered a member of the crew."

"They're certain it was the flesh peddlers who killed Francesca?"

"Unless the killer left a calling card, I don't see how they know for sure. Although it's highly probable."

"It might have been a different faction. Russo amassed a lot of enemies on his way to becoming prime minister. And my dead flight attendant might have nothing to do with the traffickers either. I have plenty of my own enemies. Don't draw conclusions without salient facts. The events might be unrelated. It could all be a coincidence."

"I'm not a big believer in coincidences."

"I'm not either, but they can't be fully discounted. When we chase red herrings, Rafael, the bodies pile up."

He's right, of course. And he's not losing his touch. He's in an impossible situation that I muddied and made more difficult by tracking the plane.

I will find you, Lexie, even if it means breaching the gates of hell. I will not lose another person I care about.

2

LEXIE

The white noise of the jet engine allows my chaotic brain to focus while I compose an email that lets Valentina know I'm gone but doesn't give away too much. Ordinarily I would text her, but if she's awake, she'll want to chat, and I'm not up to that conversation right now.

Hey gorgeous!

Just want to let you know that my bruised ego and I are on my way to London. Somehow the idea of playing house with Rafael was more glamorous than the reality. Shocking, huh? I'm making a quick stop in Quimper to pick up a wedding gift, and a birthday present for my mom. She fell in love with the bowl you sent her. I'm thinking of getting her a few more and some matching plates. Send me the name of the shop so that I don't wander the streets aimlessly.

I miss you already. Come see me soon!

xoxo

Lexie

She doesn't need to know the details of what happened with Rafael, but I have to tell her something. As it is, leaving without saying goodbye feels strange. Even so, I couldn't face her without bawling, and I don't want her to feel responsible for something that isn't her fault.

My mother does love the bowl Valentina sent, and I told my father that I would pick up something nice for her while I was in Quimper. If I show up empty-handed, he'll ask questions, and it'll be more difficult to trick his bullshit meter when we're face-to-face.

I reread the email to Valentina and press Send. It's the middle of the night, and she probably won't check her mail until the morning.

Life was simpler before Rafael and Marco and the trafficking ring that weighs on my conscience. We had few, if any, secrets between us.

I sigh deeply and turn my full attention to the real reason I'm stopping in the old city.

I'll be at the mayor's office when they open in the morning. Even if she can't see me then, I'll tell her staff who I am—who my father is—and she might be willing to meet with me at some point later in the day. Hush-hush, of course. There's no way she'll want word to get out that she met with someone so closely related to organized crime. If she won't see me, I'll make a scene big enough to interest the press—which she'll hate—and then she won't have any choice.

One thing I'm sure about is that the mayor won't risk calling the authorities on William Clarke's daughter. If she does, her days in politics are over. *Maybe worse.* It's her choice. I don't have a choice. I have to speak to the mayor. *It has to be her.* Going to the police is out of the question.

Since I was a young girl, I've been warned repeatedly that the police will stop at nothing to destroy my family. Not just the police, but all of law enforcement. My father trusts only those on his payroll—even then, he's cautious. As an adult, I understand that the relationship between my father and the authorities is more complicated than I was led to believe, but still, I would never dream of going to them for anything.

As far as Interpol goes, they don't have an office in Quimper. Plus, for all intents and purposes, they're law enforcement. My previous contacts with them have all been anonymous and untraceable. If I show up in person, even if I use my mother's maiden name, they'll know who I am right away and begin asking questions about my father. At this point, it's better to avoid them altogether.

When I'm satisfied that the plan is complete, I stare out the window into the abyss that is the night sky.

If this doesn't work, I'm going to have to share what I know—what I've been doing—with my father and deal with the fallout, ugly as it will surely be. His head will explode when I tell him.

Although I think he'll be willing—or at least that I can convince him—to help. Will Clarke doesn't permit women to be trafficked through London. No exceptions. Those who fail to heed his order do so at their own peril.

But Quimper isn't London or even the UK, and he might not see it as his purview. If that happens, I'll have to change his mind—from the cloistered tower he's going to lock me into when he finds out what I've been up to. Any punishment I've experienced up until now will seem like nothing compared to what's in store for me when he learns the truth.

"Do you need anything, miss?" the flight attendant asks, rousing me from disturbing thoughts of Anne Boleyn, a dank tower, and another unforgiving king.

"How long before we land?"

"Forty-five minutes," Anya replies.

Anya. Something about her makes me uncomfortable. I don't know why—she's nice enough. I force my mouth to curl, and she smiles back. She has a gap between her front teeth, like Cristina, the regular flight attendant.

"Although," Anya continues, "I understand there's some bad weather ahead and we might fly around it. If that's the case, it'll be a bit longer before we're on the ground. Are you sure I can't bring you some chamomile tea or a blanket?"

She's more than nice. She's very sweet. It's late, and I'm exhausted and a bit cranky. I hate personnel changes—that's all. I'm used to Cristina, who stocks my favorite snacks and sits with me when she's not busy. *I'm a baby. A baby who would benefit from a nap.*

"A blanket would be lovely. Thank you."

3

RAFAEL

*W*HEN WE CHASE RED HERRINGS, *Rafael, the bodies pile up.* Will's words keep coming back to me like street food in Marrakesh.

I'm beginning to have doubts about who's responsible for the dead flight attendant. The trouble in London doesn't sound at all like the traffickers—it sounds personal.

"Where is she staying in Quimper?" I ask Will, putting the call back on speaker as a plan forms in my head.

Between issuing orders to someone with him, he rattles off the hotel information.

"Pull it up," I instruct Tamar.

"Done," she replies seconds later, pointing to the large screen on the wall. The hotel is little more than an elegant inn. I'm sure they took it because it's easy to contain. "Here's the interior layout they provided to the fire inspectors."

"Did you take the entire place?" I ask Will. It's midweek and offseason. With a little financial incentive, a small hotel could be procured for a day or two.

"All but one room. There are VIP guests occupying the top west side, and despite a good deal of encouragement, the hotel refused to move them in the middle of the night."

Doesn't matter. We're not going to that hotel.

I mute the call while Will talks to someone on his end. "Find a new hotel. Something larger that will make it easier for us to get in and out. Make it happen quickly."

"It's Quimper, not Paris. All the accommodations are going to be on the small side. But we can probably find something that better suits our needs," she adds.

"The insurgent on the plane is Astrid Eklund," Will sneers. "Swedish father, Romanian mother. Her parents were divorced when she was three, and her mother took her to Prague, where she grew up."

An image of Misha strung up in the shack pops to mind, and I swat it away.

"She's been involved in some honey traps," he continues. "And subterfuge of various kinds. She's a freelancer. But not a killer—not yet anyway."

But not a killer—not yet anyway. "That sounds like a hedge. Is she a killer or not? If you're not sure, just fucking say it."

"What part of *my daughter is on that plane* don't you understand?" he growls. "There's nothing, not a damn thing, in her background to even suggest that she could be an assassin, and she doesn't fit the profile of a suicide bomber."

There's always a first time for everything. For Lexie's safety, we need to remain cognizant of all possibilities, but we also need to follow the facts as we know them.

If Astrid's not there to kill or to bring down the plane, she's there to gather intel and feed it to someone on the ground. That means we can use her to send disinformation to her employer.

"Does anyone on the plane know about the dead flight attendant?" I ask.

"No. That's been kept under tight wraps."

Perfect.

"Here's what we're going to do. Tell the pilot that I'm

responsible for the satellite monitoring the flight. Explain that Lexie left Porto to get away from me, and I'm tracking her. No need to keep it a secret from the guards or the fake flight attendant. Warn everyone that I'm unpredictable and resourceful, and you're concerned about Lexie being abducted."

"Not much of a stretch," he mutters.

I ignore the editorializing. "I also need you to buy some time. We're not far behind them, but I need to get on the ground and to the hotel, and once we're there, we need to come up with an exit plan."

"As soon as we were sure the flight attendant wasn't a killer, we sent word to the plane, through traffic control, about impending weather. If we need to divert them, we can. But I'd prefer we didn't. I don't want to spook anyone, and besides, I have an advance team mobilizing on the ground in Quimper. That will be the safest place for Lexie to deplane."

That depends on the information your traitor has and whether you're correct about Astrid not being a killer. "Any soldiers at the hotel?"

"Two. Brendon Symes is in charge of the ground operations. He's a pro. And loyal."

I don't think you know who's loyal, but we might need to take our chances with Symes. "Once I have Lexie, we'll need to get word to him. I might need his help getting her out. But I don't want anyone to know anything until we have her." *And I can breathe again.*

"What exactly is your plan to secure my daughter?"

"I'll let you know when I see the hotel. Answer your phone."

"Rafael," he says before I disconnect the call. "I issued a shoot order on you earlier."

Of course you did. Jesus Christ. "Shoot or kill?"

Tamar's fingers still on the keyboard as she turns to me.

"Shoot," he replies, without hesitation or regret.

"You need to retract that order. Immediately," Tamar demands, like any guard in charge of my protection would do. Like her boyfriend, she doesn't understand that I'm in charge of my own safety. *Always.*

"Don't call it off, Will," I cut in, overriding my guard, who pulls her mouth into a grim line. "We don't know who we can trust. If you retract the order, it'll raise red flags, especially since our cover is that I'm after Lexie. Leave the order as is."

4

RAFAEL

After I disconnect the call, Tamar opens her mouth as if to say something, but no words come out. Although the fire in her eyes practically singes my skin.

"Have you found a new hotel?"

"Rafael," she pleads. "I'm fully aware of the problems it presents, but that shoot order has to be retracted. In a heated moment, there's often little daylight between shoot and kill orders."

I'm fully aware. But I'm not wasting precious time debating semantics. Nothing she can say will change my mind. Lexie wouldn't be on that plane if I hadn't overreacted and kicked her out of my place.

"I don't like to repeat myself, Tamar. Have you found a new hotel?"

"We have," she replies tightly, turning the screen so I can see it. "It's not perfect, but it's better than the other place. Zé's making the arrangements. He knows what we need."

"As soon as we get there, we'll send word to Will of the hotel change, and he'll get it to the plane. That should send the rats scurrying." *Hopefully right into our trap.*

"Clarke's not exactly an amenable guy. What if he doesn't go along with the change?"

Then we're screwed. "He will," I assure her. "He'll assume that when we got on the ground, we saw something that alarmed us."

It's a risk not telling him up front. I have no doubt we were on a secure line, but he's juggling a lot of balls. I don't want to take any chances that the wires get crossed. Besides, the best way to control the outcome is to control the pieces. Some of them are in the hands of the enemy, but the rest are ours to manipulate.

"If we have to read Clarke in to appease him, we will," I tell Tamar. "But that's plan B."

She nods. "Our team is minutes from entering the city."

"Send the four best sharpshooters to the airport. Tell them to observe at a distance unless Ms. Clarke's entourage is ambushed. If that happens, they need to take immediate action. Warn them that they will likely be expected, and that there's a shoot order." It might be directed at me, but any order on me extends to my people as well. "Send the other two to stake out the original hotel. Have them alert us when Will's soldiers leave the premises, and tell them to pick up anyone who leaves after them—male or female."

That's the best scenario. The worst is that the guards are working with the enemy.

"Our people need to remain in constant contact," I add.

"What if it's just the guards who leave?"

"Then we know they're involved, and getting Ms. Clarke out of Quimper is going to be particularly challenging."

"We're two minutes from touchdown," the pilot announces through the intercom.

"We need to find a place in her room to hide until she's alone. Because once she's there, no one's getting near her room."

"Maybe I can. They'll be less suspicious of a woman."

"They're not going to take any chances. Her life's on the line, and if they fuck up, it'll be an ugly end for them." Will won't show a lick of mercy. *If they fuck it up, they better hope Will gets to them before I do.*

She nods and puts the interior layout on the big screen. "We took a section of the hotel without suites to ensure that the guards wouldn't stay in the room with her once they've swept it."

It's good thinking, but a single room means there are fewer places to disappear.

"I'll go to the roof," I mutter, studying the layout. There will definitely be somewhere to hide up there, and they don't have a large enough team to search every inch of the place on short notice. That's one of the perks of the last-minute hotel change. "From there, I'll find a way onto the balcony after her guards check the room."

"You're not serious, right?" she asks, as the wheels hit the ground with a thud, although there's no thud that can mask the exasperation in her voice.

"You have a better idea?"

"Platform beds in hotel rooms are hollow." She points to the screen. "The beds in upscale establishments are high off the floor—that means taller platforms, which leaves plenty of room for lying in wait."

I've never known Tamar to be prone to hyperbole. If she's not sure, she says so. But we're in a tough spot, bordering on desperate, and I can't afford to leave anything to chance.

"How do you know those beds are on hollow platforms? Fabric obscures the entire bottom of the bed to the floor."

"The hotel was completely renovated two years ago. I guarantee the mattress is sitting on a platform. It's industry standard. The bed skirt is for polish."

"You're sure?"

"Yes. It's too expensive to make them solid. I've seen this tactic used successfully before. Many times. Including with platforms that were not as tall as these appear to be."

It's genius. "Once I'm in, how do I get out?"

"The room she'll be in has a king-size bed."

In most of the world, that means two single beds pushed together. It certainly does in Europe.

"The cover on the platform is replaced," she continues, "leaving an inch or two open at the top of the bed for ventilation. Then the bed is made up from the outside, and the pillows positioned carefully so as not to cut off the air supply. When it's time to move, you slip your hands through and push the cover down. You can flip it if necessary, but it will be quieter if you just make an opening large enough to squeeze through."

It's a clever ruse. No question. But in practice, nothing is ever as easy as it sounds.

"I'm plenty strong enough, even with little leverage to get out," Tamar adds.

I shake my head. "I'm going in. I need you to make the bed after me." She doesn't reply, and even I realize that I sound like a misogynist. "Good thinking, Tamar. It's an impressive tactic."

She shrugs. "I didn't come up with it. I was trained by an elite agency."

That's for sure. No one would know better than Mossad how to successfully infiltrate a heavily guarded hotel room.

5

LEXIE

WHEN I WAKE UP, I gaze out the plane window, my mind wandering to Rafael even before I get my bearings. *You're going to have to do better if you expect to get over him.*

Forgetting him is going to take a concerted effort and time. *A lot of time.* Some small part of me knows I'll never be able to forget him.

For years, I've built him up to be some kind of Prince Charming. If Prince Charming is a hot, dirty-talking criminal type who oozes sin, that is.

That night in the vineyard solidified everything I'd ever dreamed about him—and more. Then those long, white-hot hours, in his apartment, that turned into blissful nights with his body tucked around mine. My traitorous pussy and my heart flutter in tandem as I remember—*it's infuriating.*

Sex can't carry a relationship forever, not even amazing sex, but it was our way of communicating all the things that were too hard for people like us to say. Although it turns out we were speaking different languages, and I didn't realize it until it was too late. *That's the lie I've been repeating inside my head so that I stop beating myself up for being weak and pathetic. So pathetic.*

I knew it was just sex for Rafael—maybe a little more than that, but nothing compared to how I felt about him. *Not even close.* Even knowing this, I interpreted every ragged breath, every groan and shudder, every trembling orgasm as something it wasn't. I put stock and importance in all of it, especially in the gentle caresses and whispered sweet nothings that came after —stock and importance they didn't deserve.

It's not that I should have known better—I did know better. It's like I believed that my pussy held some voodoo magic that would cause him to fall in love with me. It's embarrassing to admit, even to myself.

Rafael didn't lie or even mislead me. He told me exactly who he is, and then he showed me—not once, but twice. But I'm stubborn and I refused to accept any of it, until I didn't have a choice.

I glance out the window as though there's a balm somewhere in the heavens that will soothe my aching heart. If it's there, I can't find it.

We seem to be flying low, as though we're about to land—although I don't remember the landing gear being lowered, and the flight attendant isn't seated. I haven't been paying close attention for long, but it's almost as though we're circling the city. *Why?*

Maybe I missed something while I dozed. "Is there a problem?" I ask Anya when she brings me water.

"I'm not at liberty to discuss it, but"—she leans over until her mouth is just inches from my ear—"it's for your safety."

For my safety?

She captures my gaze with a quick nod as she straightens.

"Is there a threat?"

She lifts a shoulder like she doesn't know, but it's not terribly convincing. "May I get you a snack?" she asks with a practiced smile.

A snack? She's told me everything she plans on telling—at

least for now. But offering a snack means Anya suspects it's going to be awhile before we land. "No, thank you."

After she disappears, I scan the cabin for the guards. Ivy is at the front of the plane, and Callum is seated in the rear. Both appear to be on alert. Is it possible the traffickers veered from the pattern, like they did with the timing in Oslo? *Am I too late, again? Please, God, no.*

I swallow the grapefruit-size lump in my throat and peel the blanket from my legs, setting it on the armrest before going to the front of the plane.

"We're circling the city. What's going on?" I ask Ivy, taking the seat across from her.

"It's a safety precaution," she replies, her tone even and matter-of-fact.

"Why the precaution?"

She lifts her chin. "It's not something you need to worry about."

Really? I feel the ire build. My tolerance for this nonsense is even lower now, after being guarded by Giana and Sabio, who treated me like an adult invested in her own safety. *This is not going to cut it.*

"Does that mean the precaution was put in place for your safety or, perhaps, the crew's?"

Her eyes widen.

"I'm never surprised when a male guard tells me not to worry my pretty little head, but I expect more from you. I have the right to know if there's a problem."

"Of course, miss. Your father will explain everything when we land."

This is not what I envisioned when I told my father I wanted guards who interacted forthrightly with me. I should have known he would never step back and allow the guards, *my guards*, to have an honest relationship with me. *Another thing I kidded myself about.*

"I understand that you're following orders, Ivy, but I want to talk to my father, now. Before we land."

"Communication with the ground has been spotty for the past hour," she says, more forthright now, "but let's see if we can connect you from the main server in the conference room."

6

RAFAEL

"I WANT TO STRESS, *AGAIN*," Tamar says on the way to the new hotel, "it's a very, very bad idea to keep that shoot order in place. Please reconsider."

By *again*, she means for the fifth time she's raised the issue since I got off the phone with Will. She's now added two *verys* for emphasis. I plan on ignoring this the same way I ignored the four previous pleas to reconsider. It's only her training and respect for chain of command that's stopped her from telling me it's the fucking stupidest thing she's ever heard. *It wouldn't be far from the truth.* But if Will retracts the order now, we'll lose control of the narrative. I don't want that.

"Everyone understand what they're doing?"

"Yes," the two soldiers grunt in unison. They're seated in the front of the SUV and were on the plane with us. I don't know them well, but Zé handpicked them for the trip to the US after I refused to take him. I have no doubt they're capable and lethal.

"Do not forget," I order, mostly for Tamar's benefit, "Ms. Clarke's safety is our primary concern. Today, I'm just a soldier, like you."

7

LEXIE

COMMUNICATION with the ground must be better, because my father answers immediately. "Clarke," he growls.

"Dad, what's going on?"

"Lexie," he murmurs. "Everything all right?"

That's rich. "That's what I'm wondering. We've been circling the city as a precaution. What does it mean?" *Please don't let it be anything to do with the traffickers.*

"New flight crew. They're just being extra cautious."

Bullshit.

"Does this have anything to do with the traffickers who've been terrorizing the Continent?"

My father doesn't say anything. I shouldn't have blurted it. *That was a mistake.* But from the moment I learned we were circling as a safety precaution, I haven't been able to push the thought away. What if they skipped a city beginning with the letter *R* and went straight to *Q*? What if I was wrong, and another woman's been abducted?

"Why would you say that?" he says finally, in pure form. *Answer a question with a question.*

I try to read between the lines, but it's my father and he's not easy to read even in person, let alone over the phone. His tone isn't at all defensive. It's more like those times when he suspects I'm up to trouble and fires questions at me until I'm backed into a corner—step by step. *I need to be careful or he'll turn this plane around in a heartbeat.*

"It's in the back of everyone's mind. Certainly every European woman under twenty-five who has any sense. If it's not that, what is the problem?"

He's quiet again. "I hoped not to have to worry you until the matter was settled." My father draws a breath. "That bastard, Rafael Huntsman, who doesn't deserve you and never did, commandeered a satellite and has been tracking your flight."

What?

It's as though I tripped into a cavernous hole in the ground. There's so much noise as it swallows me, but I can't make sense of anything because it's all muffled sound.

I finger the angel wings in my pocket—that I took with me, just in case. *The one tie I wasn't willing to sever.*

"He's stalking you," my father continues, "and I have every reason to believe he means to do you harm."

Stalking me? No. It makes absolutely no sense. "I don't understand."

"He contacted me, looking for you when you wouldn't answer his calls. When I wouldn't give him any information, he said he'd find you. He sounded unhinged, Lexie. Completely unhinged. We've secured a hangar at the airport, and we're clearing the area before you deplane. It's not London, and the French are not proving as amenable as I'd hoped. But it won't be too much longer before you land."

"Dad, Rafael wouldn't hurt me." I don't believe it for a single second.

"He commandeered a satellite from a foreign government, Lexie. There's no telling what he might do. A few extra minutes on the plane isn't going to hurt you."

"Let me talk to him. Maybe I can help."

"No!" he roars. "Do not contact him. It took some effort, but we managed to scramble the satellite signal transmitting him information about your location. If you call him, he'll be able to track you again."

This is—surreal.

"The plane will land and taxi to a secure location surrounded by guards. After you deplane, Brendon Symes will get you to safety. I have to go, sweetheart."

With that, he disconnects the call before I can ask anything more.

"Stalkers are big problems," Ivy explains, like I might not know this. "Especially men. No one presents the kind of danger they do."

Rafael isn't a stalker. He's too arrogant and proud to chase a woman who walked away.

The argument we had before he left was contentious, but if he had wanted to do me harm, he would have done it then, with tempers flaring. *Could something have happened in the interim to make the situation worse between him and Valentina?* Maybe. It still doesn't make sense that he would commandeer a satellite to track me down and punish me.

I pull up the email from Rafael that I've been ignoring. *I have information about the traffickers. It's a matter of life and death. Contact me as soon as you get this.*

The traffickers. I knew it. They struck again. It's my fault.

I read the message again and again. It seems rational and sane—properly punctuated, no shouty capitals. Although I suppose it could be a ploy to get me to contact him. *But I just don't see it.*

Anya sticks her head in the conference room, looking as washed out as I feel. "We're about to land. You can remain here, but please fasten your seat belts."

"Not here," Ivy says brusquely, jumping to her feet. "I need you seated in the center of the main cabin when we land. It's protocol under these circumstances."

My skin prickles as I stand. *Rafael unhinged.* I think about how angry he was when we were in the kitchen at the apartment. I guess that could be considered unhinged. *What if they shoot him?* An icy shiver runs up my spine.

I turn to Ivy. "Is there a shoot order on Rafael Huntsman?"

She peers into my eyes. "He poses a serious danger to you."

Ivy doesn't confirm my fear, yet she told me everything I need to know. It has to be my father's doing, because a shoot order on someone like Rafael had to have come from the very top. *He's the only one who can call it off.*

What if it's a kill order? Oh my God.

"I need to talk to my father again before I go to the main cabin."

"There's no time," she cautions. "We're in landing mode, and there won't be a signal anyway."

My mouth is bone-dry and my hands are shaking. I'm not worried for my own safety, but Rafael—I need to warn him. *But how?* Right now, I can't even send an email, and even when I can, I'm sure my communications are being monitored. He won't get it, certainly not in time.

8

RAFAEL

I LIE in an oversize coffin for what seems like hours, waiting for Lexie to go into the bathroom. The wait is purgatory.

Each time she shifts on the mattress above, the movement echoes in the hollow chamber. It's a small sound, but frustrating. She's achingly close, but still out of reach.

I scroll through my messages so that when I get the hell out of here, my eyes won't need time to adjust to the light. I can't afford to be incapacitated, not for one second. When I get word, I need to move quickly.

We knew the guards would sweep the room thoroughly and would likely discover any surveillance we planted. If there had been an inkling that we'd be in this situation, we would have had an undetectable monitoring device with us on the trip. Fortunately, Tamar is resourceful and improvised using the smart alarm clock beside the bed for surveillance.

Lexie will be pissed when she finds out we monitored—spied on—her in the room. I don't like it for her, either, but there was no fucking choice. We have to know the coast is clear before I can move.

While the wait has been excruciating, it gave our extra team an opportunity to get here, and it allowed for important exit planning. It would be ideal if we could get her out of the country before dawn.

Despite the extra planning time, no one believes we can get Lexie safely out of the hotel without Will's guy, Brendon Symes. This isn't a circumstance where we can dress her up as a maid or shove her in the bottom of a laundry cart and pile dirty linen on her. Those tactics work only when no one is expecting them. Lexie has to walk or be carried out, and to do that, Symes will need to create a diversion.

It's hot as hell in here, and every muscle rebels against confinement. My mind begins to wander. I imagine Lexie's damp skin against mine after we've gone a few rounds. Her hair is matted to her cheeks. I sweep it away so that no part of her is hidden from me. Beads form on her forehead and above her lip as she babbles, eyes glazed. "I can't," she whimpers. But she can, and if I coax her body just right, she always gives up another orgasm for me. *Always.*

My cock twitches, and I curse, just as my phone lights up with a single word.

Now.

9

LEXIE

After stripping off every stitch of clothing, I lean into the shower and turn on the water. It's then I sense something moving behind me.

Before I can turn my head, a large hand covers my mouth and secures my body against a wall of muscle. *I can't move.*

The traffickers. My throat tightens with panic. *He's going to sell me. I'm going to die.*

The man twists so that we can see each other in the mirror.

Rafael. It takes a few seconds for my brain to register that it's really him. Although the wild black eyes in the glass do nothing to reassure me that I'm safe.

I can't stop staring at his reflection. He looks—unhinged. *Maybe my father was right.*

"Francesca Russo is dead." His voice is hoarse, devoid of empathy—or any emotion at all.

Did he kill her?

Fear claws at me as I struggle to breathe through my mouth.

"Your father's operation has been infiltrated, and it's unclear who can be trusted. You're in danger. We need to get you out of here."

You're in danger. Every cell of my being knows it's true, but the danger seems to be coming from him. I need to alert the guards—*how*? But what if he's right? What if they can't be trusted?

"If I take my hand off your mouth, can you be quiet?"

I pause as the dark eyes in the mirror bore into me. *He's unhinged.* My father's words are all I think about as I nod.

"Promise me, Angel, that if I let go, you won't scream. Both our lives depend on it."

Especially his.

Maybe he is a bit mad—I don't know. But there's a shoot order, and I have no doubt the guards will kill him in a heartbeat if I scream. I don't care how deranged he is; I won't let that happen.

Get a grip, Lexie. Rafael would not kill Francesca, and he wouldn't hurt you. My brain is cautious, but my heart knows he wouldn't do those things.

"Promise me, Lexie. I don't want to die—not without knowing you're safe." His eyes are softer now and filled with concern.

He's not a danger to me.

"I promise," I mumble into his hand and nod.

He studies me in the mirror before dropping his hand from my mouth.

I take a ragged breath and then another, as he turns me to face him. "Get dressed. We need to go."

He seems more like himself now—more controlled—but I'm not leaving with him. I don't want him shot, but my father wouldn't lie about him going to great lengths to stalk me. What if he's now decided I'm a traitor, and he needs to make some sort of example of me? The push and pull of emotions, and the panic that hasn't fully subsided, is making it hard for me to think logically.

You need to stay near your guards. Once you go with him,

anything could happen. This is a basic tenet of survival in my world. I need to lean on what I've been taught, because I can't think clear enough to make a good decision right now.

"I don't want you to die either. You need to get out of here before the guards find you. But I'm not going with you. My father said you commandeered a satellite and were tracking my flight. That's not rational behavior."

He pulls out his phone and sends a text.

"Rational went out the window after I learned about Francesca, and I couldn't reach you or your father."

Francesca. I squelch the sob with a ragged breath. "She's really dead?"

"She is."

My heart races again. Maybe it never stopped. "Who are you texting?"

Rafael holds up the phone and flashes the screen so I can see: *WC.*

"My father?"

He nods.

What if it's a trick to get me to go with him?

"What's going on? Why are you talking with my father? He said I shouldn't trust you."

Rafael winces. "We don't have a lot of time." His gaze skims my naked body, and the knob in his throat bobs. "Get dressed and I'll tell you everything."

I snatch my shirt from the floor. "Go on," I urge, making quick work of the buttons.

"Your father's men discovered the flight attendant who was to be part of your crew—dead."

Cristina? No! She can't be dead. Please don't let it be her.

"An impostor used her credentials to get onto your plane."

He's telling the truth. How else would he know that it wasn't the usual crew aboard the plane? A sense of relief begins to creep in, or maybe it's a need to trust him—to trust someone.

Before I can ask a question, three raps sound at the room door.

He holds his finger to his mouth. "Wait here."

I grab his arm. "No. I'll go to the door. There's a shoot order. Even if the guards aren't compromised, they'll kill you."

"I know about the order. Your father sent a trusted man to help us get out of here. I want to be sure it's him." He gazes at me. "Lock the door and keep my phone in case you need to call for help. Here," he says, pulling a gun from an ankle holster.

"Rafael. No. You need your phone and gun."

"I have another gun and a knife."

I stare at the weapon in his hand.

"It's a precaution, Angel. That's all." He runs a thumb over my cheek, and I'm swamped with familiar feelings—feelings that obscure all cogent thought. "Cover that gorgeous ass, but first lock the door behind me."

I don't lock the door. I crack it so I can listen, then place the gun on the vanity and dress.

"You don't have much time to get her off the property. Ten minutes, tops."

I don't recognize the voice, but that doesn't mean anything. Aside from the people who guard us, I don't know most of my father's men.

"Go down in the service elevator," he continues, "and get into the food service truck on the ramp. Don't dawdle."

"If this is a trap," Rafael grunts, "I will come back from the dead long enough to drag you into the bowels of hell."

"I follow orders," the man replies. "Godspeed."

Rafael appears, with his gun drawn. "We need to go." He slips his phone in his pocket and hands me the gun from the vanity top. "Keep this. Next time I tell you to lock the door, you need to listen."

He takes my hand and sticks his head out into the hall before leading us toward an elevator that Tamar is holding.

"Ms. Clarke's father arranged for our plane to be moved to a VIP section of the airport reserved for the French president and foreign heads of state," Tamar tells Rafael as we descend. "Once we get there, we'll be fine. At this time of night, it's a quick trip."

My father's helping him. *It's true.* I squeeze his fingers. I still don't understand what's happening, but I'm safer now than I was before Rafael showed up.

"Do you know anything about the food truck waiting downstairs?" Rafael asks.

"It's ours," Tamar replies. "And our soldiers are covering the ramp."

I feel him relax beside me, even as I clutch the gun in a shaky hand.

"Nothing's going to happen to you, Angel," he murmurs.

I'm not sure if he says it for my benefit or his. But I believe him.

When the elevator stops and the doors open, Rafael holds me against him, using his body to shield mine. Guards surround us, and the adrenaline surges, propelling me down the ramp at warp speed and into the truck.

"Go! Go! Go!" he shouts to the driver even before the door slams shut.

10

RAFAEL

MY PULSE DOESN'T RETURN to normal until we're airborne.

The sun isn't even up, and it's already been a hell of a day. But I'm not complaining. Lexie's shaken, but safe, and the fucker my men found sneaking out of the original hotel is shackled in the cargo hold, hopefully freezing his balls off.

My knife and I are jonesing to chat with him. I want to know exactly what he had planned for her, and who ordered it. But I won't have that bastard in the cabin with Lexie here.

I glance at her seated in the center of the cabin, staring out the window. We need to talk, and it's not going to be pretty. She's probably exhausted. I know I am, and I should wait, but I need answers.

As I make my way to her, my conscience pricks. Her face is ashen, and she looks worn around the edges. Beautiful still, but frayed. *And fragile.* Not so different from how she looked at Sirena the night we disrupted the ring. *Maybe the answers can wait.*

"Hey," I say, taking the seat beside her. "You okay?"

She nods. "Francesca was murdered?"

Most young women in her position would be concerned

with their own safety above all else. Not Lexie. "Yeah. Along with a seasoned guard, near home."

She squeezes her eyes tight, but a few tears escape, and I feel them in the pit of my stomach. If this had been a week ago, I would have leaned over and dried her tears with my shirt, or caught them on my lips while I comforted her. Even now I want to soothe her pain. But the waters are murky between us, and I hold myself back from touching her.

"You said you would explain everything," she murmurs, dabbing at her eyes.

"I will. Do you want to talk now, or do you need to sleep first?"

She shakes her head.

"I have questions, too, and I'm going to push you for honest answers," I warn. "You might want to be well rested for that."

If she's tired, it'll be easier to catch her in a lie or to back her into a corner so that I get the answers I want. When she's tired, she allows herself to be vulnerable around me—or at least she did—and lets the mask slip. I treasured those times when she let me see the raw parts she hid from the rest of the world. I never took advantage of her when she was like that, and I won't start now. *No matter how much I want the information.*

"I napped on the flight," she replies. "But you look like hell. When's the last time you slept?"

I snicker. "I've been busy. I said some awful things to my woman, kicked her out of my place, and she ran straight into danger. There was no way I was going to allow anyone to hurt her."

"Because you reserve that right for yourself," she says softly, more of a probe than a statement.

I shake my head. "No one has that right, Lexie. Least of all me."

"I'm not your woman." Her voice is laden with emotion. "And you didn't kick me out. I left of my own accord."

"Semantics."

"I realize this flight has to land in Porto first. But after it's refueled, I'd like to use the plane to go home to London, Rafael." The emotion is gone from her voice, and she's all business as she sits up straight. "I'll fully compensate you for the use, including the crew."

I bristle at her offer to *compensate* me for what amounts to nothing more than a favor I've done for many people. "I don't want your money. You can use my plane anytime it's available. But going to London is not an option right now."

"Why not?" she demands, narrowing her gaze. "I won't be held prisoner."

I'd prefer not to hold her against her wishes, but she's not going to London until things are calmer there.

"I'll tell you everything, and then you'll do the same," I add, meeting her gaze. "But let's talk in the conference room, where we'll have some privacy."

"Fine." She stands and glares at me when I don't follow her lead. "Let's go find that privacy you need."

I'm sure she'd rather talk out here, where she thinks I might not push her for answers others might overhear. *She's misjudged me, if that's what she believes.*

I'm not worried about the soldiers on this plane overhearing and spreading gossip. If I were, they wouldn't be here. But I don't intend to let her off the hook.

Lexie is going to tell me why she was in Quimper, even if I have to tie her to a chair and edge her for the remainder of the flight. Her whimpers and sultry pleas are mine. As is her pleasure. No one gets to listen to any of it—but me.

11

LEXIE

Rafael carries a tray into the conference room with tea and biscuits for me, and a coffee for him. He places it on the table between us and sits down across from me.

I dunk the tea sachet in the hot water while he scrolls through his phone. I'm not sure if he's actually responding to messages or dragging his feet while he concocts some bullshit story about why I can't go to London. But after a minute or two, I've had enough.

"Why isn't London an option? If it's about the plane—"

He lifts his head and glares at me. "I already told you I don't care about the damn plane. And if you ever offer to compensate me for anything again, I'll take you over my knee and slap your ass until you can't sit for a month."

The last time I was draped over his lap while he slapped my ass, I managed to hump his thigh to a blissful orgasm. *Focus, Lexie. Focus.*

"If borrowing the plane isn't the issue, then what is?"

"There's been a lot of trouble in London tonight—small things, but your father's bracing for something bigger to happen. As I mentioned earlier, his organization has been infiltrated. He's concerned about getting you into the city safely and tucked away before the other shoe drops."

Trouble in London. Tucked away is nothing more than a euphemism for *in hiding. Wait. Mum.* "Where's my mother?"

"They moved her to a secure location right away. That's all I know."

"But not my father. I'm sure he's out and about, waving his middle finger in the air, and taking every opportunity to step into harm's way."

"I don't know where your father is, but when I last spoke with him, he was looking for a traitor, not inviting trouble. Whatever is going on is serious. He knows you're safe, but you should call to tell him yourself." He hands me the phone. "It's already connected to Wi-Fi."

The last time I spoke with my father, he lied to me. A lie that could have gotten Rafael killed. My stomach rebels, the acid tickling my throat. *What if I had shouted for my guards?*

Any number of things could have gone wrong, and Rafael would be dead. I realize my father was trying to protect me, but the price of that protection was too damn high. I couldn't have lived with myself if something had happened to him—especially because of me.

With the possibilities swirling inside my head, coiling my anxiety tighter and tighter, I enter my father's number.

"I hope you're not calling because you already lost my daughter, Huntsman," my father snarls. "Because I will put that bullet in you that I promised."

It begins as a giggle, bubbling in my chest and spilling out all over the room until I'm nearly hysterical. It's not at all funny, but I can't stop. My pent-up emotion refuses to be bottled any longer. It wants an outlet, and it doesn't care that Rafael is staring at me like I've gone mad.

"Lexie?" my father says sternly. "Is that you?"

"Ye—yes," I manage. "I'm sorry. I'm a bit out of sorts. It's been a wild night."

"Are you sure you're okay?" he asks, his tone as gentle as he can be.

"I'm fine," I assure him, even though I'm an emotional wreck. "What's going on in London? I'm worried about Mum—and you."

He draws a breath. "Is Rafa there?"

"Yes. We're in the conference room on his plane."

"Anyone else there?"

"No."

"Shut the door and put the phone on speaker, sweetheart."

12

LEXIE

"WHAT'S THE WORD, WILL?" Rafael asks after putting us on speaker.

"Tyler Worthington is the traitor," he sneers.

I gasp and glance at Rafael, whose brow is knit tightly. Tyler is—was—the man my father groomed to take over his operation when he retired—or if something happened to him in the interim. I have no brothers. No cousins. And I don't have a dick that's not battery operated, so I would never be considered for the position. Not that I have any interest in being a crime boss.

"I'm so sorry, Dad. I know how much you liked him." *How much you believed in him.* The betrayal is stunning.

"Was he acting alone?" Rafael's concerned about whether the head of the snake has been cut off or if there's more trouble out there biding its time.

I'm worried too—mostly for my parents, especially my father, who is vulnerable if there are traitors in the inner circle.

"It's too early to know. There are a handful of foot soldiers he turned, for sure, but he had enough power, and my backing, that he didn't need to turn too many people to stage a quiet coup."

"He kill the flight attendant?" Rafael asks.

"It was done on his order, and he paid some gang members to cause problems for us last night."

"Cristina's dead?" I ask my father in a wobbly voice.

"Cristina's fine."

Cristina's fine. Cristina's fine. Relief floods me, but before my spirits are lifted, it hits me. "Which flight attendant is dead?"

"Anya—the woman being impersonated. You don't know her."

I don't, but still, I feel terrible. Although not as crushed as I would be if it were Cristina who had been murdered.

"The woman on the flight—what's her name?"

"Astrid."

"Astrid. She's a bad actor?"

Rafael nods and my father grunts.

"Something about her made me uncomfortable, but I couldn't put my finger on it. What about the pilot?"

"He's loyal."

"Dad, was she going to sabotage the plane?" My father's plane has been targeted before, and I lost my grandparents and others I'd known my whole life. It was gruesome. My mother held up through the search and recovery—and the funerals—but it stole some of her fire.

"Your flight wasn't targeted. She was learning the ropes and sending information so that a future flight could be compromised. Worthington had always planned on subbing her when the new flight crew came on board next month. But when we changed the timing, he had to move quickly, because once Roman, the pilot, worked with Anya—the real Anya—a seamless switch would have been impossible. They look very similar, but not identical."

Eerily similar, now that I look back on it.

"Why did Worthington turn?" I can't understand why someone who was heir apparent to a lucrative enterprise, and all the power anyone could ever want, would turn and risk losing everything—including his life. Because he will die and it will be a very public, very ugly end.

"It's rarely just one thing that turns a man. But you're getting older, and apparently he was concerned that you might marry before his ticket got punched."

I side-eye Rafael, who's doodling on a notepad, like he does sometimes. Even when it seems like he's not paying attention, he is.

"This has been in the works for a while. It has nothing to do with your friendship with Rafa," my father adds, in embarrassing detail.

I feel my cheeks warm, but Rafael seems to take it in stride, as though it's just another piece to a damning puzzle.

"Is there any connection to the bastard in my cargo hold?" Rafael asks, glancing up.

Someone's in the cargo hold? It'll have to wait until later.

"Doesn't appear to be. But we've just gotten started with the interrogation. We'll explore that avenue. Trust me. I'll let you know what we find."

We've just gotten started with the interrogation. Worthington deserves what he gets, but still, I shudder at the prospect.

"I'm coming back to London to be with Mum," I say quietly, but firmly, my tone unwavering. I'm not asking permission from either of them. "I'm sure she's lonely and worried about you out and about." It's isolating being in lockdown. She shouldn't have to be alone.

"I'd like you back in London, and so would your mother. But give me a few days until we have a better sense of how we've been compromised."

A few more days to torture people until they give up the goods.

"For now, stay in Porto—either at Valentina's place at Huntsman Lodge or at Antonio and Daniela's house. I spoke with Antonio. They would love to have you, and you'd be safe there."

Rafael sits back with a sour expression. My father's suggestions didn't include him. Although it wouldn't have made the slightest difference. My heart hasn't given up on him completely, although it's beginning to understand the term *no future*. My brain and my sanity, however, want no part of him.

"Anything else, sweetheart?" Dad asks.

"Yes. Make sure you call off that shoot order on Rafael. And don't put out any more orders like that on him. *Ever*."

Rafael's eyes light up, and he winks at me.

Just because I don't want him in my bed doesn't mean I want him dead—unless he comes around with another woman on his arm. Then all bets are off.

"Rafa?" my father asks.

"I think it's outlived its usefulness," Rafael quips dryly.

"For now."

"Dad," I admonish, even though there's something about their interaction that seems a bit light. I don't quite get it. Did he actually think Rafael was going to say, *No, keep the shoot order; it makes life more interesting*?

"My daughter's safety is your greatest concern while she's in Porto, Huntsman. Don't fuck it up. Lexie, get in touch with me right away if there are any problems."

"Tyler Worthington," I murmur after my father is off. "I'm dumbfounded. Imagine if—" I don't finish my thought because it's too painful to think about. I might have died, or my mother. We'll never know. But the one thing I do know for certain is that for Tyler to take the reins, my father would have to be dead. I wrap my arms around myself to ward off the chill.

"Fucking psychopath," says the man who's transporting a prisoner in the belly of the plane.

"What's the story with the guy in the cargo hold?"

"We think he might be involved with the flesh traders. But we're not sure."

My stomach does somersaults. "In what way?"

He pins me with his gaze. "I think you've asked enough questions, Angel. Now it's my turn. Tell me why you went to Quimper. Save the wedding present story for someone who isn't accustomed to making online purchases."

Here we go. I snatch a piece of paper from the pad he was doodling on and fold it in half, for no other reason than to buy myself some time to think. "It wasn't a lie."

"But it wasn't the entire truth."

No, it wasn't. I have nothing to lose by coming clean with him. There will never be a relationship between us. It no longer matters if he thinks I'm reckless. *What do I care what he thinks, anyway?*

There's nothing to lose, but everything to gain. I lost my chance to warn the authorities in Quimper. Rafael has much more clout in the European world than I do, and he can help—if he chooses too. *He will.* Rafael won't say it's outside his purview, like my father might. *He won't.*

I study his unshaven face, etching the details onto my brain, until I can almost feel the prickle of scruff on my fingertips. Once I tell him, there's no going back. I will forever be the reckless girl he believed me to be. *Always.*

It doesn't matter anymore, Lexie.

No, it doesn't.

With a heavy heart, I begin to form words. "There was more to the story than wedding presents."

"I'm listening," he murmurs, his tone no different from when we were in bed with his mouth grazing my temple. *"That's it. Let go, Angel. I've got you."*

I draw a jagged breath and hear the faint echoes of a tragic whimper. But somehow I find the courage to share the secret

I've held so close for so long—with the man who will judge me in the harshest light possible.

"The traffickers are going to strike in Quimper soon. I went to warn the authorities in hopes of disrupting their plan and saving an unsuspecting woman from a life of hell."

His expression is unreadable—almost blank. For a moment, I'm not sure he understands what I'm trying to tell him. It's not until he squeezes his eyes shut and lets his head fall back, with a feral growl, that I know he understood *every* word.

13

RAFAEL

THE TRAFFICKERS ARE GOING to strike in Quimper soon. I went to warn the authorities in hopes of disrupting their plan.

She did not just fucking say that she went to disrupt the traffickers' plans. I must have misunderstood. She couldn't possibly have so little regard for her life.

I take a moment to pull myself together before I go on a rampage and destroy everything on this plane. When I'm breathing again, I replay her words. *The traffickers are going to strike in Quimper soon.*

How can she know this?

"What makes you think the flesh traders are going to Quimper next?" The words come out with an eerie calm that belies the drumbeat in my soul.

"They follow an alphabetical pattern," she explains, like she's teaching a word problem to a kid.

An alphabetical pattern?

"Quimper is not next. It's likely to be Riga or Rimini, but I can't be certain. Although I am sure Quimper will be hit right after that."

Either she's insane or I am. I have dyslexia, and even though

I've learned to compensate, words can trip me up occasionally, but I don't think that's what's happening. Although what she's suggesting makes no sense. "Which alphabet are you using? Because *R* doesn't come before *Q* in the Latin one."

"It's an alphabetical pattern, but not a sequential one."

What the fuck does that mean? "Explain."

"Porto, Oslo, R-city, Quimper. *P-O-R-Q*. I traced it back almost two years. From everything I've studied, they have never deviated from that pattern. It would make more sense if I could show you the graphs and charts I created."

She created graphs and charts? Jesus Christ.

"The pattern," she continues, "is *B-D-C-F-E-H-G*—"

I hold up both hands to stop her before my head explodes trying to make sense of something that will never make sense to me—not like this, anyway. "Why are you so sure about Quimper?"

"There are only three European cities that begin with the letter Q and also follow the profile. Quarteira is in Portugal, and the traffickers were just there, and the other is Quartu Sant'Elena, which has already been a target."

"What about Queluz?"

"It's in Portugal and doesn't fit the profile anyway."

"Why not?"

"It would be easier to explain if I could borrow a computer to access my work."

I am so pissed at her, my hand trembles as I text Tamar to come to the conference room.

"You have this information stored on the cloud where anyone could connect it to you?" I'm ten seconds from shaking her.

"Of course not," she huffs, like I'm an idiot. "It's stored securely in a place that can't be accessed by anyone but me."

Can't be accessed is a relative term, but still, I'm so relieved she took precautions that I bite back the retort on the tip of my tongue.

"What other variables are you considering besides the alphabet?"

"Size, redundancy, timing." She shrugs. "I have a good sense of the pattern, but I don't pretend to understand how all the variables impact it." Her shoulders sag. "I was certain they were going to hit Oslo, but I was off on the timing."

There's a knock on the door before I can ask any more questions or mention the designer she claimed to be doing a story on. "Come in."

"You need me?" Tamar asks.

"Ms. Clarke needs a computer. Set it up so we can use the large screen."

Lexie and I eye each other as Tamar works, each in search of clues. She seems a little nervous, though still defiant. But I want answers that aren't on her face or in her body language.

"Anything else?" Tamar asks, preparing to leave.

"Tamar's going to sit in on this discussion," I tell Lexie. "She's trustworthy, and this is her area of expertise. Having her here will be beneficial to both of us."

I wait for Lexie's response, but it's just for show. Tamar needs to be present for this, and she will be, regardless of what Lexie wants.

After a long moment, Mata Hari nods, and I relax a bit. There's a fight ahead for us—a fucking war—but I prefer not to do battle every step of the way.

I glance up at Tamar, who I'm sure is wondering what the fuck is going on. Although her expression gives nothing away. "Ms. Clarke has been tracking the flesh traders."

Tamar doesn't bat an eyelash as she takes a seat. She nods, politely, like I just said *Ms. Clarke is going to Israel, and she's wondering about restaurants. Do you have any suggestions?*

I position my chair so I can see both the screen and Lexie, who has put up a color-coded graph.

"Tell us everything." I peer into her washed-out hazel eyes, narrowing my gaze. "I mean *everything*." My tone is pointed, but not as pointed as the consequences will be for her if she fucks with me on this. From the way she glares back, with her chin out, I'm quite sure she got the message.

I ask a few questions and jot down facts while Lexie and Tamar engage in a discussion that I struggle to follow. Not because of my dyslexia, but because most of it is highly technical.

Lexie's graphs and charts were created using software programs that are beyond my capabilities. Fortunately, Tamar is used to distilling complex technological information for me and the rest of the team, and she restates the jargon in ways that are understandable to the average person.

I might not be a tech whiz, but here are two things I do know: Tamar is impressed by the data Lexie has amassed, and if it didn't scare me half to death, I probably would be too. And second, I'm not sure I've ever seen Lexie so engaged or so happy. Even after everything that's happened in the last few days, her eyes are bright and alert as she shares the details of her discovery. That's what makes the next part so difficult.

The evidence Lexie collected is impressive, but not actionable. It's all circumstantial—at best—and there are huge holes in it. It's enough for me to haul some asshole in for questioning, but it won't be enough to convince the authorities to take any measures beyond those they're already taking. Tamar knows this too. But I'm going to have to be the one who breaks the news to Lexie.

"The risks you've taken aside," I say as kindly as I can, "this is a remarkable effort."

"Extraordinary," Tamar chimes in.

"Then why can't I get anyone to listen to me? I understand

why the cities operate as silos. But Interpol? I've contacted them so many times, and I've never heard a peep back." She drums her hand on the table. "I probably should have used my real name."

"No," I snap. "That would have put a big bull's-eye on your back." I scratch my forehead, because I know this is going to hurt her. "As salient as the evidence is, it's not actionable."

As her face deflates, I feel it in my chest.

"He's right," Tamar adds gently. "In theory, there's a striking pattern, but there are too many unknown variables at play. It appears a city that begins with *R* is next, but what would a practical recommendation be? Should they shut down all European cities that begin with the letter *R*? And for how long?" She shakes her head. "We need more. There has to be more. Something we're not seeing yet."

"But Quimper," Lexie says with the tang of frustration. "That's a clearer target. Rafael, you can talk to the authorities. They'll listen to you. It's important to catch them before Quimper—because if we can't..."

Lexie's voice trails off, but I can finish her thought. *Because if we can't, I'll have another victim on my conscience.*

"They're going to Quimper," she pleads. "I'm sure of it."

The room is quiet. She's not wrong. But she sees it with a hopeful optimism that's in short supply in my world. There's an innocence about it that snakes its way into my heart. I've always believed that as a child Lexie wasn't sheltered anywhere near enough, but sometimes she surprises me. Neither Tamar nor I are pessimists, but we trade in reality, not in hope.

"So that's it?" She looks squarely at me, disappointment clouding her features. "We just sit back while women keep getting kidnapped and sold into slavery?"

That's not what I want, nor what I'm thinking, but even if it were, there's no way Lexie's getting off this crusade. I either take control and let her come along for the ride, or when I'm distracted, she's going to steal the keys and drive the car headfirst into a ditch. *No survivors.*

I fill my cheeks with air and blow it out with a loud whoosh.

"All right. This is what we're going to do. For the next week, or for as long as it takes—the two of you are going to work together to gather more evidence. You've been enmeshed in this for a long time, Lexie. A fresh pair of eyes might bring clarity—especially Tamar's."

Lexie's face lights up, again, with newfound hope. But my head of IT looks like she swallowed a toad. Tamar's clearly impressed by what Lexie found, so I don't know what the problem is, and quite frankly, I don't care. It's been a shitty few days, and seeing Lexie happy—even if it's just for a few minutes—boosts my spirits.

Lexie glances from me to Tamar and back. "Should we inform the authorities in cities that begin with *R*?"

Tamar responds before I can. "There are so many of those cities that if we tell them, I guarantee the traffickers will learn everything we know and change their patterns. That will put us back at square one."

"Tamar's right. No one gets a heads-up yet."

We're essentially making a decision to sacrifice an innocent woman or two for the greater good. But it can't be helped. We have to proceed strategically. The bile rises in my throat as I contemplate the consequences of playing God. Because that's what we're doing.

"What about Interpol?" Lexie asks.

"I would have expected someone at Interpol to run with the info you sent," Tamar says, "even if they never got back to you. It might not be enough in and of itself, but they could have developed the information—set up some undercover operations. They have the resources. From everything I know, they're still operating in the dark."

"They're useless and untrustworthy," I announce flatly.

"One-half of the agency is on the take, and the other half are lazy bastards. Give me the name and contact information of everyone you alerted. Especially at Interpol."

Lexie nods, stifling a yawn.

She needs to sleep. This has been a hellish night for all of us, but Tamar and I have experienced hell before. Lexie is not a soldier—far from it.

"I kept careful records of all my correspondence," she says. "I'll pull them up."

"Not now. You should rest. Why don't you go back to the bedroom and get some sleep," I say quietly. "You're exhausted, and Tamar and I need to shift her schedule so she can dedicate the bulk of her time to working on this."

She flashes me a small smile that eases some of my anger. "A nap sounds good."

"You have time for a long nap. The flight will be making a big circle and then landing over the Spanish border. From there, we'll board a helicopter directly to Huntsman Lodge."

By now, whoever sent the asshole in cargo will have figured out that I have their guy, and they'll want him back before he talks. They'll be watching the Porto airport and the private landing strips nearby. But no one will expect us to deplane in Spain.

"I'm sure Valentina won't mind if I stay in her apartment again."

"Tamar, give us a minute." After Tamar leaves the conference room, I break the news. "You can't stay at Valentina's place."

"Why not?"

"I'm no longer permitted in her apartment, and I'm inclined to honor her wishes—for now. This means I can't secure it, or fully protect you while you're there. You'll stay at my place."

She purses her lips. "I don't think that's a good idea."

"I'll be staying at the Intercontinental." The words are bitter on my tongue. But it's a concession I make because I behaved like an asshole before she left.

She nods and heads for the door.

Lexie turns in the doorway. "Thank you for coming to get me."

Her voice is soft and sincere, and I want nothing more than to hold her in my arms and promise that I'll always find her—always. But she's not ready to hear that promise, and I'm not ready to make it—even though I would search the planet for her if she went missing.

"Isn't that why you took the wings when you left?"

She tips her head. "I took them—I don't know. A memory, I suppose. But I disabled the tracker."

I snicker. "That tracker can't be disabled with the little magnet trick you learned at Saint Phil's. I'm disappointed you think so little of me."

She sighs. "And thank you for not freaking out about what I've been doing—with the traffickers."

Oh, we're not done with that conversation, Angel. We haven't even begun. I have a lot to say on the subject, and you will listen to every terse word.

14

RAFAEL

After Lexie leaves, Tamar comes back. "She's onto something. Whoever got her messages at Interpol is holding the information close, perhaps for a little glory."

"Or they're involved in a cover-up."

"This is a dangerous proposition. I'm surprised you're allowing her to be involved."

I have no fucking choice.

"It'll be less dangerous if you're controlling the investigation. She'll report directly to you."

Tamar sits up straight and clasps her hands on the table. "I didn't want to say anything in front of Ms. Clarke, but that won't be possible."

It won't be possible? "Why the hell not?"

"I'll be tendering my resignation once we're back in Porto. But I can recommend someone who will be a good fit for her."

What the fuck? She's resigning? *I don't think so.*

"What do you mean you're tendering your resignation?" I have trouble getting out the words. "Did you and Zé have a falling-out?"

She presses her lips together and shakes her head. "I wouldn't leave a job because my boyfriend and I broke up."

"Are you sick?"

"No."

"Not playing twenty questions, Tamar. What the fuck is going on?"

She studies me without uttering a word. I hate not being in control. *Hate it.* Something's clearly wrong, but I can't fix it until I know what the problem is.

"Talk to me, Tamar."

"I don't think I can provide details without sounding insubordinate."

"This is a serious matter, and I'm not standing on protocol, and neither should you. I want to know why you're resigning. Speak freely."

"You're not going to like what I have to say."

"I got that part. Just say it."

She nods, meeting my eyes. "Protecting you is an impossible task. I always suspected that to be the case, but when you told me to stay in the waiting room at Bancroft's office, I knew for certain, and nothing that's happened since we arrived in Quimper has changed my mind."

Does she think I disrespected her in some way? That I don't think she's a capable soldier? "Do you believe I made those decisions—or any others—because you're a woman?"

"No," she replies without hesitating. "I wouldn't like it if that were the case, but it's something I could wrap my head around. You're a leader who wants to protect himself. I don't understand that."

She pauses, as though waiting for me to respond, but I want to hear everything she has to say first.

"Go on," I urge. "Lay out all the cards."

"In my former agency, we protected leaders of all levels, including the president. We did it proudly. It was a great honor.

You're not only a leader, but you're poised to step into a greater role, where you'll garner more enemies and be at greater risk for assassination. I don't believe you're going to change. I don't think you want to change," she adds softly.

I feel like I'm talking to her boyfriend. *It's fucking annoying.* "Zé's been filling your head with nonsense."

"I haven't said a single word today that I haven't experienced for myself. Besides, Zé would never speak a bad word about you—not even to me. But he's concerned. I'm sure of it. If something happens to you under his watch, he'll never forgive himself. The entire time we were in Quimper, I worried that I'd be the person to deliver the news of your death and break his heart. I can't do my best work under those conditions."

Zé would survive. He'd have a few choice words for me, but he'd survive. "Zé's tougher than you think."

"I know he's tough. That's not the point. He loves you like a brother."

"I'm not a fool, and I understand the ramifications of my behavior. Never more than when you just laid them on the table."

The room is heavy. I know that I put my people in a difficult position when I insist on being responsible for my own protection, but it's a matter of survival for me—mental survival. I carry many mementos from a horrific childhood, and I cope the best way I know.

"I don't like to dig too deep into my motivations, nor do I care to share them with others. But you leave me no choice." I pour myself a glass of water and take a drink. "Zé and I have a long history. He's been trying to protect me for most of our lives. I spent the first decade of my life with an abusive monster. I made a promise many years ago that I would never be helpless again. I don't depend on others for my safety. And I don't see that changing."

She nods. "Marlena would be perfect to work with Ms.

Clarke on the project you mentioned. And I think Tony is ready to be in charge of IT."

"You misunderstand me. I'm not accepting your damn resignation. You're too important to the team."

I get up and push in my chair before going to the door. "Do whatever you have to do to make peace with the fact that I'm an asshole." I stop in the doorway, a hand on the jamb. "For my part, I'll be more mindful of the security decisions I make for myself. Your concerns were duly noted. But don't expect perfection. It's never going to happen."

I leave before she can say another thing about resigning, because that is not happening.

On my way to the interior cabin, I stop in the galley and pour a bourbon. Lexie and I need to talk. Not about her lying and the stunt with the traffickers, but about what happened before I left for the US. The rest can wait.

I throw back the expensive bourbon like it's swill. The burn in my throat is satisfying, but nowhere near as satisfying as being around Lexie. It's probably going to require an apology to make things right. And because I'm a pussy, I grab a bottle of water and head back to grovel.

15

LEXIE

With a great sense of relief, I lock the door and crawl between the sheets in just my panties. I'm exhausted, but my mind is racing.

I'm going to work with Tamar. *Tamar, who is a brilliant badass.* If I had known this was possible, I'd have come clean sooner.

Rafael surprised me. Aside from that scary little growl, and a menacing scowl or two, he didn't lecture me on being reckless. Probably because it doesn't matter as much now that we're not together. The pivotal thing for him wasn't that I was a risk-taker. It was that he couldn't be involved with someone like that. *Someone like me.*

I shove away the thought. It's stealing the sense of peace I have from sharing the information about the ring and the relief I feel not to be working alone.

I still at the knock on the door and pull the covers higher. *Please don't be the flight attendant telling me we're going to land and I need to be seated in the cabin.* I haven't even had a chance to close my eyes.

"Yes?"

"It's me," he announces, opening the door without waiting to be invited in.

So much for the lock.

The room is dim, and when he enters, he blinks a few times, his long, inky lashes fluttering. Although it's too dark for me to see it now, when he blinks, his lashes cast shadows on his face, making him look young and a bit angelic. It's achingly beautiful. He's achingly beautiful. *Damn him.*

He glances at me, then at the clothing strewn over the chair, and back at me. I shiver and pull the covers higher still until only the upper part of my face is visible.

"I brought you some water. The body does funny things for the first twenty-four hours after an adrenaline rush. You need to stay hydrated." He holds out the bottle, and his eyes rest on the bare arm that reaches from under the covers to take it.

"Thank you," I croak.

"You should have some before you fall asleep."

I nod, but unscrewing the cap and taking a sip would require sitting up and exposing more skin than I care to. This could easily become one of those moments when two people fuck because they crave human connection—or to celebrate surviving—or because they're stupid.

He sits on the empty side of the bed, his feet on the floor, his palm inches from my hip, only a thin blanket and sheet between us. My pussy flutters, and I feel the stupid seeping into the room.

"I'd like to catch a nap before we land."

"And I'd like you to pull back the covers and invite me into the bed." He smirks. "But neither of us is getting what we want." He pauses, studying me. "I thought we'd talk, but you look exhausted. Drink some water, and I'll go."

I want him to go. Don't I?

I imagine him tugging off his clothes, pulling the blanket back, and covering me with his hard body. Nudging my legs apart, he'll slide his fingers over my wet pussy with some kind of gruff approval before rubbing his cock over my slick flesh until I beg for more. Then he'll notch at my entrance and plow all the way in, while I welcome him home. Bracing himself on his forearms, he'll roll his hips and brush the hair off my face and own my mouth. We won't talk. Not with words. We'll communicate using our bodies—like we always do. *Just feel.*

Damn you, Rafael Huntsman. I hate you.

"I'm not going until you drink," he reminds me, his voice gruff and his eyes hooded like he's been enjoying my fantasy.

I sit up, careful not to let the sheet expose me more than I already am. "I'm surprised you're not so pissed at me that you wouldn't prefer that I suffer from dehydration to learn a lesson." That should throw ice water on all the stupid in the room.

Rafael's brow furrows. "I want you safe," he murmurs, "only uncomfortable when it gives you pleasure."

His words are like skilled fingers caressing my pussy. *Stay strong, Lexie.* "Well, those days are over."

"Are they? Because I think you're aroused. I see it in your eyes. And I smell it."

I was aroused from the moment he walked in the room, but I'll never admit to it.

"That's body odor. I haven't showered recently." I take a couple of swigs of water and recap the bottle before placing it on the nightstand. Then I lie on my side and tuck the blanket to my chin. "Good night." I close my eyes, but he doesn't take the hint.

"What do you want?" I ask after a few moments of deafening silence.

"What do I want?" He pauses. "You know what I want.

That's why you're clinging to the covers like they'd stop me. But it's not why I'm here." He draws a breath. "I came to apologize for the way I acted in my apartment the last time we were together."

Apologize. Imagine that. Rafael Huntsman apologizing for despicable behavior. He's not of the same generation as my father and Antonio—who wouldn't apologize for anything, not even if their lives depended on it—although I do suspect they've apologized to their wives once or twice. No, he's not just like them, but he's cut from a similar cloth, and I know he's stingy with his apologies. *He wants something.*

"I was out of line—completely out of line. I flew off the handle, and more, I grabbed you in anger. It shames me more deeply than you'll ever know."

His sincerity floors me, dredging up warm, fuzzy feelings that I'm trying desperately to bury. But it's not easy to bury love. It's powerful and resilient and— *Why did he have to apologize?* It just mucks up everything.

"It's not something I'll ever do again," he assures me, regret wrapped around each syllable. "You have my word."

Talk is cheap. It's true, but I don't say it, because I believe him. Not because I'm foolish, although I can be when it comes to him, but because I've known him almost my entire life. Rafael's not the kind of man who raises a hand to a woman. He just isn't.

"You scared me," I admit, "because you were so out of control. Although aside from your rough hold on me, I didn't think you'd hurt me physically. But I'd never seen you like that, and it was unnerving."

He takes his hand and places it over mine, the blanket between us. "I don't want you to be afraid of me. Even that night, when I was raging, I didn't want you to be afraid. I regret making you feel that way."

"But you don't regret the things you said." The ugly words that landed like daggers in my soul.

He opens his mouth as if to speak, but doesn't say anything. It's as though he's searching for the right words.

"I regret all the problems my outburst caused, but I meant some of it."

It's a gut punch—maybe more like an elbow to the side. "You meant some of what you said, like that I'm a traitor."

He shakes his head vehemently. "No. Never. That was careless language I wielded to hurt you. It was wrong. I was disappointed. More than disappointed. From the moment you arrived at Sirena, I knew you were hiding something. But even still, I started to think about—" He scratches his forehead above his right eye, like he does when he's going to say something he doesn't want to admit.

"I started to think about some kind of future—for us. And that day, I felt like it was snatched away before we'd given it a real chance."

I don't spend too much time parsing his words, and I don't assign them any meaning. No need—they're clear. He did want something with me beyond a physical relationship—or at least he thought he did. *It doesn't change anything, Lexie. Don't give him the chance to break your heart again. Because you know he will.*

"I was disappointed too," I admit, although I'm sure he's not surprised. "Crushed. I'd hoped for more time too. But mostly I was hurt because I expected better from you."

"I expected better from you, too, Lexie. Maybe it was foolish, but I expected you to be loyal to me over all else. I understand now. I don't like it, but I get it."

He squeezes my hand before moving his away.

"I want to show you something. It's something I should have shared with you that day. Maybe sooner," he mutters.

I have absolutely no idea what he's talking about. All I know is that it's taking everything I have not to throw my arms around him.

Rafael hands me his phone. "Scroll right. There are two images. Those documents are the reason I interfered in Valentina's life the way I did. Marco was the beneficiary of the account, and we believed her life was in imminent danger."

The words he says are a blur. But Valentina already explained this to me. I get the gist of what he's saying. What he doesn't understand is that it doesn't change anything. It's like there's a disconnect somewhere. It's how he went about dealing with his concerns that caused the problem between them. I hope he doesn't think this justifies *any* of his behavior. He's not getting a damn pass from me.

"From that information, I'd have drawn the same conclusions that you did. But I would have approached it differently."

"Even knowing that the best way forward was to keep your mouth shut, and lie, because it was unclear who you could trust?"

He's holding up a mirror and challenging me to look at my reflection in the glass. "I know what you're doing, but comparing your decision to my decision about how to manage the traffickers is a false equivalency. And you know it."

"Maybe. But if we told Valentina, she would have gone straight to her husband and given him a heads-up before we had a chance to question him."

I don't respond, because of course she would have done that, and I understand that it might have put her in danger. "No question it was a no-win situation, but that doesn't excuse how you treated me. You took all your anger and frustration over the situation with Valentina and hurled it at me—never once taking responsibility for your part."

"I'm taking responsibility now, and I'm doing the best I can to apologize." He lies on the bed next to me and turns on his side. "I'm not ready for it to be over between us, Lexie. I want us to have a chance. Maybe it won't work out, but at least we'll know that we gave it our best shot."

I would love to, but I can't. I need to think with my head for once when it comes to him, not with my heart and certainly not with my body.

People say all kinds of things they don't really mean. Listen when someone shows you who they are.

"I am who I am, and you are who you are. Despite our best intentions, neither of us is going to change. I can't do it again, Rafael."

"Your feelings for me have changed so quickly? Maybe they weren't really what you thought they were." His tone isn't biting, but the words are churlish, maybe manipulative. He's not accustomed to being told no.

"Don't you dare lecture me about my feelings. You don't even have a sense of your own, let alone mine."

"I know that you scare me," he says, eyes locking with mine. "I know that you lied and put yourself in astounding peril. I know that I could care about you in ways that would be my ruin. But I'm willing to give it a shot, because I also know that I've never felt this way before, about anyone."

He runs his fingertips through my hair, and I close my eyes so I don't have to look at him.

"My feelings haven't changed," I confess, my eyes still shut. "What's changed is my willingness to act on them." I open my eyes and peer at him. "You know that saying, fool me once, shame on you; fool me twice, shame on me? For me, the third time wouldn't be about shame, but about self-loathing. If you run, I can't imagine how much I'd despise myself for being foolish enough to have sex with you again. Because that's what you're really asking for."

"I'm asking for another chance."

"I can't give you that."

"You won't, you mean." His tone is resigned, with a bitter edge.

"I won't."

He nods, gets out of bed, and tugs off his clothes.

"What are you doing?"

"Showering," he grumbles, pulling open the bathroom door. "But this discussion isn't over. Not anywhere near close."

16

RAFAEL

DAMN WOMAN. I slam the bathroom door and turn on the shower.

What did you expect? She'd ride your cock until you passed out? *No.* But I wouldn't have complained if she offered.

I went to the bedroom to apologize. No ulterior motive. But once I saw her clothes draped over the chair and I knew she was naked beneath the covers—sex crossed my mind once or twice, or a dozen times.

When the water's warm, I step into the shower like it's a baptismal font. I let the water rain on me, hoping it'll wash away my unrelenting desire for her. But I must be the worst of sinners, because it doesn't do a damn thing to curb my craving. *My addiction.* If anything, I want her more.

As I work the soap into my skin, all I smell is Lexie. Her shampoo. Her lotion. Her amber perfume. Her sweet cunt that fits like a glove around my cock. *So perfect.*

She has a choke hold on me. She's all I see. All I taste. All I smell. I'd give anything to touch her, again. I ache for it. *I ache for her.*

I palm my cock and close my eyes, imagining her here, on

her knees, gazing up at me with water droplets clinging to long, pale lashes. Her eyes flicker with lust as her tongue darts out between those luscious pink lips to lap at my crown.

Her essence is everywhere, inching closer, squeezing tighter until I can barely breathe.

Memories of her velvet mouth consume me. *It's warm and tender, with a wicked edge.* I pump my cock viciously, pulling roughly, until all I think about—all I feel—is her hot breath and the way her teeth scrape over my length as she drives me to the brink of insanity.

With a savage grunt, I submit to the fantasy, letting it take me to a place where there's only pleasure—and torment—twisting together until they're one.

My cock throbs as I curl my toes into the shower floor and surrender to her mouth like she's a *bruja* who's cast a spell over me.

As her tongue bathes my rock-hard cock, I thread my fingers through her hair, with shaky hands. *Be careful with her, Rafael.*

She draws me into her mouth, with lips like a silky vise molded around my shaft. I'd sell my soul to the devil for more of this. *Maybe I already have.*

A tortured groan snakes its way from the depths of my chest and into the steam wafting around us. Her eyes sparkle victoriously. She knows there's no turning back—not for me.

You have all the power, Angel. Own it.

She swallows me deep.

Again.

And again.

And again.

I close my eyes, clawing for control that's out of reach.

Fuck.

The tingle begins, inching up my spine, like a roller coaster making its final ascent. Every muscle tightens as I climb.

I stroke harder—*rougher*—chasing the release I desperately need.

I can't hold back a fucking second longer.

Tugging at my tight balls with quick, rhythmic pulls, I detonate, decorating the shower wall with thick milky streaks.

My heart hammers as I brace my forehead against the wall, gasping for breath.

The edge isn't gone. The desire for her hasn't waned.

I can't make it stop.

I fear it never will.

17

RAFAEL

After the helicopter landed, I took Lexie to my apartment and packed a bag while I waited for her guards to arrive. I'm sure she'll sleep for most of the day, and there's nothing I'd like more than to fall asleep wrapped around her. Instead, I've been toying with the souvenir we brought back from Quimper.

I enter a dank cave deep in the bowels of Huntsman Lodge for the second time today. Unlike the one where I questioned that feckless pussy, Marco, there are no comforts here. If the walls could talk, they would tell gruesome stories of men who took their strangled final breath, pleading for mercy that never came.

While I've never asked, I suspect this is where my brother got the end he deserved too.

The prisoner we transported in the plane's cargo hold is strung up by the arms, in the far end of the cave, wearing nothing but his briefs. The blows I meted out earlier are now swollen purple bruises. When he spots me, he begins to cry.

After interrogating Andre earlier, I warned him that when I returned, he should either be prepared to tell me everything he knows about the flesh traders, or to meet his maker after a long, excruciating death.

The truth is, he's less than a foot soldier and knows very little, but he did implicate Francesca Russo's boyfriend, Paolo, as well as Paolo's cousin. It's unlikely either of them are the mastermind of the ring. Although Russo believes Paolo led his daughter to her death.

The closer I get to Andre, the more desperate his whimpers become. With his toes barely grazing the floor and his arm sockets groaning under the weight, he's had plenty of time to ponder his fate. I don't know if he slept in the cargo hold, but the guards have kept him awake since he arrived. There's been no food, and the only water he's been permitted is when his head is pushed into a vat and held down until he nearly drowns.

Let's see if our hospitality has jostled a new memory.

"Andre. *Tout va bien?*" He doesn't reply, but I can see for myself how it's going. And more importantly, I know exactly how it's going to end.

This is the man who was sent to gather intel on my Angel—to deliver Lexie to her death—or worse. He will die not by my order, but at my hand, and I will relish every cut of the blade.

"Tell me more about Paolo."

Andre shakes his head. "I told you everything I know."

"Paolo's Italian," I begin, recounting what he told me earlier, "and he speaks to you in French with an Italian word thrown in here and there. Paolo has a cousin who speaks a little Italian, but more French, although you don't think he's a native French speaker."

It all seems worthless on its own, but when pieced together, it could give us a lead. Plus, even a seemingly inconsequential bit of information can be the key to solving the puzzle. You never know.

The problem is that men who are being tortured sometimes

tell us stories they think we want to hear. This is especially true of men who have few bargaining chips. Asking the same questions over and over in different ways will tell me if his story holds up, so we don't waste time chasing bullshit.

"Not a native French speaker. Did I get that right?"

He nods.

"Paolo approached you about a month ago while you were on your way home from a club. What color are his eyes?"

"Like I said. It was late, and he was wearing dark glasses and a beanie pulled low."

"In all the times you spoke with Paolo, he never let his cousin's name slip? Think, Andre. Think like your life depends on it, because it does." It's important to keep hope alive at this stage of the interrogation. But that's all it is, hope. Andre is not getting out of here alive.

"No. He called him his cousin. Never used his name."

"What about when you talked to the cousin?"

"He just said he was Paolo's cousin."

He might not even be Paolo's cousin. He might have introduced himself that way to get Andre to do his bidding. Or Andre could be lying.

"I only talked to him twice. The first time was when he told me to go to the hotel. And then when he said I needed to go to a different hotel. But I never got there because the guards grabbed me."

My guards grabbed him.

I lower the prisoner until he's on his feet, then give him a few sips of water. Not because I'm inclined to show him mercy, but because I want him to believe that he'll be rewarded for cooperating.

Andre rolls his shoulders, something he couldn't do when he was off the ground.

"Feels good, doesn't it?"

He nods.

"Keep answering my questions and you'll buy yourself some grace." I give it a moment to sink in. "Why did Paolo's cousin want you to collect information on the woman in the hotel?"

"He didn't say. Only that it was very important."

"I want you to listen very carefully to my next question. What do you think they wanted when they had you check out the clubs? Not the kind of information they asked you to gather. You already told us that. But why did they want it?" He might know shit, but everyone has hunches, and those hunches can sometimes be useful.

"I told you. I don't know."

I pull out my knife and wave the blade under his nose to refresh his memory. "How about when they asked you to get information on the woman at the hotel. You never wondered what they were going to do with that information?"

His head flops to the side, and he shuts his eyes.

I move toward the lever that will raise him up off the ground. He grunts.

"I wondered whether they were going to steal money, or if—"

"Or if what, Andre?"

"If they were with the trafficking ring."

Fucker. He was willing to feed them information, knowing they might snatch her. I take a few steps back so I don't end this bastard now, before we have everything we need from him.

"You were going to provide information about an innocent woman to men who you believed might be flesh traders?"

"I didn't know she was innocent. I needed the money."

My phone rings. *Will Clarke.* Just what I need.

"I'll call you right back," I tell him before he says hello.

"Do you know who that was on the phone?" I ask Andre.

He shakes his head.

"Will Clarke. British guy. You ever hear of him?"

Andre nods.

"That was his daughter you were spying on for those monsters. *My* woman."

"I didn't—"

I grab him by the throat and carve an *X* into his chest. He pisses himself, but I don't let go of his throat to move away from the puddle. "Save your excuses for Satan. Because when I'm finished, you'll burn in hell."

I pry my hand off his damp skin.

"Give this fucker another dunk or two," I instruct the guards, "and then string him back up. Don't be gentle."

18

RAFAEL

Zé follows me out of the cave into a small office nearby. "I can take another whack at him, but I think you've gotten everything there is to get."

"Which is nothing." I slam the door shut, but it doesn't give me any satisfaction.

"Not nothing. It appears that Paolo identified Andre as someone who wasn't a total lowlife, but had fallen on hard times and needed money. He put him to work. This is probably what they do in every city they target."

"It's a clever way to operate," I mutter. "There's no way Paolo's running that operation. He's too young to have enough experience to pull off something of this magnitude."

"Agreed. What about the cousin?"

"Who the fuck knows?" I grouse, returning Will's call. Hopefully he called with something useful and not just to ram his boot up my ass.

"Clarke," he answers.

"Do you have anything that connects my prisoner with your dead flight attendant?"

"No. The flight was a reconnaissance mission, period. It's as we thought. They expedited their plan when I changed crews ahead of schedule. I was the target. Not Lexie, although that traitorous bastard would have taken her or Samantha out if it meant getting to me."

"I assume his time on earth is quickly coming to an end?"

"There will be nothing quick or merciful about his end. I'll prolong the suffering as long as possible."

He won't suffer long enough as far as I'm concerned.

"What do you have?"

"My prisoner claims he was working for Paolo, the Russo girl's boyfriend. He lives in Quimper, and Paolo hired him to gather intel on clubs. Once he was done, Paolo helped him get a job at the North Star, a club popular with wealthy tourists. He was the bartenders' lackey, fetching booze when they needed it, and feeding Paolo logistical info."

"Why was he at the hotel?"

"He was contacted by someone claiming to be Paolo's cousin to report Lexie's comings and goings," I sneer through gritted teeth.

"Son of a bitch. I hope you haven't made his stay too pleasant."

"He's been receiving the Huntsman special welcome."

"Good. You need to turn that bastard over to Russo before the sun sets."

Fuck that. "He went after Lexie, not Francesca. I'll turn him over once we've extracted every bit of information from him."

"Russo's daughter is dead. He gets the lead. I don't like it any better than you. If I had my way, I'd feed him his balls myself. But that's not the way we do things."

Every nerve in my body is on edge, jonesing to go on a murderous rampage—because he's right. It's how it's done. How it's always been done, and I'm too damn high on the food chain to buck long-standing tradition for self-serving purposes.

"I understand you want to avenge my daughter—maybe

because you care about her, or perhaps because it will ease your conscience—but don't indulge boyish whims. You're better than that, Rafa. You have honor. She was Russo's daughter—he takes charge until we determine that he's running a clown show. But I don't think that's going to happen. Neither do you. Turn over the prisoner."

I want to say, *I don't take orders from you*. It's on the tip of my tongue. But I don't, because regardless of the vengeance I crave, I do have honor. He's right about that too.

"I'll send him to Russo when we're finished questioning him. We don't need much longer." I'll also need to send the information Lexie has put together—once Tamar has confirmed everything—but I don't share this with Will. When she's ready, his daughter can fill him in. I won't betray her confidence.

"Rafael," Will says with some measure of authority. "She isn't going to be any safer if you kill the bastard than if Russo puts a bullet in him when he's done. Even if Russo fucks it up and the prisoner escapes, she's not going to be in any danger."

I'm not sure if he's trying to make me feel better or if he's trying to convince himself that turning the asshole over is the right thing.

"What will put her in grave danger," he continues, "is if you decide that feeding your ego is more important than making clearheaded decisions. If that happens, you'll have more to worry about than an errand boy."

Some men would just say, *Take care of my daughter*, but Will would never ask me, or anyone, to do a job he believes is his. Instead, he prefers to threaten me like I'm some contractor he's hired. I don't give a shit. I don't need stroking from him, nor do I need to be threatened to protect his daughter with my life. I'd gladly lay it down for her.

"I've got things to do. Keep me apprised and I'll do the same." I end the call before I say something I'll regret.

“Get the branding iron we use to mark the barrels,” I instruct Zé.

I’ll turn that fucker over to Russo, but not before his skin has been defiled. Not with my knife. Not today. I don’t trust the blade not to slip and sever his carotid artery.

“Torch or electric?” Zé asks, eyeing me.

“Not the electric one.” A sense of calm takes over, soothing some of the edginess. “Build a fire.”

I want to watch the burning embers crackle and fly when I dip the iron in the flames. His final breath won’t be mine, but I’m going to give that piece of shit a taste of hell before he leaves here.

19

LEXIE

I'm in such a sound sleep, it takes me a moment to realize the buzzing is my phone, and even longer for me to remember that I'm in Rafael's guestroom at Huntsman Lodge.

The shades are drawn, and I fumble for the phone in the dark. *A UK number I don't recognize.* "Hello," I croak.

"Lexie?"

"Mum!" I bolt upright, and the grogginess fades. "Are you okay?"

"Much better now that I've heard your voice."

"How about Dad?" I hold my breath, and turn on the bedside lamp.

"I just spoke with him, and he's a bit ornery, but otherwise, he's well. What about you, darling?"

"I'm good. Totally good." In truth, I'm a bit shaken up, not so much because of what happened to me, but because of what could have happened to my father if Worthington's plan hadn't been exposed. *The traitor would have killed him.*

Mum pauses as though she's weighing my response, or perhaps hers. "You've been through quite an ordeal. Are you sure you don't need anything? A doctor? Maybe someone to help you process what happened?"

"I don't need anything. But if I change my mind, you'll be the first person I call." My mother's bullshit meter is almost as finely-tuned as my dad's, and reassuring her is always a challenge.

"I was lucky. Between Dad and Rafael—they sorted everything in time."

She coughs to hide a sob. "I can't bear to think about what might have happened to you."

"But it didn't. I'm lying in a comfy bed, between sheets with a decadent thread count, guarded by more soldiers than, even you, can imagine. Did you get a new phone?"

"It's a temporary number. But I don't want to talk about phones or sheets. Don't make light of the danger you were in."

"I'm not," I reply, sitting back against the headboard and pulling my knees to my chin. "Tyler Worthington. I still can't believe it."

"Neither can I. Such a betrayal. Your father treated him like family."

Like the son he never had.

"How's Dad coping?"

She sighs deeply. "At first he was spitting venom, but now, he seems almost relieved."

"Relieved?" That's hard to believe.

"He had an inkling something was afoot—for more than a year. Although, he couldn't put his finger on it."

A year? "Did you know?"

"I knew your father was out of sorts, and in the last six months he seemed to be getting progressively worse. He feared for your safety and mine. The fear seemed irrational at times—even for him. But I don't need to tell you what he's been like."

As Worthington's plot progressed so did my father's obsession with our safety. That makes sense. It must have been torture for him sensing the danger, but not being able to identify the source.

"So you think his behavior was a response to what was happening in the inner circle, and not about his family's killer and his cancer diagnosis?"

"I think what they did to his family weighs heavily on him, more so after the diagnosis, and I don't regret forcing him to talk about it. But the murders only played a minor role. Worthington was the real culprit. The closer he came to killing your father," her voice wobbles, "the more paranoid your father became."

"I don't think it's called paranoia when someone's actually trying to kill you."

"Maybe not," she says wistfully. "I miss you, Lexie."

"I miss you too. When can you go home?"

"In a day or two."

"As soon as I get the all clear, I'm coming home too."

She pauses. "Are you seeing anyone?" Samantha Taft Clarke sneaks it in casually, in a matter-of-fact tone. It's cheeky and not very subtle. Of course, she's heard *all* about Rafael. If not from Dad, then from Daniela. But I'm happy to change the subject from traitors and sinister plots. Although I would prefer to talk about something else—*anything else.*

"Well, are you?" she probes when I don't respond immediately.

I grin, imagining her pressing her lips together so she doesn't laugh and give herself away. "I was seeing someone, but it was over so fast, you missed it."

"Tell me about it," she cajoles, gently.

"There's nothing to tell. I fell for a man who's a younger, hipper version of Dad, who I'm always pushing back against. It didn't work out."

"It doesn't sound like it's over."

I rest my chin on my bent knees and close my eyes. "It is."

"Is that why you decided to stay at his place instead of going to Daniela and Antonio's?"

Someone ratted me out. Probably the same weasel who told her about the relationship in the first place.

"I'm staying in his guestroom and he's staying at a hotel downtown. It was convenient for everyone." I'm dismissive, but even before the words are out, I know my mother isn't going to let it go.

"I'm sure he carries scars not so different from your father's." The empathy in her voice is so thick, it's palpable.

He does. My heart aches—for my two favorite men. "Not so different," I mutter trying to keep my feelings in check.

"He risked a lot to save you," she murmurs, picking at the wound to ensure it's thoroughly clean before I cover it. *Unclean wounds become infected, and festering infections leave scars.*

"Your father issued a shoot order, and Rafael insisted he not retract it, so that they could hatch some plot to rescue you. He was desperate to save you. It even made an impression on your father, who's not easily impressed."

I'm going to strangle him—both of them. But that explains their banter about the order when we spoke on the plane.

He was desperate to save you. I clench my fists, digging my nails into my palms to ward off the emotion bubbling near the surface. Then I reach for my mask. "Don't make too much of it. Rafael loves a damsel in distress."

"I don't doubt it, but handing a stranded woman cab fare is quite different than laying down your life. He might not be the right man for you, but it's not because of the way he feels about you—or the way you feel about him. I hear it in your voice," she adds just above a whisper.

I put the phone on speaker and press my shoulders into the headboard, hugging my legs to my chest.

"It's hard to be with someone like him," I admit. "He's not easy."

"What would you do with an easy man, darling?" she asks softly.

Valentina found a man who seemed easy, one who wasn't connected to our perilous world. *Look how that turned out.*

"Are you suggesting I'm a difficult woman?" My tone is off and the sarcasm falls flat.

"I'm suggesting you're spirited and strong, and you need a partner who's a match for your energy and passion. It doesn't have to be Rafael. But you'd never be happy—or feel safe—with a doormat."

Don't worry. I'd never be attracted to a doormat. Not even a designer one from Knightsbridge. I prefer men who wrestle with demons, and take no prisoners—the sex is better.

"Men like Rafael do *nothing* in half measure," she continues. "They're overbearing, possessive, exhausting. They aren't everyone's cup of tea, and I'm sure every feminist on the planet would be horrified to know that I'm not warning you away from him. And maybe I should."

She draws a long breath. "But when it clicks with a man like that, it's something special. Something extraordinary. The kind of extraordinary that makes for the love affair of a lifetime."

She's not talking about Rafael and me. She's talking about her relationship with my father.

The kind of extraordinary that makes for the love affair of a lifetime.

I want that. I want it with him. But right now, the cost feels too great and the risks too high—almost impossible.

20

RAFAEL

THE LAUNCH IS two weeks away, and I have Tamar hunting flesh traders with Lexie. I'm insane. Not that it isn't of vital importance to stop those animals, but I have a responsibility to the company, my family, my employees, and the people of the valley who need Port to thrive well beyond our lifetime.

This endeavor will make, or break, Premier as a modern, cutting-edge port house. Its success is vital to the region. No one can convince me differently. But the monsters who killed Francesca, and who have set their sights on Lexie, are taking up a lot of brain space and I'm finding it difficult to focus on the launch.

To add to my problems, I have Tamar and Lexie working in the conference room down the hall from my office—although that has to change. I can't get a damn thing done knowing Lexie's a few doors down.

My attention never strays far from the leggy angel with a devilish gleam in her eye. More than a few times today, I've thought about sending Tamar on a fool's errand so I can beg Lexie to lick her pussy. Although I doubt she'd be into it. She's still keeping me at arm's length, and I'm still giving her space—but it's killing me.

I close my laptop and stretch my arms overhead. Valentina will be here shortly. *Something else to add to my sullen mood.*

Our relationship hasn't recovered. The worst part is that she's not seething anymore, but she doesn't bother with me unless it involves work. *Like today.* The relationship is strictly professional. I hate it with a vengeance, although most days I consider myself lucky for the crumbs.

There's a knock on my open door, and I glance up to my sweet niece, who looks so much like my mother it's sometimes startling.

If the door was open, Valentina used to waltz right in without knocking. *Not anymore.* "You don't need to knock, *cara linda*. Come in."

"*Bom dia*," she chirps brightly, a phony smile plastered on her beautiful face.

"I only have a few minutes," she says, taking a seat in front of my desk. "But it's getting close, and I have to nail down any changes by the end of the week."

The global launch will take place in Porto, with a swanky party at Antonio and Daniela's house, where Valentina and I grew up. It sends a loud and clear message that Antonio, who owns the oldest and most revered port house in the valley, and Daniela, who holds the most important vineyards in the country, are fully on board.

They've been supportive both privately and publicly, but this inaugural event is akin to warning the naysayers to get with the program or suffer the consequences. It's a huge fucking deal, and Valentina has personally seen to every detail.

"Before we begin," I murmur, coming around the desk and taking the seat next to her. "How are you?" I ignore the grimace as I turn my chair to face her.

"I'm great," she replies, again with that fake smile, "and so excited about the party and the launch." She holds out a manila envelope. "It's a hard copy of the packet I emailed you last night. It was late when I sent it, and I wasn't sure if you saw it."

"I did. No changes. It's perfect the way it is. You've done such a great job with the marketing. I'm proud of you."

"It's not like I did it alone," she replies, dismissing the praise. "But it's going to be epic." Her eyes light up, and for a few short seconds the smile she flashes me is real.

"It is. I'm so happy we got to do this together. The first of what I hope will be many modern initiatives."

She doesn't respond, and I don't push. It's too early for that—the wound I inflicted, when I interrogated her husband in the caves, is still too fresh. Any discussion we have will likely end with her angry and hurt. She'll demand a promise that I'll never do something like that again, and I won't lie to her.

"I have to go," she says, standing and smoothing her skirt.

"I'll see you Saturday night at your dad's birthday party."

Her face contorts like it did when she learned her mother's horse, Zeus, had to be put down. For a moment, I'm sure she's going to cry. But she swallows hard and composes herself. "I won't be there."

I won't be there. Family is everything to Antonio and Daniela—everything. They've instilled that value in all of us.

"It's your father's birthday. Don't punish him or your mother for something I did. If it makes it easier for you and Marco"—I manage to say his name with more geniality than I feel—"to be there, I'll stay away."

"You didn't do anything to Marco that my father didn't sanction. He knows it, and I know it." She holds up her hand when I open my mouth to speak. "But that's not why I won't be there. Marco has business in Athens and needs me to accompany him."

Sure he does. *Fucker.* "We'll miss you."

She lifts her chin and takes a breath before she nods. "I'll miss everyone too."

"I thought I heard your voice," Lexie cries, sweeping into the room and embracing Valentina, who gifts her a huge grin—not a fake one. As angry as I was at Lexie, I'm glad she has Valentina's back.

"Do you want to get coffee?"

"I have an appointment," Valentina replies, "but how about if we meet at my apartment in an hour?"

Lexie glances at me, and I nod. While my hands are tied regarding Valentina's security, the guard stationed outside the door will check the apartment before she enters.

"Perfect," Lexie coos. "I want to steal those cute red sandals for your dad's party—unless you're wearing them?"

Valentina freezes.

This should be interesting.

"Valentina and Marco will be in Greece this weekend," I pipe in before Valentina has an opportunity to change the subject. I want to see the interaction between them on this.

"You're not going to your dad's birthday party?" Lexie's eyes are wide, and her tone drips with incredulity.

Valentina pales. "I—I'll have lunch with him before we leave on Friday. It's his actual birthday. I have another meeting, but I'll see you upstairs in an hour." She rushes out the door before there can be any more questions.

"Her parents are not going to be happy," Lexie mutters, mostly to herself.

Quite the understatement.

Her brow furrows, and the wheels are turning, but she shares none of it with me.

I'd give anything to be a fly on the wall while those two are having coffee.

21

LEXIE

I APPROACH Valentina's apartment flanked by Sabio, who nods at the guard stationed outside the door. I'm used to a high level of security, but the Huntsman men are over the top. That's why my father has never had too much heartburn about me staying here without my own security.

"*Senhora* Cruz will be here shortly," the guard informs Sabio. *Senhora Cruz.* She must hate that.

"Hey," Valentina calls, rushing down the hall with two espressos from the café downstairs and yet another guard.

Over the top.

"You look hot in that wraparound dress, *Senhora* Cruz," I tease, taking a cup from her.

Valentina rolls her eyes. "Marco grew up with a different level of formality. It's not my style, but it's not worth fighting about."

We have bigger things to fight about. She doesn't say it, but the stench of the unspoken words hangs in the air like burnt popcorn.

"I feel like I haven't seen you forever," Valentina murmurs, linking her arm through mine as we wait for the apartment to be swept.

"I know. It's ridiculous. We need to change that."

"It's been hectic with the launch, and I'm trying to work from home more often."

Valentina and Marco have a great house with stunning views, but it's somewhat isolated for a girl who thrives on a city vibe. "Do you like working from home?"

She shrugs. "I miss the buzz of the office. But Marco's schedule is unpredictable, so if I'm home, we get to see more of each other."

One of Valentina's favorite things about working at Premier has always been that she gets to see her dad and Rafael every day. Although seeing more of her husband probably makes up for it.

"Ladies," the guard says after he checks the apartment, "all clear."

"Did you hear Francesca Russo was murdered?" she asks as soon as the door shuts behind us.

Did I hear? Rafael *borrowed* a satellite to track my flight and hid in a hollowed-out platform bed in my hotel room, all while there was a shoot order on him—issued by none other than my father—all so he could tell me. "I heard."

Valentina turns on the kitchen light and grabs a tin of biscotti from the cupboard. "Marco and I were listening to the BBC this morning, and it sounded like it might be related to the trafficking ring you two got caught up in at Sirena. I'm worried about you, Lexie."

"They suspect it was related, but so far, it's just speculation. The prime minister has a lot of enemies." Neither my father nor Rafael believe it's speculation, and neither do I, but Valentina has plenty on her plate. She doesn't need to worry about me.

"That's what Marco said too." She puts the tin on the island, and I help myself.

"But I don't agree," she continues, taking the seat across from me. "Going after a family member—an innocent girl—that's a bridge too far, even for most bad men. But flesh traders? It's their calling card."

"Don't discount the Bratva, the cartels, or even local gangs. It's their calling card too. But don't worry. I'm sure my father has people all over it, and Rafael's upped my security to a level that's unprecedented—even for him."

"It's not a terrible idea," she says, dunking her biscotto into the espresso.

"I'm not fighting it. What about your security? Any changes because of the murder?" It wouldn't surprise me if Antonio or Rafael added to her security detail—although I don't know if Rafael is still allowed to intervene in her security.

She shrugs. "Nothing's really changed at home, although Marco mentioned adding another guard at the front gate. All security in this building is Huntsman-sanctioned and tight. Always has been. The only change is that Rafael is no longer permitted to be involved in my protection in any way. *Nada*," she says with some satisfaction.

"Rafa agreed to that?"

"He didn't have a choice. My father agreed to it. He leaves decisions about Premier to Rafael and me, but my father still has the final say over everything that happens under the Huntsman umbrella. Although I suspect that's going to change soon. My mother's pushing hard for him to cut back, and I think he's going to do it. He was so young when he took over. I think he's had enough."

"After everything that's happened, are you okay with Rafael taking over for him?" She always was, but I wonder if that's changed too.

"Of course." She breaks a biscotto in two and offers me half.

"I have no desire to step into my father's shoes. What he does is not for me."

I get that. What my father does is not for me either. But unlike Antonio, Dad doesn't have someone at the ready to step in—at least not anymore. It still gives me chills to think about how close Worthington came to murdering him.

"Rafael's the right person to take over Huntsman Industries and to assume the responsibility for the valley and the industry." She doesn't hesitate or equivocate. Not for a second. "He's fair—unless it involves Marco. People like and trust him. He and my father have many similarities, but he'll be a more modern leader. I'm confident he'll do a great job—with all of it."

Relief and a sense of hope courses through me as she talks about him with pride in her voice. She won't stay mad at him forever.

"Once you feel he's been sufficiently punished, you should tell him what you just told me. I think he worries that he's lost you."

The evidence against Marco might have been concocted, but it was damning. Yes, they behaved like jerks. But they were in an impossible situation. I've thought a lot about it since Rafael showed me the documents, and I'm not sure that I would have done anything so different.

"I love Rafael," she admits, the words thick with emotion, "and the distance between us breaks my heart. I'm not punishing him. I'm fighting for my marriage."

Something about her tone is wistful. And resigned. As though she can't have both her family and Marco. *Is this why she's not going to Antonio's birthday dinner?*

"Are you not going to the party to teach your father a lesson?"

She glances up from her coffee and meets my eye. "I'm not like that."

No. You're not. "Is Marco?" I ask gently.

"Rafael and my father crossed a line. Think of how you would feel in his shoes," she says defensively before taking a sip of coffee. "He needs time to move past how he was treated. And he needs to know that I choose him over all else. Our marriage depends on it," she adds, almost in a whisper.

I'd like to wring Marco's neck. She would go to her father's party in a hot minute, but her husband is forcing her to choose sides. He's punishing them, but he's also punishing her in a way that cuts to the quick. To keep Valentina, who's been through so much, away from her family is just plain mean.

My respect for Marco has decreased immeasurably in the last month. I'm starting to think he's a manipulative little asshole. *But until she says otherwise, he's her manipulative little asshole.*

"What about you and Rafa?" she asks, studying me. "I know what you said in your email, but I heard there was a big blowup."

As I try to come up with something to tell her, it occurs to me that Rafael wanted me to choose him over Valentina—who is like my family. It's not much different from what Marco wants. I sigh heavily. "It was ugly, but inevitable. In some ways better to have happened sooner rather than later."

"I don't understand. I assumed you patched things up and that's why you came back."

I cradle the paper cup between my palms. "I never made it to London. My father's organization had a major shake-up. My mother was moved to a safe location. It made sense for me to stay in Porto for a bit longer."

It's not a lie, just a watered-down version of the truth. When I began tracing the traffickers' movements, I wanted to talk through my suspicions with someone. Normally that would have been Valentina. But I didn't want her involved in anything related to them, and I still don't.

Her dark brows draw together. "I'm glad you're here, but that doesn't sound good. Are you worried about your parents?"

"A little. But my father's on top of it. They've identified the traitor, which is huge, and contained most of the fallout. They just need to mop up any issues that might still arise. In the meantime, Rafael's letting me help Tamar with some research so that I don't die of boredom."

"Launch stuff? We certainly can use all the help we can get."

There's no way I'm telling her a thing about what we're doing.

I smile. "I think you have that launch well under control, girlfriend."

She beams at me but then her face twists with sadness, and she takes my hand. "I know how much you liked him, and I'm so sorry that I ruined things for you." She squeezes my fingers. "I really am."

She didn't ruin anything—at least not in the way she thinks. Rafael wants to try again. I'm the one with cold feet.

"Sorry enough to lend me those red sandals and maybe an outfit to go with them?"

She snorts so hard that coffee spurts out her nose, and we laugh until tears stream down our cheeks. For a short while, we're the two girls who shared *everything*. Not a single secret between us. Or the teenagers who pinkie-swore we'd never let a guy come between us—but we've let two.

While the damage to our relationship, so far, has been minimal, the little lies, half-truths, and omissions will eventually take a toll. They'll pile up and create a heart-wrenching barrier between Valentina and me, or even a rift. I feel it in my bones.

22

RAFAEL

"IS HE ALONE?" I ask Antonio's assistant, Cecelia.

She nods.

On the credenza behind her desk, there's what looks to be a homemade birthday cake with a few missing slices. "You baked him a cake?"

She scoffs. "I put up with him every day. That's his birthday present. If you want to talk to Antonio, you better do it now. He's free for about ten minutes. Then he has a meeting with the minister of agriculture."

The minister of agriculture. That guy has a stick up his ass so big he chokes on it from time to time. He was insulted that Premier was going to use *his* grapes to bastardize Port—until I reminded him that they were *our* grapes and we would bastardize whatever we wanted with them. *Asshole.*

I steal a mint off Cecelia's desk and knock on Antonio's door.

"Come in."

He's seated at his desk with his jacket off and sleeves rolled up, still looking like he could go a few rounds in the ring. As honored as I am to take over from him, the changing of the guard also pains me. It's a sign he's getting older, and I hate thinking about what it means.

"Happy birthday, old man," I quip, making light of my fears, because it doesn't matter how old I get, it's my Binky.

Antonio shakes his head and chuckles. "I can still run circles around you, my friend."

"Not unless you're in some kind of high-powered, motorized scooter."

I snatch the ball of rubber bands off his desk that he put there for me to fidget with after I dropped a glass paperweight, while tossing it in the air. It shattered spectacularly, and for months, he complained about finding shards of glass.

I lob the ball from hand to hand. "Listen, I'm sorry Valentina won't be at dinner tomorrow. When she told me, I offered to stay away, if it would make it easier for them to go, but—"

He looks at me pointedly. "Don't ever do that again. We're family, and we should be able to get along with one another, at least for an evening. This is on her."

It's not on her. I don't buy that. "She seemed upset about missing your party. I have a feeling this is her husband's doing."

"Oh, I'm sure that bastard is behind it. His little feelings are hurt, and he wants to punish me. I had lunch with Valentina today, and she fell all over herself apologizing and making excuses. I'll miss her tomorrow, but she's the one who's being punished, maybe even more than her mother. I'd like to slit his throat."

Of all the things Marco could do to incur Antonio's wrath, upsetting Daniela might be the worst. Normally I would say he gets what he deserves, but a pissed-off Antonio is not a good thing. He's likely to say or do something that will make matters worse with Valentina.

"We should have held off questioning him until we had all the facts." I somehow manage to get it out without gagging.

"Bullshit. Not with that kind of evidence. I'd do it again under those circumstances."

Me too, but I don't say it. There's no sense in riling him up more.

"Why is Daniela sending Thiago for Lexie tomorrow?" he asks. "She's staying at your place. Can't she just come with you?"

He knows the answer to both questions. But he wants me to talk to him about what's going on between Lexie and me. He's been doing this sort of roundabout bullshit since I was a little kid. I know how to beat this game, but better to talk about my personal business than about Valentina's.

"Lexie's staying at my place, and I'm staying at the Intercontinental. Although it's not really out of the way, and I'd be happy to pick her up. But that's up to her."

"*Ah.* She hasn't forgiven you."

I don't respond. I'm willing to take a little heat to deflect some of the attention off Valentina, but I'm not baring my damn soul.

"You've got to grovel."

I did, but there's no way in hell I'm sharing that with him. "Grovel?" I snicker. "Like buy her a piece of jewelry?" I say it in jest, although I've thought about it once or twice. She loves the angel wings—but expensive trinkets are off the table.

I want another chance to see where it goes. But she's right. I am who I am, and she is who she is. It might never work. I'm certainly not ready to make promises, and I don't want to mislead her. Unless it's for a utilitarian purpose, like to house a tracking device, jewelry feels too much like a promise. *We're not there and we might never be.*

"Throwing around large sums of money is not groveling," he cautions. "It's the kind of thing that buys you a *neither my affection nor my forgiveness is for sale* remark. I don't recommend it."

"Sounds like you're an expert. One would think that you're always in trouble with Daniela." He is, although he's mellowed a lot over the years.

"You don't need to be an expert. She'll tell you exactly what you need to do to get out of the doghouse—or, in your case, the Intercontinental. But listen carefully, because she won't draw you a fucking map."

23

LEXIE

RAFAEL GLANCES from Tamar to me. His features are tight, regret scrawled all over his face in red ink. "We need to send all the information you've amassed to Bruno Russo."

Tamar and I have been at this for the better part of a week, and while we've been able to confirm all the data I gathered, we don't have a lot of new information. It's a huge disappointment.

Tamar nods, and while I'm sure she's not happy to be passing off our findings, you'd never know it from her expression. One day I hope to be like her.

"We need more time," I plead, not just with my words, but with my tone, my eyes, every cell begs for more.

"I can't in good conscience hold it back any longer," he replies. "I suspect the Italians have their own cache of evidence, and together with what we have, they might get somewhere before the bastards strike again."

Their information might be useful to us too. Maybe I can convince Rafael to let me continue to work on it. "Will they give us their information in exchange for ours?"

"Possibly. I'm pushing for it, but if my daughter had been murdered, I'd want revenge. And if I thought sharing information would endanger that, I wouldn't give it up. I'd be surprised if Russo feels differently."

Russo should be more worried about his people oversharing. His administration leaks like a sieve—at least according to the news reports. "You don't think everything we have will get leaked, and the traffickers will go into hiding or change their pattern?" I ask, watching him carefully.

He grimaces and shakes his head. "It's possible, but I don't see it. Russo's the prime minister of Italy, not some chump who runs a card game in the alley. He's accustomed to covert operations and handling classified material. And he's fully aware of how important it is to limit this information to a few select aides. He wants to destroy those animals more than we do."

I can't argue with the last part, although I'm not sold on Bruno Russo's posse.

"Tamar, make sure that nothing you send points back to either you or Lexie. I don't anticipate an issue, but if for some reason it gets into the wrong hands, I want to protect your anonymity as well as Lexie's. When you're through, send it over a secure channel. Russo's expecting it."

"Right away," Tamar replies as she prepares to leave.

"I hate this," I say quietly when she's gone. "I've protected it for so long. It's like sending my children into a wolves' den."

"I know it's difficult to hand over your work to someone else. I'm sure you want to see it through to the end. But sharing what we have doesn't mean that you and Tamar are finished."

I was hoping that was the case. "It's not that," I explain. "If I was sure Russo wouldn't screw it up, I wouldn't have any issue turning it over. But he's under duress, and the people around him are not the brightest bulbs in Italy."

He smiles. "You're not entirely wrong, but the Italian press is ruthless on the administration because they don't feel they give them enough access. Don't believe everything you read."

"I don't," I say with a bit more huff than warranted. "I've heard one or two of the dimwits speak."

He leans over the table and takes a lock of my hair between his fingers, letting them glide to the ends. "You're a tough audience."

"And well informed," I reply in a voice that's much too breathy.

"Is that so?"

I nod. "My father and I have been debating politics for years." Some debaters argue until the bell is called. But "fight to the death" has always been our approach.

"Smart and beautiful is a lethal combination. At least I've always thought so."

His mouth twitches at the edges, and his eyes are flickering not with that *I want to fuck you* look he gets right before he owns my mouth, but with something more tender. *More deadly.* I look away so I don't succumb to his charm.

"I spoke with Russo myself," he assures me. "There are no guarantees, of course. Although I'm confident they'll handle the information carefully and that they'll give us something in return—although I doubt it'll be everything they have. But I can't promise Russo's team won't fuck this up. I can only vouch for my own people."

I adore this about him—no insincere promises to placate me.

"This is about defending his honor, isn't it? His daughter gets killed so he gets first dibs on retaliation so that everyone knows his dick still functions."

Rafael smirks, and my panties start to melt. "Why don't you tell me what you really think?"

"I just did."

"It's his privilege to lead the effort. Up to a point." Rafael drums his fingers on the table. "There was a man gathering information about you for nefarious purposes. I promise you, Angel, your father is not going to let Russo go off half-cocked for too long before he steps in. And my patience on this front is even shorter. But Russo's daughter is dead. He gets to avenge her death. That's how it works in our world."

"I know. And I would want revenge if it were my child too. I'm not complaining. I just hoped we'd be closer to ferreting them out before another woman was taken."

"You need a break from this. Tamar too. If you spend too much time in that dark corner, it'll suck all the life out of you."

He runs his fingertip over the inside of my wrist, and a small shiver runs through me. I'm sure he noticed, but he doesn't call it out.

"Take tomorrow off so you can clear your head and enjoy Antonio's party."

"I plan on it," I say, my resolve softening like butter left in the sun.

"Good." He pauses, fidgeting with a pencil. "Can I pick you up on my way to the party?"

"Daniela invited me to come over early. I said yes, because I know it's going to be weird for her without Valentina. I promised the girls I'd help with the decorations."

"Would you have said yes if you didn't have a plan to go over early?" His gaze is probing.

Probably. But then I would have hated myself.

"I'd like to tell you that I would have found my own way there. But I don't know."

It's the truth. I'd like to think that I can hold out forever, but he's so tempting, and I'm having more and more weak moments—like now.

He drags my chair closer to him and takes my hand. "What will it take for us to have another chance? What do you need from me?"

Some assurance that you won't walk away at the drop of a hat. That when it gets hard, you'll put your fears aside and fight for us. "I don't know," I murmur.

"I think you do."

I will myself to speak the words not of my heart, but of my head. "I'm not ready to try again. I might never be."

"I can wait. But as to the second part, I don't accept that. Never is nothing more than a challenge as far as I'm concerned."

His arrogance should strengthen my resolve. I should hate it. But I don't.

I'm in trouble.

He's going to break my heart again. And I'm going to let him. I feel it. But there's not a damn thing I can do about it.

24

LEXIE

"WHERE'S VALENTINA?" Vivi, Antonio and Daniela's youngest daughter, asks, and the chatter around the table stops. It's the elephant in the room, although I suspect everyone, aside from the kids, knows why she isn't here.

I glance at Antonio, whose expression is unreadable.

"Marco had business, and he needed her with him," Daniela tells her daughter. "We've already talked about this." Neither her face nor her tone gives away her true feelings on the matter. She's too smart and poised for that, but she's not happy.

I'm not happy about it either.

When I arrived, she peppered me with questions about Valentina—and Marco. I'm sure it's why she wanted me to come over early. Helping the girls decorate was just an excuse. Oddly enough, she didn't seem to blame Rafael or Antonio for Valentina's absence, like I would have expected. But she's worried.

"Didn't they know it was *Papai*'s birthday?" Vivi presses on. "They should have told them the business is off." She slices her tiny hand through the air to make the point. "I'm going to have a word with that Marco." She's so serious that the adults laugh, except for Daniela, who shoots her daughter a disapproving look that Vivi barely acknowledges.

Rafael shakes his head with a devilish smirk. He's been playful since he arrived, especially with the kids. "By the time the last one leaves for college, you'll be referring to me as the easy child."

Earlier, when the girls and I arranged the place cards we made, they argued about who would get to sit next to *Rafa*. Catarina, the oldest, was the first to fold, deciding that I was cool enough to sit near, and that her sisters could flank Rafael, who knew they were babies anyway. But right before dinner, the baby of the family, Gabe, who proved as wily as the rest of the Huntsman males, switched Anabela's place card with his. When she discovered what happened, Alma intervened to avert a meltdown. That must have been quite a bribe she offered, because Anabela sat down immediately, looking very much like the cat who got the cream.

"Valentina made me lunch yesterday," Antonio says, ignoring Rafael's *easy child* comment. "She even made a birthday cake."

"What kind of cake?" Anabela asks, because she needs to know everything.

I was that kid too.

"Chocolate, of course."

"Why didn't you bring us any?"

"Did you eat it all by yourself?" Catarina asks with a disapproving tone.

"Every last crumb," Rafael teases. "He didn't share it with anyone, not even me, and I was starving."

The three little girls turn their heads, at once, and glare at their father, who's enjoying this way too much. Valentina would enjoy it, too. She'd be egging her sisters on like Rafa's doing.

"Don't look at me," Antonio says. "I did him a favor. He's

been eating too much cake, and he's getting a little chubby around the middle. Soon he won't be able to button his pants."

The bulge that stops him from buttoning his pants is more below the middle than around it.

"*Papai,*" Anabela gasps, her eyes wide. "It's not polite to talk about how someone looks."

Vivi pats Rafael's hand. "Don't be sad," she whispers, shaking her head. "You have big muscles, and they pop out of your shirt. You're not chubby."

Rafael's face lights up with a grin that makes me smile with such intensity my cheeks ache. He leans over and presses a kiss to the top of Vivi's head. "*Te amo, cara linda,*" he murmurs. "Your father's just jealous because my muscles are huge."

"What do you think, Lexie?" Antonio asks, and all eyes turn to me. "Think that paunch around his waist is muscle or too many carbs?"

Rafael smirks, waggling his eyebrows. "Yeah, Lexie. What do you think?"

I feel my cheeks warm.

I think your body is a collection of long, lean muscle with hard planes and ridges that make my mouth water—there's not an ounce of fat anywhere.

I smile sweetly at him. "Not sure about how the pants fit, although his head might be too big for an ordinary hat."

Everyone laughs, but no one laughs harder than Rafael, who is completely relaxed around his family. And not just Rafael. Antonio's relaxed too. It's always like this when they're together here. It's as though the house has some kind of magic.

My mother is normally laid-back, but my father never fully relaxes. *Never*. We laughed plenty in my house, but I was almost always the only child at the table, and the conversation was usually very adultlike—although I was free to share my opinions. Here the kids are expected to behave during dinner, but the mood and most of the conversation is on their level—or at least geared to include them.

It's different here in other ways too. My mother was the daughter of an ambassador, and even though she's kind and generous to the household staff, and even to the guards, she follows protocol. Daniela is more like Lydia.

There's a seamless blending of staff and family that feels just right. Victor and Alma, who worked for Antonio's family when he was growing up, and now keep this house humming, are seated at the family table for the party along with Cristiano and Lucas, Antonio's top men, and their families. If a stranger walked in, they would never know that this group wasn't all related.

"Not much longer," Cristiano says, "before the big launch. It's exciting what you and Valentina have done with Premier, Rafael. We're very proud to be part of it."

Antonio glances at Rafa and nods. "Very proud."

"We didn't do it alone," Rafael replies, because even though he's cocksure and arrogant, he's also self-effacing and never hesitates to give others credit when it's due.

It's one of the things about him that I find irresistible.

"Nothing this big could have been accomplished without all your support," he adds. "And Valentina deserves a lot of the credit. She took the lead with marketing and promotion. From the beginning, she knew how to sell the idea." He gazes at me from across the table, pride shining in his face. "It's quite remarkable what young women can accomplish when given a chance. Even a fool like me can appreciate real talent."

I stare at my plate, seeing nothing while his gaze warms my skin. As angry as Rafael was about my graphs and charts, there's always been a measure of admiration and respect for the work I did. He's mentioned it more than once.

"Lexie," Daniela says from the far end of the table. "I asked

Valentina to tell you that the dresses for the gala are my treat, and a spa day, too, if you girls can squeeze in the time."

The launch will begin with a formal gala, complete with gowns and tuxes, and dancing. With the way our relationship is... Will Rafael bring a date? *That would be almost too much to bear, even for the woman who keeps telling herself that there won't be any more chances—any more opportunities for heartbreak.*

"She did tell me," I reply, forcing my lips to curl, "and it sounds wonderful. Valentina and I don't have anywhere near enough girl time these days. Thank you."

"What about me?" Vivi asks. "I'm a girl. I like spa days and party dresses."

I love all the girls, but Vivi is my kindred spirit. I hope they don't rein her in too much.

"When have you been to the spa?" Catarina asks in the disparaging way that ten-year-old big sisters can sometimes do.

"When we have sleepovers with Valentina. We have face masks and manicures. She calls it spa night."

Valentina and I had plenty of sleepovers and spa nights when we were teenagers. A few with Grandma Lydia—but nowhere near enough.

Catarina glances at me and rolls her eyes before leaning closer. "Do you think I can come with you?" she whispers so no one else can hear.

"I would love it, and so would Valentina. But we need to check with your mom."

She nods with a confident smile. "I'm almost a teenager. I think she'll say yes."

Almost a teenager is quite a stretch, but it might not matter, because I doubt shopping sprees and manicures are in my near future.

The gala is one thing. The guest list will include high-ranking political types, like the president of Portugal, plus it's being held here, at Daniela and Antonio's home. Security will be as close to impenetrable as it gets. But I can't go dress shopping or to the spa or even the pharmacy until the traffickers are caught—or at least until I'm old news for them. Right now, it's too hot for me to be out in public. Even I know that. But I don't say anything about it. Now isn't the time or the place.

"Rafa," four-year-old Gabe says softly. "I have a new tent. Do you want to see it?"

"I definitely want to see it. As soon as everyone's finished eating, we'll go check it out."

"I told Gabe you'd take him camping in the backyard." Antonio's mouth twitches while he speaks. "You know, payback and all that."

Gabe peers up at Rafael with big brown eyes, filled with innocence and hope.

"Just the guys," Rafael tells him with a wink. "No girls. No dresses. No spa days."

"Just the guys," the little cutie repeats, beaming, and my heart flutters.

25

RAFAEL

After dinner, Gabe drags me up to his room, which was once my room. While we're test-driving the tent to be sure my legs don't stick out, Daniela waltzes in.

"He doesn't fit," Gabe tells his mother, bottom lip trembling. "We can't go camping."

"What do you mean, we can't go camping? We'll just get a bigger tent," I assure him. "I'll pick you up on Saturday morning, and we'll get breakfast at the café with the bike hanging on the wall, and then we'll buy a big tent."

He beams. "Just the guys?"

"Me and you, buddy. That's it."

"I'm going to tell *Papai* that we're going to buy a new tent. A big one."

Daniela catches him for a quick hug before he scrambles out of the room.

"Hard to believe someone who is so good with children," she muses when we're alone, "and people in general, would have absolutely no sense when it comes to women."

A groan rumbles in my chest, as I get up off the floor. Daniela is closer to my age than to Antonio's, but in many ways, she's been very maternal and protective toward me. My family did some unconscionable things to hers—and to her. But she's never blamed me for any of it, and she bent over backward, from the moment she arrived, to let me know I'd always have a home here. For that, I show her more deference than most people, and permit her a little leeway to stick her nose into my personal life. But it's not a free pass. Otherwise, there'd be no end to her meddling.

But this isn't about my personal life. This is about family. I've been expecting the lecture about Marco since I arrived.

"Don't expect me to apologize for what happened with Marco. You know better than anyone that I want Valentina to be happy. But I won't look the other way when it comes to her safety."

"I'm not talking about Valentina," she huffs. "I saw the account statements. There was no choice but to question Marco."

Wait—what? I'm sure Antonio was forced to show her the evidence so that she didn't lop off his balls in the middle of the night. But our assumptions were incorrect, and she's still giving us a pass? That's interesting.

"You think we were right to question Marco?"

She glares. "Don't ask me to answer that question."

Wow. Just wow.

"I'm talking about the way you treated Lexie."

Christ. *She gets ten seconds, and then I'm pulling the plug on this.*

"How do you know about what happened between me and Lexie? Did she share my personal business with you?" She was here early, although I highly doubt Lexie bared her soul to Daniela.

"It's her business too," she chides, "and she has a right to tell whomever she wants. But she didn't say anything to me—even when I raised it. From what I understand, you were such a loud bastard that everyone on the floor heard what happened."

Antonio told her.

"You're a busy woman, and a smart one. I'm surprised you have the time or the inclination to gossip."

"I make time when it involves the people I love. And I'm not afraid to tread in the mud, if that's what it requires."

I need to pivot, because she's tenacious and I'm done with this. It's a no-win situation for me.

"Your offer to Lexie was generous and kind. Having her here is fine, because the property is highly secure, but Lexie can't go shopping or to a spa—at least not without a lot of preliminary groundwork that I don't have time for. It's too dangerous for her to be out and about."

She sighs, lowering herself to the edge of a rocking chair. "Are they ever going to catch the people who murdered Francesca Russo?"

"I suspect they're getting closer, although I don't know the specifics. But I'm certain the prime minister will not rest until he avenges his daughter's death." I pause. "I'll arrange a dress for Lexie."

She lifts her chin and peers at me before standing. "Not that Lexie can't afford her own dress, but I want to do it for them. Valentina's so excited about the launch, and they're like sisters. I've always appreciated their relationship, but never more now that I have three little girls who are close in age. It's been a tough few weeks, and I want to do something fun for them. But I understand the safety issues. I'll work around it, even if it means having a rack of dresses brought to the house."

I nod.

"Besides," she taunts from the doorway, "buying a woman a dress is a privilege, especially for a man who's not related to her. He gets to enjoy her in his gift all evening, and imagine the fabric pooling at her feet at the end of the night."

Daniela could be turning cartwheels in the room. All I see is an image of a naked Lexie in high heels, surrounded by clouds of soft fabric.

"I don't believe you've earned that privilege, Rafael," she adds, throwing cold water on my little fantasy. "But Lexie's a grown woman, and that's up to her. I came to tell you that we're serving cake soon."

She leaves without another word.

When Antonio told me he was marrying her, I wondered how a sweet little thing like her would ever survive such a powerful and formidable man. I never wonder about that anymore. I snicker before my mind returns to something she said earlier.

Don't ask me to answer that question.

I'm still shocked by that little revelation. Either Daniela feels the evidence was too damning for us to ignore, or Marco has lost some of his sheen and she doesn't trust him.

Join the club.

26

LEXIE

When I get back to the apartment, I change into a pair of boy shorts and a cotton cami that I like to sleep in, and plop on the sofa, thinking about the hot guy who sat across from me at dinner. The one who joked with Antonio and Daniela's kids—completely relaxed like he used to be all the time, before he became powerful and deadly.

Rafael got a call shortly after the kids were in bed. When he got off, he said he needed to make a stop at Sirena—something about the band having underage girls with them. I couldn't catch the words they exchanged, but when he said goodbye to Antonio, his tone was low and menacing.

Sirena. A beautiful club filled with beautiful women who will be happy to spread their legs for Rafael—and won't make him wait. *I can't think about that.* I have to do what's right for me.

He's right for you, a small voice inside whispers. It's the whisper that comes late at night after a couple glasses of wine, and you don't want to go to bed alone. It's the voice of weakness, and she rarely has anything beneficial to say.

It's the devil tempting you, my eleventh-grade dorm mother would chide when we were caught hanging out with boys after curfew. Apparently, the devil takes on many forms. I don't know much about it. I was raised in the Church of England, and while we're still big on condemning sinners, we've decided to leave all talk of the devil to the Catholics.

My phone vibrates on my stomach, and as I reach for it, a small part of me hopes it's my devil tempting me.

Valentina. It's almost a relief.

I sent her a video earlier of Vivi begging Antonio to let her stay up for a little while longer *because it breaks my heart to go to bed before your special day is over.*

VALENTINA: *LOL. What a little drama queen. How was dinner?*

LEXIE: *Not the same without you. Missed your gorgeous face.*

VALENTINA: *I missed all of you too.*

I bet you did.

LEXIE: *How's Athens?*

VALENTINA: *Fine.*

Hardly a ringing endorsement.

LEXIE: *Just fine?*

VALENTINA: *The client who said he was bringing his wife, and insisted I come too, did not bring his wife. Marco ended up going to dinner alone.*

I don't believe there was ever a wife. But I keep my mouth shut, because she's not an idiot. She knows Marco dragged her to Athens to punish her father.

LEXIE: *What did you do?*

VALENTINA: *I ordered room service, and I'm watching a movie.*

LEXIE: *I'm sorry.*

VALENTINA: *He's taking me to Rhodes on our way home to make up for it.*

Really? You're going to let him buy you off that easily? I'm not going to pile on.

LEXIE: *Ohhhh. That sounds like a VERY nice way to apologize.*

She texts me a smiley face.

Rhodes is a gorgeous Greek island, although I doubt it's

enough to make up for missing her dad's birthday. It wouldn't surprise me if her—

A loud rap on the door startles me. Giana is on tonight, and she always checks with me before the guards order food. They always order food, and I usually get something too. But I'm still full from dinner.

I text Valentina as I go to the door.

LEXIE: *Giana's here about my bedtime snack. Love you!*

"Yes?" I won't open the door until I know it's her. Protocol and all that.

"It's me."

Rafael.

I peek through the peephole. *It's him.* My lower belly clenches tight enough to wake my pussy, as I open the door, hoping some resolve blows in with him.

27

LEXIE

"Hi."

"Don't look so surprised. It's still my apartment."

I'm aware—painfully aware. "I'm only surprised you knocked."

He snickers before skimming my body, his lecherous eyes latching onto my nipples long enough for them to harden into tight peaks and push against my cami, in case he missed them.

"It's late. I didn't want to alarm you. Were you in bed?"

I shake my head. "Everything okay at Sirena?"

"Yeah. The band's manager brought in some girls he was trying to impress, and two of them weren't old enough to be in the club. He told Stella that if the girls had to leave, he would leave, too, and take the band with him. But it's all good."

His voice has that deceptive butteriness about it that lulls people who break his rules into a false sense of security. "Why do I think it might not be so good for the manager?"

One corner of his mouth curls. "I need to grab a couple things from the closet. I'll only be a minute." He glances down at my breasts again, and then directly into my eyes.

I shiver and wrap my arms around myself as I lead us

farther into the apartment. I'm sure he's checking out my ass, but at least I can't see it. Not because I don't like his heated gaze that always promises sin. But because I like it too damn much.

"I was just texting with Valentina," I tell him when we get to the living area.

His face goes blank, and I realize I shouldn't have brought it up.

"How's Athens?" he asks, recovering quickly.

"Old and hot." Valentina didn't say either of those things, but it was my impression the first time I visited Athens. I was eight, it was August, and the ruins of the Parthenon didn't impress me as much as the hotel pool. He's mouthwatering and my brain is blathering nonsense that hopefully won't reach my mouth.

I point toward the guest bedroom. "I'll just hang out in my room and let you get what you need in peace." Before I say—or worse, do—something stupid.

Rafael cocks his head. "You're using the guest room?"

"Yes. Am I not supposed to?"

"Why?" he demands, totally ignoring my question. "It's small and not as comfortable. Why don't you just take the large bedroom?"

His room. The one that was *our* room for a short time.

Because it's hard enough to be in the apartment—you're everywhere. But in the bedroom? There are too many memories there. I keep the door closed and I don't peek in.

"I like the showerhead better in the guest bathroom."

His eyes twinkle.

Oh God. "I mean—it's not what you think."

"No judgment here," he says wryly. "You should use whatever showerhead makes you feel good."

"I'm going to lie down." Because even though I don't think I could possibly embarrass myself any more than I already have, I'm not taking any chances. "Good night."

I don't wait for a response before grabbing my e-reader and hightailing it out of there.

Not five minutes pass before he calls, "Lexie, I'm leaving. Come bolt the door behind me."

"I will. As soon as I finish this chapter. I'll do it the moment I'm done." I don't care about the book. But after being at Daniela and Antonio's, it feels lonely here, and I can see myself blurting out something foolish like, *Do you want to watch a movie?* Bad idea.

"I want to sleep tonight. Hearing the lock click behind me would help that cause."

Fine. I throw on a robe over my pajamas and trek into the hall.

He has two dress shirts on hangers in his hand. "I know this has to be an inconvenience for you. Your things here, and you somewhere else. I appreciate it."

"It's not much of an inconvenience. My office is downstairs."

"Did you get what you needed?" I ask, glancing at the pressed shirts.

He stops dead in his tracks a few feet from the door. After a long moment, he turns and takes a long stride toward me, dropping the shirts in a heap on the wood floor. For every step forward he takes, I take a step back until there's nowhere to go. Before I can blink, I'm caged against the plaster, his hands on the wall just above my head, and his mouth hovering over mine.

"No," he mutters with a raspy breath. "I did not get what I needed. Not even close. How long are you going to do this to me—to us—because I know you want it as bad as I do."

"You're arrogant," I chide with as much *oomph* as a wilted flower.

He runs a thumb over my cheek, and I suck in air like I'm dying.

"Don't answer the door dressed like this again."

"Like what?" I croak as though I'm brain-dead.

He tugs open the robe and circles my nipple until I gasp. "Like this."

"Giana's on tonight," I blurt.

"Good thing. If Sabio saw you like this, I'd have to scoop out his eyeballs. You won't like having to adjust to a new guard."

"You're a Neanderthal."

"You're mine, Lexie. I'm willing to indulge you until you come to your senses. But no one, *no one*, will touch you, not even with their eyes, without paying a penalty."

"I'm not the one who's lost my senses. I should slap some into you."

He lifts his chin and turns his cheek to me, pointing at a random spot on his face. "Go ahead, Angel. Turn my skin red—although I warn you, when you're done, it's my turn, but it'll be a different cheek I'm reddening."

"You're a pig," I murmur, arching closer to his hard body. My pussy aches for a little taste of a muscled thigh.

"And you're going to moan and whimper," he continues. "Do you know why?"

I shake my head.

"Because while one hand is prettying your skin, the other is going to be teasing your pussy."

"No," I murmur in a voice that's so sultry, it sounds like yes. *Maybe I did say yes. If I don't find it in me to resist him in the next minute, I won't be able to find it at all.*

"Get out," I whisper, pressing my hands to his chest.

"Is that what you want? Me to leave?"

When I don't respond, he lowers his mouth above my ear. I feel his warm breath on my skin.

"Let me take care of you. If you don't like how I make you feel, you can send me away then."

No matter how much I will my head to move from side to side, it bobs up and down.

It's all the encouragement he needs. In a heartbeat, the flimsy robe is on the floor and my back is flush against the wall, with his hand threaded through my hair, and his mouth—*oh God his mouth*—it's the best kind of wicked, sending delicious zings straight to my pussy.

"You're mine," he says gruffly as he pulls the camisole over my head and tosses it aside like it insulted him.

I want to be his. I want him to be mine. Although I haven't figured out how we do that without destroying one another—without destroying me.

But for tonight I'm not going to think about it. Instead, I'm going to let him take care of me, and maybe he'll let me take care of him too. The rest can wait until the morning.

28

RAFAEL

SLOW DOWN, good sense warns, but it's drowned out by my throbbing cock and the unrelenting desire pumping in my veins.

We're not moving from this spot. There will be no long drawn-out seduction. No flat surface to rest on. I'm not giving her an opportunity to change her mind. *I'm going to fuck her, right here, against the wall.*

I yank at her tiny shorts, while placing a call to send the guard away. It doesn't matter that it's a female guard. *No one gets to hear her whimpers, but me.*

"Take a break," I bark at Giana, as I glide my fingers over Lexie's slick cunt, flicking her swollen nub until her eyes flutter shut.

After ending the call, I toss my phone onto the discarded robe. "Look at me, Angel." She's flushed and her eyes are a swirl of browns and greens and unfettered lust. "I'm not going anywhere tonight besides your pussy."

Her lips curl softly at the edges and a sultry mewl escapes. She palms my cock, rubbing a firm hand over the thickening shift. My trousers separate us, still, her touch feels like heaven —but I'm too damn aroused to let it go on for too long.

With one hand, I pin her wrists overhead and rake my free hand through her hair. "I've missed you, Angel." I slide my tongue into her hungry mouth, and she arches off the plaster. Her whimpers are so sultry, I feel them in my balls.

"Rafa," she gasps. "I need you." *The sweetest words I've ever heard.*

"Oh, you're going to have me. Every inch, in every hole, before the night's over. But I want to taste you, first, pretty girl."

I find her nipple, sucking greedily on one, and then the other, until I'm confident she feels it between her legs. My mouth skates down her belly, leaving a trail of kisses in its wake. As I lower myself to my haunches, I take her cock tease shorts with me, and help her out of them.

Lexie's head is glued to the wall, her mouth like a tight O that I ache to shove my cock through. "Rafa," she moans as I stroke her inner thighs, nudging them apart.

"Spread your legs for me," I urge, hooking her slender leg over my shoulder. "Open your eyes, Angel. I want you to watch while I feast on your cunt, right here in the foyer."

She's wet and her arousal is all I can think about. *All I smell. All I taste.*

I lick her from back to front, again and again, catching her clit on my tongue. She trembles, and digs her fingertips into my scalp for support. "When I'm done, I'm going to fuck you against this wall like a pretty little whore. You'll like that, won't you?"

"Yes," she moans in a breathy voice. "Yes."

"You're going be so needy, you'll beg for my cock."

I clamp my lips around her clit, and slide two fingers inside her. She squeezes them so goddamn hard my dick weeps for a turn.

When her thighs clench, I withdraw my fingers and my mouth. "No. No," she whines as I stand. "I'm almost—"

I kiss her, letting her taste herself on my tongue and quieting her briefly. "You'll come when I say you're ready, Angel."

She presses her pussy into my leg searching for some friction. I'm not even sure she's aware of what she's doing. "Does that pussy need a little attention, already? Would you like to grind against my thigh?"

My Angel gazes into my eyes, with the flush of arousal staining her flawless skin, and nods. "Yes."

She's shameless, and it's so goddamn sexy. I slide my mouth over her throat. "Maybe later. If you're a good girl."

Not placated by maybes, Lexie tears at the buttons on my shirt, and I pull off my pants, because I'm craven too.

Pressing my body into hers until she's flush against the wall, I find her mouth in a frantic coupling.

When her whimpers become helpless, I offer my hand, stroking her tight little cunt just the way she likes it when she's close. Gripping my arms for leverage, she sinks her teeth into my shoulder, grinding her wet pussy into my hand.

Without warning, I swat her ass. "Stop squirming. You'll take what I give you, until I tell you otherwise."

She mewls, and I feel the sharp intake of breath on my neck as she struggles to let me set the pace.

"That's it. Such a good girl." I run my mouth along her jaw, murmuring. "Do you know how hard I get when you let me control your pleasure? Rock hard. All for you. I'm going to take such good care of you tonight. Your pussy is going to be so tired and sore when we're done." She moans. "Don't worry, I'll soothe it with my tongue until it's all better."

"Please, Rafa. Please."

Her pleas are driving me to the edge, much too quickly.

"You beg so sweetly." I sweep the matted hair off her face. "What do you need, Angel?"

"Fuck me." *Fuck me.*

I palm my cock to keep myself in check. "Ask nicely."

"Please fuck me. Please." *Oh, baby. I love how you beg.*

I'm done denying either of us. "Anything for you."

I lift her up, and she wraps her legs around me. "Hold on tight, Angel." Using the wall to brace her, I lower her onto my leaking cock, sheathing myself inside her hot, tight walls.

Lexie groans as I slide home. The sound is deep and clawing, echoing around us.

She's beyond aroused, and this is going to be over much too soon if I don't find some control. I tighten my grip on her, and force myself to pause. But despite my efforts the control I crave is just out of reach.

"This is going to be hard and fast, and you're going to come all over my cock like a good girl."

"Now!" she cries. "Move, Rafa!"

With one hand cupping her ass, and another between her shoulder blades, I brace her on the wall and give her everything she begged for—and more.

"That's it. Squeeze that pussy around my cock, Angel."

When she does, I suck in one breath after another, fighting for control. "Take what you need," I rasp. "Squirm all over me."

She digs her nails into my back, as I thrust savagely, mesmerized by the pleasure reflected in her beautiful face. As she begins to unravel, I dip my head and suck on her throat, marking her. *She's mine.* By the time the sun rises, I plan to mark her in every way known to man.

Lexie tightens around me, clamping down almost painfully, and cries out her release. I roll my hips as she trembles, but I'm too far gone to hold out any longer.

Like a demon, possessed, I use her like an animal. Taking and taking and taking until my balls burn for release.

She clings to me, whispering into my damp skin. "Your cock feels *so* good. Come for me, Rafa. Deep inside my pussy." Her voice is so sultry that I can't resist. I hold her steady, and with a few brutal thrusts and a rumble in my chest, I empty myself inside her.

She cries out again, and buries her face in my neck while her pussy pulses around my shaft.

"It was perfection," she pants, gasping for breath. "I don't want it to be over."

I don't know if she's talking about the relationship or the sex. Either way, my answer is the same.

"We're not done, Angel. I'm just getting started."

29

RAFAEL

WE'RE TWEAKING the plan for launch security, but all I can think about is the sexy blonde who begs so sweetly for my cock. I'm about to cut this meeting short to go find her, when my phone rings.

"Prime Minister Russo, how are you?"

I put the phone on speaker and glance at Zé, whose ears perk up at Russo's name.

"It's a new day, Rafael," Russo says with conviction. The sense of defeat he had the last time we spoke is gone. "We captured the monsters who murdered my little girl and were responsible for terrorizing the Continent."

Captured, not arrested. He might be the highest-ranking Italian official, but Francesca was his daughter, and he will mete out justice the same way I would.

"We got every last fucking one."

He's awfully confident, but I need more details before I'll be convinced. "That's impressive. How did you manage what no one else was able to accomplish?" I keep the skepticism out of my voice. I don't want to make an enemy of him.

"We didn't do it alone, of course. We amassed our own intelligence, together with what we received from Clarke in London, and others in Oslo. We received assistance from all corners. European leaders paid their condolences not with flowers and prayers, but with intelligence. The information you sent was invaluable. I'm indebted to you.

"The end of this scourge serves as a memorial to Francesca. God rest her soul and forgive me for not having dismantled the ring before it hit home." He sighs. "Let that be a lesson to you, son. Europe is a family, and if we don't take seriously the threats against our brothers and sisters, those threats will eventually find their way into our homes."

Russo's in a reflective mood, and I let him pontificate. But he still hasn't told me a damn thing to make me sleep better tonight.

"Paolo was found with his throat slit. It appeared that his death was at his own hand, although there are far easier ways to die."

My jaw tightens. I hope he doesn't believe Paolo was in charge of a fucking trafficking ring. "Are you suggesting Paolo was the kingpin?"

Zé peers across the desk at me and shakes his head, his lips pulled into a thin line. Neither of us believe a kid was running that ring.

"No," Russo scoffs, and I relax a bit. "But he was the man responsible for my daughter's death. Miles Vander Gant was the kingpin."

Was. "Did he survive long enough to be questioned?"

"We got what we needed from him."

Russo doesn't say *We got everything from him*, because he's experienced in these matters. No one ever gets everything. Not even a skilled interrogator with state-of-the-art tools.

"They would hire a local to help select the right club, and then put someone on the inside who could assist, as needed." *Fuckers.* "Sometimes it was the same person. The errand boys never lived long enough to collect a payday. They also had a few trusted teams, like the people you caught at Sirena, who would lure targets into the trap."

Targets like Lexie. I would have liked to have spent some quality time with Vander Gant.

"They ran a lean organization," Russo adds, "especially given the terror they caused."

Those assholes put in a lot of advance work, when they could have sauntered into a club, found a target, and convinced her to leave with them. Although that would have put them in a venue with security for longer periods of time—which was risky—and depending on the night, they might not have walked away with a victim. *It would have left too much to chance.*

"I'm assuming they chose their targets in advance?"

"Not initially. They honed their tactics as time went on."

"Did you find out anything about why they moved onto wealthy targets?"

"They could be sold for a higher price. It was always the plan."

First they practiced using girls whose families didn't have the resources to go after them.

I lock eyes with Zé, whose expression has darkened considerably since the call came in.

"Vander Gant's deputy led us to an Interpol agent who had been burying information."

"Fucker," Zé mouths.

"It's a big agency, and he couldn't keep everything under wraps, but he hid information that could have helped break the ring sooner. He was found dead this morning in London."

"You didn't have an opportunity to question him?"

"That was done by a business acquaintance of yours." *Will.* "I have no doubt he did a thorough job."

I have no doubt either.

"Only one dirty agent?" *Possible, but unlikely.*

"I can't say with certainty, but with the ring gone, they've been neutralized. I guarantee that if there are others, they'll be on their best behavior."

For a little while.

"Who ordered the hit on Paolo?"

"Vander Gant denied it." Russo sniffs. "It did look like a suicide, but as I said earlier, there are easier ways to kill yourself."

Zé rolls his eyes. He doesn't believe that Paolo died by suicide any more than I do. *It takes a lot of balls to slit your own throat. Someone was cleaning up.*

"Did you find Paolo's cousin?"

"Almost everyone we questioned knew Paolo. No one knew anything about a cousin."

Andre had no reason to lie about that, but whomever he talked to could have lied to him. We've always known it was a possibility. But still, it feels like a loose end.

"Rafael, I honored the promise I made to you. We used the charts you provided as a road map to question Vander Gant. He gave up enough details on the victims that we'll be able to trace most of them."

"Trace, but not locate?" It's a punch to the gut, and I'm sure Zé feels it too.

"That will be more difficult. The women were sold through an online auction on the dark web, everything was encrypted, and money was exchanged through untraceable wire transfers. They have no idea who the buyers are."

The whole thing makes me sick.

"Interpol has agreed to contact the victims' families provided that I keep their culpability out of the news."

Those bastards aren't worried about one dirty agent. They're worried there might be more. "Are you going to keep quiet?"

"Yes," he says firmly. "A month ago, I would have enjoyed their humiliation. But now? There's no point.

Francesca is gone forever, but at least I know what happened to her, and I know where she is. It's more important for us to give the families something than it is for me to gloat."

It's good news, but it brings no real comfort. The emotion continues rumbling inside like lava in a volcano. Not ready to blow, but on the precipice. *I should be more relieved.*

"Before he departed this world, Vander Gant threatened that we could kill him, but we couldn't kill the cause."

"The cause?" *What the fuck is that?*

"He suggested this was some kind of political payback."

"That's it?"

"We pressed him, but it was the end, and even adrenaline couldn't keep him alive. If he had anything meaningful to trade, he would have done it sooner. Trust me. It wasn't a good time for him."

It's not uncommon for prisoners to make those kinds of threats. The cowards make them early, hoping to bargain, while others save them for the end, as a parting shot to leave the interrogator with doubts that will eat at him.

"You're confident it's over?" *Because I'm not.* Men who believe blindly in a cause are the least likely to give up useful information.

"I'll sleep well tonight."

Russo has other daughters, a wife, and sisters. If he's wrong and they're not finished, they'll seek their revenge with any one of them. *He won't risk it. But I can't shake the thought that this was some kind of cause.*

"I know it doesn't bring back Francesca, but you've done a great service to many."

When we end the call, I lean back in my chair and stare at Zé, my gut still churning.

"You don't believe he cut it to the ground and destroyed the roots?" my top man asks carefully.

"I'm not sure. He wanted them so badly. What if there's some measure of magical thinking involved?"

"Russo is a ruthless son of a bitch. He doesn't strike me as the kind of man who's inclined toward magical thinking."

"Normally I'd agree. But they murdered his daughter right under his nose. It wasn't a shot across the bow, it was a full-frontal assault, meant to neuter him. I don't think we have any idea what's going on in his head."

You destroy a powerful man by taking women he loves—women he's vowed to protect. It's a tactic that's been used since the beginning of time, and it's still used by those without honor—because it works.

"What do you think about Vander Gant suggesting this was some type of a cause?"

"I don't like it. It was the only thing Russo said that gave me pause. We'll poke around," Zé adds, standing to leave. "I'm sure others will too."

I'm not so sure. Everyone wants it to be over. It's been a pox on the Continent. Tourism has taken a hit. This news is going to be celebrated across Europe, and if he really did destroy those fuckers, it certainly is a reason to celebrate.

"Poke around—but do it quietly. I'll have Tamar see what she can find on Vander Gant."

"Rafa," he says from the doorway. "Even if Russo didn't clean up everything, I think we're going to find that he cleaned up the worst of it."

Maybe it's because something that has consumed me since the night they showed up at Sirena—with Lexie—is done, just like that. Or maybe it's the fact that the woman who's back in my bed might be one step closer to leaving my protection, with everything that entails, including returning to London. As much as I don't want her to go, I still can't make up my mind if, in the long run, it's for the best—for both of us.

I thought I'd have more time to figure it out.

30

RAFAEL

ON MY WAY TO share Russo's news with Lexie and Tamar, I make a detour to Antonio's office, striding past Cecelia. "I need to see him."

She must sense something in my demeanor, because she waves me on without a single question.

While there's no real urgency, the news is going to become public soon. I want to run it by Antonio before I tell Lexie. I don't want to say anything to get her hopes up, or worse, lull her into a false sense of security. I need a gut check, and he's just the guy to give it to me.

"Got a minute?" I ask, entering his office without knocking.

He glances up and pushes his laptop to the side. "Always."

I take the ball of rubber bands off his desk and plop down in my favorite chair.

"What's going on?"

"Russo called. He brought down the ring."

Antonio sits back, arms folded across his chest, expression unreadable, even to me. "Is that right?"

I nod. "There might be foot soldiers here and there, but he

claims they captured the animals at the top and most of the vermin below. It'll be announced shortly."

"Who was the mastermind?"

"Miles Vander Gant."

He shakes his head as though the name means nothing to him. I've never heard of him either. Although I don't rub elbows with those kinds of monsters. At least, none that I'm aware of.

I tell Antonio everything Russo told me. He listens carefully, and critically, I'm sure, giving every detail his rapt attention. When I'm finished, he studies me like I'm a curiosity.

"I would expect you to be ecstatic. Why aren't you?" he asks.

"I am." My tone is a tad too defensive.

Antonio raises his chin, his keen gaze steady as though he's trying to untangle my jumbled thoughts and feelings.

"What's bothering you?" There's a sense of disquiet woven into each word.

"This doesn't feel too easy to you?"

The crease in his forehead eases as he shifts forward, elbows on the desk and hands steepled below his chin. "Easy? All of Europe has been hunting those bastards for a couple of years. Eventually, they were going to run out of luck."

"They eluded capture for a long time—even most of the errand boys. All of a sudden, they're finished? These are the same bastards who managed to kill three suspects, in *two* separate prisons, within minutes of one another, so they couldn't spill their guts. Yet the entire enterprise collapses overnight, like a house of cards? That doesn't bother you?"

The more I think about it, the less convinced I am.

"It wasn't overnight. But when you capture the kingpin and his top lieutenants, everything collapses. This isn't like a crime family with heirs apparent and intricate succession plans. Russo's a powerful man who was determined to find his daughter's killer. He put more resources into it than anyone has, and it sounds like he had help from all over Europe. But in the end, I suspect a dead daughter was the greatest incentive. I can appreciate that. I wouldn't have stopped to piss if I were in his shoes."

Antonio is the shrewdest man I know. He questions everything—always. There's no reason to believe Russo fucked this up.

"Their end didn't give me the sense of satisfaction I expected. But I'm sure you're right."

"The end wasn't satisfying because someone else meted out justice."

Maybe the stirring in my gut isn't a warning. Maybe it's a twinge of regret because I didn't have the opportunity to butcher the animals myself.

"I don't agree that their capture was easy," Antonio continues. "But like you, I'm always concerned when it seems too easy. Although, Rafael, sometimes it is just easy. Having said that, you're wise to question anything that gnaws at you. That's one of the reasons I have complete faith in your leadership."

A sense of satisfaction washes over me. When I was younger, I spent so much time and energy working to become the kind of man that would make him proud. But the truth is, he was always proud of me. I might have done things that disappointed him, but I was never a disappointment in Antonio's eyes. His unconditional love is one of the greatest gifts he gave me.

"It's over," he says. "Take a deep breath and stop worrying so much about Lexie—because that's what's at the heart of your concerns."

If I had half a brain, I would let the comment about Lexie roll off my back. But I glare at him from across the desk, and the flicker of amusement in his eyes tells me he knows he hit a nerve.

"You have a big launch right around the corner. Don't take your eye off the ball now."

"I've been consumed by this, but I haven't taken my eye off the ball. The launch is proceeding on schedule, and the new product is going to wow the Americans, much like it wowed the Europeans. Maybe more."

He nods, not bothering to hide his admiration. "Have you told Lexie the traffickers were caught?"

Antonio knows Lexie was chasing them, and he also knows that she and Tamar have been digging for more information. The latter giving him less heartburn than the former.

"Not yet. I was on my way to talk to them, but I stopped here first."

"I spoke to Will yesterday." He gauges me carefully, but I give nothing away. "Things have settled down in London. Now that this is over, will she be going home?"

His prying buys him another glare.

"I don't know." The words are bitter in my mouth, and they sound no less bitter to my ears. It's up to her. "Tamar would like to make her a permanent part of the team."

"That's an interesting idea. Lucas says she's a natural, curious, with raw talent and great instincts and tenacity."

A compliment from Lucas is rarer than snow in the Mediterranean.

"Doesn't surprise me," Antonio quips. "I was there the day she learned to ride a bike. Lots of scrapes and bruises, but she was a stubborn little thing. What's going on with you two?"

He sneaks the last part in seamlessly—and shamelessly.

"What happened to men are entitled to privacy? That was always your big thing."

"Still is. But another one of my big things is that fools don't need to suffer alone."

I could blow him off. But that's not how our relationship works—on either end. We don't allow each other to hide, even if it's uncomfortable. "I don't know if it's going to work."

"Relationships are hard. A strong woman who knows her

own mind is tough. Maybe you're better suited to one-night stands with women who think that every word that comes out of your mouth is genius. You know, the ones who live to suck your cock, even when you're an asshole. Although, I found the thought of that kind of *devotion* was much more interesting than the reality." He shrugs. "But everyone's different. It might be your jam."

"My jam?" I scoff. "Next thing you're going to tell me, you're a Taylor Swift fan."

He sits forward, drumming his fingers on the blotter. "What are you afraid of, Rafael? That one day you'll wake up and she'll have disappeared?"

31

RAFAEL

The words are a sharp blade plunged into my heart by a hand skilled at eliciting the truth—a man who takes no prisoners.

"Don't be an asshole," I snap in a voice that's too loud and brimming with emotion.

He raises his brow in warning, which I heed out of respect.

"It's not much of a stretch." My voice is hollow, belying the sorrow that's crept in. "She's a risk-taker like my mother—and yours."

His expression tightens, and his eyes reflect the anger and grief—and the regret—that are my constant companions.

"My mother died when some son of a bitch who had it in for Will blew up a plane over the Atlantic. And your mother didn't disappear because she was a risk-taker. She disappeared because she married a monster. That's why she's dead."

It's true. Every word. But that doesn't make it less painful.

"We don't know how or why my mother died." *Or even when. We don't even know with absolute certainty that she is dead. We don't know a fucking thing—not really.*

"We don't know the details. But we do know your father was responsible."

No question. We know that whatever happened to her was on his order. The bastard ordered the demise, if not the death, of a woman he once vowed to love and protect. My mother told me, herself, that he loved her before they married. She was sure of it. But things changed. He changed.

Although I find it impossible to believe that he loved anyone, or that he was capable of that emotion. I never saw any evidence of it. *None.* He was an ogre. As was my brother, and my Uncle Hugo, Antonio's father. They were evil personified—I've thought about it a lot over the years. Tried to find something—just one thing to hold on to—something to give myself a shred of hope that I didn't inherit the gene. *That I might be different.* But I could never find a damn thing.

"What if my father didn't start out as the devil? But he hated her causes and crusades, and that hate tarnished everything. I heard the fighting." *His fury. Her screams.* "Eventually things went from bad to worse—until she disappeared."

"What he hated," Antonio replies, "was that he couldn't control her. That she had a brain and a goodness about her. The rest were the excuses of a coward. If it hadn't been her crusades, he would have found another reason to hate her. He was a devil who tortured his wife, and an innocent child. Your mother's disappearance is your father's sin. Not hers."

Fury engulfs me, and I slam my fist on the desk. "Of course what happened wasn't her fault."

"You're not him."

His voice is as gentle as it's ever been, but his anger is easier to take than his empathy. When I can't stand it anymore, I go to the windows and brace my arm along the frame.

It's a clear day, and the view over the old city is unparalleled from this spot, but I see nothing. Antonio's not like his father, but he has it in him to be. He's just made different choices. *What if I can't? What if I succumb to my demons?*

"What if I'm just like him?" I ask, my back still toward him so he can't see the nakedness I feel. "What if I've inherited his psychopathic tendencies and they get worse with age? It's not a huge stretch. I crave vengeance like an addict craves their next fix. I've reveled in ending a life more than once." *Dozens of times.* "How is that any different from him?"

"You don't kill innocents. Not only do you not kill them, you go to great lengths to protect the weak and vulnerable. You. Are. Not. Like. Him."

"Don't be so sure," I sneer, turning to face him before unearthing my greatest shame. "When I confronted Lexie about telling Valentina that I'd questioned Marco, I grabbed her roughly and held her by the arm in a way that I'm sure left a bruise. I scared her to death, and she doesn't scare easily." I'll never forget the fear in her eyes. Not if I live to be a hundred.

Shame rages inside me. But Antonio doesn't blink at my confession.

"When I learned she was hunting traffickers, I wanted to shake her until the fury eating at me subsided. All I could think about was pacifying my wrath. I didn't give her well-being a single thought. If I'd put my hands on her that day, I would have done serious damage."

"But you didn't."

"Not that time. But what about next week, or ten years from now when I'm tired of having the fight—or just tired in general? What's going to happen then?"

"Your father's blood runs through your veins, but so does mine. Neither of us wants to be a man who beats innocent women and children. But I know the fear. I know it well. I know how it eats away at your soul in the dark."

His eyes have a faraway look, and I have no doubt he lives with demons of his own.

"You would never turn your fists on a woman you're supposed to love and protect."

"But I've wanted to," he whispers. "More than once. But no. I wouldn't. And neither would you."

He's so sure of his self-control. So sure of mine. But he doesn't know what I feel inside. Fear, anxiety...it goes by many names, but its face is always—*always*—rage. I often mask it with humor or an outward sense of calm. But it's rage—not just simple anger. *Rage.*

I don't have confidence in my ability to keep it contained over the long haul—not with someone like Lexie, who pushes all my buttons.

"I can talk to you until kingdom come, but it won't do any good. I couldn't see the truth until Daniela forced me to confront the demons and promised that she would stand between them and my better angels."

"I don't understand the point you're trying to make. It makes absolutely no sense."

"And it never will, coming from me. Only Lexie can give you the assurances you need."

More gibberish.

Next time I need a gut check, I'll check my own fucking gut.

32

LEXIE

TAMAR HAS me working on a gnarled mess of facts, but I'm pulling every thread carefully, like my life depends on it—and it might. Even if it doesn't, someone's life does.

"Hey," Rafael says, strolling into the office with two days' worth of scruff on his jaw.

Facial hair is such a good look on him that I'm thinking about hiding his razors.

"Where's Tamar?" he asks.

"Valentina needed her to get a layout of the hotel in Boston where everyone's staying during the launch. Zé needed something too." I lift a shoulder. "She should be back in about an hour."

He pushes aside a folder and parks his gorgeous ass on the edge of my desk. It's a welcome interruption. "What are you working on?"

"I'm trying to find any and all connections between the victims. Things I might have originally missed." Using a small remote, I put the chart up on the wall screen. "Low income, middle income, upper income, and obscenely wealthy. The middle-income group has the broadest range. Most of the women who were abducted are from that group. At least the ones we know about." I'm not sure we'll ever know the name of every woman they abducted. It's heartbreaking.

He studies the chart. "There might be women unaccounted for in the low-income group."

"That's always the way it is. I don't know why it would be any different here. Plus, they started with women from poorer families. Who knows how many went missing before someone caught on. The highest income group has the fewest victims. But from what we know, they were just getting started there."

"They were practicing up until then." His response exudes confidence, like he knows something that I don't.

"Could be. What makes you so sure?"

He gazes at me, his features softening. "Bruno Russo brought down the ring."

The blood whooshes in my ears, and I feel almost light-headed. "He brought down the ring?" My brain is processing in slow motion. "Really?"

He nods, a small smile playing on his lips.

When it finally registers—fully registers—I leap up and fling myself at him. Rafael catches me in his strong arms and holds me against his chest. The heat of his body adds to the surge of euphoria.

After a few moments, I pull away, reluctantly. "Are you sure? Absolutely sure?"

"I didn't see the evidence for myself, but I had a long talk with Russo, and I ran our conversation by Antonio, after. I have no reason to doubt the prime minister's word."

There's something about the way he's qualifying everything that's unsettling. *I didn't see the evidence for myself. I have no reason to doubt his word.* It's almost as though he's hedging. "I feel a *but* coming on."

"No buts."

The emotion hits like a tsunami, and a few tears that I can't contain fall.

Rafael drags me against him, holding me like he's never letting me go. "You're safe from the worst of it, Angel."

He presses a kiss to the top of my head, his mouth lingering in a gentle caress that seems to go on forever. It's as joyous as his words. *You're safe.*

"I can go out again, like a normal person?"

"If you mean like a normal person whose father is a crime boss, then yes."

I feel his mouth curl.

"But let's give it a couple of days before you start traipsing around town."

I pull back so I can see his face. His jaw is tighter than it should be if the news were all good. "You're still worried."

"They're going to make an announcement today, and after that we'll have a better sense if the rats start to scurry deeper into the sewer or if one or two remain aboveground spreading plague."

It's like I'm on a carnival ride, at the low point after the giddiness of the descent. "So they didn't get all of them?"

"It appears they got everyone of consequence."

"Appears," I repeat softly, stepping back, because it's impossible to think about the ramifications in the safety of his arms.

"Russo's confident."

"But you're not?"

He pulls me between his legs until we're nose to nose. "I have a lot to lose by being overconfident. I won't take that risk. For now, I'm taking a more cautious approach."

I have a lot to lose by being overconfident. He means me. Ordinarily I would spend too much time overthinking the meaning behind his words—the sentiment—and maybe later I will, but right now—

"Russo said that the charts you made have been a great

resource for them. They'll also help ensure that all the families are notified."

"Doesn't Interpol have a list of victims' families?"

"There was a mole at Interpol—at least one," Rafael sneers. "He buried information. I don't think anyone knows how much or the nature of what was lost."

Bastards. I blamed myself, but maybe this was why they ignored my emails. I'm sure the mole found a permanent underground home, or rather, someone found it for him. "Let me guess. Russo can't tell the families that Interpol had a traitor."

Rafael shakes his head. "He cannot."

"Have you spoken with my father?" He'll never relax when it comes to my safety, but at least he'll be relieved that I'm no longer in imminent danger.

"After I speak to Tamar, I'm going to call him. Russo mentioned that he was helpful in bringing those fuckers to justice."

Bringing justice to them is more like it. Thank God. I think about Francesca, who was just a girl, and about the woman in Oslo I was too late to save—and all the others. And I think about this beautiful man, right here, who risked his life to protect me. *If something had happened to him...* I push the thought away. It's heart-wrenching to think about. I hope every bastard involved, in any aspect of it, suffered terribly—for hours, days even. If that makes me a vile human being, so be it.

I peer up at Rafael and ask a question that is beyond all boundaries in our world. A question my father would *never* indulge—not even from my mother. But I'm desperate to know. *Desperate for vengeance.*

"Were the bastards tortured before they took their final breath?" If my father, or Antonio, or Rafael were leading the charge, I wouldn't need to ask. But Russo is a politician, and in the end, he might have done what was politically expedient.

Rafael narrows his gaze but doesn't say anything. Just when I've given up hope of a response, he takes firm hold of my hips. "They got the end they deserved on the order, or perhaps at the hand, of a distraught father. Don't ask for more, because I don't have details, and even if I did, it's not something I would ever share."

"Because I'm a woman."

He shakes his head. "No. Because I'm a man bound by honor. You know this."

I do.

Honor. An unspoken code shared by men who live among the shadows. They move in and out of the dark, effortlessly, avoiding the bright light like it's the enemy—and in many ways, it is.

"Do you want to call your father?" he asks, his eyes softer. "He'd be happy to hear from you."

I'd love to call him, but it's not a good idea. He'll want to know when I'm coming back to London, and I'm not ready to have that conversation. "He's probably gotten wind of it by now, and he's going to want to discuss the particulars with someone other than his daughter. You should call him."

Rafael nods, watching me through a mournful lens, as though he shares my inner turmoil.

"I thought I'd be so happy they were caught, and I am, although more relieved than anything. But it also feels almost surreal." I glance at my laptop. "I'm not even sure what I should do now."

"It felt surreal for me too—so much so that I began to question whether it was real. Everyone needs some time to process it—especially you. It's not like winning a prize. They caused terror and misery for nearly two years, and women are missing. Their capture and death does nothing to change that fact."

"Do you think they'll find any of the women?" *Please say yes.*

He tucks a lock of hair behind my ear. "I think it's a long shot, at best."

My shoulders slump as another wave of emotion threatens to pull me under. *There's no happy ending, Lexie. Face it.*

Rafael tips my chin up until I meet his eyes. "Why don't you finish what you're doing." He points to the screen on the wall. "The more we understand the similarities, the better chance that we'll be able to figure out who they all are—even the early victims. We might never find a single woman, but we'll know their names, and we can let the families know what happened. That's important too."

Rafael knows firsthand what it's like to be a victim's child, who wakes up every day wondering. My father, too. Although Dad knows what happened. He just doesn't know who's responsible. Rafael, on the other hand, knows who's responsible, but he doesn't know what happened to his mother. I think that might be worse.

I run my fingers over the stubble, gracing his jaw. "I agree. It's vitally important."

He takes my hand and slides it to his full lips, placing a tender kiss on my fingers. While he holds my gaze, his mood shifts, and he seems distracted by his thoughts—or perhaps by his demons.

"Hey," I whisper. "Where did you go?"

33

RAFAEL

WHEN I SHARED Russo's news, she leaped at me without thinking. She trusted that I'd catch her. *She trusted me.* It filled me with a sense of purpose—and a swarm of other feelings I'm not prepared to name.

I knew as I held her against me that I'd never let her go—that I had to make it work. *Somehow.*

"Have dinner with me, tomorrow. I'd like to take you to one of my favorite spots."

She cocks her head. "Like a date?"

"Not like one, Angel. An actual date. It doesn't seem right that you've let me have so much dessert without buying you dinner."

We both snicker because it's such an outdated concept. But she deserves more, and with the danger lessened, I have no excuse not to give her more.

"You're right," she teases. "You should have to work for treats, like the dog you are."

I snort and take her silky hair between my fingers. "No matter how fucking entitled I act, you should always make me work for it. Don't put up with my bullshit."

"You mean like when you threaten to scoop out someone's eyes for looking at me?"

"That's not bullshit. You're mine, and nobody gets to look—or touch—if they want to keep their body parts."

She draws back to punch me in the arm, but I catch her wrist before she can land it and go in for a kiss. At the last minute, the little vixen turns her head and denies me.

"Dogs who piss all over everything to mark their territory don't get treats."

"I'm going to rue the day I told you to make me work for it, aren't I?" I murmur, before pinning her bottom lip between my teeth.

"Every day," she says, taking a small step away from me.

It's jarring—not just physically but emotionally—to feel her back away.

"You haven't answered my question."

"*Have dinner with me tomorrow* isn't a question."

She's obfuscating. But I'm not letting her slip any further away.

"*Will* you have dinner with me tomorrow?"

She scoffs, and her mouth curls into a small fake smile to cover myriad feelings. But as I stare into her eyes, I get a glimpse of the chaos inside. The nonstop chatter in her head. *Sex is sex. But a date? A real date. I'm not sure that's a good idea. What if he bails? I'm scared.* Those are the words she's using to build a wall between us, although I doubt she ever admits to being scared—even to herself.

The need to stop the destructive inner monologue that I'm imagining, to reassure her, to take care of her, drives me to a place I'm loath to go. A place with soul-baring, unfamiliar feelings, and so many other things that could spell my ruin. *But there's no fucking choice.*

"On the plane, I asked you what it would take for us to have another chance. What you needed from me to make it happen. Do you remember?"

She nods. "I remember."

"You never answered me. So I've been winging it." *I hate winging it. It feels too much like being out of control.* "It's not a long-term plan for a relationship. Not a solid one, anyway."

"I don't know. You're winging it pretty well, Huntsman."

That mask has got to go, even if I have to yank it off myself.

"For now, maybe. But if you're not honest about your feelings, I'll eventually fuck it up." *I might anyway.*

She rubs her lips together and gazes at me, as if weighing her options—or maybe her words.

"What I need is some assurance that you won't walk away at the drop of a hat. That when it gets hard, you'll put your fears and misgivings aside and fight for us."

This isn't something she came up with on a whim. She's thought about it long and hard.

What I need is some assurance that you won't walk away at the drop of a hat. That when it gets hard, you'll put your fears and misgivings aside and fight for us.

It sounds a lot like *I need you to stop being a pussy and man up, Huntsman.*

I can do that, because I might be many things, but I'm not a fucking coward. I'm a soldier at heart. I know about loyalty and perseverance. And I sure as hell know how to man up. *Although this thing between us? It's a different kind of battle—one that I have no experience fighting. I need the road map that she's never going to give me.*

"I love you," she murmurs. "But I'm not looking for a promise of forever. I'm looking for a commitment toward making the relationship work. If you can't promise to fight for us, there can be no more chances. My heart can't take another battering. Neither can my self-esteem."

Oh, baby. The rawness in her voice seeps into the depths of my soul.

I love you. That alone should scare me the fuck away, but it doesn't. I step to the edge of the cliff, ignoring the murky water below, and dive in headfirst—like a fucking moron. *Reckless.*

"I'm not going anywhere, Angel. Even if I wanted to, I can't get you out of my damn head. You're under my skin. I've got it bad." The words are low and gruff, but every one heartfelt.

It's not the kind of admission a man like me makes often—if ever. It's unguarded, and weak, leaving me exposed—and vulnerable. It cost me. No question. But remaining quiet will cost me much more.

The layers are raw and painful as they're stripped away, mine and hers. It's both uncomfortable and freeing, and the silence that follows is almost reverent. Not so different from the confessional booth.

My Angel's quiet and lost—wading through the discomfort, for while there's purity in truth, it's blistering just the same.

Lexie swallows hard. "What can I do to make it easier for you?" She's tossing me a safety net because she knows the value of what I just showed her.

I don't have to search for the words to respond, because I've thought a lot about it too.

"You can remain locked up in the apartment—every day and night, wrapped in layers of Bubble Wrap. That would make it easier on me."

"Really?" she huffs, incredulous.

Before she can rip me a new one, I hold a finger to her lips.

"But the woman who consumes my waking thoughts and finds her way into my dreams burns too bright for that. She gets her energy—her light—from chasing sex traffickers"—*God help me*—"and debating political ideology that I will *never* be on board with. You're not built to sit on the sidelines any more than I am." I draw a breath. "What I need is for you to trust me to do right by you. To be honest with me—always. To come to me with the hard stuff—even if it means we're going to have an argument that will take days and several rounds of hate sex to fully recover from. We both run, Lexie. We just do it in different ways."

She links her arms around my neck, standing so close my cock twitches against her belly. But it's her eyes, wide with sincerity, that cause a muscle in my chest to clench.

"I will be honest. I promise. I will trust you—I do trust you. That's why I never go anywhere without these." She pulls a chain from under her shirt, with the angel wings dangling from a clasp.

I take the charm between my fingers. It's no more than a few grams, yet I nearly buckle under the weight.

"No matter what happens between us, as long as you keep the wings close, I'll always find you, Angel. You have my word."

"I know," she says, raking her fingers through my hair.

There will come a time when her promise, her trust, and her loyalty will be on the line, as will mine. It might not happen right away, but it will happen. That'll be the real test.

But even if we fail, I'd scorch the earth to find her.

34

LEXIE

I SPENT a good part of yesterday, and today, too, getting accustomed to the fact that the traffickers are dead. It was all over the news last night. Young women dancing in the streets and raising glasses in clubs all over Europe.

But what about all the women who are still missing, dead, or praying for death to save them? *I won't forget them.*

While I'm relieved that there will be no new victims, at least not by their hand, they weren't the first monsters, and they won't be the last.

I slide several silver bangles on my wrist and swipe cherry gloss across my lips. I don't know why I even bother. It doesn't stay on for long, and it's certainly no match for Rafael's kisses.

Rafael.

I love you. That part wasn't meant to be said aloud. I was mortified. But the feeling lasted just a second or two, and by the time I said my piece, I was glad it was out in the open.

I didn't expect him to say it back. I don't want him to say it at all until—unless—he means it.

But what he did say—*that* I never expected. *I'm not going anywhere, Angel. Even if I wanted to, I can't get you out of my damn head. You're under my skin. I've got it bad.* And *you're not built to sit on the sidelines any more than I am.* It's true. I'm not. But it's almost as though he's accepted it, accepted me, in a way that most people can't. *Not even my parents.* It's hard not to love a man who allows you to be yourself.

When I hear the knock, I glance at the clock and slip on a light, short jacket. Rafael's going to love the dress I'm wearing, but I don't want him to get the full effect until later.

"Yes?" I ask, because it's protocol, even though I know it's him.

"It's me."

His deep tenor makes the butterflies in my stomach take flight.

I'm a little nervous. Unless we're spilling our guts, I'm normally comfortable around him, but this is a date. *A first date.*

Considering his cock has been in my mouth—and in a few other places too—I should be embarrassed that he hasn't bought me dinner yet. Well, technically he has, but— *Get a damn grip, Lexie, and let the man in or there will be no dinner tonight either.*

I take a big breath and open the door for my date, who's talking to Sabio with his eyes on me.

In a black shirt rolled to the elbows—always rolled to the elbows—and a pair of jeans that look like they were made for him, he's pure sin. *The kind of sin that he's taught me to love.*

"Hi," I say, like a shy waif.

"Hi, beautiful," he murmurs, stepping inside, and brushing his lips across mine before the lock snicks. "I don't tell you that anywhere near enough." He deepens the kiss—or maybe I do—and when my back grazes the wall, it evokes memories of the last time we stood in this very spot. *Starving for one another. Taking and taking until the edge was off.*

I pull back to catch my breath. "You're quite beautiful yourself."

One side of his mouth curls. "We need to go. Otherwise, we'll never make it to the restaurant."

I nod and reach for the purse on the credenza. Rafael doesn't say a word about it, but his expression flickers with light when he notices the cork and fabric purse as we walk out the door. *The Judite Furtado original design, he asked her to bring me.*

"No one goes in. I don't care who they are," Rafael instructs Sabio, who nods respectfully. "Don't leave your post until we return."

"What if he needs to pee?" I ask when we're out of earshot.

"Not my problem, and not yours. I want you to have a relationship with your guards that makes you comfortable, but you're permissive and indulgent with them. They need an occasional reminder that they've been entrusted with an important assignment, and that there are boundaries and protocols. Otherwise, they'll become lax and undisciplined—especially Sabio, who is very capable, but arrogant."

The king of arrogance throwing stones—that's rich.

"I'm surprised," he says wryly, glancing at me. "You haven't asked where we're going. I would expect you to be pestering me about it."

I shove his arm. *I haven't asked because I don't care. You're taking me to your favorite spot, and although I've often wished for this kind of intimacy, it's more than I hoped for.*

"I'm full of surprises," I quip. "I thought you knew that."

"Oh, I do," he murmurs under his breath as we approach the elevator.

Giana is waiting with Zé, who is holding the elevator for us. *Great.* Nothing like a Grumpy Gus to kill the vibe.

"Good evening," Giana says pleasantly, flashing me a discreet smile as I step into the carriage. Zé, on the other hand, doesn't utter a damn word, although he catches Rafael's eye and nods. Rafael nods back, his eyes conveying a message I can't decipher.

On the short ride, they have an entire conversation in an unspoken language that only they understand. It's unnerving and scintillating at the same time, and I can't look away.

When we get to the garage, there are three nondescript SUVs parked near the elevator, along with several guards. In an uncharacteristic public display of affection, Rafael takes my hand and leads me to a sleek black Bugatti.

He opens the passenger door and helps me inside, but not before his mouth grazes my ear. "You're too damn tempting. I'm not sure we'll make it through dinner," he murmurs, his hot breath sending a small shiver through me.

To anyone watching, his behavior has been innocent enough, and certainly this isn't the first time the guards have seen him with a date. There have been dozens and dozens of women in and out of his life—his bed. *Maybe hundreds.* Rafael has a long history with women that's been well-chronicled by both the Portuguese and London media. I don't allow myself to dwell on what came before. But this is the first time he's openly treated me like a woman rather than a family friend or a little girl.

"You're driving? It's just us?" I ask as he gets in the car.

"There's not a lot of room in here for passengers, so unless Zé's going to sit on your lap—and that is not happening—yes, I'm driving."

"I'm sure Zé hates you driving with a passion." *One more strike against me.* I wouldn't care whether Zé likes me or not except he's so tight with Rafael.

"We're not going far, and we'll be flanked by security. I never go anywhere without guards—and neither do you, right, Angel?"

"Of course not."

Rafael side-eyes me and scoffs before pulling out of the garage, sandwiched between the SUVs.

"So quiet." He turns on some jazz and reaches for my hand.

"I expected a comment about the car making up for a tiny dick."

I laugh and glance at him across the console. He's grinning. *I want more of this.* "I was saving it for the return trip after I'd eaten dinner. I didn't want your feelings to be hurt if I brought up that, *uh, um*, unfortunate fact, and change your mind about feeding me. There's no food in the apartment."

He squeezes my fingers. "I could pull over and remind you how small my cock is, if you'd like."

"You've gotten all the treats you're getting until you shell out for dinner."

"The treat would be for you." His eyes twinkle madly, and I feel the flutter between my legs.

"You really have no business accusing Sabio, or anyone else, of being arrogant."

Rafael flashes me a panty-melting smirk, or at least they would melt if I was actually wearing panties.

"Do you cook?" he asks, like he's expecting the answer to be *no*—which would be correct.

"I'm not sure if what I do with food and a pan could actually be considered cooking." I shrug. "But I make a mean pasta with butter, cheese, and toasted breadcrumbs. Do you cook? I only ask because Giana mentioned the stove in your apartment looks like it's never been used."

"I'm going to have to talk to Giana about spilling my dirty secrets." He gifts me a cheeky smile. "I can reheat almost anything without ruining it. But I usually get something out. If not, my housekeeper Josefina keeps the pantry stocked. I'm not fussy, so I'll never starve."

"I'm surprised you don't have a housekeeper who comes in more than once a week."

"I'm never there." His jaw tenses. "But you're there every day. I'm sure it would be nice for Josefina to come in more often. I'll talk to her," he adds.

"You don't need to make any changes on my account. I'm neat and organized. Living at boarding school, you learn to clean up after yourself if you don't want to lose privileges. You know how it is."

He turns in to a parking lot and pulls up behind a black SUV. Zé gets out and disappears into the restaurant, along with several guards.

Rafael looks relaxed behind the wheel, like he enjoys being there.

"Do you normally drive?"

"Normally? *No.* But I appreciate the freedom of being in the driver's seat. When I feel like taking a drive, Zé hops in and we take off, usually followed by a couple of guards. It's not exactly freedom, but it's the closest thing a man like me gets."

He sounds almost wistful.

Men like my father and Rafael seem to have all the freedom in the world, and in some ways they do, but it's not as unlimited as I often imagine.

"Do you know how much it shocks me that you don't go off without guards? It always has."

"I'm responsible for my own safety, but unlike you," he says, tugging at my hair, "I don't go anywhere without backup. When I was a teenager, someone ran Antonio's car off the road, into the river. He had his driver with him, but no guards. He almost didn't make it. If they could get to him, they can get to me. I have too many responsibilities to let some fucker take me down."

I was a little girl—about five—but I remember when it happened. I was with Grandma Lydia when she got the call. She was taking me to a production of *Beauty and the Beast*, and we were having lunch before the show. I'll never forget the horror in her face, or the way her hands shook as she shepherded me out of the restaurant. It must have been scary for Rafael too. If Antonio had died, it's likely he would have been forced to go back to live with his father. *It would have been awful.*

Zé comes out and gives a thumbs-up.

Rafael helps me out of the car and tosses his friend the keys before we go inside.

35

RAFAEL

When I help Lexie with her jacket, my hand grazes her exposed back, and my cock jumps to life. She's wearing a dress that reaches her neck, but it's deceiving. Her shoulders and arms are exposed—as is her entire back. *Fuck me.*

"This dress is cheating," I whisper, after handing the jacket to Lena, who owns the small restaurant with her husband.

The impish smile she gives me makes me smile too.

Her makeup conceals the freckles on her nose, but I know they're there, reminding me of sass and fun, and of how young she is, compared to me. *How inexperienced.* Something I lose sight of too often.

"It's the perfect evening for eating outdoors," Lena gushes, leading us to the back of the restaurant.

When we step outside, Lexie's jaw drops as we follow Lena across the stone patio to a table a few yards from the surf. Her gaze moves from the lit votives to the torches buried in the sand, and finally to a firepit designed to ward off any ocean chill. All other light comes from the moon reflecting off the water and her beautiful face.

"It's magical," Lexie purrs to no one in particular.

Lena winks at me. I told her what I wanted, then left the details to her and her husband, Elliot, who does all the cooking. I've never bothered with anything like this, but I knew she'd get it right.

It's almost impossible to impress someone like Lexie—although I'm not interested in impressing her. I'm interested in surprising her and in making her smile.

I don't let Lena help her get seated. I do it, letting my hands linger on her skin. When she trembles at the touch, it takes everything I have not to drag her into the ocean and fuck her beneath the waves.

Before she disappears, Lena motions to what looks to be a soft wrap on the back of Lexie's chair. "It's lovely tonight, and the fire should be more than enough, but it's there in case you need a little something extra."

"My heart skipped a beat when I saw all this." She waves her arm through the sultry air, her gaze following it to the ocean. "I don't need to taste a morsel to know why this is your favorite restaurant. With this view, it doesn't matter if they serve a perfectly cooked filet or soggy fish-and-chips."

She's right, and I'm pleased she sees it the way I do. The food is great, but I come for the view, and with her across the table from me, it's never been better.

"The owners are good people, and the view is breathtaking no matter how many times I see it. But the food is good, too, and unpretentious. Plus, the tourists don't know about it."

"I'm surprised it's not crowded on a Friday night. Wait a minute." She smiles shrewdly, narrowing her gaze. "You rented the restaurant for the evening."

It's not a question, and I don't respond. I'm becoming more confident that Russo did his job. But I won't take chances with her safety, even if it means paying a popular restaurant to close its doors for part of the evening.

"My family doesn't often go out to dinner in London," she

says softly, "unless it's a special occasion. When we do, it means closing the restaurant—or at least part of it. Most people don't recognize my mother or me. My father's been zealous about keeping our photos out of the media—especially mine."

Zealous—the understatement of the year.

"But his face is very recognizable," she continues, "and he doesn't travel light. When he's with us—everything's a big production."

I enjoyed studying in London, but it's easier for people like us to go about our business here. There are more opportunities for a normal life.

"Porto is much smaller than London. Most of the time it's easy to be out and about—although not without some advance planning. Still, it's rarely necessary to shut down an entire restaurant."

Her brow furrows. "But it was necessary tonight. Is that because you think the traffickers are still a risk?"

I could tell her that I asked them to close because I wanted us to have the place to ourselves. It would go a long way to easing the lines on her forehead, but I won't lie to her.

"From all we've found, Russo cleaned up everything, at least the most dangerous elements. But we haven't had enough time to turn over every rock. You're far too precious to take chances with, Angel."

I reach across the table and take her hand, rubbing small circles over the inside palm with my thumb.

"They didn't close for the evening. No amount of money can make that happen on short notice. And I'm not arrogant enough to ask," I tease, coaxing a smirk from her. "They just didn't do a late seating. Except for one table inside. A couple is celebrating their fortieth wedding anniversary, and I didn't want to spoil their plans. Karma and all that."

"*Karma and all that*," she mocks. "Admit it, Huntsman...you have a good heart."

"There are plenty of people who would disagree with you."

"Only because they don't know you."

She gives me more credit than she should. I pride myself on being fair, but there's nothing good about me.

"Don't put me on a pedestal, Angel. It could come crashing down on you. My heart is anything but pure."

A waiter brings Port tonics and tapas to the table, ending that conversation.

Lexie holds up her drink. "Cheers," she says when I touch my glass to hers.

"*Saude*," I reply, taking a sip of what I'm quite certain is a cocktail made with Huntsman white Port.

"This looks yummy," she says, helping herself to a croquette.

"You get what you get here. But I've never been disappointed. Elliot goes to the market and to the dock each morning, and dinner is whatever catches his eye and imagination. He cooks like your mother or grandmother might cook."

"Clearly you've never had my mother's cooking," she jokes, taking a bite of croquette.

Every inch of this gorgeous woman is spirited and fun—and so very fuckable. If we get through our main course tonight, it'll be a damn miracle.

She turns her head toward the ocean and closes her eyes, soaking in the briny scent and the spray. "This is heaven."

"I think so too. When I was a kid, and anxious about something"—*like when my father let the strap fly or locked me in the attic*—"I'd call up the smell of the ocean or the sound of the surf to calm me. Even now it's the first place I go when I have a lot on my mind."

"That's why you spend so much time at Sirena. From a distance, it looks like it's part of the sea."

I nod. "It's exactly why I bought Sirena." *But now I have another Siren who calls to me.* I don't spend as much time there as

I used to—or even as much as I should. I spent my nights there, because once Antonio told me he wanted to put the succession plan into motion, I had to curtail some of the whoring or at least put a lid on it. I didn't have much reason to go home—there wasn't a stunning blonde who challenges me at every turn waiting in my bed.

"The ocean always renews my spirit," she admits. "But the city has a pulse I thrive on. Some people like to be alone. They crave solitude. That's not me."

It's not me either.

"Do you miss London?" I sit quietly, gauging her reaction, although my mind isn't quiet. *Are you going back now that things have calmed down, or will you stay here with me?*

God, I'm a pussy. If Antonio knew the half of it, he'd put a different succession plan in place.

I'm a fool who has let a woman crawl under my skin and set up shop. The worst part is that I have no plan to evict her. *I'm not even sure I can.*

36

LEXIE

"I LOVE LONDON, but I love Porto too. I've spent so much time here over the years it feels like a second home, and the Huntsmans are essentially family."

The question was benign—at least I thought so—and my response uncomplicated. Yet he considers my words carefully, weighing each one, as he takes in my demeanor like someone searching for clues.

"I asked about London, because I'd like to offer you a job—or rather, Tamar would like to offer you a job."

"A job?" I clarify, because surely I misunderstood, and before I start jumping up and down for joy, I better check.

"You'd work for Premier as a member of Tamar's team. You'd report to her, not to me."

He wants me to stay. I want to stay, too, but can it be that simple? Nothing between us has ever been simple—at least not since I was nineteen and started fantasizing about him. But working on Tamar's team would be life-changing. I could learn so much from her. Although it can only work if—

"Is Tamar fully on board or did you twist her arm to give me something to do?"

There's a tug at the corner of his mouth, and he shakes his head. "If you think Tamar would be willing to babysit, you don't know her very well. Offering you a job was her idea. She believes you have natural talent and good instincts. Apparently, Lucas does, too, and he thinks everyone's an idiot, so that's quite a compliment."

Lucas is intensely focused. It can be a little scary. When I was young, I was always a little reticent around him, and then after he walked in on Rafael and me in the vineyard, I avoided his gaze as much as possible. If I work for Tamar, our paths will inevitably cross. I'll see more of Zé too. *Ugh.* As unpleasant as the prospect is, it can't be part of the equation. I'm a big girl, and I won't make life choices out of intimidation.

But there's a potentially bigger problem that has to be part of the equation. Clarke Enterprises and Huntsman Industries do a lot of business together, but I doubt their interests always dovetail. I'm not getting involved in anything that puts me at odds with my father's company.

"I won't do anything that goes against my family's interests."

"I would never put you in that position, and neither would Tamar. Family's family. Besides, when your father isn't threatening to kill me, we work together." He raises his brow. "And it'll happen more often when Antonio retires."

I wish my father would retire, but he's not going anywhere soon. Especially now that the heir apparent turned out to be a traitorous weasel.

"Premier is a lawful entity," Rafael continues, "as is Sirena. Anything unsavory is done under other entities that won't be part of your portfolio."

Unsavory. I almost laugh. What he means is that anything illegal, immoral, or punches your ticket to hell falls under a different umbrella.

But it's true about Premier. I don't know whether it was always like this, but I do know that since Valentina became

Rafael's partner, Premier has had a squeaky-clean reputation. There's no way Rafael or Antonio would allow her to get her hands dirty.

"What do you think? You want to work for Premier? It's a good company, lots of perks, and the CEO is God." His expression is full of mischief, but he's pushing me for a response.

I laugh. "He's not God. He just thinks he is."

I heard everything he said about the job, and I don't think he's lying, but I do think he wants me to stay in Porto—at least for now—and he might have been painting it in the most favorable light. Rafael knows how much I admire Tamar. He thinks I'll jump at it.

"My first inclination is to say yes," I reply with a playful smile, "and to thank you for the opportunity in ways that are not fit to discuss in public."

His eyes sparkle.

"But can I think about it?" Before the last word is out, the sparkle is gone.

"Take whatever time you need." His tone is supportive, but the fingers drumming on the table say something different. *He's impatient for an answer.*

He'll have one, but not until I have a heart-to-heart with Tamar.

37

LEXIE

Dinner is delicious, and the rest of the evening is as spectacular as the moon's shadow dancing on the ocean. The discussion is light and flirty, filled with innuendo that makes my nipples pucker.

Every time Rafael leans across the table to fondle my hair, or skates a finger down my arm, or when he gazes at me until my skin burns, I want to grab his hand and lead him behind the rocks, where we can be alone.

We pass on coffee and dessert because the kind we're hungry for is not on the restaurant menu.

When Lena hands Rafael my jacket, he tucks it under his arm. "You won't need this. I'll keep you warm."

Yes, please.

With his hand in the hollow of my back, he leads me outside, and the pulse between my legs kicks up a notch at the feel of his open palm on my skin.

Guards flank us as we make the short walk to the car. He never takes his hand off me, not even when Zé hands him the keys.

When we're in the car, Rafael leans over the console, cups

the back of my head, and kisses me. His tongue slips into my mouth, and no corner is safe from his exploration. The longer the kiss goes on, the more aroused I become—until I'm toying with crawling onto his lap, unzipping his pants, and impaling myself onto his cock, which I know is rock hard. When I brush my hand over it to see if I'm right, a deep rumble escapes from his lips, and I swallow it.

"I need you," he murmurs, rubbing his thumb along my throat.

The windows are blacked out, and I don't think anyone can see in, but I'm not quite brave enough to let him fuck me in a parking lot, surrounded by guards—*and Zé.*

"We should go back to the apartment," I somehow manage.

He nods and pulls away, and I almost whine at the loss of him.

"I'm staying over tonight," he announces as we leave the parking lot with a trio of black SUVs. "I want to fuck you until we pass out, and every time I wake up during the night, I want to slide into that needy pussy until you clench around my cock and purr like a satisfied kitten."

"Such a romantic," I tease, my inner thighs damp from his filthy words. "You can stop wooing me with hearts and flowers. I already decided that I wasn't letting you go back to the hotel."

"Not letting me, huh?" He squeezes my thigh. "You're becoming quite impertinent, Angel. There might be a spanking in your future."

My belly tightens at the delicious threat. One that holds no menace—only pleasure. As long as I don't challenge him in public, he couldn't care less what I say to him when we're alone. I think he enjoys my impertinence.

As we turn onto a deserted stretch of coastal road, Rafael slides his hand up my thigh, inching toward my pussy. He draws a ragged breath when he discovers my surprise.

"Too slutty for a first date?"

"Oh, Angel," he murmurs, gliding his fingers over my slit. "You're in for it now."

Without wasting a second, he pulls the car to the side of the road, adjacent to a knee-high ledge of rock, and presses a button on the console before I can ask a single question.

"Problem?" Zé asks, his voice tight.

"Not a single one," he replies, circling my clit as I struggle not to make a sound. "Close the road between the grotto and the lighthouse."

"What's the plan?"

"You're on speaker," Rafael cautions.

Zé's quiet for a moment. "Would you like us to sweep the area?"

"I don't need anyone to sweep the area. You're in front of me, so you know there's no danger—unless you're worried a fish is going to jump out of the water with a gun. A half-mile stretch in each direction. Not an inch less."

"How long do you want it closed?"

He presses his fingers harder. *Faster.* I throw my head back and arch off the seat.

"As long as it takes."

He disconnects the call abruptly and turns to me, cradling my cheek in his large hand. "Do you know why I need an entire mile?"

I shake my head. An entire mile? *No.* Although I know exactly why he doesn't want gawkers driving by.

"Because I'm going to fuck you until you scream, Angel. No one gets to hear your pleasure. It's all mine."

He gets out of the car and comes around to my side, opening the door, then extending his hand to help me out.

I had anticipated car sex, and I was all in, and sex on the beach would be great, too, but it's impossible to scale those rocks in the dark. "Where are you taking me?"

"I already told you what I was going to do. But I know how

much you love to hear the filth. How wet it makes you. Do you want to hear me say it again?" He kisses me, long and rough, until my knees buckle.

When he drags me toward the front of the car, my eyes dart over the area.

"You're safe here," he whispers. "No one can hurt you besides me."

No one can hurt you besides me. I feel the pulse of the words between my legs. A veiled threat meant to make my heart beat faster, and the arousal curl tighter. *Predator and prey—that's his game tonight.*

There's something in his eyes as he lifts me onto the hood of the car, nudging my knees apart until I feel the cool air caress the wet flesh between my legs. *Something feral.* Something I should be afraid of—but I'm not.

His hot mouth skates over every inch of exposed skin while his hands roam my body, freely, as though it's his privilege. He's going to push my boundaries. I feel it in the intensity radiating from him. *Predator and prey.* But I'm on fire, and right now, I don't give a damn.

I cling to him and lift my legs to wrap around his hips. But a sharp pain in my calf stops me and I cry out, pushing him away.

"Did I hurt you?" His voice is raspy, and I hear the concern.

I shake my head. "My leg. It's a cramp," I reply, kneading the tight muscle.

He's perfectly still. Almost as though he's paralyzed.

"You didn't hurt me. I moved my leg—and it must have been the position I was in."

My assurance seems to spark some life into him, and he takes my calf in his hand and massages the muscle with tentative fingers that feel foreign. There's nothing about Rafael that's tentative—certainly not the way he touches me.

"What's wrong?" I take his hands. He doesn't respond, but I wait quietly because there's a storm brewing inside him—I feel the vibrations and see the turmoil in his face. It calls to some instinct deep inside me that desperately wants to be his safe harbor.

While I wait for him to finish with my leg, that's fully recovered, and say something—anything—the fog rolls in, shrouding the moon in puffs of lacy smoke. There's an eeriness about it that suits the moment.

Rafael turns his attention from my leg to my face. It's an abrupt switch, with verve, but without the gracefulness with which he normally moves.

"Promise me, Angel," he says, his fingertips caressing my face ever so lightly. "No bullshit. Promise me that you will not let me hurt you. That you won't put up with a single second of it. That you won't let me slide, inch by inch, until I've destroyed you. No free passes. Not a single one."

His voice is low, twisted with desperation and regret, but there's a roughness about it too. Everything about this moment is more somber, more serious than it was yesterday when he told me, *ordered me*, not to put up with any bullshit from him—but it's all related. This is coming from somewhere inside him that I'm not sure I can reach. He's asking for something that's beyond the words—but I'm not sure what it is, and I don't know how to respond.

I cup his jaw, reaching inside myself for humor, but it doesn't come. "Please tell me what has you like this."

"You have me like this." He shakes his head. "When I heard you cry out in pain, it shook me to the core. I don't want to hurt you, Angel. Ever."

"You didn't."

"You have to be the guardrail," he pleads, peering into my eyes. "I need to know that you will never, *never*, let me hurt you."

He means physical pain. That's what he's talking about. It starts to make sense. These feelings are tied to his family.

Don't worry. I'll protect us both.

"You might break my heart, but you won't hurt me—not like you're suggesting. But if you need to hear it, fine. I'm plenty strong enough to stand up to you, Rafael Huntsman. I will not be your punching bag. Don't you worry. I will never allow you to destroy me."

Rafael tips his head to the side while stark emotion fills the space between us. He cradles my face in his hands. "I don't deserve you."

I lift my chin. "I decide what I deserve." I place both hands on his chest. His heart is pounding when I find his mouth in a kiss filled with promise. A kiss that whispers *I won't let you down.* A kiss that conveys everything my heart wants to say. Because this is how we communicate best.

I place my fingertips on his stomach, pressing into the unrelenting muscle. "I believe you promised to fuck me until I screamed." A small, impertinent smile tugs on my lips. "Time to put up or shut up."

He growls, and I feel the earth shift and the burden lift from his shoulders as he nips at my ear.

"It's dangerous to summon the demons, Angel."

"Angels and demons are nothing more than two sides of a single coin. One cannot exist without the other." With both hands, I pull his face within inches of mine. "Are you waiting for me to beg?"

"You will beg," he assures me in a tone that makes my toes curl. "But it's too early for that."

On the hood of a Bugatti, surrounded by ocean mist and fog, Rafael Huntsman eases me onto my back and buries his face in my cunt.

His touch is no longer tentative. It's skillful, and knowing, and insistent, bringing me all the pleasure I can handle.

He licks me with long, firm strokes, teasing, until I'm

squirming, my ass polishing his obscenely expensive car with my arousal.

When he lifts his mouth before I come, I gasp in horror. "No."

"Oh, I'm not done. Those sweet little moans are the kind that make my cock so happy it weeps. But you haven't screamed for me yet, Angel."

He undoes his pants and drags me closer to the edge of the hood. With my legs braced on his chest, he buries himself balls-deep in one long thrust, using his fingers to caress my swollen clit. I whimper, and he stills inside me before rocking his hips in a slow, torturous tease.

"We're going to wind you up nice and tight, Angel."

The fog clears, letting the moon bathe his face in soft light. *He's beautiful. So beautiful.*

His hips move rhythmically, a controlled roll made to prolong our pleasure. "It feels so good," I cry, arching off the cool steel.

"So good, Angel. So fucking good."

He lists forward, tilting my pelvis and plunging deeper as he sucks a nipple into his mouth. When he finally lifts his head, the cool breeze coaxes the bead tighter.

"I'm so close," I beg. "Please."

"Not yet, baby. You're not ready."

His thumb flicks across my clit. *"Ahhh!"*

"Before you come for me, every muscle in your body is going to be coiled so tight, you'll be afraid to let go, because when you do, it's going to rip you apart." My walls tighten around his cock, and he curses. "But you'll be brave," he says through clenched teeth, "and you'll let go *for me*, when it's time, won't you?"

His breathing is ragged, and he struggles to stay in control. Even half out of my mind, I revel in the power I have over him, until I'm bucking wildly.

"That's it. Come closer to the edge. I've got you, Angel."

I thrash like a feral creature, but I can't stop myself. It's as though a force has taken over my body.

"You're so beautiful when you're wild." His voice is pure gravel. *Sin in all its glory.* "Suck on my fingers. That's it, taste yourself on my skin."

I'm overstimulated. The delicious sensations lick at my flesh, as I teeter between heaven and hell. I bounce on the car as every muscle contracts.

"Let go, Angel. Be brave." He rubs my clit and his hips buck —all without a shred of mercy. "It's time. Give me your screams."

And I do. *I have no choice.* My body can't tighten any more than it already has, and I can't hold back any longer.

"Now, Angel," he pants. "Now."

Writhing on the hood, I come spectacularly. My body convulses as he rips the orgasm from my body along with an earth-shattering scream.

But Rafael's not done. He fucks me savagely as I tumble farther and farther into the abyss.

A single scream echoes in the breeze while my body contracts and unspools, splintering, as he finds his release inside me.

38

RAFAEL

I STAND by the bed and watch her sleep, the wrinkled white linen tucked around her naked form. She's always so peaceful in sleep. The energy that normally buzzes around her is dormant, as though recharging.

Last night I learned something new. Fools don't have to suffer alone. *Antonio was right.* Sharing what's inside, with the right person, makes you stronger, not weaker.

I also learned that while Lexie is soft, pliable, and loving, she's also tough and strong, and fearless—and so many other things.

Sure, we're all a bundle of personality traits, some harmonious, others seemingly incompatible. But what makes Lexie different from the average person are the extremes to which she embraces all aspects of her personality. Not favoring one over the other—not choosing to show the world more of one than the other—that's what most of us do. We pick and choose who sees what. Yes, she sometimes does it, too, using sarcasm and bravado to hide her hurts, but that's different from hiding her personality.

I've been trying to understand her by shoving her in a box.

But she's much too complex, too untamed for that. It's what made her seem so confounding—so much of a contradiction. But she's not. She's simply who she is.

"Hey," I say softly, lowering myself to the mattress and brushing the hair back off her face. "I brought you some tea, but you really don't need to get up. Nothing requires you to be in the office on a Saturday morning."

She rubs the sleep from her eyes and sits up to take the tea. "Thank you." She wraps her hands around the warm mug and inhales. "There's so much happening between now and the launch, and I'd like to finish my project before I leave for the US."

I used her hard last night and kept her up half the night. Most women—most people—of her stature would sleep in, and worry less about work. She certainly doesn't need the paycheck.

Lexie peeks up at me through thick lashes. "Thank you for last night."

"I'm happy to own your pussy, anytime, anywhere."

"Not that."

"Really? I thought that was the highlight of the evening."

"The capstone." She gives me a bashful smile. "Thank you for knowing how much I needed to get out of here, and for making it happen."

It's not what I expected her to say. I thought she would talk about how I shared a part of myself last night that makes me feel weak in the light of day—or would certainly weaken me in the eyes of others. But I should have known. Lexie understands the importance of strength in our world, and she has no interest in weakening me.

"I'd do anything for you, Angel. I can't believe you haven't figured that out yet."

"I'm starting to believe it," she says with a tender smile that I feel in my chest.

"Speaking of getting out of here. I want you to be my date for the gala, and the US launch. I know Valentina invited you to both, but I'd like you to be by my side. As crazy as you make me, nothing relaxes me more than when you're close by."

"Not even the ocean?"

"Not even the ocean." *Nothing.*

I squeeze her leg, wanting nothing more than to yank back the covers and lose myself in her, but I've got plans with a little boy who would be crushed if I canceled.

She sits up taller against the headboard and flashes me a beautiful smile. "I'd love to be your date—for all of it."

I didn't expect her to turn me down, but the excitement in her voice is a bonus. "I'll send you the itinerary. Valentina can fill you in on the particulars, if she hasn't already. Buy whatever you need."

"I already have a dress for the gala, but I was planning to pick up a few new things for the trip."

"Work out the shopping details with your guards. And spend my money, not yours."

"I can—" She starts to protest about the money, but something changes her mind.

While my dick doesn't shrink in the presence of a woman who has a fatter bank account than I do, she doesn't. Although at some point, she'll inherit vast wealth. More money, less money—I don't care about any of it. I want her to buy whatever she wants, because it makes me happy to make her happy. What's the point of having money if it doesn't make you happy?

I lower my head and run my tongue along her clavicle, placing a small kiss at the top. "I'd love to crawl back in bed with you, but I promised Gabe that we'd get breakfast before going to the sporting goods store for a tent. I can't disappoint him."

"Those kids think you walk on water. You're so good with

them. You're going to make a great father." She flushes. "I didn't mean—oh God."

I snicker. "Everything doesn't need a qualification. I don't think—for a single second—that you're jonesing for me to put a baby in you."

She shakes her head. "I'm nowhere near ready to be a mum."

"But you want kids one day?" I ask, in part to ease her embarrassment, but also because I'm curious.

"Me?" she asks with a wry smile. "A houseful."

"A houseful?" I chuckle.

"I'm an only child, of parents without siblings. I've always wanted a brood running around, traipsing mud into the house, and making a lot of noise. You're surprised."

So many pieces to the puzzle that's Lexie. "I am."

"Because you don't think I have a maternal bone in my body?"

"I did not say that. I just—"

"Just what?"

"Just keep on surprising me, Angel. It's good for my soul." I slide my hand to the nape of her neck and claim her mouth. When she yields to me, I deepen the kiss, knowing that not all surprises are equal.

39

LEXIE

Spend my money, not yours. It's another way of saying, *Let me take care of you*, which he says often. It always seemed to be about sex—at least that's what I assumed. But that's just part of it—the surface layer. It actually means something else. Something all-encompassing. *Profound.*

Let me take care of you in a way that I couldn't take care of her. He's never actually said it, but I'm starting to think that's what it means. That's where the fear of hurting me comes from—I'm sure of it. His father might be in hell, but before he got there, he left wounds on Rafael's soul, so pervasive that they've never healed. Maybe they never will. Maybe they'll fester over a lifetime, eventually poisoning him and everything he holds dear. *Like what's happening with my father.*

I've been battling my father's demons for a long time—without much success. I'm not sure I have the strength left to battle Rafael's. I'm not afraid of a fight, but I don't think this is one I can win. *Love is a powerful force, but it does not conquer all.*

"Good morning," Tamar says brightly, dragging me out of my head. "I heard you'd be here this morning."

"Let me guess, you spoke with Rafael."

She smiles. "Yes. He wanted to let me know that he spilled the secret about working for me—for Premier."

"Was he not supposed to?"

She sighs. "I'm trying to teach these men how to stay in their lane, but I'm not having much success. Will you come on and help?"

I pause, because in the last couple of days he's spilled a lot of things, and I haven't had much time to focus on this particular one. It's an extraordinary opportunity, but a big step too. Not because of my freelancing work, but if things don't work out between Rafael and me, I'll have turned my entire life upside down.

"You have misgivings?" Tamar is not only perceptive, but she's up-front, which is another reason I like her.

"I'm excited about the opportunity to work with you. You're so talented, and I could learn so much—I've already learned so much. But I'm sleeping with my boss's boss, and if things don't work out, my life will have been upended."

"I know the feeling. I left a job that I loved, colleagues I admired, and my family, to take a job in another country, worlds away from mine. I didn't have a single friend here. And to top it off, I was pretty sure Rafael wasn't excited about having a former spy work for him."

"What helped you decide?"

"I knew if I passed on the opportunity, I'd always wonder how my life would have turned out if I'd taken it. It would have eaten at me when things weren't going well, or anytime I was bored or unsatisfied." She shrugs. "I don't like regrets."

I think about my London flat, which I spent months decorating until it felt like home, and my friends I've known forever, my family too. "What about regretting that you took the chance and didn't stay in Israel, in a life that you already knew you loved?"

"In my life, I've only regretted choosing safety, never choosing growth—even if I fell on my face chasing a dream."

There's so much she could teach me—not all of it work related.

"How do you make it work, living and working with Zé?"

"I work for Rafael and Valentina, although I report to Rafael, for the most part. As much as I'm sure he hates it at times, I don't report to Zé. I'm the only one." She raises her brow with a small smile.

"He respects the boundaries," she continues, "and so do I. If our relationship ends tomorrow, I'll still have a job. It would become complicated, and I might eventually have to work remotely—but I'm in IT, so it could work." She gazes at me. "I won't lie to you. There are times, because of my relationship with Zé, and Zé's relationship with Rafael, that life becomes very challenging."

I'm sure I'll face similar challenges.

At this point, I really have only one major concern. I glance at Tamar. "Will I be a member of the team, or just a girlfriend who needs a hobby?" *Despite all the upside, this would be a deal-breaker for me.*

"I like you, Lexie. But I don't have time to play house with you and Rafael. You'll be a member of the team. Rafael agreed to that. Although—" she says carefully.

"Although?"

"He was very clear that you'll never become a guard or even a soldier. You can go to the range with the team and also learn some survival skills, but your work will not involve ninja tactics. His words, not mine. He was also clear that there will be times, like during the launch, that your 'job'"—she punctuates the word with air quotes—"will be to have fun."

"Did *the boss* have any other stipulations that will make your life more complicated and annoy me?"

"He is *the boss*, and you are his woman. Not many men in

his position would allow any of this to happen, and that would be a shame, because you have so much potential."

"Rafael is never off—even when he's having fun," I tell Tamar. "If you need an extra pair of hands at three in the morning, I hope you won't hesitate to call me because I might be having *fun*."

She grins.

"What's so funny?"

"You. You're so refreshing. If I need you, I'll call you." She pauses. "There will be sticky wickets, and a learning curve, for all of us, one that I suspect will be rocky in places until it flatlines. If we want to make this work, we're going to need to trust each other and communicate openly."

"I agree."

"Does this mean you're taking the job?"

As we've been chatting, I realized that while I have some concerns, I'm mainly projecting my worries about the relationship not working out onto the job. This is an opportunity of a lifetime. I'm not turning it down.

"Yes!"

"I'm happy to hear it," she says sincerely. "Welcome aboard in an official capacity. There will be some paperwork to fill out so you can be paid for your work, as you should be."

I don't really need the money, but I've always loved earning a paycheck, even the pittance from freelancing. There's something empowering about it.

"Since Rafael handed you a gun in the hotel room without blinking, I assume you can handle one."

There must have been surveillance in the bathroom. It probably saved my life. I push the thought away.

"I've been trained to use a gun, and I have advanced self-defense skills. Although I've gotten lazy, and they could both use some polishing."

"There will be an opportunity to improve your skills. Even

if you don't work here, given who you are, you should keep those skills sharp." She stands. "One more thing. I'm a stickler about chain of command. As is Rafael, which will make this endeavor easier for all of us. I'm your boss. You take orders from me. You have a problem, you come to me. Rafael can usurp my power at any time, of course, but I don't think he'll do that."

"I understand."

"Good." She smiles. "You can start as soon as Monday, in your new capacity, if that works."

I want to make a remark about not having any fun scheduled for Monday, but I decide against it. "Works for me."

40

LEXIE

It's late morning when I get a photo of Rafael and Gabe grinning from inside a souped-up tent in the sporting goods store. I grin until my cheeks ache.

Gabe has rich brown eyes, and Rafael's are bright blue, but there's a strong resemblance between them. They could be brothers. Although their childhood experiences couldn't be more different. Gabe has two parents who love each other madly and love him with all their hearts. That was not Rafael's experience. He had only one parent who loved him—until she disappeared.

I glance at my new boss, contemplating whether it's better to keep my mouth shut or ask. I almost always choose ask.

"Tamar, before I officially start on Monday—can I talk to you outside our roles?"

"You can always talk to me, even after Monday. If you're out of bounds, I'll tell you."

I draw a breath, hoping she doesn't freak out like Zé. *Here goes nothing.* "Are you still searching for information about Rafael's mom?"

She peers at me, slack-jawed. "Wow. You don't pull any punches."

"I think this is one of those things that's always difficult to get down, even if you sugarcoat it."

A shadow creeps over her face, and she nods but doesn't say anything. I probably should have kept my mouth shut, but it's too late now. The damage has been done, so I forge ahead, albeit with a bit more grace.

"I know from my parents and my grandmother that Antonio and his team searched for a long time. I also know from Valentina that when you were hired, it was to be part of your job. I'd like to help. I doubt I can accomplish anything that you and Lucas haven't been able to, but her disappearance impacts my relationship with Rafael, and it might impact our future. But more than anything, I want him to have some peace."

She draws a breath through her nose and shuts her laptop.

"Lucas and his team looked for years, but by the time they got the case, it was old. When I got it, it was older still. In truth, Premier has really grown under Rafael's leadership, and there hasn't been a lot of time to work on it—especially in the last two years." She sits back in her chair, eyeing me.

"But Rafael never asks about it anymore," she continues. "I'm not paid to be an armchair psychologist, but I'm not sure he really wants to know."

He's torn. Or protecting himself because finding her seems like a pipe dream at this point. "Has he asked you to stop looking?"

She shakes her head.

"He might be conflicted, Tamar, but he carries the past like a cross."

She gathers her hair into a ponytail and flips it over one shoulder. "There might be some time for you to work on things that have been put on the back burner," she says, without specifying what those *things* might be, "but not until after the US launch. We can discuss it then."

A smidgen of guilt creeps in when I remember how angry Zé was when I asked him about this very thing. I need to tell her so she's not blindsided.

"In the spirit of full disclosure, there's something I should tell you."

"Go on," she urges warily.

"When I asked Zé about the search for Vera Huntsman, he was furious. We were in the elevator, and he flipped the switch and let me have it—no holds barred. If I was intimidated by that sort of thing, I'd have wet my pants. If you allow me to work on it, he's going to be fit to be tied. I don't want to cause any problems between you."

She snickers. "You know those sticky wickets I mentioned?"

I nod.

"This is not one of them. I don't take orders from Zé."

41

LEXIE

"YOU'RE COMING UP?" I ask Valentina as we slide out of a bulletproof SUV, flanked by guards. While we didn't have time for a full spa day, we had lunch at the spa and had our nails, hair, and makeup done for the party tonight.

"I'm going to get dressed upstairs and go to my parents' house from here."

"Is Marco coming by, or is he meeting you there?" I ask as the elevator doors open.

"Marco can't make it tonight," she replies breezily, as if I asked if she's taking a purse with her.

There are a dozen questions on the tip of my tongue, but I glance at the two guards with us in the elevator and don't say another word. But it doesn't stop me from steaming quietly. She's worked so hard for this moment. *That bastard better be on his deathbed.*

The elevator dings, and we get off, but the guards follow too closely for me to ask anything personal.

I've been with Valentina all afternoon, and she didn't breathe a word about Marco not coming. She was in good spirits. Her usual self. I didn't suspect a thing. *Maybe you're so wrapped up in your new job and in Rafael that you didn't notice.* Maybe, but I'm paying close attention now, and I don't see a single chink in the armor.

We wait outside her apartment while one of the guards does a sweep.

"Have you decided which shoes you're wearing?" she asks.

Shoes? Your husband isn't showing up for one of the most important nights of your life, and you want to talk about my shoes?

"I think you should go with the gold sandals," she adds. "They're perfect with the dress, and they'll be more comfortable than the silver ones."

Now I know how Alice felt when she fell into the rabbit hole.

"I think so too. You know what," I say, with much more cheer than I'm feeling. "We should crack open a bottle of champagne and get dressed together. Like old times."

"That's a fabulous idea," she squeals, like she doesn't have a care in the world.

Valentina isn't a big crier, but she's been very emotional when it comes to problems in her marriage. She's confided in me more than once about them, but if I wasn't going to the party tonight, I don't think she would have said a word about Marco bailing on her.

She's protecting him. I don't like it.

"I'm going to get my clothes, and then I'll be over. Five minutes," I call over my shoulder. "Chill the bubbly."

I didn't invite her to Rafael's because she won't want to get dressed there. She talks to him as little as possible, and although it eats at him, I don't think he still blames me. If he does, he certainly doesn't show it.

What I can't shake is that we spent hours together, laughing and gossiping, and making plans for the US trip, and I never noticed anything. Not a ripple. *How is that possible?*

IT TAKES me longer than five minutes because Sabio had to check the apartment before I could enter, and then I had to pull together everything I need.

Sabio offers to take my tote, but I hand him my dress instead so I can text Rafael on my way to Valentina's.

LEXIE: *Getting dressed for the party next door with my BFF.*

RAFAEL: *Don't bother with panties on my account.*

LEXIE: *I won't be going anywhere near Antonio and Daniela's without panties.*

RAFAEL: *Pity.*

LEXIE: *What time should we leave?*

RAFAEL: *5:15 at the latest.*

RAFAEL: *You'll have more time for makeup if you ditch the panty idea.*

I shake my head at the phone and knock on the door before taking my dress.

"You took so long," she says when she opens the door, "that I drank all the champagne. Want a beer?"

"I've always known you were a lush." Before the lock snicks, with all the subtlety of a bull in a china closet, I blurt, "Why isn't Marco coming?"

Her face falls. "I don't want to talk about it."

"Oh, we're talking about it, girlfriend," I grumble, following her into the kitchen.

She sighs. "You have three minutes to be in my business." She holds up her watch. "Starting now."

"Why isn't he coming?"

"He has a conflict." She's very matter-of-fact.

A conflict? This is a big event. The guest list includes the prime minister and the president, and every muckety-muck who was lucky enough to snag an invite. But it's especially important for Rafael and Valentina—and he has a fucking conflict?

"A conflict?"

She nods. "That's what he said. Although I suspect it's because the gala is at my parents' house and he's not ready to face my father."

What a coward. Maybe Rafael's right about him.

Valentina takes a rag and a bottle of cleaning spray from under the sink and begins to scour the countertop. She looks like a housewife from the fifties, hair coiffed and makeup perfect as she scrubs a counter that doesn't have a crumb or even a speck of dust on it. *She's stressed to the max.*

Tonight is bad enough, but tomorrow we're leaving for the US. We'll be gone for ten days. It might not be quite as embarrassing for him not to be there as it will be for her tonight, but it will make a whirlwind trip more stressful. *He better be on that damn plane.*

"Is he still planning on making the trip to the US?"

"Of course," she replies, but not with the conviction of someone who's certain.

"What else aren't you telling me, sweetheart?"

She shakes her head. "There are some things that are best kept between two parties in a relationship."

That's totally lame in this circumstance, but I let it slide because I don't share every detail about my relationship with Rafael, even with her.

"I'm here for you. Anytime. If you change your mind and want to talk, I'm here."

She takes a breath. "I just spent forty minutes in a makeup chair. I don't want to ruin the war paint."

It's part of the armor.

I'm crushed for her. But she's determined not to let that asshole ruin tonight, and I need to get on board too.

I glance in the mirror. "It does look a little like war paint," I say in jest. "So do you have some bubbly we can sip while we pour ourselves into our dresses?"

She waggles her eyebrows. "Pink champagne?"

"*Ohhhh*. Now you're talking."

She pulls a bottle from the cooler, and I take two coupes from the bar, because they're more fun to drink from than flutes.

"A toast," I say, raising my glass. "To you and all the hard work you've done to get to this day. I'm so proud of you."

She puts her glass down and hugs me tight, and I hug her back, grateful for waterproof mascara and the touch-up kit the makeup artist sent home with us.

"Let's get dressed," I coo softly, but long moments pass before she releases me.

42

LEXIE

ONCE WE'RE DRESSED, I put a little more gloss on my lips and collect my things. "Are you sure you don't want to come with Rafael and me?"

"No." She waves me off. "I would just be a third wheel."

"Never."

Her parents' house isn't just around the corner, and I hate for her to make the trip alone.

"I can sit between the two of you if that makes you feel any better. You know, like when you sat between me and that biatch Melissa Blair at the Christmas concert so I wouldn't slap the shit out of her."

"*Oh my God.* I forgot about that. What did she do to piss you off? I can't remember."

"She said that we shouldn't use the proceeds from the concert to buy presents for poor kids because they should get used to their station in life early."

Valentina groans. "She was a bitch."

"I'm sure she still is. But you did save her fake nose that I wanted to break—and me, from getting kicked out of school. It's my turn to repay the favor."

"I can't, Lexie." She sniffs, picking up that damn cleaning spray again. "It's bad enough I'm going to the party. If I show up with Rafael, it's over."

I stop dead in my tracks, peering at her.

Her eyes are like saucers. *It's bad enough I'm going to the party.* She didn't mean to let that slip. "Marco didn't want you to go to the party?"

She lifts her chin. "Where did you get that idea?"

From you, sweetheart. "Isn't that what you just said?"

"No," she replies, waving me off again.

She can't even look at me. *Marco is officially on my shit list.*

"What time are you getting there?"

"Rafael wants to leave at five fifteen. Your mother said she wants pictures before the guests arrive. What time are you planning on getting there?"

"On the late side. Otherwise, my parents won't stop with the questions, and there's no way either of them will abide by the three-minute rule. But they won't ask in front of guests."

She has way more faith in Antonio's social graces than I do. He'll ask whatever he feels like asking. That's the truth.

I pull out my phone and text Rafael while she pretends to look through her mail so she doesn't need to deal with any more questions about her husband.

Lexie: *How about if I meet you at the party?*

Rafael: *Why?*

Lexie: *Valentina and I are still dressing, and then we'll go over together. Girl time.*

But I delete the message before I press Send. I promised to be honest with him.

Lexie: *Marco isn't coming.*

Rafael: *Fucker. Is she okay?*

Lexie: *She's holding up. I'm concerned if her parents push too hard, she'll fall apart. I don't want her to be alone when she walks in the house.*

Rafael: *What can I do?*

Lexie: *Less is more.*

Rafael: *My phone's on.*

"Well, my date's meeting me there," I say with a smile that I'm not really feeling. "It looks like you're stuck with me."

"Lexie," she scolds, a hand on her hip, "you shouldn't have changed your plans."

"Shush." I grab the bottle of champagne from the ice bucket and dry off the condensation. "Can you bring the glasses, or are you going to stand there with your hand on your hip all night like an affronted maiden?"

43

RAFAEL

I LINGER near the bar with my second bourbon of the young evening. Valentina worked her ass off to make this happen. She poured her heart and soul into every detail, not just with the launch, but with the product development too. It's her dream as much as it is mine, and I'd like to beat that piece-of-shit husband of hers for stomping all over it.

While I didn't hear the door, the little girls are squealing in the foyer, which means the big girls have arrived. I toss back my drink and follow the squeals that will lead me to an angel. *My Angel.*

I stop at the edge of the foyer to admire the stunning blonde in a plum halter dress that skims every luscious curve before it grazes the floor. She takes my breath away.

When Lexie notices me admiring her, she gifts me a smile that sparkles brighter than the amethysts dangling from her ears.

We don't take our eyes off each other as I cross the room. When I bend to kiss her cheek, the amber in her perfume wafts softly from her skin, beckoning me closer. "You might not have come with me," I murmur, "but you will be leaving with me."

"I'm counting on it," she replies, only for my ears.

I force myself from her to say a quick hello to Valentina, who can barely get a word in, before she's whisked away by her sisters to make a French braid or some other nonsense.

Before the girls decide they need Lexie, too, I take her hand and make a beeline for the stairs. "Let's go find somewhere quiet so I can see if you took my suggestion about panties."

"We shouldn't leave Valentina alone until the guests start to arrive. The whole point of me coming with her was so Daniela and Antonio wouldn't ambush her."

"There won't be an ambush. No one's going to say a word about Marco. I talked to both her parents. I even made Antonio practice what he was going to say when she arrived."

Lexie bursts out laughing. "Practice? I wish I could have been there."

"I don't want to know where you're going, or what you're planning on doing," Daniela calls to us from the bottom of the stairs, "but remember there are children in this house, Rafael. And there are pictures in twenty minutes."

"Don't worry. With the kids in the house, I'd never dream of doing anything that you wouldn't do."

"Lexie, you look gorgeous. Slap him for me, please."

"Thank you. You look gorgeous too. Red is definitely your color."

Lexie's still talking as I drag her up the stairs.

"Where are you taking me?"

"To the turrets."

"Rafael," she whispers. "We really shouldn't."

"Oh, Angel. We really should."

We climb to the top of the turret where Antonio now keeps his racing simulator. It's the one I used as a secret fort when I first came to live here.

"I'm not convinced Marco is coming to the US," she says when we're alone.

I kiss her until the only thing I can think about is her coming around my cock, those sultry sounds she makes filling my old fort. "We don't have long. I don't want to waste time talking about that fucker."

When I run my fingertips down her arms, she shivers, and my cock pushes against my zipper. "You look like a princess—beautiful and sexy, and I want to stay up here and do dirty things to you all night."

"But then we'd miss your big moment."

"It's a trade-off I'd be willing to make, Angel."

She averts my gaze, brushing her hands across my chest. "You're so damn hot in a tux. If we were anywhere else, I'd let you do whatever dirty things you wanted. But not here," she adds softly.

I rest my palms on her breasts, acutely aware of the thin fabric shielding them from me. Using my thumbs, I draw tight circles around her nipples until they pucker.

I've fucked lots of women before, and during parties like this. Sometimes accidents happened and dresses got snagged or stained, and hair and makeup ruined. As long as there weren't tears accompanying the spoils, it never bothered me. But tonight, the small packet of lube and the butt plug in my pocket are weighing heavily on my conscience.

Not here. Not with her. She deserves more. My better angels are brawling with the devil, but my cock continues to thicken, because it knows how this ends. *How it always ends.*

Lexie's pupils are dilated, and she has the flush of arousal. It wouldn't take much to persuade her to take off her clothes, but she's right. Anyone could walk in on us. As long as it wasn't a child, I wouldn't care. But she would—especially if it was Antonio.

She deserves something better. Take care of her. Above all else, take care of her.

I hold her hand against my hard cock. "I want you. But cum

does not go well with purple silk, so I'm going to wait until I have you in my bed tonight, Angel, alone. I'll hold back now. But I won't hold back anything later. Not a thing. Every inch of you will be mine. Every hole."

She takes a ragged breath that I feel in my balls.

"I want you to think about that all night. Every time you catch my eye from across the room, I want you to remember how hard my cock is under this jacket and how much you're going to whimper and plead when I get you alone."

She licks her lips, and the unfettered lust in her eyes is making me second-guess my decision.

"I'm yours later," she whispers. "Every inch."

Five small words, alive with the promise of submission. My self-control is shattering.

Take care of her. It's your most important job.

"Let's go downstairs before I change my mind about waiting."

44

LEXIE

WE'RE the last ones to leave, and by the time we say goodbye to Daniela and Antonio, Rafael's jacket is off, his tie loose, and I don't know what happened to his cuff links, but his shirtsleeves are rolled to the elbow. He's gorgeous—my dirtiest fantasy come-to-life, and I crave the prickle of his stubble on my inner thighs.

Rafael leads me outside through a door that's used mainly by the family, and into the back of a waiting car. He mutters something to a displeased Zé, and a moment later, Giana slides into the passenger seat beside the driver.

I suspect Zé's pinched expression has something to do with my guard being in the car instead of him. He's not happy, but his boss doesn't appear to be having any of it.

When I grow tired of trying to decipher what Rafa and Zé are discussing on the curb, I slip off my sandals that are nowhere near as comfortable as I'd hoped, and wiggle my aching toes.

"Take the scenic route to the lodge," Rafael instructs the driver when he gets in the car. "Stay along the river," he adds before raising the partition between the seats and turning all his attention to me.

Along the river—the long way back. He wants to play. *Me too.*

Rafael turns on some jazz, then cups my face, brushing his lips over mine. "We're finally alone."

"Not exactly." My voice is low and husky like I've been up all night smoking cigarettes and drinking whiskey.

"Close enough," he quips. "They can't see anything and unless you scream, they won't hear anything either." He palms my breasts and crushes his lips to mine in a sensuous assault that leaves me gasping.

"Is that why you replaced Zé with Giana?" I ask when we come up for air.

"Even I'm not talented enough to make you come while Zé's in the front seat." He smirks.

The man is arrogance personified. But it's not a lie—he is talented—in every regard. "You're so cocky."

"Enough talking. Hand over your panties." He holds out an open palm, his fingers twitching impatiently.

Happy to oblige.

I open my purse and pull out the purple lace thong I removed just before we left the party, and hold his gaze while I drop it into his hand.

His lips quirk. "Oh Angel. Were you hoping I'd fuck you on the way home?" He brings the thong to his nose and inhales. "Is your pussy wet and swollen—aching for me to make it feel better?"

He's an insolent bastard and I'm beyond aroused. The threats he made in the turret have had me aching for him all night.

I'll hold back now. But I won't hold anything back later. Not a thing. Every inch of you will be mine. Every hole. I want you to think about that all night. Every time you catch my eye from across the room, I want you to remember how hard my cock is under this jacket and how much you're going to whimper and plead when we get home.

Every time he glanced at me during the party, all I could think about was his cock and how much I wanted it.

He presses his lips to my throat, nipping at the flesh, before placing a small kiss on the bruised skin.

"How could I not be aroused? All evening you gave me these smoldering looks like you wanted to devour me."

"I did," he murmurs. "Still do."

"I'm yours," I whisper, resting a hand on his pounding heart. "Take me."

"Be careful what you ask for, Angel." He nips my bottom lip before pulling back. "If you expect to wear that dress out of this car tonight, you better keep it out of my way."

I narrow my gaze and gather the billowy silk fabric above my hips. He steadies me while I straddle his lap, one knee on either side of his thighs. When I'm astride, Rafa grasps my hips and lowers me, until my bare pussy is kissing his trousers.

"Are you going to leave a wet, sticky stain on my pants?"

I suppose I should feel embarrassed and the tiniest part of me does. But Rafael's taught me that there's no shame in pleasure. No shame in taking or giving. No shame in my body or his.

I nod, unbuttoning his shirt to press kisses to his chest.

There's a sharp intake of air when my mouth connects with his warm skin. His fingers dig deeply into my hips, and I revel in the heady feeling of power, fleeting as it will surely be.

Without a word, as though it's his God-given right, Rafael reaches behind my neck and unties the top of my dress, letting the bodice fall to my waist. "So beautiful," he coos, his fingertips grazing the tops of my breasts. "So smooth and creamy. Luscious."

My pussy clenches at the awe in his buttery timber.

Sweeping back my hair, he tugs at the locks until my head

tips, leaving a large swathe of neck exposed. With a dark smile ghosting his lips, he skates his mouth over the flesh. It's a gentle caress that lulls me into a blissful trance, until he clamps down, marking me with his lips and teeth.

"Every inch of you is a treat, but nothing is as delicious as your sweet cunt. Not even your flawless skin."

It's hot in here. *So hot.*

Clutching his open shirt, I wiggle against his erection, but his trousers are in the way of my prize. *I want his cock. I need it.*

Half-crazed, I reach for his zipper. "Do it," he urges, not that I need encouragement.

His cock springs free, impossibly long and heavy, red and swollen, impatient, like it's been waiting too long for some love.

As soon as it's out, he takes it in hand—which always drives me wild, and he nestles it between my freshly waxed labia. "Slide your cunt all over my cock. Make me wet and slippery with your juices, Angel." He presses his shoulders into the seat adjusting his hips so I can move freely.

I rise to my knees, clinging to his muscled arms for leverage, and slide up and down his thick shaft. My movements are primal and exact, and although my legs are quivering, it's not enough. "Rafa," I whine, sinking back into my heels.

"Are you ready for me?"

Long past ready.

"I'm tempted to make you wait until you're in my bed. But I'm too selfish and impatient, and you're too damn tempting."

I rock into his cock and pull back quickly.

"Such a tease," he tuts, tugging my hair and reaching for a lever overhead. The rear moonroof opens, and a million stars shine on us, along with a cool breeze.

I bury my face in his neck and breathe in the warm sandalwood of his cologne. "Will they hear us?"

"They don't have their windows open. But it doesn't matter because soon you won't care who hears."

I might already be there.

Rafael reaches for his jacket and takes a velvet pouch and a packet of lube from the pocket. He removes a jeweled butt plug, that matches my dress, from the pouch.

"I was going to have you wear it during the party to remind you that I own you, and that all your pleasure is mine.

I moan, wiggling into his cock. "Why didn't you?"

"I didn't want to spoil your dress or to stress you. It wasn't the right time or place for that kind of play."

I love this man, with all his contradictions.

"But you'll wear it now," he demands, opening the lube and spreading it on my back passage, before coating the plug.

While we've only tried anal sex a couple of times, we've used plugs many times—although not usually while we fuck—we save the beads for that kind of play.

"This is the perfect size. It'll make you even tighter than you already are, Angel. The plug is going to feel so good while you ride my cock. Would you like that?"

"Yes." My voice is a whisper, lost to the wind.

"Hold onto my arms and stick out that gorgeous ass, so I can slide it in."

I follow his directions blindly—I've been aroused for so long, I'm in a dream-like state.

"Push out while I push in," he reminds me, "so it'll slide in nice and easy."

His voice is hypnotic, and I do as he asks without a single thought.

"Such a good girl." Rafael pulls out the plug and slides it back in, fucking me with it while he strokes my clit.

"*Oh.* Oh, my God," I pant, overwhelmed by the dueling sensations.

He kisses me—and helps me upright. The plug feels enormous while he tongues my nipples.

"Hump my cock, Angel. Let me see how aroused you are." I grind my pelvis into him, clenching my buttocks.

"Such a filthy little slut," he murmurs sweetly, and I feel the gush of arousal. I love being his filthy little slut and pretty little whore as much as being his good girl. *Maybe more.*

He hoists up my hips. "Hold my cock steady." His voice is a rasp.

I circle the taut base with my fingers, as he impales me on the thick shaft. My fingers uncurl, as I sink deeper, taking every gorgeous inch. *He's mine.*

When I bottom-out, we groan in unison. It's low and guttural.

He's deep. I'm so full. *So full.* I need to come—even if it hurts.

I draw small circles with my hips and sway them side-to-side. Rafael guides my movements with a gentle touch.

Slipping his hand between us, he teases my clit until I'm ready to topple. When I'm right there, he edges his fingers back so that I have to take him deeper, and buck harder and faster to reach them.

"Bastard," I cry.

"Hang on tight," he warns, before moving a hand behind me to rock the plug.

"You're the devil," I mutter.

"I'm going to fuck your ass with this plug, Angel. You're going to come so hard around me. He slips his tongue into my mouth, and pulls out the plug then pushes it back in, again, and again, and again while I bounce on his cock, chasing my orgasm.

As my body tightens and spools, he rubs my clit until there's no going back. His fingers are relentless, even as I tremble.

"Oh, Angel. You're so beautiful when you're wild. Untamed. So fucking sexy when you take what you need."

He doesn't let me ride out the orgasm for too long, before

he takes firm hold of my hips and moves me like a ragdoll, until his body jerks and he finds his own release.

Rafael wraps his arms around me, holding me against his chest while we catch our breath. Eventually, he pulls back and rests his forehead against mine.

"Don't ever leave me." His voice is raw and his chest flayed wide open. It's a prayer straight from the soul of a man who shuns prayer and every notion of a merciful God. My heart clenches.

"Never." My voice is soft, but resolute. "You're mine as much as I'm yours. It's written in the stars."

I speak from the heart and my words are sincere—every one of them. It's as much assurance as I can give him. But I'm not sure it's enough to satisfy either of us.

We both know that in our world, tomorrow is promised to no one. *Fate be damned.*

45

RAFAEL

When Lexie and I board the plane to the US, Valentina and that pussy husband are already there. While I own a smaller plane, this jet, which is more appropriate for transatlantic travel, belongs to Premier—which means it belongs to both Valentina and me.

The first thing Lexie did when she woke up this morning was text Valentina to see if Marco was coming, so it's not exactly a surprise that he's here. But I am surprised the fucker would have the balls to travel with me.

I suppose the other option, traveling on the Huntsman plane with Antonio, was even less palatable. *Although if I were him, I'd be more concerned about Daniela wringing his scrawny neck.* She had some choice words for Marco last night, and she didn't once stop Antonio when he went off about him.

"Why don't we sit up here?" Lexie says, waving at Valentina.

When I'm not in the conference room, I prefer the back of the plane, especially when others are onboard. But I don't think I can be that close to Marco in his stupid artsy shirt for six hours without knifing him. Lexie knows it, too, because I'm sure she'd be happier sitting with Valentina.

"I need to have a word with Zé and Tamar." I touch her hip and brush my lips against her ear. "I'll be back before we take off."

"Sure you will," she quips. "Do you think Tamar needs help with anything?"

"This trip is all pleasure for you," I whisper into her hair before I go. "All pleasure."

She flashes me a smile filled with passion, and warmth, and trust, and so many other things that I might not deserve, but that I crave from her. It feeds my soul.

"Bring Ms. Clarke a pot of Earl Grey, with cream and sugar," I tell the flight attendant on my way through the cabin.

I turned off Lexie's alarm before dawn, when I woke up, so she could sleep in a bit this morning. It was late by the time we passed out last night. We were at it longer than wise, considering we had a morning flight.

"Give me an update," I demand when I enter the conference room where Tamar and Zé have taken up shop.

"I spoke with our people on the ground in Boston and in New York," Zé begins. "No issues whatsoever. The hotel in Boston is secure, as are the venues. We're in good shape."

The trip is Boston, New York, Chicago, and Los Angeles. It's ambitious, but we wanted to launch on both coasts, and in the middle of the country. In six weeks, we'll travel to Charleston, Dallas, Austin, and Seattle. Boston is where our US headquarters is located, and that's why we chose to do the first and largest events there.

We took over an entire hotel overlooking the Boston Common to accommodate our large entourage and invited guests. After the first leg, the group gets smaller. Antonio, Daniela, and the kids are joining us in Boston, then flying to Disney World before returning to Porto. *Maybe they can take Marco with them since he's such a fucking baby.*

"Nothing that bothers either of you?"

"So far nothing," Tamar replies.

"Nothing more than usual," Zé mutters.

"We need to keep our eyes on the East Coast, but we shouldn't lose sight of Chicago or LA either."

"I don't plan on losing sight of anything," Zé replies.

He's been in charge of the security for all of us and for the events—with some help from Lucas and Cristiano, who have staged operations in the US in the past. Managing security for something of this magnitude is a huge fucking deal, but there's no one I trust more than Zé to protect the people I care about.

I glance at Tamar. "Anything new on the traffickers?"

She cocks her head. "Nothing. Is there some reason you're asking?"

Yeah. The safety of the blonde who owns my dark heart. "Just checking."

"I put all research on hold while we're traveling. But the more information we have, the more it looks like they might really be finished."

"I agree." *So do Will and Antonio.* "But let's not get too complacent. If we're wrong, Lexie is still a target."

"If we're wrong, you could be a target too," Zé adds with a pointed look. "Don't worry. Security's not complacent. Everyone understands that we might not be out of the woods. They hear it every day."

I'm certain Zé never forgets that we need to stay alert. I'm also certain that his people have had it drilled into their heads.

What worries me is that even elite security, seasoned guards and soldiers, can stay on high alert only for limited periods of time. The amount of security we need to make a trip like this, and to keep everything at home well-guarded, is staggering. We're spread a little thin, and that doesn't leave enough time for meaningful breaks or days off. My people are good, but they're not robots. This is especially true of Zé and Tamar, who have been working nonstop.

"When we get back, I want you both to take some time off. Go to Israel, the South of France, Antarctica—anywhere that catches your fancy. I don't care where. Just get out of the country and recharge your batteries. Take my plane. Vacation's on me. Consider it a well-earned bonus."

They both nod, and Tamar even smiles, but I'm sure I'll need to order Zé to leave the fucking country before he's willing to take a vacation.

"If that's it, I'll get out of your hair. Let me know if anything comes up."

I grab a couple of waters from the flight attendant on my way to the cabin. Hopefully Lexie's not too hopped up on caffeine from the tea. Maybe I can persuade her to go back to the bedroom and take a nap with me. We'll need a nap after I initiate her into the mile-high club.

When I enter the main cabin with my dick primed just from thinking about my naked angel, Valentina is sitting up front with Lexie. I glance toward the back of the plane, but Marco's not there. With any luck, someone shoved him out the rear door without a parachute.

Valentina starts to get up as I approach. "Sit," I tell her. "I need to stretch my legs."

"Everything okay?" Lexie asks.

I nod and turn to Valentina, who looks well rested. "I just checked in with Zé and Tamar. Everything is good on our end. Are you excited?"

Her face lights up. "Totally. Last night, I spoke with Julia, who's in charge of coordinating the large event, after she reconfirmed with all the vendors. Everything's on track. The planner coordinating the smaller events gave me a thumbs-up too. I also spoke with our communications people to go over everything again. The appropriate media will be at each event, and press releases will go out accordingly. It will be all over social media starting tomorrow morning."

"It's going to be perfect," I tell her. "You've done amazing work. I'm so proud of you."

She blushes. "You've done a lot of the heavy lifting."

"Team effort by my people." Lexie beams. "I'm so proud of both of you. It's going to be epic."

"Where's Marco?" I ask, admiring the swell of Lexie's breasts, that I want to cradle in my hands while sinking my teeth into that tendon where her shoulder meets her neck. It never fails to get a response from her that makes my balls tight.

"He has a headache," Valentina replies. "He's lying down."

A headache? I'm going to murder that son of a bitch.

The plane has two bedrooms. One is being used to store luggage, electronics, and other sensitive materials that we didn't want to carry in the belly of the plane. It's not available for the nap, or the pretending-to-take-a-nap I had planned for Lexie and me. I should probably just be grateful he's not back there with Valentina. I don't care if they're married. It turns my stomach.

"You ladies hang out. I'm going back to the conference room and get in a little work." If I can't be alone with my woman, Zé's not going to be alone with his.

"Rafael," Valentina calls before I get more than a few feet away. I turn around. "Lexie told me that you read my parents the riot act before we got to the house last night. Thank you."

"No big deal."

She raises a brow. "I don't know. Sounded like a big deal to me. You made my father practice. Is there a recording of that somewhere?"

I snicker and wink at Lexie.

"Seriously. Thank you."

"You don't need to thank me, *menina*. I might be an asshole, but I'd do anything to save you pain."

I glance at Lexie, who looks like an angel, her light casting a glow so bright that it softens any bitter feelings Valentina still harbors toward me. I smile at her before I turn, cursing that cockblocker Marco under my breath.

It's a six-hour flight, I remind my disappointed dick. *He can't sleep the entire time.*

46

LEXIE

It's a gorgeous day—sunny, warm, and no humidity to speak of—and a group of us—mostly women and children—are relaxing by the hotel pool. Marco's here, too, and I counted about a dozen guards. Even though we've taken over the hotel, security has been tight.

Vivi and Anabela are taking turns jumping into the water, and I'm contemplating joining them, when Valentina's phone vibrates. She picks it up and blinks a few times as she reads the screen. "Excuse me," she says, slipping on a cover-up and sandals.

"Everything okay?" Daniela asks from the edge of the pool, where she's sitting with Alma, watching the kids.

"Fine," Valentina replies, striding toward the door, followed by a guard. But she doesn't look like everything is fine. She's pale and white-knuckling her phone.

"Want me to come with you?" I ask, reaching for my sarong.

She shakes her head. "It's the caterer for tomorrow night. They have a question."

Why is the caterer contacting Valentina instead of Julia, the party planner? It's her job to coordinate the vendors so that everything is streamlined through one person. That way, nothing slips through the cracks.

Daniela glances at me as Valentina disappears into the building. I'm sure she's thinking the same thing I am.

I sit back on the lounge chair and glance across the pool at Marco, who seems to be engrossed in a book. I wonder what a man like him reads. Art heist thrillers? How-to manuals? *Our Bodies, Ourselves*?

I need to stop. Rafael's bad attitude about him is rubbing off on me. The truth is, Marco's been fine on the trip.

Last night, there was a family dinner with a few close friends included, and earlier today Premier hosted an event for mixologists and bartenders. He was pleasant and doted on Valentina, rarely leaving her side.

Tonight's events include a cocktail party for local and national distributers, and a dinner with club owners. The goal is to make everyone feel special so that they'll want to carry and promote the product. Tomorrow night is the big bash.

I pick up my phone to see if there's a message from Rafael, who's making calls in the three-bedroom suite they're using as a command center. He promised when he was done, we would do a little sightseeing. "Check out the spots where those traitorous colonists plotted their coup," he teased this morning as he tossed me over his shoulder and into the shower.

Fifteen minutes pass, and Valentina's still not back. I tie on the sarong and slip into my flip-flops.

"Let me know if there's something I can do," Daniela murmurs as I walk past her on my way inside, Giana at my heels.

I have no idea where she went, but if I can't find her, I'll have Giana text her guard.

But it's not necessary. Valentina's in an alcove outside the locker room, pacing, her phone to her ear, and her hand shaking.

"What's going on?"

She holds up a finger. "This is Valentina Cruz, again. I just spoke with the caterer, and there seems to be some misunderstanding. Call me as soon as possible."

"Everything okay?" Marco asks from behind me.

I should be pleased that he came to check on her, but something about his tone—or maybe his demeanor—irks me.

"No," she answers, anguished. "Everything's not okay. The caterer's business manager contacted me at the pool. Despite the cancelation, they need to be paid in full tomorrow. She hasn't been able to reach Julia, and she wanted to be sure that I understand the terms of the contract."

"What do you mean *cancelation*?" I ask.

"I don't know," she replies softly.

"What did Julia say?"

"I can't reach her. I left a message."

She's not answering her phone the day before a huge event? Last I heard, there were over a thousand guests attending. Anything could go wrong. Why isn't she available?

"When did you last talk to her?"

"The night before we left. Everything was all set. We weren't scheduled to talk again until tomorrow morning—unless something came up."

"Maybe she has another event?"

"I don't think so. She was supposed to be doing some off-site work for the party. Putting together party favors and place cards—that kind of thing. She rented space in a nearby warehouse."

I glance at Marco, who hasn't said a single word to help get to the bottom of this—or to reassure her. He's just standing there watching us, as though he's waiting for someone to pass the popcorn.

"Maybe Rafael can send someone to the warehouse to see if she's there. If it's an old building, the cell service might be bad."

"I'm not sure where it is. Maybe Tamar can figure it out—we paid a rental fee for the facility. She might be able to track it down that way."

"Are you sure you didn't cancel the caterer by mistake, sweetie?" Marco asks.

What in the ever-loving fuck? I glower at him.

Valentina blinks a few times, like she's thinking about it, and then shakes her head. "No."

"Of course she didn't make a mistake," I say brashly.

"What's the problem?" Daniela asks, approaching.

"The caterer for the big event was canceled a couple of days ago. I can't reach the party planner."

"Canceled?" Daniela's tone sets my hair on end.

We've been thinking it's a misunderstanding—Daniela is thinking sabotage. *She's probably right. Misunderstandings like this don't happen.*

"What did Rafael say?" she asks, her hand on Valentina's arm.

"I haven't had a chance to tell him."

"You go talk to him, and I'm going to talk to your father, who's with Gray and Delilah. They might be able to help sort this out, if you can't reach Julia."

Gray is one of Antonio's college buddies, and Delilah is his wife. Valentina's close to both of them, especially Delilah.

"That's a great idea," Valentina says, nodding.

It is a great idea. Gray's father was the US president who was assassinated more than a decade ago, and they have the connections to fix, well, almost anything.

"Even if the caterer is still willing to do the party—" Valentina stops midsentence, uneasiness clouding her features.

"You need to let Rafael know right now," Daniela tells her daughter before heading to the elevator.

Valentina shuts her eyes, and her throat ripples as she nods.

"He's going to freak out," Marco says flatly, like it's a foregone conclusion. "Why don't you hold off on telling him until you see if your mother can pull a rabbit out of a hat."

"He's not going to freak out," I assure her, side-eyeing Marco. "He's resourceful. He'll be able to help too. You're partners," I remind her. "You need to tell him." *Or I will.*

"Of course I'm going to tell him." She doesn't even glance at her husband, who has a disapproving look about him.

"He's in the command center. Do you want me to go with you?"

"No." She shakes her head. "I'm a big girl."

"Did you take your medicine?" Marco asks gently.

Medicine?

She nods and heads toward the bank of elevators.

"She's disorganized," Marco murmurs when she's out of earshot. "I'm sure she let some ball drop."

You fucking prick. "Why would you say something like that?" I take a step back so that I don't slap him. "She's not disorganized. And even if she was, she needs our support, and that includes being positive. What medicine did she remember to take?"

He cocks his head. "She didn't tell you?"

If she told me, I wouldn't be asking you, dickwad. "No."

"I'm not surprised. Antianxiety meds."

Antianxiety meds. My chest hurts. *Why didn't she tell me?* "When did she start taking meds?"

"A few months ago, maybe. The anxiety has been going on for a while. At first, I thought it was the wedding, but it never went away. I finally convinced her to see someone, and they prescribed antianxiety meds and a sleeping pill."

How did I not know this?

"I realize it's easy to scapegoat me for everything that goes wrong, Lexie. But she was put in an untenable position. Who would put someone with so little marketing experience in charge of something of this magnitude? She was set up to fail. Maybe on purpose."

He's blaming Rafael without actually naming him. *No damn way was she set up to fail on purpose. Marco is a weasel.* But I can't allow myself to be distracted by his bullshit. Valentina's my biggest concern right now.

Valentina has been anxious, but from everything she's confided in me, I assumed it was because of the issues with her marriage. *Oh God. What kind of friend have I been?*

She doesn't have a ton of experience, but she has great instincts, and she's had an army at her disposal to assist her.

"That's why I didn't go to the gala at her parents' house. I can't bear to see how stressed she is. Besides, she's been doing a lot of hand-wringing about what Rafael did to me."

What Rafael did to me—he's such a pussy. I have absolutely no sympathy for him.

"I thought it would make her more stressed to have me there. I'm sorry, Lexie. I know you're together, but Rafael's hard on her. I don't like him any more than he likes me."

I doubt that's possible.

My head is spinning, and I can't discern fact from fiction. Rafael adores her, and he would never put her in a bad position —no one can convince me differently. But is it also possible Marco isn't the villain we've made him out to be?

I glance at him, and while he seems sincere, he called her disorganized, which is a blatant lie, and he was only too happy to tell me about the meds. I'm not cutting him a break.

"I'm going up to see how I can help."

He doesn't follow me.

47

RAFAEL

VALENTINA KNOCKS as I'm finishing my last call of the afternoon, and I beckon her into the makeshift office.

She looks like she's been battered by the waves and dumped on shore. My chest tightens. "It sounds like you handled it. I'll call you back in a few minutes," I tell Xavier, who's been updating me on a minor security breach at Sirena last night.

"What's wrong?" I ask Valentina, tossing my phone on the desk and going to her.

"I screwed up, Rafa. I don't know how it happened, but I screwed up. I'm so sorry."

She's shaking. Whatever has her like this isn't some small hiccup.

I put an arm around her. "Let's sit down, and then you can tell me what has you so upset. Whatever the problem, I'm sure we can fix it." *I've already sharpened my blade.*

"The caterer's office contacted me," she begins.

I listen intently as she tells me a story that puts my nerves on edge. The more she talks, the harder my blood simmers. By the time she finishes, it's at a full boil. This was not a mistake or a misunderstanding. This was a deliberate action meant to sabotage the most important launch event.

"I-I-I was prescribed some medicine for anxiety, and I don't normally take it because it makes me foggy. But I took it the night of the gala, along with a sleeping pill, which I never take."

Antianxiety medicine? Sleeping pills? What the fuck?

Valentina is normally poised, but she's fidgeting nonstop. It's painful to watch.

"I don't know," she continues. "Maybe I canceled them by mistake. Maybe I did something. Misworded an email. I—"

I won't allow her to blame herself for this. *Not for a fucking second.* Someone's going to pay for putting her in this position. I take her hands. "Listen to me, sweetheart. This wasn't a screwup. This sounds like sabotage."

"Sabotage?" Her features crinkle. "Like what Scott Bancroft tried to do with the bank accounts? It doesn't seem quite the same." She peers into my face, eyes wide. "Do you think he could be responsible?"

No, it doesn't feel quite the same. But it's the first place I'll be looking. I thought he'd been sufficiently warned, but maybe my knife didn't cut deep enough to leave a scar. "Maybe."

"Do you think anything else might have been sabotaged?" she asks, bracing herself for bad news.

She was so excited on the plane. *God help Bancroft if he's responsible.*

"Not sure." I pause to organize my thoughts. "This is what we're going to do. I need you to spend the next hour trying to get through to the caterer. Start out being nice with them, but if the business manager still refuses to put you in touch with the caterer herself, turn up the heat. Tell him if you don't get a call back from her within the hour, they won't see a cent. If he continues to put you off, say he's left you with no other choice than to go to every media outlet in the state so that others are protected, and that we'll be forced to sue them for breach of contract. I don't think it'll come to that."

She nods, taking notes on her phone. "I'll keep trying the party planner too."

"Are we okay for tonight?"

"Yes. Different caterer. And it's a different party planner too. I checked with her on my way up to talk to you."

"Good. I also need the information about the warehouse you mentioned. I'll send someone over to see what's going on."

"I have a packet from the party planner with that information, and other specifics—including names and contact information for all the vendors. I'll confirm everything," she says, scrolling through her phone.

Now that she has a plan forward, she seems less stressed, which makes me less stressed. "Focus on the caterer, and I'll round up some people to help with all the other details. We'll pull together as much support as you need."

"I can't find the email with the attachment."

The stress is back, along with confusion. *Great.*

"Is it the same packet you gave me?"

She nods, her eyes glued to the screen as she searches. "Do you still have it?"

I don't tend to keep emails after I've read them—but my assistant never throws out anything. "I'm sure Noelia has the hard copy. I'll have her scan it and send it to you."

She nods but continues to search her phone.

"Don't waste any more time looking for the email. And don't spend more than an hour on anything else. Delegate whatever you can. Then get ready for tonight. We're going to go to that cocktail party, and we're going to charm the hell out of every fucking person in the room, until they're begging us to carry our product."

"Hey," Lexie says as she enters in a sarong.

I can't take my eyes off the knot that's holding it up. *A single knot between me and her sexy little body.*

"Gray wants to talk to you," she tells Valentina. "They're sending up a party planner from Charleston who's coordinated some big events for them. She'll work with your person to sort things out. I can help too. I'm not as good at this as you, but I can take direction."

Valentina couldn't ask for a better friend than Lexie—and I couldn't ask for a better partner.

Valentina nods, but she doesn't move.

Lexie puts a hand on her shoulder. "Gray's next door in your father's office. You should go."

I stand, hoping to prod her, and she finally gets up too.

"Thank you," she whispers, eyeing me for a moment before giving me a heartfelt embrace.

Valentina and I have always been close. I knew eventually we'd move beyond the cold war. I'm just sorry that it had to happen like this.

"It's all going to work out," I assure her when she pulls away. "You'll see."

"I'll be right there," Lexie tells her as she leaves.

"What do you think happened?" she asks when her friend is gone.

There's a bit of tang in her tone, and I'm sure she doesn't buy the misunderstanding bullshit.

"I don't know, but I'm sure as hell going to find out. Will you keep an eye on her?"

"I'm not planning to leave her side."

I wrap my arms around her and pull her close, inhaling the sweet scent that is Lexie. "Thank you."

"For what?"

"For being you."

"You can thank me when it's all done. I know exactly how, too."

"You're getting awfully cheeky, Angel," I tease, fingering the knot on her sarong. "Don't think just because we're away, I won't find a way to put you in your place."

Her eyes glitter. "I look forward to it."

Antonio clears his throat from the doorway, and Lexie jumps. "You two don't have enough to do?"

48

RAFAEL

"WHAT EXACTLY IS it that you need?" I glare at him.

Lexie untangles herself from my hold and gives Antonio a small wave on her way out.

"What the fuck is going on?" he asks gruffly, parking himself at the edge of the desk.

"I have no idea."

I text Zé: *Need you in my office. Give me five minutes. Bring Tamar.* "If we were in Porto, I'd say it was a distraction."

"What about that asshole Bancroft?"

He seems to be first on everyone's list. *Too easy.*

"No one else stands to lose as much as Bancroft, but I'm not convinced. I was exceedingly direct when I met with him. My knife and I were clear about the consequences if he caused any more trouble. The guy pissed his pants. Don't get me wrong, it's the first place we're going to look, but I don't see it."

"If not one fucking thing, it's another," Antonio grouses.

"Did you know Valentina was taking antianxiety meds?"

He blanches.

I should have kept my fucking mouth shut.

"Did Lexie tell you that?"

I shake my head. "Valentina."

"No. I didn't know. And if her mother knew, I would know."

I suspect that's right.

"She said the meds make her foggy and she's worried that she might have canceled the caterer by mistake."

"Bullshit."

"I agree."

"Do you think the party planner is involved in this?"

"I think it's suspicious as fuck that she can't be reached. She was carefully vetted before we settled on her. But I've only talked with her once. We need to find her."

"I can send Cristiano to look for her. Better to let Zé continue to focus on security here. Cristiano can take one of the local guys we're using."

"We have no idea what they're going to find. We need to send people we can trust."

"The man I'm thinking of was part of the team we had on Daniela when she was in the States."

Perfect. "That would be great. Can I borrow Lucas?"

"Whatever you need."

Tamar and Zé are in the doorway.

"We need to go to that cocktail party like nothing happened," I tell Antonio, beckoning my team to enter. "Maybe you can spend a little time propping up Valentina."

"AT FIRST GLANCE, it appears the email originated with Valentina," Tamar explains. "But it was easily traced back to Bancroft. Although—"

"How easily?" I demand before she finishes her thought.

"I would say much too easily, but it's the first place I looked, and I knew how to get in because we just did it."

I can't believe he'd pull this shit again so soon. I'm going to kill that son of a bitch.

"Are you sure that the digital fingerprints are Bancroft's?" Zé asks.

"I'm sure. But I'm not sure this isn't some kind of ploy. There could be layers of encryption that lead us to dozens of others. I spent five minutes on it—there's no way I can be certain he's responsible."

"What were you going to say before I interrupted you?"

"This seems like the work of a woman—and an amateur. Canceling a caterer...it has a mean girl flavor to it." She shrugs. "It doesn't feel like something a man would do."

She's right. Although I'm glad she said it and not me. "Bancroft's not much of a man, but I agree."

"Me too," Zé adds.

"Antonio's sending Cristiano to look for the party planner. She might be able to shed some light on this—if we can find her." But, if Bancroft is behind this, I doubt he killed her.

"Security measures need to be tighter than planned tomorrow," I caution them, although I have no doubt Zé's already on top of it, "and for the rest of the trip. At the very least, someone wanted to embarrass us. Boston is our first stop, and they zeroed in on the high-profile event with over a thousand guests. If we fail, and a caterer not showing up would be an epic failure, we would immediately be dismissed as lightweights, not at all ready for prime time."

"Bancroft's already in town for the celebration," Zé mutters.

We invited all our competitors, and many of them will be here. Not to wish us luck but to scope out the competition. It's irresistible. Even still, I didn't think Bancroft would have the balls to show up.

"Arsonists like to show up at the fires they set," Tamar adds.

Maybe that's why Bancroft came—he lit the fuse and came to watch us burn.

"Should we pay him a visit?" Zé asks, getting out in front of the inevitable. He's still pissed I didn't take him with me last time, although, as it turned out, having him on the ground was a godsend. Otherwise, I might not have heard about Francesca's murder until it was too late—for Lexie. I shove the thought away. There's enough happening right now to send me into a rage. I don't need to add fuel to the fire.

"Not yet. I promised Bancroft pain if he fucked with me again, and I never break my promises. Let's wait until we have more information before I disembowel him."

49

LEXIE

"Do you know Valentina's taking antianxiety meds?" Rafael asks, pouring us a nightcap.

"Yes." I'm still smarting about it. Not because of the meds but because I had to hear it from Marco. *Did she think I would judge her for taking care of her mental health?* I take out an earring and drop it on the dresser. It reminds me of when we spent hours at the spa and she never mentioned that Marco wasn't going to the gala. *Maybe she doesn't trust me.*

There's more distance between us since I moved in with Rafael. No question. While I hate it, I'm not leaving him because it's hard for her.

He hands me a tumbler. "When did she tell you?"

There's something almost accusatory in his tone, and I stop fiddling with my earring to look at him. "She hasn't told me. Marco did."

"Marco?" he asks, running a finger along my lower jaw.

It's an intimate gesture, but it feels almost foreboding. I don't like the tenor of this—at all.

I gaze at him in the mirror. His features are tight. "You know, her husband."

After the whole fiasco with the caterer, we were all a bit on edge before tonight's events, but they went off perfectly. Valentina relaxed as the night went on, and Marco stuck to her like glue.

In the elevator, on the way to the room, a *very* loose Rafael promised to do delicious things to me while Zé and Sabio looked straight ahead and pretended to ignore us. He stood behind me with his head lowered to my ear so they couldn't hear him, but there was something titillating about it—and arousing. Even so, the mood in the room has gone from sultry to stank. Or maybe it's just my mood that's soured.

"Why don't you ask the question that's really on your mind?" I step away from him. "You want to know if I kept it a secret from you."

He grasps my wrist, gently, and pulls me closer until we're facing each other, almost touching. "I'm curious. Would you have told me, if you'd known?"

I don't know. "I helped put Gabe down for a nap earlier, and even cranky, he's less needy than you."

One corner of his mouth curls—not in a smile, but something darker.

"You promised not to keep secrets from me."

When I don't answer right away, because I'm still thinking about it, he decides that my silence is my response. I feel the shift in his demeanor.

And you promised not to scare me—but here we are. Although I'm not scared. I'm just pissed we're having this conversation. *I don't know if I would have told him. It's not a simple question.*

"Do you remember that promise, *Angel*?"

"Don't be so literal. Surely you won't expect me to tell you what's in the boxes under the Christmas tree. Because I won't. You'll need to wait until Santa comes down the chimney like everyone else."

"Gifts aren't secrets. They're surprises."

God, he's annoying.

"You might be entitled to my secrets, but not to anyone else's."

"Valentina's not just anyone."

"No. She's not. She's like my sister, and for some reason she didn't see fit to tell me that she was struggling with anxiety. Maybe she thought I was going to blab to you." I move back, but this time I cross the room, putting plenty of space between us.

"I don't want to fight," he says quietly, following me. "You're a good friend to her. The best. I'm happy she has you."

He knows I'm hurt that she didn't confide in me, and he's being gentle. This is why it's hard to stay annoyed with him for any length of time.

"She made it through today because of you," he adds, running his fingers through my hair.

Not just me...you, too. I don't say it because I'm still feeling churlish.

"Everyone stepped up. Even Marco was very supportive of her. He has been the entire trip."

"Especially the other day when he didn't show up at the party at Antonio and Daniela's. But I guess that doesn't count because it was the night before we left."

He can't talk about Marco without at least one biting remark.

"He didn't go to the party because she's been so stressed about the two of you crossing paths. He wanted to make it easier on her."

"Did he tell you that too?" he asks, much too carefully.

"He did."

"I'm tired of talking about that feckless pussy."

He takes my arm as he sits on the edge of the bed and pulls me onto his lap, but I'm not feeling it. I understand that he wants me to take his side over Marco's, every time. It's childish, but I get it. What I don't like is his attitude about secrets, and I'm not ready to let it go.

"I don't know whether I would have shared the information about Valentina's mental health with you, unless things were out of control. But I stand by what I said earlier. You're not entitled to other people's secrets."

"Is that so?" He nudges my thighs apart before gliding his fingers over my pussy.

My lace panties are the only thing separating us. Small zings of pleasure are already starting, but I won't let it distract me. *That's what he wants.*

"And not just other people. I'm also entitled to some privacy. You don't need to know every time I fart."

He pulls his head back, but his fingers don't still. "You fart?" His nose is scrunched. "If I had known sooner, I would have never gotten involved with you."

I slap him on the arm.

"And you're not entitled to know my every thought, just like I'm not entitled to know yours. It has nothing to do with honesty or loyalty."

Rafa's fingers are magic, and I squirm on his lap, while he works the churlishness out of me.

"I don't entirely agree, but you can stop now." He presses a kiss to my hair. "You made your point."

"Good. Otherwise, we're going to have a problem, Huntsman."

He throws his head back and laughs out loud. "Oh, are we?" His thumb finds the seam of my pussy and rubs the thin fabric into the wet flesh. "Are you threatening me, Angel?"

I shake my head, trying not to moan as his fingers move faster. *Harder.* "It's not a threat. It's a promise."

He takes hold of my hips and sets me on my feet.

"It didn't sound at all like a promise. No one threatens me, Angel." His eyes are dark, but they sparkle with mischief. "If you don't want to be punished, you need to find a *nice* way to apologize."

His voice is a low rumble that makes my pussy ache for his touch. Only he would pick a fight, and then, after he's proved wrong, would expect a blow job in apology. *Cheeky bastard.*

I'm ready to put this discussion aside. I'm too distracted now—too aroused to squabble.

"If you need a suggestion, I can help," he purrs, his hands on my ass and his eyes glittering playfully.

Intense Rafael is heart-stopping, and I'd hand my panties over to him anytime, anywhere. But playful Rafael? He owns my heart.

"I make a demand or two, and you need to snatch back the power," I tease, running my finger over his lips.

"Is that what you think this is?"

I shake my head. The one thing I've discovered is that when I'm on my knees—especially if I'm on my knees—I'm the one with all the power. "No."

Without once releasing his gaze, I shimmy out of the scarlet cocktail dress, exposing my breasts to him. His eyes are dark, with swirls of lust that set me ablaze. I hook my finger into my panties and slide the red lace down my legs, maddeningly slow.

He groans as he admires me, and all I think about is touching him. *Owning him.* It's powerful and heady, and I can't get enough.

"Tease," he murmurs as I finger the ends of my hair, putting on a little show—for him—always for him.

When I sense his patience for sitting is frayed, I fall to my knees and swallow his cock.

No long licks. No swirls of my tongue. Neither of us has the patience for that kind of teasing tonight.

"Fuck," he mutters, threading his fingers into my hair.

I breathe through my nose, as he hits the back of my throat, again, and again, but I don't gag. It feels like victory.

"Touch yourself, Angel," he grits out. "Rub that wet pussy for me. I want to feel your whimpers around my cock."

I slide my free hand between my legs and stroke mindlessly, concentrating only on the thickening shaft in my mouth. *Smooth. Throbbing. Impossibly big.* So long and thick I gag, now, but I don't stop.

"Such a good girl," he pants, and I feel the muscles in his lower abdomen contract.

He tugs on my arm, stealing my fingers from my drenched pussy and into his mouth. "So sweet. Your cunt is so tasty, Angel." When he sucks on my fingers, I feel it between my legs.

As I tighten my lips around his cock before I pull back, his hips jerk and he draws a long, shaky breath that makes me feel like a skilled courtesan. *He's right there. Mine for the taking.*

I dip my head, taking him deep, and swirl my fingertips over his tight balls. A tormented growl twists from his chest, and I feel his surrender. He grips the edge of the mattress and explodes on my tongue with a guttural groan and a symphony of curses.

With his head tipped back and his eyes closed, I bathe his cock with my tongue. Each tender caress brimming with the love I feel for this man.

50

RAFAEL

"Good morning," I say brightly to Scott Bancroft, who recoils like he just saw the devil himself. "Aren't you going to invite me to join you for coffee?"

I take a seat in the sunny atrium before he can find his voice.

He's ashen—gray's not a good color on him. I snatch a grape off his plate and pop it into my mouth. "We have a problem."

"I-I-I didn't do anything."

"Come on now. Did I accuse you of anything?"

He doesn't respond.

"Did I?"

He shakes his head.

"No," I tut. "I didn't. Not yet, anyway."

"What do you want then?" he asks, terror dancing in his eyes.

"We'll get to that. Eat your breakfast before it gets cold." I pick up his knife and run my finger along the blade. It's a table knife with a flat edge and not much of a blade.

Bancroft takes a forkful of eggs, but his eyes are glued to the implement in my hands.

"This knife looks harmless, but you'd be surprised at what you can do with it. Nice flat-top good for popping out an eyeball. Digging it out, anyway. With a little elbow grease, I bet you could wedge it into the slit of a man's dick. You know, the place that makes your knees weak when a woman tongues it." I glance at his chalky face. "Maybe you don't know."

"My wife will be joining me soon," he says, like I might hightail it out of here.

Not a chance.

"That's nice. I've never met her. You can do the introductions."

"I never told her anything about what happened in my office. I-I-I didn't tell anyone."

"Don't you have security, Scottie?"

He shakes his head. "It's expensive."

"You're right. Although I think it's worth every penny. You really should consider it."

He's sweating like a pig by the time his wife arrives. She's a petite woman, maybe sixty, and unlike him, she's well dressed. She'd be considered attractive if her lips weren't puckered.

I stand to greet her. "Rafael Huntsman, and you must be Mrs. Bancroft." I wait for her to put out her hand, but she doesn't. *Oh, Elizabeth, you don't want any more strikes against you.*

"It's a pleasure to meet you," she replies with a pinched smile.

"The pleasure's all mine." *All mine.*

"I was just telling Scottie that we have a problem," I explain once we're seated.

"What kind of problem do you have?" Elizabeth tips her head. "I hope it has nothing to do with the big party tonight."

She should find some new hobbies, because she sucks at the kind of subtlety subterfuge requires.

"I'm sorry. I didn't mean to give you the impression that *I* have a problem. *You* have a problem."

Liz lifts her snotty little chin. "I'm going to call the manager," she announces, standing.

I put my hand on hers. "I *really* don't recommend that. Not before you hear what I have to say."

Even when I touch his woman, Scott doesn't breathe a peep. *What a coward.*

It takes her a moment, but she puts her scrawny ass in the seat.

"You upset my niece yesterday. I hate when that happens. Instead of curling her hair or whatever it is that women do before a cocktail party, she had to chase down caterers and party planners. And have silly conversations about table linens. It was a real drag."

"I don't know what you're talking about," she huffs.

Like hell you don't. "But you do know that computers and cell phones, all electronics, really, can be traced, right? Someone fucked with the party plans for tonight. We traced it all back to you. To your email address. It wasn't even that hard."

"I didn't do that," she cries, like a haughty bitch, looking to her husband for help. But she gets nothing from him.

"Keep your voice down, or I'll call the police and the FBI. Your picture will be all over the media within an hour, and you haven't had your makeup done. You don't want your friends to see you like that."

"All I did was make one phone call to change the color of the tablecloths."

"What?" her husband growls.

It's the first thing he's said since she arrived. Most men would have said something by now to try to protect their wives.

"Hush now," I chide. "Let Elizabeth talk. Don't be rude. You know how much I hate rude behavior."

I turn to her. "You changed the color of the tablecloths?"

I already know she did, but I want to hear what else she has to say. She had the cloths changed to the color of their brand.

Somebody made it look like Elizabeth Bancroft was responsible for everything, but after hours of digging, Tamar and Lucas couldn't tie her to anything but the linen. Still, I came to see for myself.

"You don't understand. Foreigners are breaching our territory and selling their products. We can't compete against the entire world, Mr. Huntsman."

Fucking hypocrite. "You distribute your product all over the world. You do realize you're a foreigner in all those countries?"

The idea seems to surprise her. "It's not the same."

"It's exactly the same. It's the free market. Capitalism. When it works in your favor, great. But when it works against you, there's a problem."

"You don't understand," she whines.

"I understand very well." *And soon you'll understand me.*

I stand and push in my chair, my hands wrapped around the top of the ladder-back. "I'm not a man to be trifled with, Mrs. Bancroft. When my business interests are put at risk, I go for the jugular—not the tablecloths. Enjoy your breakfast."

Zé, who was standing a few feet away, catches up to me. "Anything?"

"She confirmed what we already knew. They're not responsible for anything but the puke-yellow tablecloths. But we need to find out who is—I'd feel a hell of a lot better if we could locate the party planner." *People don't just disappear.* Even Valentina is beginning to think something happened to her.

"Keep your focus on security," I mutter, "but when you have a minute, begin the process of ruining the Bancrofts and what's left of their crumbling empire. Get Tamar involved and whoever else you need."

"Define ruin."

"Take everything. Everything. Make it hurt. Funnel the proceeds to charity. Something that feeds kids."

I was willing to allow their business to bleed out naturally, but I'm tired of dealing with those fuckers. They're done wasting my time.

51

LEXIE

We've been back for several days, and Rafael's still on a post-launch high. The trouble in Boston aside, it went better than expected—much better. The reviews were glowing, and the press gushed all over Rafael and Valentina. Everyone loves a feel-good story, and those two, young, hip, and beautiful, teaming up to modernize the staid Port industry is the very best kind of story.

"Are you asleep?" Valentina asks, nudging my foot with hers.

It's Sunday, Marco's away, Rafael is at Sirena, and the two of us are lounging on opposite ends of the sofa in her apartment.

"No. Just thinking about the US trip. Have you had time to process it all?"

"Not really. I'm still a jumble of emotions—exhausted, ecstatic, triumphant. So many things all wrapped up in one."

She seems like her old self today. On the way to LA, we took a nap in the bedroom on the plane—something that made neither Rafael nor Marco all that happy. It might be the only time they found common ground. While we were lying in bed, Valentina told me about the "soul-destroying" anxiety.

She couldn't explain why she hadn't confided in me before. Marco thought she should keep it between them so that nothing got out before the launch. He suggested that her father or Rafael might decide it was too much for her and pull her off the project. Rafael might have added people to her team or pressured her to delegate more, but there's no way he would have forced her off, and he wouldn't have allowed Antonio to do it either. But Marco sees only what's on the surface—he can't see beyond that—or he doesn't want to.

The whole thing is a little strange, since he was the one who told me about the meds. I've spent a lot of time around Marco, especially before they were married, and I don't remember ever getting a weird vibe from him until recently. Maybe I'm more in tune to it now that Valentina has confided in me about their problems, or I've picked up on it because Rafael is such a bastard about all things Marco.

"The only thing that bothers me," she adds, "is the party planner. I think about Julia a lot. We'd been in touch for a year, weekly, and then in the last six weeks, almost every day. I find it hard to believe she took a bribe and disappeared. I worry something happened to her."

Not even Rafael is willing to guess if she's a culprit paid handsomely by a competitor or a victim of foul play. Although if I pressed him on it, I'm quite certain he'd say the latter. Cristiano checked her place, and I saw the exchange between Rafael and Antonio when they learned that the apartment wasn't disturbed and her things appeared to be all there.

"They're still looking for her. Hopefully it won't be long until they find her, and you can stop worrying." *Although I have a terrible feeling she's going to turn up dead.*

"Are you up for another whirlwind trip?" I ask, changing the subject.

"It's a challenging way to roll out a new product." She laughs. "It would have been less exhausting to do the entire

East Coast or West Coast and then the middle of the country—three separate trips. But this way we didn't have to pick favorites, and I think the frenzy adds to the youthful vibe. Unlike those awful tablecloths Mrs. Bancroft tried to stick us with."

"Awful? How dare you! That's the color of their brand."

"You know," Valentina says, "what she did was terrible and mean-spirited, and it nearly pushed me over the edge, but part of me understands how awful it would be to watch your family business—one that had been around for almost a century—become irrelevant."

"I agree. But it's been on a death slide. You guys didn't destroy their company."

"No. But their ciders and wine coolers were what was keeping them afloat, and they're going to lose the market share now."

Bancroft Spirits is the least of Premier's problems. Valentina knows it too. "The Bancrofts aren't the only enemy—someone else went to a lot of trouble to embarrass Premier."

"Premier's success makes it a target." She sighs. "Huntsman dealt with these types of things forever, because they've been on top for so long. The only reason no one ever pulls this kind of shit on them anymore is because my father would make an example of the culprits. When I say example, I mean parade them through the streets of Porto before executing them in the public square."

We both snicker, because as much as Antonio would love to put on that little display, he would never do anything quite so public. Although the end would be brutal for them, just away from public scrutiny. When Rafael finds out what happened in Boston, it won't be much fun for the culprits either. *I have no sympathy.*

"How about you? Did you have fun?"

"It made my heart full to watch you and Rafael together. You guys are such an amazing team."

They were so great together doing interviews. Rafael spoke from the heart when he talked about how special it is to share a dream with Valentina. And Valentina's love for him shined through when she explained how he gave her the opportunity to take the lead in an industry still dominated by men. I couldn't get enough of them together.

"I never thought I'd say this, but you and Rafa make a pretty great team too."

An excellent team. My mind drifts to the *very* special goodbye we enjoyed before he left for Sirena.

"What are you smiling about?" she asks. "You're thinking about him naked, aren't you?" She whips a cushion at me. *"Eww."*

I laugh.

"I'm only grateful that you have your own room here, because otherwise I'd be so grossed out, I'd have to buy a new bed."

I almost tell her about the massage candle on the island, but I wouldn't want Rafael sharing any dirty details with Zé, so I keep my mouth shut.

"Do you want a glass of wine?" she asks, getting up.

"Sure."

I want to ask her about her relationship with Marco, but even though I'm not probing for dirty details—not those kind of dirty details—it feels too nosy right now. Although I'd like to know more about how he treats her when they're alone.

Our grandmother Lydia often said, *It's hard to know what goes on in someone else's marriage from the outside, no matter how close you are.*

It might be true, but I have a feeling Valentina and Marco are still struggling. She's not crying anymore, at least not to me, or maybe it's the meds making her feel more in control.

Although she told me on the plane that she doesn't like the way they make her feel, so she doesn't take them every day. *It's all unsettling.*

She hands me a glass of rosé and plops back on the couch. "Could we be any lazier?"

"I don't know. I fetched some wine. We're drinking it. That's something."

My phone buzzes, and I pick it up.

RAFAEL: *Let's plan the vacation tonight. I'm up for anything that includes you naked.*

"Now that the traffickers are history," I tell Valentina, "Rafael wants us to take a vacation."

"Where are you thinking?"

"I don't know. Somewhere warm where there's a beach and places to explore."

"What about Rhone? Marco and I only spent a night there, but it was gorgeous. I'd go back in a heartbeat."

The ocean is soothing for Rafael. I want to go somewhere where we're surrounded by waves. "What's the beach like?"

"I have pictures." She pulls up the photos and hands her phone to me.

"The beach is gorgeous."

"Pristine."

I scroll through the photos and stop at one with Marco and a man who looks vaguely familiar. I sit up and hold the screen so she can see. "Who's that with Marco?"

"A client he met with while we were there. You know Marco. He's always working. He can turn even a night away to apologize into a work thing." She shrugs. "It's hard on him that my family has more money than his. He feels like he has to play catch-up."

Most of what she said went right over my head. The longer I stare at the image, the more my gut churns. "What's the client's name?" I ask, trying not to give anything away with my tone.

"I don't know. Marco never said. I can ask him."

Every cell in my body shrieks, *No!* Where did that come from? "Don't bother. I'm sure I'm mistaken."

But I'm not sure. He resembles the photo I saw of Paolo —Francesca Russo's boyfriend. But I saw it for only a brief second—and I was too preoccupied with keeping Francesca safe to absorb the details. I didn't care about her boyfriend at the time. I shouldn't care about him now either. Paolo's dead.

52

LEXIE

I CLOSE the file and sit back, dozens and dozens of images passing before my eyes like old movie frames. The research on the trafficking victims is finished—at least my part. Tamar is going to take another look at the file, and then she'll send it to Rafael, who'll turn it over to the proper authorities.

In some ways, it's strange to be done with the awful business, but I'm thrilled to put it behind me and start something new, preferably something less dark and soul-sucking. Although Tamar agreed to let me get up to speed on Vera Huntsman's disappearance, and there's only darkness there. I suppose it's the nature of the work. *No unicorns or sparkly glitter anywhere.*

Before I meet with Tamar, I make a double espresso. I need a big hit of caffeine. I had a nightmare last night and couldn't fall back asleep for hours, not even wrapped in Rafael's strong arms.

Valentina and I were running on the beach, and two men were chasing us. They were wearing masks that made them look like monsters. One of the men cornered me. I fought back and managed to pull off his mask. It was the client Marco had been talking to in Rhone. I don't need Freud to analyze that dream.

I haven't been able to shake the man's face since I saw it on Valentina's phone. It's been bugging me. I'm sure I know him from somewhere—*he can't be Paolo.* Maybe I know him from London. Eventually I'll figure it out. But for now, I have a meeting with my boss.

"SEND me the file on the traffickers," Tamar says as we're wrapping up. "I have time this afternoon to take a look at it."

"I'll send it as soon as I get to my computer," I reply, preparing to leave. But a nagging feeling stops me from going anywhere. "Did you ever have a déjà vu experience?"

She looks at me curiously. "Yes. Why do you ask?"

"When I was going through some photos on Valentina's phone, I saw a man who looked like Paolo, from the picture Francesca showed me." It sounds particularly ridiculous saying it out loud, especially to Tamar, who is a serious person.

"You told us that you couldn't remember what he looked like."

"I couldn't. And when the photos of him were published in the media, after he was killed, it didn't jar my memory at all. But yesterday, as soon as I saw the photo, I knew it was someone I'd seen before. I don't know why, but it made me think of Francesca's photo. I'm sure it's nothing. Tying up the case has me a bit out of sorts, I guess." *I sound like a moron. Way to go, Lexie.*

"Déjà vu is a subconscious message. Something we've experienced in the past—and I don't mean a past life. I'm not a fan of woo-woo, but an experience that's stored in our brain is closely related to a gut feeling or instinct. I wouldn't create a battle plan around them, but I never ignore those feelings either."

"Even if I wanted to, I couldn't ignore it. It has me a bit spooked."

"Did you ask Valentina about the photo?"

I nod. "It's one of Marco's clients."

"Who else was in the photo?"

I wouldn't have brought it up if I didn't want to talk about it with her, but she seems to be taking this more seriously than I expected. "Marco and the man. There was a family walking on the beach behind them. That's it."

"Were they posing for the camera?"

She's observing me carefully. It's a bit odd.

I shake my head. "It was candid, taken from a distance. Why do you ask?"

"Unstaged photographs tend to tell us more than staged ones. They're almost always truthful. Was this a recent photo?"

Oh God.

"It was taken on her trip to Greece."

"Did Valentina have anything to share about the photo?"

I'm starting to feel as though she has suspicions about the photo too.

"No. She offered to ask Marco about the man, but I told her not to bother."

"Why?"

I shrug. "I don't know." *I've been too anxious to explore it.*

"Why, Lexie? Allow yourself to think about why you didn't want her to ask Marco about the man."

"I got this terrible feeling. I didn't want her involved." I feel myself flush. I must sound like a foolish girl to her.

"Have you mentioned any of this to Rafael?"

"No. I try not to talk too much about Marco with him. Rafael's not a fan."

She nods. "You said they were at the beach. In Athens?"

"Rhone."

"Rhone," she repeats, drawing out the word.

R. Oh God. My heart begins to panic. I can't just let this go.

"Tamar, is there any way you can pull up Valentina's photos? I know she stores them in the cloud." I can't believe I just asked someone to hack Valentina. *I'm sorry, sweetheart. But I don't want to involve you in this if I can help it.*

"Of course there's a way. But Valentina's my boss. I can't go rifling through her personal belongings."

"I apologize. Forget we ever had this conversation." *I'll figure something else out.* I stand to leave.

"I don't think it's wise for either of us to forget about this conversation. Ask Valentina to send you the photos. Make up an excuse."

I don't want to lie to her. *You just asked Tamar to hack her—well, not exactly hack. I'm a mess.* "I'll text her."

"Do it now," she urges.

"You're worried?"

"Not yet. But if the man in Valentina's photo is the man from Francesca's, it means he was in close proximity to your friend. That's a big problem. Rafael and Valentina need to know."

"Can you hold off telling Rafael?" *Because if he goes after Marco, again—*

"I can hold off for a short while. Very short."

I have no idea what *very short* means, but there's no time to waste.

LEXIE: *Can you send me the photos from Rhone so Rafa can see the beach?*

VALENTINA: *I'll do it when my meeting ends.*

LEXIE: *Thanks.*

"She'll send them after her meeting," I tell Tamar. Hopefully I'm mistaken.

Tamar nods and turns her screen to me. "Look familiar?"

I recognize the image as the man the media claims was Francesca Russo's boyfriend. Otherwise, it doesn't ring a single bell for me. *Nothing.*

"He's not the man in Valentina's photo, and I don't think he's the man in Francesca's either."

"Forward the photo to me as soon as Valentina sends it."

53

LEXIE

AN HOUR LATER, my phone buzzes. *Valentina.* I close out the file I'm working on and scroll through the pictures she sent. They seem to be all here—except for the one of Marco and the mystery man.

LEXIE: *What about the picture you took of Marco in the hot pose?*

VALENTINA: *You want to check out my man? ;)*

LEXIE: *Got my own hot man. And I'd love to show him those waves.*

It's true about lies. Once you start, you can't stop. I hate this.

VALENTINA: *He'll have to use his imagination. When I told Marco you thought his client looked familiar, he freaked out and made me delete it.*

My chest feels like a boulder was dropped on it.

LEXIE: *Why did he freak?*

VALENTINA: *Client confidentiality or something.*

LEXIE: *Thanks for the pics. Talk to you later.*

Even before I press Send, I'm on the way to Tamar's office, my heart pounding. *Calm down, Lexie. Client confidentiality is a real thing.*

I knock, so anxious I'm bouncing on tiptoe. Tamar motions for me to come inside.

"She told Marco I thought the guy looked familiar, and he made her delete the photo," I blurt. "He was upset. What does this mean?"

"Maybe nothing," she replies calmly. "But we need to run it by Rafael."

I'm going to vomit. *Breathe through your nose. Nice even breaths.*

"Are you okay?" Tamar asks, stepping closer.

No. She must think I'm some kind of lightweight.

"I'm fine. But their relationship is just getting back to normal. He's going to jump to every conclusion and drag Marco back into the caves. We need more before we go to him."

"Did she look in the cloud or in the trash for the photo?"

"I don't know. But I can't come up with a reason to ask her to do it without alarming her. And I don't want her to say anything more to Marco."

"No. The less he knows the better."

"Isn't everything backed up and stored here?"

"I can only access it for work matters."

"Not safety?"

"Not without telling her."

One blow after another. My head is throbbing.

"But as part of your training," she continues, "I could teach you how to access material from our backup storage. What you do with that skill is your business." She pauses. "Although, under any other circumstance, I would fire you, and I can't promise that Rafael or Valentina won't."

The least of my problems is being fired. I'm more concerned they'll never talk to me again—or to each other. But if it's Paolo in the photo, that means Marco knew him. Maybe it's an innocent connection, but Tamar doesn't strike me as someone who jumps to conclusions, and she's concerned.

"Let's do it." The guilt is so thick I could choke on it. *I'm such a terrible friend.*

"Lexie, when you're done, whatever you find, it goes straight to Rafael. I'm telling you this as your boss, and your friend."

I nod even though I'm not convinced there isn't a way around it.

After a short lesson where I take a few notes, I access Valentina's information.

"What you need is right here," Tamar says, pointing to the files. "Start hunting."

I'm sick to my stomach as I search through Valentina's personal information. Fortunately, it's a photo, and I have an approximate date, so my snooping is limited, but still, I feel awful.

For what feels like hours, I look, and look, and look. But I find nothing. Not in the trash. Not in the cloud. *Nothing.*

My head feels like it's going to explode. I take Tylenol from my purse and wash it down with a large swig of water.

"Do you think she has another phone that's on a separate account that we don't have access to?" Tamar asks.

"She has one phone."

"It's time to talk to Rafael," she says firmly, and my heart sinks.

"We're going to cause a problem, and all we have is a feeling." *I should have kept my big mouth shut.* "He's going to jump to every dire conclusion, some we haven't even considered."

"When's the last time you deleted something off your phone and it disappeared within a day? Totally disappeared without you taking the necessary steps to make it happen?"

I don't say anything as my fear of telling Rafael and my guilt about ruining their relationship, again, take hold.

"Never," Tamar replies to her own question. "It's gone from her device and from the backup. It's a system breach."

She's right. There's no other way to look at it. Marco—or someone—wanted that photo gone. *Completely gone.*

"Would you mind if I talk to him first?"

"I think you should. But it has to happen right now. Otherwise, I'll have to intervene."

54

RAFAEL

"Hi," Lexie says from the doorway of my office.

I've been expecting her since she texted to say she needed to see me right away. I made a joke about how I've always dreamed about having her under my desk, and she responded with a smiling devil emoji.

I assumed my greedy angel wanted a little afternoon pick-me-up. I know I do. But standing in the doorway, with pasty skin and shoulders hunched, I don't think she's here to have her pussy licked.

"Hey," I say softly so that I don't frighten her away. I jerk my head toward the sofa. "Let's sit over here. Do you want something to drink?"

She shakes her head.

A meek Lexie is not something I'm accustomed to seeing. "What's wrong?"

"Promise me," she pleads, "that you'll hear me out before you go off half-cocked."

The hair on the back of my neck rises as I imagine scenarios ranging from *I'm pregnant*—which I actually wouldn't mind at all—to *there's someone else*—which would send me on a murderous rampage. "Let's hear it."

"Not until I have your word."

I want to tell her that there's no way I'm making that promise, but I also want to hear what she has to say, and I don't want to waste time negotiating. "I'll hear you out. You have my word." *But once you're through, all bets are off.*

She peers up at me like she needs a lifeline. "Do you remember when I told you how beautiful Rhone was?"

She's changed her mind about where we're going on vacation? A small part of me relaxes. *A very small part.* She's ashen and her lips are dry. Lexie wouldn't hesitate to tell me she changed her mind about something so inconsequential. "Yeah. You saw the pictures Valentina took."

Her teeth sink into her bottom lip, and she chews on it for a moment. "Marco was in a photograph with a man Valentina didn't know."

I have no fucking clue where this is going, but I know it's not going to be as sunny as a Greek island.

"Let's sit down." I take her by the arm and lead her to the sofa. She props on the edge, her hands clasped in her lap. *Lexie's not a hand clasper.*

"What about the man?"

"He looked familiar. At first, I wasn't sure from where. But the longer I looked, the more convinced I was that he looked like Paolo, Francesca Russo's boyfriend."

What the fuck did I just hear?

There's so much noise in my head, it's about to detonate. "Say it one more time," I mutter, while I try to wrap my mind around it. She's upset, and maybe I misunderstood.

"The man in the photo," she begins, then proceeds to fill in details that have me reeling. I see the turmoil in her face with each word that emerges. She's on the verge of tears, something I've rarely seen. I want to comfort her. I want that so much, but

I'm caught in a storm and need all the energy I can harness as I try to sort through and make sense of what she's telling me.

By the time she gets to the deleted photo and starts to sob, I feel the magnitude of the problem deep in my marrow.

I pull her onto my lap. "Don't worry. I'm not going to let anything happen to Valentina, and certainly not to you." *Valentina didn't just put herself in danger when she asked Marco about the photo. She implicated Lexie too. Unwittingly, of course, but it doesn't matter. The damage is done.*

"I'm not worried about me." She sniffs.

"You don't need to worry about anyone. That's my job. I'm going to have Tamar and Zé come in, and we're going to figure this out."

I pick up my phone and call Tamar. "Get Zé up to speed, and I want you both in my office.

"Why don't you take the rest of the day off? Just relax. When I get home, we'll have dinner on the terrace."

She shakes her head. "I'll go crazy up there alone. I'm part of Tamar's team. Let me help."

Not a fucking chance. "Listen to me. I'm going to do what's necessary to get to the bottom of this, even if it means pissing off Valentina again. I don't want to compromise your relationship with her. It's too special."

Another tear trickles down her cheek, and she swipes it away with the back of her hand. "This is why I was nervous about telling you. Next time, she might hold her grudge against you forever."

It would kill me, but I'm willing to risk it. "Would you prefer that I do nothing? Hope for the best? That's the alternative." I keep my voice controlled, because I know it was hard to come to me with what she feels is a betrayal, and I want her to come to me every time—with anything that makes her heart heavy.

She stares at her hands, and I pull her closer. "No. I'm worried for her, Rafa."

I nod. "I'm worried for you, too, Angel. If something happened to you because I sat back so Valentina's feelings wouldn't be hurt, I couldn't live with myself. But I won't go in half-cocked—isn't that what you said?" I tip her chin until we're nose to nose. "I prefer to do things with my full cock."

She smiles, and some of the tension lessens.

When there's a knock on the door, I put her on her feet. "If you prefer to be in your office, I'm sure you can find something to do. But don't leave the building today. Stay out of the public areas—don't give the guards a headache about it." I pull her against me, and her body molds to mine. *Trusting me.*

Fucking Marco. The thought of that bastard brings a new wave of anger.

When another knock comes, we pull away, and I open the door for Zé and Tamar.

"Do you have anything special you need me to work on?" she asks Tamar.

"I think with what we discussed earlier, you have enough to keep you busy."

"Good catch, Lexie," Zé says, nodding at her.

For a minute, she looks taken aback at the compliment. "Thank you."

55

RAFAEL

As soon as she leaves, I call Giana. "Two guards on Ms. Clarke at all times. She's to stay in the building for the foreseeable future. It's nonnegotiable. If you have a problem enforcing those orders, come to me immediately." I end the call, toss the phone on my desk, and rub my hands over my face.

When I lift my head, Tamar and Zé are sitting stone-faced across from me.

"Any thoughts?" I ask, getting up to pour myself a drink to steady my nerves.

"The photo was taken before Russo wrapped up things, and Paolo, or who he thought was Paolo, was found dead," Tamar begins.

"How accurate do you think Lexie's memory is of this? Do you think she's having some kind of PTSD reaction?"

"I suppose it could be a delayed trauma reaction, given that she just closed the file today. But PTSD doesn't normally present like this. Plus, something about the photo alarmed her. Even if it wasn't Paolo."

That was my gut reaction too. It might not be related to the traffickers, but something about that guy spooked her—the guy with Marco. Lexie doesn't scare easily.

"Sweep Valentina's apartment, her car, her office—everything that we can get access to. I want eyes on her at all times, Zé. Can we get surveillance into their house?"

"Not that won't be picked up in a thorough sweep, if Marco has one done."

"We can try to monitor the house from the neighborhood," Tamar adds. "But it'll require human assets on the ground—they could be detected. Plus, it won't give us anywhere near what we would get if we were doing it from the inside."

"Do the best you can."

It feels too much like a hope and a prayer. Neither of which are my style.

"I'm going to concoct some bullshit about the upcoming trip," I tell them, "and see if I can get Valentina to spend long hours here. I'd like to keep her in this building as much as possible. She'll be safe while she's here."

"Are you going to question Marco?" Zé asks.

The next time I question Marco will be with my knife. *I'm certain of it.* My gut is churning the way it does when I'm approaching trouble. But I won't act hastily this time.

"No. And I don't want to involve Antonio yet either. His patience will be thin, and he'll want to interrogate Marco right away. I had to let that slimeball walk once. Not doing it again."

They nod.

"Anything on the breach of the backup system?" I ask Tamar.

"Technically it wasn't a breach. They got in through Valentina's account using her password. It doesn't appear they went anywhere besides her backup data. But my people are still looking, and they're tracing the digital prints."

"What's your gut telling you about this?" I ask the two best minds on my team.

"It's telling me we should consider all possibilities carefully before dismissing them," Tamar replies, "including the missing woman in the US and the traffickers. Lexie had a visceral response to that photo. She's not a flake. But we shouldn't get distracted by shiny objects that lead us into dead ends."

"That's not your gut, Tamar, that's your brain." It's what makes her a valuable member of the team. Zé and I often proceed on instinct and on what experience has taught us—in many ways it's the same thing.

I turn to Zé. "What about you? See any connection to the traffickers?"

"Marco's up to something. I feel it in my bones. But trafficking? Those are special fuckers." He rubs his chin. "I don't see it. But I'm not confident enough to fully discount it either."

"Wait a minute," Tamar mutters from the edge of her chair. "We tried to find the photo from Valentina's phone. But what about the one from Francesca's?"

"How are we going to get it?" Zé glares. "The device is probably long gone, and hacking the prime minister is a bad idea. The Italians are still on high alert. Russo has other daughters, and they're worried about a copycat. They'll crucify us if you're caught."

Not crucify *us*. Crucify *her*. That's why he's so dismissive. It's a protective instinct. But from her posture, Tamar's about to dunk on him.

"I don't need the phone, or to hack into anything," she tells Zé with the same look Daniela gets before she tells her husband to take a seat and listen.

"Francesca's phone was checked for surveillance devices the night she showed up at Sirena's," she continues. "I'm sure it was backed up before my team messed with it. It's protocol."

I don't know much about IT protocol. But she's right about the surveillance devices. We checked both women's phones.

Tamar's team found a tracker on Francesca's but nothing on Lexie's besides the tracker her father had installed.

"You produce that photo, and you have a job for life," I say in jest. *She has a job for life whether or not she wants one.*

"Some women have all the luck," she tosses over her shoulder, striding out of the office. "I'll be back in ten minutes."

I glance at Zé, who clearly doesn't mind being shown up by her. "What are the chances there's a backup of Francesca Russo's phone in our system?"

"If it's Tamar's protocol? I'd say near certain. If not, some chump is getting his ass handed to him."

The muscles in my neck loosen a bit. Identifying the man in the photo could help us determine whether there's danger, and if so, what kind. But if Marco has *anything* to do with that ring that almost grabbed Lexie, I'm going to gut him, and I don't give a shit what Valentina thinks.

56

LEXIE

When Tamar texted me to come to her office, I'd made it through only a few pages of the file on Vera Huntsman—mostly biographical information.

A small part of me was conflicted as I read. I felt like I was snooping into Rafael's early life, and I doubt he'd like it. It's a thorny situation and I'm not sure how to handle it. But for now, I have other problems.

When I get to Tamar's office, Rafael is leaning back on the edge of the conference table, gripping the lip, and Zé's in a chair.

Rafa winks at me, and I relax.

"We'd like you to take a look at a series of photos," Tamar says from her computer. She points to the large screen on the wall. "Do you recognize this man?"

The man looks to be in his twenties, with dark hair and blue eyes. He's attractive, but I've never seen him. "No," I reply. "He doesn't look even vaguely familiar."

Tamar changes the image before I can ask any questions. "What about this one?"

I shake my head. "No."

I'm savvy enough to know this is some type of identification, and I'm sure it has something to do with the photo I described from Valentina's phone.

"This one?"

The moment the picture hits the screen, even before I fully grasp the features, my heart stops and a gasp escapes into the quiet room.

"Do you recognize him?" Tamar's voice gives nothing away.

I nod, my eyes glued to his profile. "I think so."

"You're not sure?" Zé asks. "It's important that we get this right."

I move closer to the screen. The man is wearing a black T-shirt, and he's smiling at something away from the photographer. His head is turned. "Where did you get this photo?"

"We can answer your questions after you've had a chance to identify the men in the photographs."

Rafael steps behind me, his hands on my hips. "We don't want to bias the identification," he murmurs. "Take your time. It's okay if you don't remember, or if you're not sure. Do the best you can."

I stare at the image for what seems like an eternity, trying to make a connection between the man on Valentina's phone and the photo Francesca showed me and this man up on the screen. *Think, Lexie. Think.* I try to recall the images, but I can't be sure.

The longer I analyze the image, the more uncertain of the connections I become—and disappointed in my inability to remember something so vital.

"This isn't the photo I saw on Valentina's phone. The man talking to Marco wasn't smiling." My voice feels shaky, and Rafael's presence behind me is like a warm embrace, supportive, imbuing courage and strength. "But it's him. I'm sure of it. Although I'm not certain that he's the man Francesca said was Paolo. I think he is, but I got such a quick look, and I wasn't really paying attention. I can't say for certain."

"No worries," Rafael whispers. "Identifications are always tricky."

Tamar shows me three more images, all young men. None of them are familiar. When she's done, Rafael pulls me closer, my back to his chest, and places a kiss on the back of my head before releasing me. I miss his supportive presence the moment he steps away.

"These photos are all from Francesca Russo's phone." Tamar puts up the photo of the man I recognized. "Does that knowledge change anything?"

Glancing at the screen, I rack my brain, trying to remember something—anything—about the photo Francesca showed me. "I don't know. I think I remember the black T-shirt, but I can't be sure. I wish I could be of more help."

"You were a huge help," Rafael says, and Zé nods.

"When you saw the photo"—Tamar tips her head toward the screen—"you gasped. It was an involuntary reaction. You might not remember him, but some part of your brain does."

It's almost a relief.

"This isn't the man who the Italians captured, is it? The one they thought was Paolo?"

"No," Rafael says, his jaw ticcing.

"What now?" I look from one to another, but their expressions give me no clues as to anything.

"We'll enhance the photo and then run it through facial-recognition software," Tamar replies. "It could take some time to get an identification."

"But you will be able to ID him, right?"

"Probably," Rafael adds, "but the chances are always better when we're working with the entire face. The profile shot will make it harder."

Of course. "What about Valentina? Are you worried for her safety?"

"We're handling it," he replies cautiously. "You don't need to worry. Leave that to me."

"Lexie," Zé says almost sternly, "it's of the utmost importance that you don't share any of this with anyone, especially Valentina."

I don't understand this line of reasoning. Keeping her in the dark just adds to the danger. "Don't you think a heads-up would be helpful? How can she take any precautions if we don't warn her about Marco's *friend*?"

"We have no idea who the man is," Rafael adds, "or if Marco is involved, or if Valentina is in any danger—although we're proceeding as though she is. But if we tip her off, and she decides to go to Marco and he's involved, or even if we can convince her to keep quiet but she starts to act strange around him, the danger for her increases exponentially. If I thought she would take our concerns seriously and stay away from him, I'd tell her in a heartbeat. But I can't take that risk."

I'm not sure he's right. Valentina and Marco's relationship has splintered some. Although I'm not sure there's enough of a chasm to make her leave him. But not telling a grown woman she might be in danger seems irresponsible.

I glance at Tamar, who's standing near her desk, examining the nearby floor, lips pulled into a tight, grim line. She doesn't agree with Rafael, but she won't go against him, at least not with me here. And forget Zé. He'd never take my side over Rafael's.

I'm going to revisit this privately, but until then I won't say a word. Honestly, I'm not even sure that I could convince her of the danger Marco's client poses—and I doubt she'd believe Marco might be a danger. I'm too tied to Rafael for her to fully trust me about anything related to Marco.

57

LEXIE

THE OFFICE PHONE buzzes while I'm preparing a memo for Tamar. Although I don't recognize the number, it's internal, and I accept the call. "Alexis Clarke."

"Hey," Valentina says, sounding upbeat. "Can you meet?"

"Sure. But why are you calling my office from that phone?" She always calls my cell phone, and given the whole thing with Marco and his client, everything that isn't her usual behavior is worrisome. It's not just me. Everyone's worried.

Rafael's managed to keep her in the building, although she insisted on sleeping at home the last two nights. There was nothing he could do without coming clean, and he's adamant it's a mistake to read her in.

Marco's away, which in some ways is a blessing. Rafael added a ton of extra security around her house, and I would bet my life that every device she owns is feeding information to him.

"I'll explain when I see you."

"Do you want to meet upstairs?"

"I'll come to you." She disconnects the call before I can agree.

A few minutes later, she's in my doorway, looking more than a little worn around the edges, with dark circles not just under, but around, her eyes.

I feel the color leave my cheeks. She was so chipper on the phone that her appearance catches me off-balance. "Come in," I squeak.

Valentina shuts the door behind her and braces her back against it as though she needs it for support.

I don't move. I can't. "You're scaring me."

"Marco was the person who canceled the caterer."

The blood whooshes in my ears. "What? How do you know?"

"Two nights ago, I accessed the alumni portal on Saint Philomena's website to see if they'd done a tribute to Francesca." *I did the same thing last week.* "I haven't been on it for ages. I didn't spend as much time at the school as you did, although I keep up with the news and with a handful of people —here and there."

What does Saint Phil's have to do with Marco and the caterer? "I don't understand how this is connected to Marco and the caterer."

She nods. "I'm not sure I understand, either. But I've spent the last thirty-six hours trying to piece it together."

That explains the dark circles. There was a time not that long ago when she would have come to me immediately, and we would have figured it out together. *She's here now. You can help now. Focus.* "Why don't you come in and sit down?"

"I'm good," she replies, shoulders dug into the door and a faraway look in her eyes.

"So you accessed the portal," I prod when she doesn't say anything. As much as I want to know, I'm almost afraid to hear the response. "What did you find?"

"You know how when you log in, it tells you the last time you were on the site and the device you were using?"

I nod. The Saint Phil's alumni and student portals have layers of security to protect the identity and personal information of the girls who attend—girls from wealthy, powerful families, ripe for kidnapping and blackmail. The tight security doesn't end at graduation.

"Someone used my log-in information to access the site from my tablet. Not just once, Lexie...dozens of times over the last six months."

"Are you sure?" It's such a dumb question, but my mind is racing, and I can't think of something smarter to ask.

"I'm sure. And I'm also sure it was Marco."

My heart lurches, but she's composed—more composed than I am.

Other than her back holding up the door and the dark circles, she doesn't seem out of sorts, like she's been, on and off, the last couple of months. *Maybe the medicine is helping.* I take a deep breath. "How did you pinpoint it to Marco?"

"He's the only one besides the staff who has access to the tablet. It's the only device I own that isn't connected to the Huntsman network. I use it for personal matters that I don't want the IT people to get a glimpse of, or for things like the Saint Phil's site, where we're prohibited from logging in to the secure areas on public computers."

I don't mention how there's a connection between the last few trafficking victims and Saint Phil's. I don't want to alarm her. But it's all I can think about—that and the photo.

"Did you ask him about it?"

She shakes her head. "He's still away. And I want a plan in place before I confront him."

Her voice is strong and controlled, without sadness, disbelief, or even anger. It's almost eerie how calm she is in the face of what is still new information.

"The Saint Phil's thing is troubling, but I still don't see the connection to the caterer."

"Once I discovered that he'd been using my log-in, *for months,* I purchased a new phone and a device with cellular service so that I didn't need to log in to the Wi-Fi at home. I kept digging and digging. I found all kinds of incriminating evidence, although I'm not a tech genius, so I'm sure there's more to find."

She's on a mission. That and the meds are probably what's keeping her from a meltdown. I can't stand talking to her from across the room. "It's lonely over here," I tease, patting the seat near my desk.

"Tell me about the caterer," I continue when it becomes clear that she needs the distance. *I don't know why she feels she needs it, but it makes my heart hurt.*

"A week or so before we went to the US, Marco asked me a bunch of questions about the caterer. In hindsight, he didn't ask about things you might expect, like what kind of food she was serving or what time we were eating. Things men want to know." She balls her hands into tight fists. "He wanted the name of the company and where it was located—that sort of information." She pauses. "Details that weren't readily available because it had all gone through Julia, the party planner. Don't you think that's odd?"

"It's a little odd." But not so odd that she would have been suspicious at the time.

"I had Freitas, in IT, search a week's worth of my emails to Julia—in the backup system. I recognized everything he pulled up—they were all still in my inbox. Except for the one canceling the caterer."

My mouth is dry, and I take a few sips of water, which threatens to come right back up.

"You think he's been using your tablet for nefarious purposes, but he didn't use it to send the email to the caterer?"

"I think that son of a bitch wanted that email to be found. He deleted it from my outbox, but it had been backed up. He expected Rafael to have someone check my email and the backup server for evidence that I'd made a mistake. What Marco didn't count on was that Rafael never considered the possibility. He never thought it had been my mistake."

She stalks over to me and pulls a prescription bottle out of her pocket and spills the contents onto the desk. Her hand is shaking. Either the sense of calm never existed or I couldn't see her trembling from across the room.

"Is this your antianxiety medicine?"

She takes out her phone and looks for something. After a few moments, she hands me the phone. "That's the pill I was prescribed. It's not the same as these, is it?"

I look carefully from the screen to the pills on the desk. They look the same to me. I enlarge the image, and that's when I see the difference. The pills on the desk have a pale-blue dot at the base of the letter *P*. The pill on the screen has a mint-green dot.

"It looks like a blue marking on this one, and a green on this." I gaze at her. "Is it possible it's the way it shows up on the screen?"

"It's not," she replies, taking back the phone. "Look at this. Five milligrams have the green dot, ten the purple, twenty is red, and thirty is blue."

"Someone switched the pills," I whisper, my stomach in knots.

"To something six times greater than what I was prescribed." Her voice is low, and that eerie sense of calm has returned.

"It could have killed you."

"Probably not," she murmurs. "But it explains why I was so foggy and confused every time I took them. And you know who was always nagging me to take them?" she sneers.

"Marco," I say softly.

"My husband. The man who promised, before God and my

family, to love and cherish till death do us part."

For the first time, I hear the wobble in her voice.

"Okay." She takes the seat beside my desk. "Now that you know everything, help me make a plan."

A plan? Does she want to kill him? I know I do. But that's probably unwise.

"What kind of plan, sweetheart?"

"I want to figure out the best way to confront him. I haven't slept in a couple days, and I can't think clearly. I need your help."

No. No. No. "You can't confront him."

"Can and will. Then, after he admits to drugging me, and selling information about Saint Phil's alumni, I'm going to call the authorities, and he can rot behind bars for the rest of his miserable life."

Selling information? He could be—to the traffickers. Maybe that's his connection to Paolo. "Valentina, stop."

She glares at me.

"For a minute."

"I won't stop until the bastard is behind bars."

"What makes you think he's selling information?"

"Because he's always trying to come up with money-making schemes. Money is all he cares about. I used to blame myself, because my family is so much more well off than his. But fuck that. I'm done making excuses for that monster."

"I understand why you want to confront him. I would too. But he's dangerous. Too dangerous for you to take on yourself. You need to talk to Rafael, or your father."

"No," she barks. "I'll take care of this, Lexie. And don't you dare breathe a word of it to Rafael. I might be the stupid girl they think I am, but this is my mess, and I'll take care of it. I can't change the past, but I can stop him."

Don't you dare breathe a word of it to Rafael.

Oh God. Here we are again.

58

RAFAEL

"Any news on the facial recognition?" It's a ridiculous question, because of course Tamar would have come to me right away if she had something. But my patience is holding on by a thread. Even under the best of circumstances, I hate waiting.

"Some false positives. That's it. I think we need to prepare ourselves that we might never have a match. There aren't many facial points to make it work, but we'll know more in a few days."

"Are you still monitoring Marco's whereabouts?"

"He's still out of the country, as far as we know. He's not scheduled to return until Friday. We're going to have to tell Valentina when he returns. I agree with Lexie. The best way to protect her is if she knows there's danger."

I don't agree. Not in this case. Although there might come a point when we have no choice. She can't be around him. He's dangerous, or at the very least, his friends are, and our hands are tied when they're alone. But I'm going to hold off until I'm backed up against a wall. I don't trust that she won't run to him the minute I tell her. This is not only about her safety, but it involves Lexie's too.

"We need that ID, Tamar."

"I know."

"I'll be at Sirena. Contact me the moment you hear anything."

59

LEXIE

As soon as Valentina leaves my office, I'm overcome by a sense of urgency to tell her about the man in the photo she took in Rhone. *I have to.* It might convince her that Marco's the kind of dangerous that's beyond anything we know, and she can't confront him.

Rafael will kill me for telling her. I push the thought away. *This is too important, and I don't have time to ask permission or to win him over.*

She's not gone a minute before I'm chasing her down the hall.

"What is it?" she asks when I catch up to her.

"There's something you should know." My voice is low, and every word causes a small fissure in my heart. *I need to be able to trust you, Lexie.* "Let's go back to my office."

She nods and follows me. We don't say a peep on the short walk back. I try to organize my thoughts, but all I hear is Rafael's voice. *I need to be able to trust you, Lexie.*

When we arrive, I shut the door while Valentina takes a seat. Guilt claws at me, the pain of the sharp talons almost too much to bear.

"You look like you're going to faint," she says as I sit beside her. "Whatever it is you have to say couldn't be worse than that my husband's been selling information about my classmates, trying to ruin my career, gaslighting and drugging me."

It's close. "The picture of Marco and the man in Rhone you showed me?"

She shuts her eyes and swallows hard. "What about it?"

"I recognized him because I'd seen him before. On Francesca Russo's phone—her boyfriend, Paolo."

Valentina peers at me, her brow crinkled. "Paolo, who her father said set up her murder?"

I nod.

The silence is blistering, and all I can think about is the excitement in her voice when she called me after her first date with Marco. How we shrieked and gushed over the ring the day he proposed, and the hours and hours and hours we spent planning the wedding. *My soul bleeds for her.*

When she stares into space for too long, I take her hand.

"He was part of the trafficking ring," she whispers, her voice so soft I can barely hear it. "Do you think that's who Marco was selling information to?"

Yes. "I don't know." We don't know, and I don't want to overstate the facts. It's not right. "But it's suspicious."

She stands and cups her elbows, pacing the room. "It's worse than I thought. I gave him the benefit of the doubt about everything. I wanted to prove my family wrong about him. If I hadn't been so stubborn, so full of pride, Francesca, and maybe others, would still be alive."

I leap out of the chair, rush to her, and clutch her upper arms. "No! You're not doing this. None of it was your fault. And we don't know how it's connected. That's why it's important to talk to Rafael."

"No," she says, firmly. "We're not doing that. He's not going to clean up after me. Do not breathe a word to him. I'm serious, Lexie."

"Valentina, I love you, but you're not being reasonable."

"I'm tired of being told I'm not reasonable or thinking logically. That's Marco's MO. So just stop."

That's how he's been gaslighting her. "I'm sorry. I shouldn't have said that."

She nods. "Rafael will go straight to Marco. Do you have any idea how much Marco despises Rafael? He hates everything about him."

The feeling is mutual.

"Marco will die before he gives Rafa any information."

She underestimates Rafael.

"He's never giving up any information to him. But I know how to get him to open up. He'll tell me everything we need to know."

She's dead serious. And delusional.

I'm speechless. This is like a horror movie where the stupid girl gets in the car with a stranger and you shout *No! No! No!* at the screen and hide under a blanket so you don't see him slit her throat.

I need a solution that she'll agree to. *Think. Think. Think.*

Tamar. "Let's talk to Tamar. She works for you, and she can help trace the digital prints. Right now, most of what we have is speculation. We need hard evidence."

It's probably more than speculation, but at this point, I'll say anything to move her away from the idea that she can manage this herself.

"She won't be able to keep something like this from Rafael." She pauses. "But you can trace the digital prints. You're good at that kind of thing, Lexie. So good that Tamar has you on her A team."

Even if I could do it, then what? I can't keep Valentina safe if everything she thinks is true.

"I'm too inexperienced. I could fumble through, but I would leave digital prints of my own that he could trace back, and that would put you in more danger."

"I don't care about the danger. Women are dead, and maybe worse, because of me. I'm not hiding behind layers of protection. I need your help. I want us to figure out everything we need to know before I confront him. He'll admit to it. I know what pushes his buttons. I want to capture it all on tape so we can take it to the police."

Oh my God. This is nuts. Even by my standards. "Valentina. Think this through. If he's responsible in any way, for any of it, he's not going to be foolish enough to tell you, unless he plans on killing you after. I won't help you do that."

"You've built Rafael up to be something all-powerful. Marco won't tell him shit. I'm telling you, if what you told me about the photo is true, more women will die. I can get him to talk."

The idea of her confronting Marco is a nonstarter. But I don't respond, because Valentina's functioning on fumes and not thinking clearly. She's taken some huge emotional blows in the last thirty-six hours and she's talking nonsense. It's almost like she's having a breakdown.

Valentina grasps my arms. "Fine. I understand that you don't want to help. But don't betray me to your boyfriend. I'll never forgive you if you tell him. I mean it."

Don't betray me to your boyfriend. I'll never forgive you if you tell him. Sharp words with an unimaginable sting. *Never* is a long time. I can't imagine our friendship, our sisterhood, will completely sever, but the fracture will be deep and painful. Betrayal always is—and that's how she'll see it. *And if I don't tell him, that's how he'll see it too.*

It doesn't matter what I do. I'm screwed. As the realization hits me, I chew on the inside of my cheek so I don't cry. The last thing this situation needs is me a blubbering mess, unable to think straight.

Her shoulders are squared and her head high. She's been thinking about bringing him down for the last day and a half. She's dug in. If I don't agree to help, she's going to go after him herself. I have no doubt. "You haven't heard a word I said, have you?" I ask.

"I heard everything. But I need to do this, Lexie. I will not be a victim. And I won't be the woman who stuck her head in the sand while her husband did bad things to innocent people. I know how he thinks better than anyone. I can stop him. He snaked his way in through me, and I'm going to stomp all over him until his life is hell."

I need to buy time to figure out what to do. "I'll help you," I say softly. "I'll help you."

60

RAFAEL

I TRY to spend a couple of afternoons a week in my office at Sirena, even if what I'm working on is Premier business. While I'm proud that we created a safe place for guests, my heart's no longer in it—not the way it was before Lexie came into the picture. Fortunately, Xavier and Stella are pros, and I don't have to worry that the standards I set are slipping.

My phone vibrates, and I glance at the screen.

TAMAR: *We have a match.*

I stare at the four small words with their life-changing possibilities.

Lexie will be out of danger, and she'll be free to do whatever she likes—including returning to London. Valentina will be safe, too, but the life she planned is likely to be in tatters.

Even welcome news wields the point of a sharp blade.

I want to hurl the phone at the window and watch the glass shatter in a million pieces. But better sense prevails, and I call Tamar instead.

"What's his name?" I demand.

"Philippe Moriarty."

"Who the fuck is that?"

"I don't have a lot yet." I hear the banging of the keyboard in the background. "He uses an alias, Michel Caron, which I traced to a French company called Triomphe."

None of this means a goddamn thing to me.

"Philippe and Marco Cruz might be cousins," she adds, with the unmistakable ring of alarm.

Cousins. I sink back in my chair. "How do you know this?"

"I'm not entirely certain. But while I've been waiting for the ID, I did some research on Marco."

"Marco was thoroughly vetted when he started dating Valentina." *Thoroughly vetted.* Tamar did the background check herself. It wouldn't have required much to set me off, but he was clean, as was everyone around him.

His father is a Portuguese citizen whose family has been here for generations. He's a paper pusher for the local government. There was nothing about him that sent up a single red flag. Marco's mother is a French citizen who moved to Portugal after she married. She's not close to her family—it's only her father. When Marco was a teenager, he began spending time in France with his grandfather, who's in his sixties. I met him at the wedding. He was shrewd and arrogant, and liked to put on airs. *Marco's a lot like him in that way*. But, otherwise, he seemed relatively harmless. I can't remember any other specifics, but Tamar will have a copy of the report.

"We looked closely at him," she says, "his friends, his immediate family—everything about them. But we didn't dig deep into the family history—not of the extended family, anyway. Now with the possibility that a cousin is involved, we should."

"When you say family history, are you talking about his great-grandfather?"

Marco's great-grandfather was a criminal who died in a French prison. I learned about him in a European history class, long before I met Marco. He stole valuable artwork for the Nazis during the war, primarily targeting museums and galleries in European countries that were members of the Allied coalition. While Italy didn't become a member until later in the war, Italian private collectors who were sympathetic to the Allies' cause were looted as well. Marco's grandfather was also involved, but he never went to prison.

"Exactly," she replies. "There's a professor of art history in Paris that I'd like to reach out to. He's an expert in stolen artwork from World War II. My former agency consulted with him many times. If he knows anything about the family, it could save us a lot of time."

"Do it. I'll be back at the Lodge in forty-five minutes."

61

LEXIE

I race around the apartment, putting together an overnight bag. Valentina and I are going to make a plan to capture Marco on tape. It's ludicrous, of course, and I'm hoping after a good night's sleep she'll see it too. If not—I don't even want to think about the choices I'll be left with. They're atrocious.

I have to get her to see reason, and soon, before something bad happens to either her or to an innocent person—another innocent person. *Like the party planner.* We didn't even get to discuss her today, but with what Valentina shared, I fear she's dead.

I grab my phone and text Rafael: *I'm going to stay with Valentina tonight. She can use the company.*

Rafael: *At her apartment?*

Lexie: *Yes.*

Rafael: *Great idea. I'll be working late.*

Lexie: *I'll miss you.*

Rafael: *I miss you every second you're not close enough to touch.*

My heart clenches.

Rafael: *Neither of you should leave the building tonight.*

My heart unclenches. He's so damn bossy.

LEXIE: *Yes, sir.*

He must be swamped, because he would normally have some quick, dirty retort.

I reread the thread with a twinge of wistfulness. I need to protect our relationship. *You can start by being honest with him.*

I wasn't entirely forthcoming, but I didn't lie.

I'm staying next door for many reasons. Valentina shouldn't be alone. Despite her outward poise, she must be dying inside, or at least she will be when she stops focusing on vengeance and begins to think about all the implications. She's teetering on the edge—but I think it's because she hasn't slept since her world bottomed out. It's certainly not helping.

I also don't want to have to face Rafael tonight, with the information about Marco weighing so heavily on me. He'll know something's wrong, and I don't want to lie to him.

I take a quick look around the apartment and shut the door behind me, the bitter trail of betrayal dogging me to Valentina's door.

62

RAFAEL

"ACCORDING TO PROFESSOR VIERNERY, sometime after Marco's great-grandfather was charged with war crimes," Tamar explains to Zé and me, "his children—a boy and a girl—seventeen-year-old-twins, went under the radar to avoid the backlash. They weren't just shunned by the upper crust, but they were harassed, threatened, and maybe even assaulted. Marco's grandfather was still a suspect at the time, and he believed that fleeing France, separately, was the only way to protect himself and his sister. They were very close, but he never saw her again after they left Paris."

I'm willing to be patient because Tamar doesn't talk to hear herself talk. There must be a point to this family saga, but I'm not seeing it.

"Viernery has interviewed Laurent Benoir, Marco's grandfather, extensively over the years. He said Benoir is polished on, the outside, but that he lived on the streets of Ireland for several years after he left Paris, and did what he had to do to survive. Because of his father's highly publicized trial, he was forced to remain in hiding, even after the authorities decided not to charge him. Viernery said that he's still a bit of a pariah and is extremely bitter about losing his sister and social standing in Paris. Benoir believes that life was stolen from him."

"How does the cousin fit in? Isn't Marco's mother an only child?"

"The cousin is the grandchild of Colette Benoir, Laurent's sister. He and Marco are second cousins. Colette died before her brother found her, but she had two daughters, both with children. Three granddaughters and a grandson."

"Let me guess. The grandson spent time in France with Laurent too."

"Yes. He's the only one from Colette's family that wanted a relationship with Laurent."

"Do you think Laurent Benoir is involved?" I ask, racking my brain to remember everything I can about the old man.

"Hard to tell."

"What if the professor is right, and he's holding some kind of grudge?" Zé asks.

"And terrorizing Europe is payback," I add.

Zé peers at me. "They took his sister away from him, and now he's taking their women and rubbing it in their faces."

"And earning some cash along the way to make up for everything else that was taken from them—money, valuables, status." I complete the circle. This is how Zé and I operate best. We see the world similarly—except when it comes to my safety.

"You two have gotten *way* ahead of yourselves," Tamar chides. "It's an interesting theory, but we have no evidence to support it." Unlike her boyfriend and me, Tamar's a stickler about tangible evidence.

I suppose someone has to be.

"Well then, find the evidence."

She huffs. It's quiet and not at all disrespectful. Zé glances at her, the edge of his mouth twitching, and from the way she glares back, I half expect her to throw up her middle finger at him. He must get his balls busted as much as I do.

"It might be far-fetched, but we can't discount the grandfather," I say, mostly for Tamar's benefit. "Pursue all leads and find out exactly where those three fuckers are so we can keep close tabs on them."

"You don't want to pick up Marco?" Zé asks, tugging at his earlobe. He's jonesing for a piece of him.

Me too.

"Not yet."

My decision has nothing to do with Valentina's feelings and everything to do with her long-term safety, and Lexie's, and the safety of countless other women as well. I want to put an end to this madness once and for all.

If we pick up Marco too soon, everyone else involved will head underground, and the danger will remain, lurking patiently until we're distracted. Then it will pounce with a vengeance. We need a little more time before we grab that fucker. But when we do, Zé can have a piece of him—a small piece. The rest is mine.

63

LEXIE

VALENTINA and I spent hours last night hashing out a plan to get Marco to confess, not only to everything he did to her, but to selling information to the traffickers. She was particularly focused on the latter.

The plan we came up is amateurish and will *never* work. Yesterday I hoped that Valentina would come to her senses after a good night's sleep, but she's even more dug in this morning.

"We need to practice with the recording equipment," she says, firing up the espresso machine.

Oh God. "First I need to find it and sneak it upstairs. It might take a day or two." I intend to stall as long as possible.

"Remember, Marco's back in a few days."

I haven't forgotten. There's a big red circle around the date in my mind. "Are you going to work up here today or go into the office?" She's like a dog with a big juicy hambone, and I'd prefer she went to the office, where there is at least the possibility of a distraction.

"I haven't decided," she replies, rubbing lotion into her cuticles like it's a calling.

She didn't want to look at me while she answered my question.

Valentina has a sixth sense about things. When we were younger and felt particularly hemmed in by our parents, we used to joke about running away, and she would support us by telling fortunes. It's why this entire thing with Marco is so bizarre. It took her a long time to catch on to him.

"It might be nice to get out of the apartment, even for a few hours."

"Hmm," she replies, still avoiding my eyes.

Has she sensed my heart's not in the plan? Is she going to go off and do something stupid as soon as I turn my back?

Oh, Valentina, I know you believe you're the best person to bring him down, but he's a dangerous son of a bitch. And I doubt we even know the half of it.

I can't wait for her to see reason. I need to act.

With much trepidation, I touch the angel wings dangling from the chain between my breasts. I wear them like the devout wear a medal of Saint Joseph to protect them.

She needs this more than I do. *Rafael needs her to have it more than he needs me to have it.*

"I'm going to the office," I tell her, carefully pulling the angel wings out from under my shirt and unclasping the chain. "I'll hunt around for the surveillance equipment while I'm there. But first I want you to take this."

Her brow crinkles. "Why do you want me to take the necklace Rafael gave you, that you wear all the time?"

"There's a tracker in it," I murmur. "We're dealing with something that's more evil than either of us can imagine. If something goes wrong, I want to be sure we can find you." I stand behind her and secure the chain around her neck, my hands a bit unsteady.

"I'm not going to take any unnecessary chances," she assures me in a whisper.

I don't believe her. It's not that I think she's lying, but if the moment presents itself, she won't be able to resist.

I finger the wings when she turns around. She could leave the necklace behind, and I can't do a damn thing about that. But if she takes it, she won't be able to disable the tracker, and neither will anyone else. She can't disappear. I don't want to lose her, *but Rafael won't survive it.*

"The charm unclasps from the chain. Bad people might take your clothes, and they'll want your phone and jewelry because they know there might be trackers hidden in them." I can't believe we're having this conversation. *It's surreal.*

"If you need to, you can hide the charm inside your body," I continue. "Just don't wait until the last minute to do it or you might lose your chance." I don't let myself think about how *very bad people* might find it, even hidden in an orifice.

"What about you, baby?" she asks, touching my arm. "I don't want anything to happen to you either."

The emotion is swirling around us, and we reach for each other at the same time, wrapping our arms tight.

"I have other tracking devices, and I'm not in as much danger as you might be."

"I have other trackers too." She pulls away. "I'm giving this back to you."

She reaches for the clasp, but I stop her. "We don't know what's been compromised. Promise me, Valentina, that you'll keep this with you, no matter what happens. Think about your family. Especially your mom—she's been through so much. Promise you'll keep it with you at all times."

She holds up her finger so we can pinkie-swear like we did when we were kids. It's a small, fleeting comfort to link fingers with her. She's on a mission, and I don't think she's anywhere near as concerned about her safety as she should be.

I recognize the feeling.

We hug goodbye, and when I close the door behind me, I wonder if it's the last hug I'll get from her.

I'll never forgive you if you tell him.

64

LEXIE

"Hi," I call from Rafael's doorway. It's so early Noelia's not in yet.

When he sees me, he smiles. It's a balm for my aching heart.

"This is a nice surprise. I missed you last night. Why are you still standing in my doorway?" he asks, taking long strides toward me.

He's wearing a fresh shirt, but he hasn't shaved recently and doesn't appear to have gotten much sleep last night. But he looks divine just the same. Although how he looks isn't important right now.

I'm swamped with the feeling you get when you're bone-tired from a long ride through a rough storm. You pull around the bend, and the place where all your cherished memories and keepsakes live comes into sight. It doesn't matter if the structure has been freshly painted, or if it's fraying at the seams. You're home. That's all that matters. *He's become my home.*

Rafael runs a palm over my hair, his brow furrowed. "What's wrong?"

"I need a hug." I twine my arms around him, and he holds

me close, neither of us speaking for long moments. I don't allow myself to think about what I'm about to do. I just soak up his warmth.

"Come with me," he says, much too soon, and leads us to the sitting area in his office. I sit on the couch, and he pulls a chair up until we're almost knee to knee. "Talk to me, Angel."

I thought about what I'd say last night, and then again on the way here.

But my head is spinning. I don't feel quite as safe as I expected—not emotionally. What if he doesn't see this like I do? *Then I'll have betrayed Valentina's confidence for nothing.*

He holds my fingers between his. "Lexie, I can't help if I don't know what's going on."

I nod. I decide to let his own words about trust guide me.

"Do you remember the day I told you what I needed so we could have a chance?"

He tips his head to the side. "I not only remember the day, but what you said too."

"After I finished, you shared what you needed. You said you need me to trust you to do right by me. And you need me to be honest with you, and to come to you with the hard stuff." I draw a breath, forcing the fear and anxiety from my body as I blow it out. "Do you still need those things?"

The knob in his throat bobs. He doesn't know where I'm going, and it's making him uneasy, but he's being patient. "Absolutely."

"I brought the hard stuff."

He nods and lets go of my hand, sitting back in his chair. The distance between us feels cavernous, and I haven't even gotten started.

"Waiting's not going to make it any easier."

No. It's not.

I take in enough air to carry me through to the end, because if I stop, even to breathe, I might not have the courage to finish.

"Marco's responsible for canceling the caterer, he's been accessing Saint Phil's site for at least six months using Valentina's log-in information, and he switched her antianxiety pills for pills that were six times stronger." It tumbles out and stretches between us like a soiled carpet that neither of us wants to step on.

He paled at the mention of the pills—something I've never seen him do. After a few seconds pass, he leans in toward me.

"How—how do you know this? Did Valentina tell you?"

I nod. "That's why I stayed there last night. That, and—"

"And?" he asks gently, rubbing a thumb over his jaw.

"She wanted to make a plan to confront Marco."

"What?" he booms, startling me. "Where is she?"

"Upstairs."

He picks up his phone and places a call. "Lay eyes on Valentina—immediately. Let me know when it's done."

My heart sinks as he takes a step toward blowing up my relationship with Valentina.

He ends the call, throttling the phone, his jaw ticcing.

"So you and Valentina have been scheming to bring down a psychopath?"

He's talking to me like an angry parent would talk to a teenager the police busted at a wild party. I don't like it, but it's the least of my worries right now.

"I was buying time, hoping she'd come to her senses and talk to you. But this morning she was still obsessed with trapping him. She wants to bring him down. She thinks she's the only one who can do it."

The phone buzzes, and he holds up a finger before taking the call. "Yeah." He swallows and his features relax. "Do not, I repeat, do not let her out of your sight. Expect her to try to slip security. If she's successful, I'll hold your entire team responsible."

I shudder because he means *your entire team will die.*

He tosses his phone on the table beside him. "Finish what you were saying."

"She feels responsible, Rafael."

"Responsible for what? That he drugged her?"

His tone is biting, but there's no time to lick my wounds. *There's more hard stuff to share.*

"When I was trying to convince her that he was too dangerous to confront," I explain, my stomach in knots, "I told her about the man in the photograph with Marco."

He stares into my eyes, and although his expression is stoic, his eyes flicker dangerously.

"I had to. She—she has a thirst for vengeance that I've never seen from her, and she wants him punished at any cost, especially for any involvement with the traffickers. Valentina thinks he sold information to them. She believes that she's the only person who can get him to admit what he's done. If we don't help her, she's going to take matters into her own hands. I'm certain."

He stands up and steps behind the chair, white-knuckling the upholstered back.

"Oh, I'm going to help her. Don't you worry."

He's venomous, and I lean back in my chair to move farther away from the ugliness that's sure to come. Because I can't let him fix this in the way he wants.

"This is the very hard part," I say, in a strong voice with my head high. "She needs to be the one who cleans up the mess. She won't be able to live with herself otherwise. I'm very worried about it."

He narrows his gaze. "Are you saying she's at risk for suicide?"

"I'm not saying that. But I don't know." I pause. "She needs to be part of whatever you do. You need to make it happen. I'm trusting you, Rafael," I plead with every cell of my person.

"When did she first come to you about this?"

"Yesterday morning."

"You've known for twenty-four hours but you didn't come to me immediately—instead you concocted a plan to bring down Marco? What the fuck, Lexie?"

I wince.

Reckless. There it is.

"I told you that you weren't entitled to anyone else's secrets, but I made an exception because the circumstances are dire and because I trust you. It's not just her physical safety on the line, but also her long-term emotional well-being, and my relationship with her is at great risk too. I'm trusting you with all of it." *Please don't let me down.*

He grunts and throws his head back. "What plan did you two geniuses come up with?"

It's snarky, but it's something. "Valentina was going to confront him, and we were going to record his confession so she'd have something for the authorities." It sounds even more ridiculous now than it did upstairs.

"You are fucking kidding me," he sneers. "She would never survive that plan, and neither would you."

"I know. Why do you think I'm here?"

"Go upstairs. Keep your phone with you in case Tamar or Zé have any questions."

That's it? You're just going to dismiss me? Not a chance.

"What are you going to do?" I ask, my eyes boring into him.

"I'm going to make a plan with my team that doesn't involve you or Valentina getting killed."

"You can't leave her out of it."

"Don't tell me what I can and can't do. If you think there's any way I'm allowing either of you to be involved in this, you've lost your mind."

And if you think I'm going upstairs to have some tea and a biscuit while I watch a show on Netflix, you've lost yours. I'm not leaving before you agree to allow Valentina to help in some way.

"I promised her."

"I didn't."

Prick. "So much for I need you to trust that I'll do right by you. You promised if I came to you with the hard stuff, we'd figure it out. I betrayed my friend's confidence because I trusted you to help. But I was wrong. When it gets hard, trust is a one-way street as far as you're concerned."

He slams the heel of his hand on the back of the chair. "Think about what you're asking me to do."

"I'm asking you to let her be part of it in some small way. I'm asking you to extend her the same courtesy you extended to Prime Minister Russo. When he was wronged, you allowed him to take the lead so that he could regain his footing and hold his head high, even when it would have been more expedient to take matters into your own hands."

The fury rises from the depths of my soul. "Is it so fucking hard to do that for Valentina—who you love?"

He glowers at me but doesn't immediately respond. He knows everything I said is true. If she were a man, not only would she get to be involved, she'd get the lead.

"This is the crossroad, Rafael. You're either a modern leader or you're not." It's a cheap shot, but I'm out of ammunition, and it's all I have left.

"We have no idea how deep this runs," he says carefully. It's almost a plea for me to see reason—his reason. "Marco isn't some kind of criminal mastermind. If she gets involved, she becomes a target in the way Francesca was—and in the way you are. It's too fucking dangerous," he growls.

When I have my answer, my battered heart and I get up and start toward the door with as much poise and dignity as I can muster. The disappointment is staggering, and I have to concentrate not to teeter.

Rafael grabs my arm as I pass. His grip is enough to stop

me, but it wouldn't be enough to hold me if I shook him loose. "Lexie. Listen to me."

"I've heard enough. I need to tell my best friend that I betrayed her confidence for nothing."

"You can't do that."

Don't tell me what I can do. Isn't that what he said?

"She might do something foolish to beat me to him," he adds, but it doesn't soften me.

I yank my arm away. "If she does something foolish, it'll be on your conscience, not mine."

I storm out, not stopping until I reach the elevator. I don't even glance at Sabio, who's following closely.

I have nowhere to go. I can't leave this place—not that I would ever dream of leaving Valentina alone for hours while she ruminates. But now I need to sit with her and pretend I didn't open my big mouth. Because, of course, he's right. If I tell her Rafael knows, it will only increase the pressure to bring Marco down sooner.

I thought he'd help. I really did. *God, I'm pathetic.*

When people show you who they are, believe them. I finally get it.

65

RAFAEL

"HOW DO you want to handle this?" Zé asks after I tell him and Tamar the entire story, including how Valentina wants to get Marco to confess.

I sit back in my desk chair and stretch out my legs in front of me. I glance from Zé to Tamar. "I'm not sure."

My hair stood on end as I recounted everything Lexie told me.

But something else happened too. Once I put aside my fear for their safety, it began to make some sense to me. Not the part about confronting Marco so he'd confess. That's the stupidest idea I've heard in a long time. *Maybe ever.* But Lexie is right about one thing.

Valentina was the one wronged. We allowed Russo the opportunity for vengeance, and we would have shown any man the same respect. Why wouldn't we extend it to a woman?

I can't come up with a single answer that doesn't prick my conscience.

I was too hard on Lexie too—and it's eating at me.

She came to me, as I asked. Yeah, she waited, but so what? I would have waited to see if Valentina changed her mind too. But she's insisting on something I'm not sure I can give.

It takes a bite out of my soul each day she's at risk. Now she's asking me to put Valentina at more risk—and herself too. I don't have it in me to worry about both of them falling into the hands of those monsters or being killed. *I don't.*

But somehow I have to figure it out. Otherwise, I'm going to lose her for good—if I haven't already.

"Is there any way we can come up with a plan that allows Valentina her revenge without putting either her or Lexie at any more risk?" I choke out the words like a cat chokes out a hair ball.

"I was hoping you'd ask," Tamar replies immediately. "I've been thinking about that while we've been sitting here."

"Are you going to share?" Zé asks, annoyed.

I'm sure his initial reaction to involving Valentina is the same as mine.

"What if we fed Marco some disinformation to lure him out?"

"Like what?"

"I don't know. We know he's monitoring her devices. What if we had Valentina and Lexie texting that they were going to slip their guards and go to the beach for the night—or something like that, but believable. They could go back and forth with the concocted story, reeling him in. We'd have to feed him a scenario he couldn't resist. If he logs in to their conversation in real time, we can pinpoint his exact location and also see who he contacts. If we're lucky, they'll make a plan and share the details with us."

I shudder to think of what the plan might be. "You're not suggesting that they actually go away to bait him?"

"Of course not."

"It could work," Zé mutters.

Maybe. But I hate any plan that involves luck—especially

when the stakes are so high. Although I suppose almost any operation we've conducted has involved some measure of luck.

"If Marco and Philippe aren't the masterminds, they could lead us to the person who is," Tamar continues, "but that means we'll need a lot of resources—more than we have available—in order to scoop everyone up at the same time. That's what we'd have to do. Otherwise, they'll go underground."

She's right. If we do this, everyone needs to be swept up within seconds of one another. It's the only way. *I know people with a lot of resources.* Whatever assets Antonio has are mine. And Will has more resources than we have combined. I have no doubt they'll both assist, even if I have to kick them in the ass. Of course, I'll have to provide details of what's transpired. *That ought to go over well.*

"Are you sure we can make this work?" I ask my team.

"Obviously it needs fine-tuning, but all we're looking to do is to catch him while he's online and capture his location so we can monitor his communications," Tamar replies. "This isn't that complicated. It's not like tracking terrorists in the desert mountains."

Which I'm sure she's also done. I glance at Zé, who nods. I'm beginning to believe we can pull it off, too, but I'm not convinced it'll be easy. "We get one shot at this. What if the communication is encrypted?"

"That's why we have her," Zé quips, cocking his chin in Tamar's direction.

The edge of her mouth curls, and she nods.

"The grandfather is definitely involved," he mutters, as though he's thinking out loud.

It's what my gut is telling me too.

"I'm coming around to that theory," Tamar replies.

"Did you find something that changed your mind?"

"All circumstantial, but it's piling up."

It must be really piling up, because a piece or two of circumstantial evidence isn't normally enough to sway her.

"All right. Let's do it."

They nod, and Tamar's shoulders loosen. She believes this is the best way forward. And I believe in her.

"Do me a favor. Text Lexie and ask if she's spoken to Valentina." I'd text her myself, but Tamar's more likely to get a response.

"I can text her if you want. But she's not going to tell her. She's too concerned that Valentina will figure out a way to act alone. I bumped into her after the two of you spoke. She seemed upset, so I pulled her into my office, and we talked about the perils of sharing the information. She didn't need to be convinced."

"She's with Valentina?"

"I believe so."

Perfect.

"Before she left my office, Lexie offered me her resignation. She thought she'd be on the outs with both owners of the company by the end of the day. It was all very professional."

She's not planning on staying in Porto. It hits me like a punch to the gut, even though I saw it coming. "How did you leave it with her?"

"I recently learned that when an employee tries to resign, you don't have to accept it. So I didn't."

I snicker. Tamar's getting a fucking raise.

I stand and push in my seat. "I'm going upstairs to corral a couple members of the amateur sleuth society to help us. Text me when you two have hammered out the details of Operation Marco."

66

RAFAEL

BY THE TIME I knock on Valentina's door, I have my own plan —*Operation Lexie.*

When Valentina answers, her eyes are a bit sunken, probably from lack of sleep, but otherwise she looks fine. Better than the woman standing behind her, pale, with hunched shoulders, which hits me like a punch to the gut.

"What are you doing here?" Valentina asks. "I thought you were in meetings all morning."

Supposed to be, but my entire morning schedule was shot to hell the minute Lexie arrived at my office door. "I need to talk to both of you."

Valentina's expression betrays nothing. But the stark distress in Lexie's expression shatters a piece of my soul. *She thinks I'm going to tell her friend that she came to me about Marco.*

"Why don't we sit in the kitchen?" I suggest.

I touch Lexie's lower back as we go in, and she flinches as though my hand is fire. The very last thing I want is for her to flinch at my touch.

I'm going to make this right, Angel. You trusted me to do right by you, and I intend to do just that. Your relationship with Valentina is too important. She's going to need you now, more than ever. And our relationship is important too—you're important to me—more important than I ever imagined possible. I need you a little more each day.

Valentina and Lexie sit on one side of my favorite island, and I sit across from them. "I have some bad news regarding Marco."

"What kind of news?" Valentina asks without a flicker of concern for his well-being.

What she doesn't ask is if there's been an accident, or if he's okay, or if I killed him on my way upstairs. The sorts of questions one might ask when they hear the words *bad news* and the name of their spouse in the same breath.

This is tougher than I expected. While it appears that she doesn't give a shit what I say about him, and on some level she might not, she's married to him. They've been together for several years. *That bastard's end is going to be brutal.*

"We have some evidence that Marco's been involved with the trafficking ring."

Lexie blinks a few times, like she's surprised I didn't out her immediately. *Have faith in me, Angel.*

"You certainly aren't obligated to hear me out," I add, "either of you, but I hope you will."

Valentina sits up tall, and clasps her hands on the counter, but Lexie is cautious. "What kind of evidence?" Valentina asks.

"A Huntsman server was compromised—the one where we store the backup data. A single photograph was deleted from your devices. But we were able to retrieve it." The latter part isn't exactly true, but one of my goals is to shield Lexie, and if it takes lying to Valentina to do that, I will.

"Marco and the man he called his client." Valentina's tone is dispassionate.

Lexie was right about her affect being off. Valentina's normally bubbly, and personable, and a bit impish. She's also passionate and often wears her heart on her sleeve—or rather, in her expression. I'd say she's treating this like a business meeting, but her attitude is much too cool and calculating even for that—at least for her.

"We've identified the man in the photograph as Philippe Moriarty. He and Marco are cousins."

Lexie's jaw falls, but Valentina doesn't blink. Although she perches forward, giving me her rapt attention.

"We matched Moriarty's image to a photo from Francesca Russo's phone." *Again, fast and loose with the truth.* "He was her boyfriend—or at least he purported to be."

I give Valentina a moment to absorb the information before I ask, "Is that name familiar?"

"No," she replies, absentmindedly chewing on the edge of her finger. "As far as I know, Marco doesn't have cousins."

"They're second cousins. Their grandparents were siblings." I pause. "Philippe has ties—several ties—to the traffickers, and we think Marco does too."

She glances at Lexie. Something passes between them, and I'm not sure what it is, but I just confirmed their suspicions about Marco. That's probably what it's about.

"I expected this to come as a shock to you." I turn all my attention to Valentina, gauging her reaction. "But you don't seem very surprised."

She shrugs. "Maybe I'm not."

I wait for her to say more, to tell me about the caterer, or the pills, but she doesn't. I gaze at Lexie, who's less ashen, but still cautious—like I'm a wild card.

"Here's the thing." I glance from one woman to the other. "We have a plan to round up what we hope is the remainder of the ring, and that includes Marco. But we need your help." I pause.

"I know it's a lot to ask, Valentina. He's your husband. But we have one bite of the apple. I think you know I wouldn't ask if it wasn't important."

From the way she's behaving, I know it wasn't necessary to lay it on so thick—she's done with Marco. But I want to convince her to be part of my plan rather than go off on her own. She needs to fully buy in.

She doesn't bat an eyelash. "Anything, Rafael. What do you need me to do?"

Lexie shuts her eyes, and I see the relief. She knows Valentina has swerved away from her foolish plan. I feel a great sense of relief too.

"We need the two of you to communicate back and forth, through text. You'll feed Marco some disinformation—something that will lure him out if he's actually involved the way we think he is. We're expecting he'll contact others with the information you provide, and Tamar can trace the contacts. I'll be honest, the details of how that's going to happen are a bit high-tech. I'm sure she can explain it to you, or even Lexie can do a better job than I can. When I came upstairs, the plan was still in the early stages of development."

They both seem to be in their own heads, and I'd give anything to know what they're thinking—especially Lexie.

"I need an answer before the end of the day. Time is of the essence, and if you don't want any part of this, I get it. We'll figure something else out. If Marco isn't involved, no harm will come to him." I add this in case Valentina, who normally has a soft heart, becomes concerned about his welfare. She might be done with him, but that's different from wanting him dead.

"He's involved," my sweet niece snarls. "I wasn't surprised earlier."

She takes Lexie's hand before she proceeds to tell me the story. Caterers, hacking, pills...everything in bloodcurdling detail. It's no less chilling the second time I hear it.

Every muscle in my body is tight. I slam a clenched fist against the quartz counter when she talks about how foggy and confused she was when he drugged her. I don't give a damn what she thinks. He could have killed her. Maybe not by overdose, but she could have fallen down the stairs, or in the shower, or even off her horse.

"With your help," I say when she's through, "we can end this quickly."

"Will he go to trial in Portugal?" she asks.

Venom rushes through me. "There will be no trial, sweetheart."

"I want a trial," she demands in a way that suggests there will be no negotiation. "Marco is bitter about how his family was wrongly shamed and shunned all over Europe because of what his great-grandfather did. I want him shamed again. Death would be too good for him."

Not the kind of death I have in mind, but I don't utter a peep.

"And," she continues, "I want an opportunity to confront him after he's captured."

As long as he's in our custody, we can make it happen safely. Although I'd prefer she never shares the same air with him again. But I'm not dying on that hill. "It can be arranged."

"I don't need time to think about it. I'll do whatever you need to bring him down."

Whatever concerns Lexie had about Valentina, or about me outing her, seem to evaporate when Valentina agrees to get on board with my plan. A tear escapes from the corner of my Angel's eye, and she swipes it away, but not before I feel it in my chest.

"What about you? Are you up for a little sting operation?"

She nods. "I'm not sure anyone could possibly want those bastards more than me."

No one's more invested, that's for sure. "Okay." I slap my hands on the counter and stand. "Tamar will be coordinating your piece of the operation. When we have a better sense of exactly how this is going to work, she'll be in touch. I expect it will be sometime later today."

They nod in unison.

"I need to get back to work." I turn to Lexie. A ghost of a smile plays on her lips, and I want nothing more than to coax it out so I can bask in it forever. "Walk me to the elevator?"

She gives me a reluctant smile. "Sure."

I embrace Valentina for a long time before letting go of her. Once this is over, I hope that our relationship can be what it was—maybe stronger.

"It's not the plan you had for your life, and I'm so sorry, sweetheart. But you're strong, and there are lots of people who love you, and we'll be right by your side as you get through this. And you will."

"I know," she murmurs, standing on tiptoe to kiss my cheek. "Thank you for not giving up on me."

"That's never going to happen."

I turn to Lexie. "Ready?"

67

RAFAEL

"THANK YOU," Lexie says as we make the short trip to the elevator. "I know it wasn't easy for you to involve Valentina."

I take her hand as we walk. "Once you shoved the bit about Russo in my face and called me out for not being a modern leader, seeing the light was easier than you might think."

"Somebody had to do it," she quips with that sassy smile that makes me want to rip her clothes off.

I squeeze her hand.

When we get to the alcove where the elevator is located, I send the guard away and back Lexie into a corner, caging her with my body. "I love you." The words emerge raw and unapologetic. And they scare me more than women who chase traffickers and slip security. But I love her. It's the bottom line.

Her eyes sparkle while she traces the contour of my face with her fingertips. "You're as full of surprises as I am, Huntsman."

She snakes her arms around my neck and owns my mouth like she owns my heart.

"I'm so damn grateful you came to me even though everything was on the line for you," I rasp when we come up for breath. "I want you to do that again, and next time I'll respond better. It'll take some practice. But I'm a quick learner. I don't want to lose you." *I can't lose you.*

The emotion is thick between us, when I slide my hand into Lexie's hair and cup the back of her head, just above the nape.

"I almost ran," she whispers. "I was going to leave once I knew Valentina was okay. You were right. We're both runners."

"I'm reformed," I murmur. "Even when you said you told Valentina about the photo, I grappled with the idea of trust, but I wasn't going to run."

She tips her chin, gazing into my eyes, assessing my sincerity.

"We had a fight," I assure her. "That's all. We need to be confident that the relationship can survive arguments, big blowups—the verbal kind—because we're going to have plenty." I brush my mouth over hers in a kiss that seals my promise to fight for us.

When I pull back, a mischievous smile blooms on her face. "Is this where the several rounds of hate sex to fully recover comes in?"

Every muscle in my body uncoils, and I laugh. She might end up being my ruin, but what a way to go. I love this woman—everything about her.

"I'd drag you into that elevator and flip the switch between floors to give you a little taste of how good makeup sex can be, but I need to call your father about resources so we can end this nightmare for good. It's not over yet."

68

LEXIE

WE'RE in the command center, deep in the bowels of Huntsman Lodge. Neither Valentina nor I have been here before. But it's clear Lucas, Cristiano, Zé, Tamar, Antonio, and Rafael, who's standing behind me in a headset, are regulars.

We're all seated except for Rafael, who's talking to my father with his hands on my shoulders.

I glance at Valentina. Her head is on her father's shoulder. Antonio has a protective arm around his daughter, daring anyone to fuck with her. Once today is over, she can begin the healing process, but it's not going to be an easy road.

I'm on pins and needles as I glance around, looking for distractions as we wait for the operation to begin.

Wall screens circle the room. The three we're most interested in are directly in front of us. Marco, Philippe, and their grandfather, Laurent, will be apprehended simultaneously. The cousins will be taken prisoner in Portugal, outside a club at the beach, where they're expecting Valentina and me to show up. Laurent will be captured in Scotland by my father's men.

There's a private plane waiting at a nearby airstrip, not far from the club, to take Valentina and me to a Scottish castle paid for from the proceeds of the flesh trade. The plane will be confiscated by Rafael's soldiers too.

"Go! Go! Go!" Rafael barks into the headphones, tightening his grip on me.

There's silence in the room, as all eyes dart from one screen to another. My heart and mind race until I'm enveloped in a muted fog.

It takes the Huntsman soldiers seconds to grab Marco and Philippe, neither of whom put up a fight. But it wouldn't have mattered. They didn't stand a chance.

My father's soldiers are not faring quite as well. The castle is fortified with guards—although they were expecting it—and there are fewer shots being exchanged now. *Hopefully that's a good sign.*

Rafael's talking to someone, but it's just background noise.

My father's men used some type of diversionary device that produced a lot of smoke in the castle. It's started to dissipate, and the images from inside are becoming clearer.

The soldiers are going room to room in search of Laurent. They don't seem to be encountering any more resistance, but it's taking forever to find him.

After more time passes, the soldiers signal they can't locate him. My soul shrivels.

He's gone.

A tornado rips through me, and I want to destroy everything in sight. *The fucker escaped. How could that have happened?*

"There he is," Antonio roars, pointing to an image at the corner of the screen. The soldiers are closing in. Unless he has some type of secret passageway—castles often do—he's seconds from being apprehended.

"Zero in on that fucker," Rafael growls, and in seconds the image takes up the entire screen. *The monster of all monsters.* He's wearing a suit with an ascot and a fedora. *A fucking ascot.*

Soldiers enter the room, and Laurent lifts something off the desk—a gun. Before anyone can react, he shoves it under his chin, and blood cascades in every direction.

Valentina screams. Maybe I do too. I'm not sure. Rafael pulls me off the chair and into his side, continuing to issue orders into the headset.

I bury my face in his chest as I cling to him. His heart is racing too.

"It's over," he murmurs. "You're safe, Angel. Those fuckers are never hurting anyone again."

I begin to sob, the pent-up emotion spilling out. *It's over.* Not just for me, but for everyone. Those women, toasting and celebrating in clubs a few weeks ago, weren't safe then. But they're safe now.

I turn toward my friend, who's being comforted by her dad. She's safe too.

"It's over," Rafael whispers into my hair.

But it's not over for him. He'll be the one to decide Philippe and Marco's fate. Whether he indulges Valentina and turns them over for trial remains to be seen.

69

RAFAEL

I ASKED Lexie's mom to stay with her while I deal with Marco and Philippe. Samantha knows better than anyone what it's like to wait for days while the man you love stands on the threshold of hell, doing the devil's work—wondering if he'll return to you largely as he left, or if the toll Satan extracts for the privilege leaves anything of his soul.

It doesn't matter that my prisoners have earned a gruesome end. Killing men, especially when I'll rejoice in every cut, is evil in all its glory. There will be a price to pay for those wails and delicious screams that will soon echo in my veins.

It gives me great comfort to know Lexie's mother is with her.

I enter the cave where Marco is chained. He's still dressed, and he hasn't been beaten—yet. That won't happen until Valentina's had a chance to see him and ask whatever questions she has for him. I'm not wild about it, but I'm allowing it, especially since I won't indulge her second request.

She's not going to like it, but there will be no trial.

It's not simply that I want to mete out justice myself—although I do. I have a responsibility to my family and to our company. A trial will only prolong everyone's misery, especially Valentina's.

I'll interrogate the prisoners myself, and the men who were plotting to auction my woman off like a head of cattle will die, not on my order, but at my hand.

"Marco," I say with good cheer. "How goes it?"

He looks almost indifferent, and doesn't respond.

"In case you're wondering, this is the cave where we question prisoners. Can you see the difference?" I point toward the wall where the implements of torture hang.

Still nothing.

Valentina will be here shortly, and I pull on his bindings to make sure he can't hurt her. I'm rough about it, and he winces, which gives me great pleasure.

"If you beat me," he sneers, "I'll make sure I tell the authorities about it."

"Beat me"? You're getting a lot more than a beating, asshole. I smirk. "Oh dear. I hate to disappoint you, but the only authority you'll be speaking to is me."

The wheels are turning now. He's drawing conclusions. Soon he'll begin to barter.

"I have information about the buyers that will help get back some of the women. But I'll only speak to Interpol."

Interpol? Not a fucking chance.

My knife is calling to me. Fortunately, I left it outside the cave. I knew I'd be too tempted to use it prematurely. I don't want Valentina to live with the bloody image of her soon-to-be deceased husband.

"Abducting and auctioning innocent women must have made you feel like a powerful man. But let me tell you something." I grab him by the throat. "Before you take your last breath, you're going to tell me everything you know." I let go of him before I crush his windpipe. "Everything."

The door opens, and Antonio comes in with Valentina, who

looks a bit wan but otherwise like herself. She's been staying at her parents' house, and her mother has been fussing over her, which has helped.

Antonio, however, is not happy. He thinks this is a worse idea than I do, but Daniela, like Lexie, thinks it'll be good for Valentina.

I hope they're right.

I meet them halfway. "You don't have to do this, *menina*."

"I want to. He took so much from me. He's not taking my opportunity to confront him."

"He's all yours," I say, motioning toward the prisoner.

She squares her shoulders and marches toward her husband, head high.

Good for her.

Antonio starts to follow, and I grab his arm to stop him. "He's bound securely. He can't hurt her. Let her go."

He snorts like a rabid dog, but he doesn't move.

"I want some time with him too," Antonio snarls.

"We can do that."

"I didn't ask for your permission," he hisses.

"Valentina," Marco murmurs as soon as she approaches. "Thank God you're here. I'm being set up. You know how much your family hates me."

She doesn't say a word while he blathers.

"We can move away from here. Just us. We'll be so happy. You know how much I love you."

He's desperate. But Valentina is patient. She has all the cards, and she knows it. I see it in the way she carries herself.

Maybe this was a good idea.

Although it hasn't changed Antonio's mind. He's a restless bear, and I don't know how long I'm going to be able to hold him back.

"I set you up," she informs him proudly. "Do you know why, Marco?"

"Why would you take their side? I love you."

"Love me?" she sneers. "You drugged me. And you tried to fuck up the launch I cared so much about. You gaslighted me. You made me feel like I was having some kind of breakdown. And if that wasn't bad enough, you traffic women!" she shouts. "You were going to traffic my best friend. I set you up, you monster, and I hope you burn in hell."

"You're a stupid whore." He spits on her.

You fucker. You just bought yourself more suffering than even I had planned.

We're done.

"Stay right here," I say to Antonio as I rush toward her, but he doesn't listen. I stop when she starts in my direction. "She's finished," I mutter to her father. "Let it be on her terms."

Valentina takes a few more steps and pivots to reach the wooden club we use to subdue prisoners when we're chaining them. Without a glance in our direction, she strides toward the prisoner and takes a healthy swing at his knees.

Marco howls, and she takes another swing and another. His bindings are so tight he can't even thrash to escape the impact. He's at her mercy.

She bats at him like he's a piñata, and catches his balls. "Ouch," Antonio snickers, and I snicker, too, as Marco's screams vibrate off the walls.

Neither Antonio nor I move a muscle while she takes her revenge.

When she's had enough, she returns the club to its place against the wall and comes over to us. She's shaking and sweating, and her father wraps her in an embrace.

"Do whatever you want with him," she tells me. "Whatever is best for Premier. I don't care what happens as long as he burns in hell."

"Let's go," Antonio says, wrapping a gentle arm around her.

She pulls away from her father before they get to the exit

and turns to me. "I have something for Lexie." She reaches into her shirt and pulls out a familiar chain—and the angel wings.

My heart stops. If Valentina has the tracker, then Lexie doesn't. *For how long?*

"Lexie made me take it. She was worried I'd put myself in danger, and that I'd be..." Her voice trails off, but the image of her being abducted hangs heavy in the air, weighed down by Marco's occasional yelps. "I'm sure she misses it. Tell her I don't need it anymore."

I take the necklace and slip it in my pocket. "I will."

I'll process this later, when those fuckers are in hell.

70

LEXIE

RAFAEL'S BEEN GONE ALMOST a week. I haven't spoken with him since he left.

I know what it means when these men disappear into the caves for days. It doesn't happen often, but when it does, they return in tatters. At least my father always did.

I'm not sure how I would have coped without my mother for company. She fed me breakfast, sent me to work for half a day, and then did her best to distract me with movies and shopping and sightseeing. But despite her heroic attempts, all I thought about was Rafael, and the turmoil twisting inside him, as he dances with the devil.

Mum left this morning, and it's deathly quiet—just me and my soul-crushing thoughts. Without Rafael's larger-than-life presence, the apartment is a mausoleum, desolate, with a pervasive sense of loneliness and despair. It's almost unbearable. I could have gone to Daniela and Antonio's with Valentina, but I want to be here when he comes home.

"You need to be patient," my mother reminded me when she hugged me goodbye. "He's going to need you. Take good care of yourself while he's gone, so that when he returns, you'll be strong enough to take care of him."

"How? How do I do that?" I pleaded, desperation choking every syllable.

"You accept the man who returns to you. You allow your love to heal his wounds, and you embrace the scars. If you can't do that," she touched my cheek, "then you don't belong with him. If you stay, you'll be miserable every day of your life. So will he. I don't want that for you, darling."

This life hasn't been easy for my parents, and I know it won't be easy for us either.

I've always considered myself a strong person. I know how to dig in my heels and fight. But what she described feels more like a war than a brawl, and Rafael already has so many festering wounds and scars.

My love might not be enough to get us through.

I'M READING in bed when I hear the apartment door shut. I've been praying for this all week. Yet, I don't move. I'm not sure I even breathe.

My heart pounds as the familiar footsteps approach the bedroom.

When a haggard Rafael appears in the doorway, I leap out of bed and into his open arms. "I've been so worried about you. I love you," I repeat over and over, clinging to him.

He holds me for an eternity without a single word, while I pray that he's not irreparably broken and that my love will be the balm that heals his soul.

His heart hammers as I comb my fingers through his wet hair. *How many showers did it take to scrub the blood off his skin? Too damn many.*

"I need you," he mutters, carrying me to the bed and laying

me gently on the mattress.

He's not a man who does gentle, but everything about him seems subdued. *Flat.* Devoid of any spark or color.

His eyes are lifeless craters, circled in black, the shadows slithering behind them. He looks exhausted, but not beaten. There's no defeat, just disquiet. It sits heavy in my chest—and on my shoulders.

With the silence growing louder, Rafael strips off his clothes, leaving them where they land. He removes something from a pocket before joining me in bed.

"This is yours," he murmurs. "Valentina said to tell you she doesn't need it anymore."

He starts to put the necklace on me, but his hands are shaking, and he can't manage the clasp. My stomach clenches. The only time I've seen his hands shake is during sex, when he's struggling for control.

I take the chain from him and put it on.

"Why did you give it to her?" he asks, brushing the hair away from my eyes so he can see the truth.

"She was in grave danger, and I worried she was going to get caught up in something and we'd need to find her."

"You were in grave danger too. Trust me. But you knew that," he says carefully, "yet you gave your tracker to her."

I lift a shoulder.

"Why?"

"I knew if she had it, there'd be a good chance you'd be able to find her if she went missing. I-I-I didn't want another woman you loved to disappear. I couldn't bear the thought of that happening to you again."

This conversation is too much, and the swell of emotion is beginning to crest.

"Do you think it would be any different if you disappeared? Do you think I'd be any less distraught?" His voice is a rasp with a desperate edge.

I did think that.

"I wouldn't be." He pauses. "If something happened to you, it would be like my beating heart ripped from my chest." The passion is back. It doesn't tiptoe in. It roars. "Don't ever give those wings to anyone, Angel. No one's safety is more important to me than yours."

He nudges me onto my back, kneeing my thighs apart, and crawls on top of me, his cock wedged between us. I hook my legs around his hips, digging my heels into his muscular ass, to pull him closer. *I love this man with every cell of my body.*

In one graceful move, he rears up, then lowers himself, plunging into the depths of me. His groan is low, primal and raw, as he slides, sheathing himself inside my walls—giving me everything that's too heavy to bear. *Everything.*

I accept it all. The pain. The torment. The hatred. The lack of remorse. I take every last remnant of his vengeance. *Everything.*

As he ruts deep, I anchor myself on the precipice, between him and the devil who wants his soul. *You can't have it. It belongs to me.*

The sweat drips from him, while I cradle his face in my hands. "Come back to me, Rafael." It's not a plea but a demand. "You're mine. I love you, and I'm not giving you up."

Something in his eyes stirs at my voice, and his thrusts become less violent. Less tortured.

Braced on his forearms, he rolls his hips, and finds my mouth with a kiss that robs me of all breath. *Don't leave me,* it pleads. *I love you. I need you. Let me take care of you.* The whispers linger long after our lips part.

Rafael gazes at me with a love that's all-encompassing—ferocious, demanding, and unapologetic—but not smothering. It might not be for everyone, but I'm home—and so is he.

Right then, I know for certain that we're both reformed runners.

EPILOGUE I

18 Months Later

Rafael

"WE NEED TO TALK," Lexie murmurs, as I step onto the terrace of the home we moved into three months ago. There's no hello. No music. No sass. No kiss that starts out innocent and ends with me ripping off her clothes. Nothing but the uncertainty in her voice, and a vibe that makes my skin prickle.

"What's going on?" I watch her pour bourbon into two etched tumblers. *She doesn't drink bourbon.* But since there's no one else here, I assume the talk she wants is one that requires the extra *oomph* that dirty water provides.

I don't let my imagination run free. I don't allow myself to think about a single possibility, as I take the bottle from her trembling hands and replace it with a tumbler.

With a fingertip tracing the curved rim, she bows her head and stares into the amber liquid as if summoning courage.

"Hey." I tip her chin up, so I can read those expressive eyes. But all I see is more uncertainty, cloaked in a nervous edge. I feel her torment in the pit of my stomach. "What's wrong, Angel?"

She doesn't utter a word. *She's conflicted. I see it in her face. I feel it in my bones.*

The silence is blistering, and it's becoming difficult to rein in my imaginings. This doesn't feel like *I'm sick*, or *I want us to live in London.* This is different. But I can't put my finger on it.

"Say whatever it is you have to say, Lexie. I'm a big boy, and I doubt there's anything you can say that will surprise me." *At least I hope to fuck not.*

She takes my hand, still cupping her chin, and squeezes the fingers as she gazes into my face. Her neck ripples as she swallows. "I might have found a link to your mother."

It takes me—I'm not sure how long—to process. It's akin to slogging through a swamp, pitch black, with deadly snakes and other poisonous creatures nipping at my heels as I trod. But I can't move faster and there's no escape.

I might have found a link to your mother. I'm not sure what I feel. I'm not even sure I feel anything at all. It's not the celebratory moment I expected.

She lowers our joined hands to her heart.

My head is swimming and my lungs aren't functioning in a way that's compatible with life.

I fed your whore mother to the dogs, my father sneered at me, seconds before his brain was splattered onto his office wall. Even ten years later, it haunts me. Not his death, but his words.

"Might have?" I zero in not on the possibility that I could soon know what happened to my mother, but on the possibility that it's another dead end. Maybe it's because I've chased so many leads into alleys that went nowhere, or maybe it's because I don't want to know. *I'm afraid to know.*

What if the truth is something more painful than the unknown? *Is that even possible?* What if she wasn't the saint I remember? Will the shrine I built, inside my head, implode, leaving craters that never heal? *Not even with Lexie's love.*

She nods.

"Let's sit." My voice is strained to the point where I almost don't recognize it. I take her hand and somehow lead her to a chaise, where I sit with my legs up and pull her onto my lap, holding her against my chest. *I need her warmth to chase away the pervasive chill rattling my bones.*

"Talk to me, Angel."

"I took over the case file a year and a half ago. Tamar had her hands full and it left so little time to work on anything not directly related to Premier."

Maybe by design. My subconscious protecting me from news that would wreck me. News that would make me weak. Vulnerable to my enemies.

"I asked to work on the case." She rubs her palm up and down my forearm as if to soothe me, but it's not working. "I wanted you to have closure. I couldn't bear the thought of you ending up like my father, plagued with questions until his last days. Are you angry with me?"

"Of course not," I reply, because it's a rational response and the right thing to say. But in truth, there's a small part of me that is angry.

I'm two men. One furious, aching to lash out, and another who's numb inside—feeling nothing as he goes through the motions of a conversation he doesn't want to have. I'm standing on a strip between them, one foot on either side, teetering over a snake pit, and holding onto the word *might* for dear life—even though something inside knows that I'll soon have answers. *Ready or not.*

I run my mouth over her hair. I can't stop touching her. It's as though I'm a tiny boy toying with the ribbon on my blanket when my father's voice gets too loud.

I can't indulge myself in this way. It's making me weak.

"Lexie, I need to get up. It doesn't have anything to do with you. I just need a little space while we talk."

I ease her off my lap, onto the chaise, and take a seat nearby, resting my forearms on the generous wooden arms and my feet on the flagstone to ground myself. "What did you find? Tell me everything."

She folds her legs like a pretzel, struggling to get comfortable. "I combed through everything Lucas did—Antonio and his team were thorough and methodical. They left no stone unturned."

Lucas, on Antonio's order, searched for the better part of a decade. Antonio looked too, as did Cristiano, and my Aunt Lydia. Later, Zé and I searched, chasing down every clue, but we came up empty. When Tamar got involved, my mother had been gone for so long that it seemed fruitless to examine the same dead leads. Besides, by that point, I was tired of bad news, so I found other things for Tamar to do. *That's the truth.*

"Once I retraced everyone's steps, without any luck," Lexie continues, her face pale, but every word spoken with respect and empathy, "I opened a new file and started from the beginning."

Zé and I did that, too. We looked at everything with fresh eyes—took nothing at face value.

"Your mother was well-known in all corners of the valley. So many people loved her. It would have been impossible to send her away without anyone knowing where. Even if your father killed her—someone would have known something."

The frustration in her voice is one I experienced many times too—we all did.

"I felt strongly," she continues, "that money had to have changed hands, somewhere, to buy that kind of silence."

Unless he fed her to the dogs.

"Do you remember Vincente Costa, who worked for your Uncle Hugo and your father?"

Vincente Costa. The man who would drag me to the attic without a consoling word, after my father beat me. I was a little boy, terrified of the attic, but he never once showed me any kindness. I hope he's rotting in hell.

"Yeah. I remember him."

"He paid off his mortgage two days after your mother went missing, and his brother Afonso's house was paid off eight days later."

What? Why didn't we know about this? "How do you know?"

"Because all the records are now online."

Fuck. She's right.

For centuries, real estate transactions in Porto and the Douro Valley were subject to arcane laws because property history was often hard to trace in a way that satisfied both buyers and sellers. Sales took forever to be completed, if they were able to be completed at all. There was no such thing as clear title or a quick sale.

A law was passed five years ago, requiring local government and banks operating in the Douro Valley to put all real estate transactions from the last seventy-five years online, to make it easier to buy and sell property. Unless they were given special dispensation, the process had to be completed by the end of last year.

"How did you access the bank information?"

"The usual way."

Meaning either she or Tamar, or perhaps Lucas, hacked into it.

"Who paid off the mortgages?"

"The money was funneled to Vincente through a company called H.A.H. When I asked about it, Lucas told me it was a shell company that belonged to your Uncle Hugo. It no longer exists, but he was able to dig up the ledgers, and I eventually matched a payment made to Vincente a few days before your mother disappeared—although I couldn't find any direct payment to Afonso."

Direct payment. But you found something. "What do you mean direct?"

"Afonso had a five-thousand-dollar mortgage. Vincente probably paid him from his own proceeds. I found the withdrawal, but no record of a deposit."

"How much was the payment to Vincente?"

"Thirty thousand euros."

My mother's death was bought for thirty thousand fucking euros. *Don't get ahead of yourself, Rafael. She hasn't said one definitive thing.*

"Lucas also said that Vincente Costa was someone who your father would have turned to if he needed help—with that sort of thing," she adds in a whisper.

No question. "I don't disagree. But Afonso didn't work for either my father or Hugo."

"No. He was a farmer."

"Is he still alive?" *Say yes. Give me something to hold on to. Someone to torture.*

She sighs. "No. But his wife, Maria Elena, is still alive. She lives up north, in the same house."

"Did you contact her?"

She shakes her head. "No."

"If Antonio's team had the ledgers all along, why wasn't the payment discovered before now?"

"The dates on the transactions—at least how they were entered into the ledger—didn't correspond with any kind of reality. Your father and uncle used that company to hide things in plain sight. They falsified the dates using a code."

A code—Lexie's specialty. They were evil, but they weren't stupid. "And you cracked the code."

She nods.

"Who else knows about this?"

"Lucas has some details, and I expect that means Antonio does too. But other than us, the only person who knows everything is Tamar. I was doing official Premier business, and I had to tell her. Besides, I wanted to run it by someone we both trusted before I brought it to you. What if I was wrong?" She draws a long, shaky breath. "I thought it should be your decision about whether to contact Afonso's wife, and Tamar agreed."

Lexie takes a piece of paper out of her pocket, and hands it to me. "This is the address."

I unfold the paper and stare at the swirls and scrawls, before sliding it into my back pocket. *The answers I've searched for my entire life were less than forty kilometers away the whole time.*

My first inclination is to turn over the bar cart and watch the glass shatter against the stone. But it was a housewarming present from Valentina, and Lexie will be crushed if I destroy it.

"I need some air."

She doesn't comment on the fact that we're in an open-air terrace. "I'll come with you."

"No." I shake my head, and touching her arm, I press a kiss to her forehead. "I need some time, alone, to decide what to do."

"Please don't go by yourself to see her," she pleads, reaching for my hand. "Take me with you. I'll wait in the car."

"I don't even know if I'm going." *It's a lie I tell both of us.*

"I love you," she says, not calling me on my bullshit. There's no pity in her voice or in her face. Just strength and resolve. "I need you to come back to me."

"Always," I assure her, going back through the house, my thoughts and emotions tangled in my head.

Before I reach the garage, I've made my decision. Despite what I said earlier, it was always a foregone conclusion.

"SENHORA COSTA?" I say to the hunched woman who comes to the door with a cane. She appears to be well into her seventies —perhaps older.

"Yes."

"My name is Rafael Huntsman. I believe you have information about my mother."

She nods and steps aside. "Come in, *senhor*."

It's almost as though she's been waiting for me.

I follow her through the spotless, modest house. When we get to a small parlor, she points to a chair for me to sit. "Would you like a coffee or perhaps some cheese and wine?"

It's customary to accept food and drink from the host, but I'm not here for refreshments. I shake my head. "Tell me what you know about my mother's disappearance."

She sighs deeply and lowers herself to a chair perpendicular to where I'm seated. "My husband, Afonso, was Vincente Costa's younger brother."

I draw a breath to steady my nerves.

"Afonso was a good man—not like his brother."

I'll be the judge of whether he was a good man, not you.

"His one flaw is that he did everything Vincente asked. Everything. And Vincente was a bad man."

She's right. The son of a bitch did my uncle's dirty work and later my father's. But I don't give a shit about the Costa family dynamics. "*Senhora*, I've waited a long time for news about my mother. Get to the point."

"Vincente was ordered to kill your mother and dispose of the body. For his loyalty—and I'm sure his silence—your father agreed to pay off his house and to give him some additional money so he could take his wife on a trip. I don't know if any other arrangements were made."

A trip. I can barely breathe.

She fiddles with a small gold cross that hangs from a chain around her neck, while her lips move like she's saying a silent prayer. It's as though she needs divine assistance to finish the story. When she's done, she peers up at me.

"Vincente was always greedy, and he decided to sell your mother instead of killing her."

So he could double-dip. Rage swoops in, and it takes everything I have not to wrap my hands around the old woman's neck and strangle her.

"Your mother had two babies and she wasn't so young, anymore," Afonso's widow continues, "but she was from an important family, married to an important man. Vincente believed he could get good money for her in a Spanish brothel near the border."

I white-knuckle the arms of the chair to keep myself seated, because if I murder her now, I'll never know my mother's fate.

"He brought her here one afternoon. I saw the brothers carry a cage covered with a green quilt into the old barn. My husband told me that Vincente was selling a calf and he needed to store it here for a few days. The barn was dilapidated. We didn't use it for animals anymore."

Not good enough for animals, but good enough for my mother.

I want vengeance. *Ache for it.*

The worst of the culprits are dead. My father, my uncle, and the Costa brothers—all gone. *She's here.* I've never taken my knife to a woman—although today might be the day. The craving claws at me until I'm nothing more than a ball of fury waiting to roll right over this bitch.

"I'm just a woman, but I knew that even skittish calves are not transported in cages. When I asked Afonso about it, he brushed me off like I didn't know anything about cattle. But he was so nervous, he was sweating as he spoke. I didn't believe him. I knew Vincente was up to something."

I'm jonesing for her to get to the end, but she needs to tell me the entire story, and I need to hear it.

"After Afonso was asleep, I went to the old barn and lifted the blanket off the cage." She grips the arm of the chair. "Your mother was chained inside, naked, with her mouth covered in tape. I froze when I saw her. Vincente had dragged my husband into his filth before, but nothing like that."

I brace my elbows on my thighs and cover my face. *This is a fucking nightmare.*

"I recognized your mother—at least I thought I did. Such a beautiful, kind woman treated like an animal. As I pulled off the tape from her mouth, I began to cry."

"But you did nothing to help her," I spit out. "Just gave her a few tears."

"We made a plan for the next day," she replies immediately. "I was to go to the open-air market in the morning. Your Aunt Lydia's maid, Alma, shopped there a few times a week. I was to find Alma and tell her everything, so that Lydia could help."

This is on par with Valentina and Lexie concocting a plan to bring down Marco. "Lydia? What could she have possibly done against my father and my uncle?"

"Your mother was sure her sister would know what to do. It's not like I could go to the police. They wouldn't have gone against your family. Your mother didn't want the authorities involved—she was sure we'd all end up dead if we involved them."

It's probably true. Not probably—it is true.

"Did Vincente come back before you could tell Alma?" If she had told Alma, my Aunt Lydia would have known, and she didn't.

She shakes her head. "During the night, a bad storm came through with furious thunderclaps and lightning that lit the sky for miles. It was as though God unleashed his wrath."

Something I'm seconds from doing.

"Before I left for the market," she continues, "I snuck into the barn to bring her some breakfast. She didn't wake up when I pulled off the quilt and called her name."

I hold my breath, bracing myself for the news that I've been dreading since I was eight years old.

"As I looked closer, your mother seemed stiff." She pauses. "There was no new damage to the structure, but lightning might have struck through an open window, although it was probably a ground current. We'd lost livestock that way."

Struck by lightning in a barn not fit for animals. I clench my fists, my jaw ticcing wildly.

"I ran to get my husband. Afonso cut the lock on the cage, but your mother was already with God." She makes the sign of the cross. "May her soul rest in peace."

With God? Fuck that. What kind of God takes a mother from a child and leaves him with monsters?

An image of my mother pops into my head—the last time I saw her. She's smiling, her hand on my shoulder as she sets a plate of homemade sausage and eggs in front of me. "Rafael, *meu amour*, eat everything on your plate so that you can run fast on the soccer field and score lots of goals."

She was a great mother. A great woman. Selfless. Kind and loving. Nothing Maria Elena Costa told me changes those facts. *Nothing.*

But there will be no vengeance for me. As much as I'd like to flay someone, alive, it won't be this woman. I make the decision not for my soul, but to honor my mother, who would want me to spare her. Maria Elena Costa helped in the best way she knew, in the face of powerful men who would have killed her as easily as they would have killed my mother.

"What happened to her body?"

"Vincente and Afonso buried her at the edge of the woods and put a covered fence over the area so that animals wouldn't dig up her remains. After Vincente left, I made my husband dig her up and we took her body to the Church of the Immaculate Conception. We buried her in a pauper's grave. I have a yearly Mass for her soul on the anniversary of her death, and for years I kept the area around the grave in good condition. But now—" She points at her legs.

"Did the priest know who she was or what had happened?" Because if so, I'll burn that goddamn church to the ground.

"I don't think so. We told him that she was a woman who had run from her husband and took shelter in the barn."

"Where in the cemetery is the grave?"

She gets up, and I follow her to a small decorative table with a statue of the Blessed Virgin, a prayer candle, and a Bible. She opens the Bible and pulls out the coordinates of the burial site, and presses the paper into my hand.

"Take care of her," she says softly. "She was a good woman."

I don't know whether to thank her or to bury my knife in her chest. In the end, I do neither.

As I open the door to leave, *Senhora* Costa tells me one last thing. "Your mother spoke of you and your brother that night. She worried that your father had his hooks too deep into your brother. At first, she contemplated suicide, so as not to involve her sister. She was worried about Lydia going up against her husband and your father. But in the end, she couldn't bear to leave you. She loved you, and your brother too, but while she feared it was too late for him, she believed you could still be saved."

Up until now, I've managed to swallow the emotion, by rolling it in vitriol, but it's precariously close to getting the better of me.

I turn and leave without another word.

NOT SURE HOW I got to the cemetery. It's a blur.

She believed you could still be saved. It's all I allow myself to think about—the idea of her dying alone, in a cage, is too much to take in right now.

I pull up in front of the unassuming white church and get out of the car. No one's around to stop me. Not that anyone could stop me. I have a purpose now, and that purpose is helping to keep the worst of my emotions in check, but it wouldn't take much to derail me.

The frogs are croaking as I go around back to the cemetery. With a heavy heart, I scale the fence, and follow the coordinates to my mother.

It doesn't take me long to find her.

The grave consists of a flat stone that the earth has grown around, almost swallowing the humble marker. It doesn't have her name, just the words Loving Mother and the date of her death.

I plant my feet—more uncomfortable than I've ever been—unsure what to do. I'm not the kind of man who prays. God isn't a part of my life.

Eventually, I lower myself to my haunches and gently wipe the dust from the stone. *Loving Mother.*

She was.

When my thighs ache from the crouched position, I sink down into the unkempt grass. The silence is uneasy as I struggle to find my way.

The moon is a glowing crescent and the stars shine bright, too, but they have no answers for me, and they offer no guidance.

"I've missed you," I whisper, in a quiet prayer. "I hope you're somewhere safe with Tia Lydia and Maria Rosa for company. Somewhere where no one can hurt you."

I feel the sting behind my eyes, and on a sniff, I push it away.

"You have a granddaughter," I continue, telling her about

Valentina. "She's beautiful and sweet and looks so much like you that sometimes it takes my breath away."

At first, I have trouble forming the words, but once I start, they come spilling out.

"I met a woman. Her name is Alexis Clarke. Everyone calls her Lexie, but I call her Angel. She's beautiful, and courageous, and full of goodness and spunk. Her soul is a lot like yours. Actually, she's so much like you—or at least what I imagine you would have been like if you'd been allowed to follow your heart and speak your mind. You'd love her."

I'm quiet for a while, until the heaviness in my chest returns, as though there's more I need to tell her.

"I don't hurt women or children, but I'm not a good man." It's hard to admit, because she wanted that for me. "It's not my destiny. Although even with all my flaws, and I have plenty, I do have honor. You weren't here to save me, but Antonio stepped in. He taught me to be the kind of man that would, mostly, make you proud."

The sky gets dark, before the rain begins. It's just a drizzle, but even so, my shirt eventually sticks to my body. But I don't move from the ground.

I sit with her for hours, sometimes in silence, sometimes sharing bits and pieces of my life as though she's actually here. It's nearly dawn when Lexie finds me.

My Angel approaches gingerly and sits beside me, lacing her fingers through mine. Neither of us speaks for a long time. The silence is respectful, almost reverent.

"You shouldn't have come out here alone," I chide, softly.

"I didn't. Tamar and Zé are with me."

I look over my shoulder, and my best soldiers, my friends, keep watch, in the distance.

"Come here," I murmur, pulling Lexie between my legs and wrapping my arms around her. "I love you."

She squeezes me. "I love you too. I hoped to bring you peace. Not pain. I never wanted that."

"To get to the peace, I need to go through the pain. I'm not there yet, but a small part of me is already beginning to feel lighter." I press a kiss to the back of her head, inhaling her scent. "Thank you."

The rain starts to come down harder, and while it's cleansing, it's also cool, and I don't want Lexie drenched. "I've been here a long time. Why don't we go home?"

She nods, and I stand and pull her up off the ground. Snaking an arm around her waist, I drag her to my side, where she belongs.

Before we reach the exit, I glance over my shoulder, one last time.

The cemetery doesn't have enough shade trees and her grave is too low. I'm sure it floods when it rains for more than a day. She deserved better in life, and she deserves better in death.

I was too young to save her then—but I can take care of her now.

EPILOGUE II

Eight years later

Lexie

WE'RE VISITING my parents in London when I get a text from Valentina with the confirmation I've been waiting for before I blab the news to Rafael. He's huddling with my dad, and although my father hasn't threatened to put a bullet in him in ages, I'm still sure he'd like to be saved.

The library door is ajar, and when I hear my father make an offer, I stop myself from knocking.

"I'm dead serious," my father says pointedly. "I want you to take over my business. There's no one I trust more not to fuck it up."

My father isn't prone to hyperbole, nor is he effusive in his praise. It took some effort, but they've forged a strong relationship over the last several years based on mutual respect and their love for me. I couldn't be happier.

Dad's right about my brilliant, sexy husband being the right man to take over for him. Rafael has the Huntsman empire humming. Sure, there are plenty of headaches, but he's a modern leader with twenty-first century ideals that the company and the industry desperately needed.

"I'm flattered," Rafael replies, "but my business is in Porto. Too many people depend on me. I can't move to London."

"I suspected you were going to say that. What if you put someone you trust here, and you manage the big picture from Porto. It would require frequent trips to London, but you own a damn fleet of planes. Besides, it'll make Samantha happy to have everyone here more often."

Only Samantha? I cover my mouth to suppress the chuckle. The truth is no one would be happier than Dad to have us in London more frequently.

"I could put Zé and Tamar here," Rafael replies, after some time passes. "It would be a great opportunity for him and easier for Tamar to visit her family from here. Her parents aren't getting any younger."

"Zé is exactly who I was thinking about, too. He's been with you a long time. Think he'd be willing to change gears?"

"Before we get too far down this road, you need to make the same offer to your daughter that you made to me."

"Are you out of your fucking mind?" my father roars. "Just when I think you have some goddamn sense, you say something stupid. Do you think I want this filth all over my daughter? Is that what you want for her?" *Some things never change.*

"It's her birthright," Rafael replies flatly, in that calm way he has when he's made up his mind. "She's an adult, and she doesn't mind a little dirt. But it's up to her. I won't agree to anything until she's been given a chance to step into your shoes."

I love this man with every fiber of my being.

"Lexie's smart and tough. I'll give you that. But she doesn't have the experience necessary to take over something of this magnitude."

"She's more capable than you think, and she can learn like anybody else. Neither of us ascended to power with a fucking clue."

"You really think she wants to be a crime boss?" my father hisses.

"Ask her."

I knock when I've heard enough.

"Come in," my father calls.

"I came to see if you two are playing nicely, or if a stint in time-out is necessary."

Rafael gifts me with a panty-melting smirk, and I squeeze his shoulder, before I take the seat beside him.

"I'm glad you're here," Dad says, albeit reluctantly. He knows Rafa's not budging, and he's cornered. "I want to talk to you about something."

"Is everything okay?" I ask, handing Rafael my phone with the text that Valentina sent.

I turn to him, and grin as he makes sense of the sonogram images. When he does, his face lights up and he reaches over to squeeze my wrist.

It took some time for her to trust again, but even before she was quite there, she met a man who was everything she didn't know she needed. They're having a daughter, who will be born a few weeks after our daughter.

"Are you two going to play lovey-dovey, or can I have a moment of your time, Lexie?"

"Of course," I reply, sitting up. "I'm listening.

"A girl," I mouth to my husband, before turning my attention to my impatient father.

"I'm ready, or at least I will be in the next year, to turn over my business. Is leading a criminal enterprise something you'd be interested in doing?"

Rafael rubs an incredulous palm down his face, and I burst out laughing. "Well, when you put it that way, how can I resist?"

Dad glares at Rafael, who is much too amused for his own good.

"I'm not interested in taking over your enterprise. I have a lot on my plate, but..." Now I have their rapt attention. "I'd like a piece."

Rafael shifts in his seat, and I can feel his eyes on me, but he doesn't say a word.

My father looks like he just took a big bite of raw liver, and he doesn't even know I'm pregnant. "What piece would that be?" he asks, carefully.

I twirl the beautiful engagement ring on my finger. It was the ring my grandfather gave Lydia when he asked her to marry him. One of the prongs had come loose, and it was at the jeweler when she died. Antonio held onto it for more than a decade. Right before we got engaged, he gave it to Rafael, insisting his mother would want me to have it. I was honored, and I wear it proudly every day. It reminds me of Grandma Lydia and everything she believed in. *We have a moral imperative to make the world better for women, safer, especially those of us with so much.*

I meet my father's probing gaze. "I'd like to work on efforts to end human trafficking. I already do that through Huntsman Industries, and I'd love to expand my efforts to the UK."

Rafael isn't crazy about my work, but most of it's behind the scenes and I'm exceedingly careful to stay out of the spotlight. He rarely protests because he knows it's not just a job, it's my calling. And more than anything, he wants me to be happy and fulfilled.

"Dangerous business." My father flashes Rafael a threatening look.

"Especially for the victims," I reply, with all the cheekiness he expects from me.

Before I can say another word, two young boys and their little sister barge into the library.

"I didn't hear a knock," I say, brow raised.

"They don't need to knock in this house," my father mutters, smiling at the little darlings. He's much more permissive with them than he ever was with me.

"*Papai*," six-year-old Liam, who looks just like his daddy, cries. "We finished lunch. We were so polite, Grandma gave us a cupcake."

"A cupcake at lunch?" my husband gasps, his mouth twitching.

"Just a small one." Liam uses his fingers to demonstrate how tiny the treat was.

If he's to be believed, my mother's stocking cupcakes for mice.

"Did you save me one?" I ask.

My big boy nods with a sparkle in his eye that's so much like his father's. "The lemon one with a rose. It's beautiful." He's almost as good to me as his father is. "Can we go outside now?"

Rafael promised the kids he'd take them out after lunch. He never breaks a promise, not to me, and certainly not to them.

I smile. "When the adults are finished talking."

My father beckons Liam over and gives him a hug that makes my heart swell. "We're done talking."

Not to be outdone, two-year-old Marina is clamoring for some attention from her favorite mark. Rafael scoops her onto his lap and presses a kiss to her forehead. "Are you ready to go outside, *cara linda*?"

"Yes!" she giggles, batting her eyelashes at her *papai*, who she has wrapped around her finger.

Rafael reaches his hand out to our four-year-old, who's always a bit shy on the day we arrive. "Should we play some football?"

Antonio's little head bobs up and down as he gazes up adoringly at his father with eyes the color of Valentina's and his Grandma Vera's.

"All right, then. Time to go outside." Rafael stands, and hoists Marina onto his shoulders, then turns to me. "Work out the details with your father." He glances at Dad. "We'll talk more after the kids are in bed tonight."

After I steal a few kisses from my babies, and one from their hot-as-sin dad, the boys follow Rafael out of the library like he's the Pied Piper.

I place a protective hand on my belly and smile until my cheeks ache. Not about the work I'm about to convince my father to allow me to do, although that makes me very happy. But about the best man I know, who makes my ovaries explode every time I watch him with our kids. They bring out the best in him, and he brings out the best in them.

Rafael is living proof that being an amazing husband and father isn't about what's in your genes, or the role models you've had—it's about what's in your heart and soul. *Another thing he and my father have in common.*

I glance out the window at my husband playing with our children, and then at my dad. Two powerful men who have helped me become a strong, independent woman, despite their fear for my safety. One, by example, and the other, by embracing me as I am—both loving me beyond measure.

THANK YOU FOR READING! If you loved A Sinful Empire, you'll also love JD and Gabrielle's story: Depraved

A FINAL WORD FROM EVA

First, thank you for sticking with the series, and with me! I hope you loved the twisted journey!

A Sinful Empire was a passion project, conceived in the wine caves of Porto, and born from the darkest corners of my soul. I often bled on the pages, and I shed plenty of tears as I wrote. I love these characters with all my heart, and it was a great joy to tell their stories of love, passion, evil, courage, and fear—angels and demons—cloaked in power and powerlessness.

Throughout the series, I explored the facets of power, with its myriad definitions and qualities—seizing power, joining power, fear of power, demanding power, lack of power, sharing power, and empowerment. It's a complex idea, nuanced, with subtleties that are easily overlooked. While I wrote, I often asked myself: Who really has the power? The answer often surprised me.

My next stop is Kentucky, where Bourbon is king and dynasties rule. Jake is a self-made billionaire, a country boy at heart, and arguably, the most tortured antihero I've written to date. He grew up poor, did a stint in jail, and after he accumulates vast wealth, he returns home to settle a score. Jake's willing to do whatever it takes to exact vengeance, including destroying the daughter of his arch-enemy—although she has a plan of her own.

For up-to-date information about me and my work, sneak peeks, exclusive giveaways, and fun, I invite you to join my newsletter Eva's Monthly News and my AMAZING Reader Group JD's Closet!

xoxo
Eva

ACKNOWLEDGMENTS

I'm honored and blessed to have so many fabulous people on my team and in my corner. I am forever grateful for your kindness, generosity, wisdom, and support. Thank you to everyone who helped bring A Sinful Empire to life!

An enormous, super colossal thank you to Dawn Alexander for guiding me through the process with the utmost patience and good humor. You kept me on track and honest, and when it felt like the timeline for Envy, and later for Wrath, was closing in too quickly, your encouragement and faith in my ability to finish, helped restore my faith too. Thank you from the bottom of my heart!

A big thank you to James Gallagher for meticulously editing Pride and Wrath, redlining all those commas I love. Your exactness and mastery of the most technical grammar is unparalleled. I also want to thank you for being so accommodating. By now, I guess you know I always change the ending, at least once.

Faith Williams, your thoroughness and attention to detail is incomparable. You are the polish that makes the story shine. Every time I get a manuscript back from you, I feel as though I need to send Cali MacKay a case of wine for introducing us.

A heartfelt thank you to Virginia Carey who I trust to be the very last set of eyes on my books before release. When you say a manuscript is ready for publication, it is. More, I cherish your support and friendship.

A giant thank you to Murphy Rae! You are an extraordinarily talented designer, professional, easy to work with, and just plain lovely. Thank you for taking a humble piece of fruit and turning it into something spectacular!

Thank you, thank you, thank you to Danielle Rairigh and Tami Thomason, who Beta read Pride and agreed to Beta read Wrath—if only I had finished it on time. Your insight and unwavering support during the process is something I'll never forget. You are THE best!

A huge thank you to the Bloggers, Bookstagramers, and Booktokers who have given the series so much love. I SO appreciate your generosity and kindness, and I will always be grateful for everything you did to help launch A Sinful Empire. Thank you for your tireless energy and generosity of spirit!

To all my author friends who helped in big and small ways —THANK YOU!!! I continue to be amazed by how willing busy women are to lend a hand or soothe a soul. Sending you so much love!

To the badass members of JD's Closet and Bad Boys in Books, there is nothing in my book world that gives me more joy than you! I'm humbled by your seemingly endless love and support, and your patience. I'm not sure I deserve such kindness, but I gobble up every morsel you toss my way. Your light shines brightly on me, and on each other. Thank you for your positivity and goodness, and for making the groups a safe place for everyone.

A heartfelt thank you to the readers—to everyone who read the series, reviewed, and told your friends about it! I am truly grateful for all the love you've shown my characters, and me. You fill my soul and inspire me to keep writing even on days when the words don't come easily. I'm going to Kentucky, next. Bourbon country. I hope you'll join me!

To Andy—the cliffhanger king and the love of my life.

Thank you for your patience and support, especially as deadlines loom. It's been a great ride—not the books, but the marriage—and there are still miles to travel. *Te Amo.*

ABOUT THE AUTHOR

Eva Charles is the *USA Today* bestselling author of steamy romantic suspense with dangerous billionaires and strong heroines.

When she's not writing, trying to squeeze information out of her tight-lipped sons, or playing with the two naughtiest dogs you've ever met, Eva's creating chapters in her own love story.

Sign-up for my monthly newsletter for special treats and all the Eva news!
Eva's VIP Reader Newsletter

I'd love to hear from you!
eva@evacharles.com

MORE STEAMY ROMANTIC SUSPENSE

A SINFUL EMPIRE SERIES

TRILOGY (COMPLETE)

Greed

Lust

Envy

DUET (COMPLETE)

Pride

Wrath

THE DEVIL'S DUE (SERIES COMPLETE)

Depraved

Delivered

Bound

Decadent

CONTEMPORARY ROMANCE

NEW AMERICAN ROYALS

Sheltered Heart

Noble Pursuit

Double Play

Unforgettable

Loyal Subjects

Sexy Sinner

Made in the USA
Las Vegas, NV
04 September 2023

77080082R00215